Rhoda Nathans

(Continued from front flap)

On why he devotes considerable space to flops as well as hits: "Too often no representation is given in cultural histories to the trash that makes the world go 'round."

On distinguishing flops from hits: "The only differences between a *Follow the Girls* and a *Guys and Dolls* are talent, good taste, and a point of view."

On the well-made musical: "The seams of musical craftsmanship didn't show [in *Oklahoma!*] because this one wasn't a patchwork in the way that nearly all musicals had been before."

On the poorly made musical: In *Call Me Madam*, "the song cues were so obvious you could hear them in New Jersey."

On the producers of poorly made musicals: The makers of "such fluff as *The Girl From Nantucket* and *Louisiana Lady* apparently chose their locales after examining the local costumer's trunk."

On what the musical in America is all about: "When the United States sent two musicals to play the Brussels World's Fair in 1959, the chosen ones were *Carousel* and the later *Wonderful Town*. The pairing is a statement of sorts, for these two embody the two basic kinds of musical, the uptempo city show and the sentimental romance."

Better Foot Forward

Better Foot Forward

The History of American Musical Theatre

Ethan Mordden

Grossman Publishers

A Division of The Viking Press

New York 1976

First published in 1976 by Grossman Publishers
625 Madison Avenue, New York, N.Y. 10022
Published simultaneously in Canada by
The Macmillan Company of Canada Limited
Printed in U.S.A.

Library of Congress Cataloging in Publication Data
Mordden, Ethan
Better foot forward.
Bibliography: p.
Includes index.
1. Musical revue, comedy, etc.—United States—History and criticism. I. Title.
ML1711.M7 782.8′1′0973 75-45081
ISBN 0-670-15974-3

The author wishes to thank the following people for helping him to locate essential material: Lehman Engel, Julie Haydon, Richard Horner, John Kander, Evelyn Lear, Stephen Sondheim, and Edward Thomas. Most particularly, he salutes Dorothy Pittman and Daniel Okrent; they well know why.

ACKNOWLEDGMENTS:

Chappell & Co., Inc.: "We're Gonna Be All Right," Copyright © 1965 by Richard Rodgers and Stephen Sondheim; Williamson Music, Inc., and Burthen Music, Inc., owners of publication and allied rights. "A Lady Needs a Change," Copyright © 1939 by Chappell & Co., Inc., Copyright renewed. "That Great Come-and-Get-It Day," Copyright © 1946 by Chappell & Co., Inc., Copyright renewed. "Come Home," Copyright © 1947 by Richard Rodgers and Oscar Hammerstein II, Copyright renewed; Williamson Music, Inc., owner of publication and allied rights. "You Too, Can Be a Puppet," Copyright © 1957 by E. Y. Harburg and Sammy Fain; Chappell & Co., Inc., administrator of publication and allied rights. Untitled musical composition from "The Golden Apple," Copyright © 1953 by Jerome Moross and John Latouche; Chappell & Co., Inc., administrator of publication and allied rights. "The Usher from the Mezzanine," Copyright © 1964 by Betty Comden, Adolph Green, and Jule Styne; Stratford Music Corporation, owner; Chappell & Co., Inc., administrator of publication and allied rights for the Western Hemisphere. All used by permission.

T. B. Harms Company: "That's How It Goes" from *A Tree Grows in Brooklyn,* Copyright © 1951 T. B. Harms Company, all rights reserved. "Some Sort of Somebody (All of the Time)" from *Miss Information,* Copyright © 1915 T. B. Harms Company, Copyright renewed, all rights reserved. Used by permission.

Mrs. George Jean Nathan and Fairleigh Dickinson University Press: "Follow the Girls" from *The Theatre Book of the Year 1943–1944,* © 1944

(Page 369 constitutes a continuation of copyright page.)

To my parents—
often delighted, never surprised

CONTENTS

AN APOLOGIA BY WAY OF A PREFACE

First off, I have to deal with a question the reader might naturally ask if he should hear somewhere that I haven't been a regular attender of Broadway musicals for the last seventy-five years. How, asks the reader, can someone still in his twenties talk about "sumptuous scenery" or "inferior musical direction" circa 1920? How does he know? He wasn't there!

Ah, but. Others were to leave a virtual live memory of the proceedings—photographs (often very extensive sets of them for a given production), recollections (you develop a knack for learning whom to trust), contemporary reviews, for starters. Most of the actors who worked on Broadway from the twenties onward did at least some movie work, so yes, I think one *can* understand the kind of magic Marilyn Miller, to pick one example, must have exerted on her public. Records too document the American pop music scene from the earliest days of the century, and underground tapes exist of live performances as far back as the thirties. Someone even filmed chunks of *Dubarry Was a Lady* and *Red, Hot and Blue* from the front of the orchestra—without sound, alas. But the material is mainly what counts, and all of that remains: as sheet music, complete scores, published librettos, and private scripts if you know where to get them. Luckily, actors never throw anything away (except their lives).

En bref: no, I wasn't there, but I had everything I needed to re-create the old days short of a time machine. The only thing I didn't do was talk to anybody who was involved. Actors especially are impossible about the shows they were in, and directors, designers, conductors, and such have their little axes to grind as well. Producers are okay, writers and composers often reasonable. I did cadge an hour with a certain musical director, composer, and savant who *was* there to find out if putting a show together in the forties was any different from the way it is now (it wasn't), and I had to interview a few of the more distinctive theatre composers for a magazine article at the time, so it was inevitable that I hear a personal comment or two. But, ultimately, this book does not emphasize the human side of musical comedy production as much as the hard realities of music, lyrics, and script—to whatever extent one can speak of hard realities in an industry so locked into whatever works at the moment, especially in the race for success in weeks of tryouts.

This cast-versus-material point is a big one, for musical comedy has always depended on stars—some musicals, anyway—and the question of where art ends and show shoppery begins is a tricky one. Furthermore, it is a fact that great material can die in a poor production. Actors matter, as *A Chorus Line*'s fanatic supporters thought the show illustrated. They're all wrong, of course: people matter—actors are freaks. *A Chorus Line*'s final statement is that no matter how interesting you are, unless you're the big cheese behind which choristers prance you will be packaged as part of a mob, characterless. Good as *A Chorus Line*'s actors were, and riveting though Michael Bennett's staging was, the show was powerful for the same reason such shows always are: the music, lyrics, and book worked.

That's why I have avoided the usual cast listings and chatter about personality. Such credits can be found elsewhere, they add little to an understanding of our musical theatre as an art form, and they're boring to read anyway. A trifle like *Happy Hunting* would never be revived without Ethel Merman because the show itself was twaddle, but *Gypsy* was as good with Angela Lansbury as it had been with Merman, because the show itself was so good. If *A Chorus Line* comes back to town in twenty years, it will be as exciting for those New Yorkers as it was for us, even without Donna McKechnie, Carole Bishop, Priscilla Lopez, and Sammy Williams.

I must also account for my extensive quoting of critics when I maintain, at times, that theatre critics are generally . . . hmm, we need a mot juste here . . . creeps. However, the first night business in the thirties and forties wasn't as rotten as it is now. Today few critics comprehend musical theatre except as a source for cheap thrills, but things were a little different back a ways. After reading the boys of decades past at some length, you learn who was able to understand what sort of musical: Percy Hammond for romance, Stark Young for social commentary, and so on. Matters got less trustworthy later on, and nowadays the situation is scandalous, especially as regards the position of *The New York Times* as possibly the only influential source of theatre opinion for Broadway's public other than the New York television stations, which show brief segments of the performance on film (and let's face it: ten seconds of the real thing on videotape says more than most critics can in a whole review).

I have yet another disclaimer, this one on movies. Film buffs may wonder why so little is made herein of movie musicals but anyone who has seen a few such items who isn't totally bonkers won't wonder at all. For the record, Hollywood filmed most of Broadway's musical hits from just after the start of the sound era, mostly retaining only the title, a song or two, and possibly the plot germ. With very few exceptions (almost none of them adaptations, incidentally), movie musicals were chaotic and asinine. Even worse, adaptations from Broadway that utilized the film medium fully threw out nearly everything of value from the stage (*Cabaret,* for example, one of the few great movie musicals all the same), while those that tried to re-create stage business weren't even movies (although *Li'l Abner* is at least a historically useful record of what the original show looked like).

So, I turn to the recording industry. Whether a fox-trotting 78 of one measly vocal chorus or an LP album complete from overture to exit music, records are prima facie evidence and so far have been Broadway's sole mementoes with the sensation of human life in them. More on this subject follows a bibliography for those who want to fill up the holes left gaping in this volume, especially as regards reference material. As to the paucity of lyric quotations, this resulted from the unshakeable rapacity of certain music publishers; to accommodate their demands, this book would have cost its weight in caviar. And my apologies to the thousands of actors I never got to mention. It just isn't that kind of book.

Now for a note on the title of this opus. Most ostensibly it is a grammatical correction of the name of that incorrigibly youthful George Abbott musical of 1941, *Best Foot Forward* (better of two, best of many; you can't put a best foot forward unless you've got three feet). The phrase itself harkens back to a palmier day of butter-and-egg-man musical comedies, when the dance director, auditioning hopeful chorines for their quota of physical primacy and steel glee, would call out, "All right, girls, best foot forward, now." The more apparent legs conduced to employment.

Less whimsically, this "better foot" connotes the musical's rather poky maturation. We're talking about a middlebrow art form here—swank and flamboyance and warmth, yes, and sometimes even wisdom, but until recently it all adds up to better rather than best. The indelible works of art come at the tail end of the volume, and up to those last chapters it can only be better—better, I say, not best—foot forward.

Better Foot Forward

Overture

It really begins with *Show Boat*. Jerome Kern and Oscar Hammerstein II wrote the first organic musical comedy, an artistic entity that was *about* something, that told a story through words and music instead of merely alternating them. Way back then, almost fifty years ago, *Show Boat* existed in a virtual vacuum, for nothing like it had ever worked out so beautifully before. The history of the musical up to 1927 is a great, slow advance from sappy story-and-song contraptions to transcendent music dramas—in short, art.

The idea of investing plays with music is a relatively old one, even in the United States, but it wasn't done that often or that well. By the end of the nineteenth century it was a busy little industry, doing well by cutting capers, but the plays themselves were undernourished and the music was often a hodgepodge of songs and dances acquired by a hack arranger on a foray through the public domain. The thriving medium had only just learned to walk; it had some distance to travel before it would turn into an adult art form.

Maturity came slowly, with the gleaning of useful elements every two or three years from experiments both native and imported—the buoyant charm of *Evangeline*'s dancing cow, the wit of W. S. Gilbert, the romantic finesse of Lehár, the gaudy routines of Weber and Fields, the zip of George M. Cohan, the decorative eye of Joseph Urban. But American musical comedy wasn't American until the last echo of the zither gave out in the 1920s. When Kern, Gershwin, Berlin, Porter, and Rodgers surfaced with a new sound, Hammerstein, Hart, another Gershwin, and Porter and Berlin again had the words ready; then, not suddenly, but fitfully and encountering no little resistance, they junked the hussars and laundresses for sheiks and flappers, hoofers and shopgirls, Peggy-Anns and Johnny Johnsons, farmers and whores.

Any developing artistic form has its lean times, and there were a few—we're in one now, in fact—when artistic development gave short weight and the form was struggling to reestablish itself. But the nineteen-twenties and thirties were boom times, with some wonderful new theatrical sortie every season. If the experiment worked, others would try it, build on it, transform it, and step by step, musical comedy evolved a method of being a number of different things at once and still telling a cogent story through dialogue, lyrics, dance, design, and eventually even a stylistic concept.

After *Show Boat* did it, other shows followed by doing it in other ways. Before 1927, the history of the musical is mainly the story of how the elements of writing and production asserted themselves and were assimilated into a format; after 1927, it is mainly another story, not so much "What happened then?" but rather "How else could it be done? How better? How can it be more American? More modern? More timeless? More current?"

So there's this . . . format walking along, and sometimes it takes a giant step forward and means something, and sometimes it doesn't and is just something nice to be at. Those giant steps matter a lot though, because ultimately they have added up to a marvelous live medium based on the very best of what popular American culture is. This is how we see ourselves. This is what we are.

1

Beginnings

Picking an arbitrary, pre-*Show Boat* time and place to go back to—the mid-1800s in Manhattan—isn't arbitrary in the least. In fact, it's an ideal jumping-off place for a history of musical comedy, for while the form has its essential roots in the eighteenth century, it didn't really get going until the second half of the nineteenth, shortly after New York had won out over Philadelphia as the theatre capital of the nation, with all the enterprise and activity the position implies.

The primeval cries of "Hey, kids! Let's put on a show!" could be serviced at first only by ballad opera, a play strung with popular songs in the English fashion. Everything about American theatre was in the English fashion back then, not only the plays but the leading actors as well, imposing their traditions and shtick on the colonial stage while native apprentices watched, learning, in the wings. Not until Royall Tyler's *The Contrast* in 1787 was there a truly American play, written with an ear for local speech habits and tackling a local subject. Set in New York City, this mesozoic comedy of manners pitted the Country against the Town via a favorite American trope, the Yankee bumpkin who solves the evening's problems with a mixture of folk wisdom, naïve integrity, and down-home logic, thus putting the city folks in their place and instilling the virtues of rural America. Destined to infest the lively arts in this country forever after, he was king of the early theatre in such guises as Nimrod Wildfire, Jonathan Ploughboy, and even *A Yankee in Poland.* He turned up in another prototypical comedy, Anna Cora Mowatt's *Fashion,* in 1845, and nearly a century later he was reincarnated by James Stewart in Hollywood's tonics for the escape-hungry audiences of the Depression. Though the totally unnaturalized English ballad opera made little of this fellow, his point of view came to be a significant thematic source for the serious musical theatre from the late 1920s on. In general, musical *comedies* would be set in cities, the more artistic *romantic* musicals in a sort of cloud cuckooland, whence the urban jungle was regarded with undisguised dismay. One can almost imagine Jerome Kern or Richard Rodgers composing a melody for Cowper's famous broadside, "God made the country and man made the town"—and Kern and Rodgers did, too, though not exactly in those words.

Charleston, an active theatre center, was the site of the first American performance of a ballad opera in 1735, *Flora, or a Hob in the Well*—English, naturally. Though the songs thrown into the play were spot bits with little relevance to the story, *Flora* was the only "book show" around, for concurrent musical entertainments didn't even have the foundation of a story line. A century later, the depression of the 1840s led the traveling blackface minstrels to team up into five- or six-man companies (larger corps in the big cities), and there was also the music hall, which became vaudeville in the 1880s simply by changing its name.

It would be hard to pin down just what sort of viewpoint

these antique endeavors operated from. Ballad opera tended to sensation, while the minstrel shows offered such items as "Essence of Old Virginny, Unequalled Plantation Dance," "Conga Cola," or simply "On the Levee" by way of authentic Southern flavor (any attempt to portray the South realistically was left to the melodramas based on *Uncle Tom's Cabin,* which rendered Southern life even more realistic than it was). Population centers such as New York, Boston, and New Orleans presented their music-theatre-minded customers with opera, but of course opera wasn't in English. Grand opera busied itself with the comings and goings of counts and mad ladies, comic opera with the apparently riotous but basically respectable middle class, and there was ballet, too, inevitably French. Like ballad opera and plain old opera, the ballet had as little to do with America as it possibly could.

Another foreign importation, but one that really caught on and was finally subsumed by American settings and stories, was the musical extravaganza. This offshoot of the French and English court masques originally had music as its focal point, but by the 1800s it had become largely a pictorial enterprise, emphasizing eye-filling scenery and exciting stage effects. The "spectacle," as it was first called, got its local start in 1824 at the 2000-seat Park Theatre with *Cherry and Fair Star.* This primordial musical achieved the triumphant run of 33 performances, not a bad showing for those days. *Cherry and Fair Star* was a far cry from *Girl Crazy* or *Naughty Marietta.* For one thing, it had virtually no plot, relying more on decor than music or dance to make its effect. What little continuity there was is preserved in the programmatic scene titles, "Descent of the fairy queen in her ambient car" vying for attention with "Arrival of a Grecian galley amid the acclamations of the spectators on the ramparts." The audience was treated to an assortment of unrelated images, including a fire-breathing dragon, an immense butterfly that flew off with the heroine, a temple of icicles, and a fairy vision. At one performance a fake waterfall accidentally caught fire, but the public was apparently too entranced to flee, despite the serious threat that theatre fires posed in that time.

Cherry and Fair Star never lasted through revivals or touring companies, which were already customary, but the spectacle format slowly caught on, assisted by ballet companies from abroad who could absorb the demand for scenic thrills without having to modify their programs. Every few years another spectacle or "pantomimic fairy play" would show up with mountains of canvas and a vague plot line based on the apparently inexhaustible exploits of enchanted characters. There was frequently a primitive sort of musical score of interpolated numbers picked out at random—popular tunes of the day and the day before, borrowings from the classics, and last-minute specials by local hacks.

The "extravaganza" floated over from France with the Ronzani ballet troupe in 1857 as "The Laying of the Atlantic Cable," only one of several acts on the bill that night. The Ronzanis quickly faded from view, but the word "extravaganza" caught the public's fancy and the imaginations of theatre managers. In 1866 an extravaganza called *The Balloon Wedding* took over Wood's Theatre for weeks of woefully empty houses, making it one of the earliest big box-office failures in the history of the musical.

The first really good extravaganza, *The Black Crook,* came along nine months later. Its phenomenal success insured the continuation of the musical spectacular for over fifty years, although the form was finally superseded by less grandiose musical farces and the totally bookless revue. But grandiosity was still the musical theatre's calling card in the 1860s and the big theatre managers were amassing piles of flats and wing drops to show off to New Yorkers eager to be enthralled with the further adventures of the rank and file of fairyland. *The Black Crook* was an amalgam of *La Biche aux Bois,* a ballet, "direct from Paris," and a knuckleheaded melodrama by Charles M. Barras, who had once seen a performance of Weber's gothic opera *Der Freischütz* and had never gotten over it. By a happy accident of the sort that makes good copy for historical annals, the ballet company's theatre burned down and *The Black Crook*'s producer, William Wheatley, decided to beef up his ghastly Barras property with the stranded dancers. Over Barras' objections, ballet infiltrated his scenario, and wherever the dancing master didn't impose a *pas* the music director put in a song. Furthermore, Wheatley went off to London to purchase elaborate stage machinery for the production, still called *The Black Crook* but getting less black, and less crooked, daily. No one knows where Wheatley got his backing, but his total outlay was estimated at $25,000 to $55,000, an incredible sum for the time.

As it happened, Wheatley's hunch paid off, for *The Black Crook* scored by far the biggest success of any musical show up to then, making front-page headlines and dominating conversations at the best dinner parties. The first performance, on September 12, 1866, at the gigantic Niblo's Garden, lasted five and a half hours, unusual not in length, for an evening's entertainment, but because it was the only item on the bill. No curtain raiser, no entr'acte, no minstrelsy "olio," no one-act comedy chaser—just Barras' absurd Faustian thriller laced up with, among other things, a "Grand Ballet of Gems," a rapturous "Pas de Démons" for the incantation scene and a hurricane in the Harz Mountains, thanks to Wheatley's wind machines and a great deal of gauze.

Like other extravaganzas of its day, *The Black Crook* made no attempt to integrate its elements of drama, dance, and song, but unlike the others, it had a story with a beginning, middle and end. In fact, most people felt it had too much story, especially in Act One. Chimerical thud-and-blunder melodrama was already past its prime in the Northeast; Barras' script was screamed out in the flamboyant, galloping style typical of a degenerating art form on its last legs. But by the time the long evening drew to a close, the combination of ballet, spectacle, and lowbrow songs had cast its spell, and the pretty French girls in tights didn't hurt, either.

The critics praised everything about the show except the drama, dismissing that as rubbish, but they went into ecstasies over the corps de ballet—a chorus line numbering one hundred. The *World* likened Niblo's Garden to a "vast paradise of houris," while the staid *Evening Post* warned that the beauty onstage was "perhaps less concealed than would be deemed proper by those of stout views as to where dresses should begin and end." The relatively low-cut costumes were considered shocking enough to send the public scurrying to the box office, some of the women heavily veiled to avoid detection by their equally prurient friends. The usual monitors of public decency thundered from their pulpits and in newspaper editorials, adding hugely to Wheatley's weekly take.

Of the musical score itself there is little to admire. The musician credited with the bulk of the work was one Giuseppe Operti, an immigrant band leader, who wrote some incidental music ("March of the Amazons" went over well) and scrambled around in music shops for most of the songs. There were a few interpolated numbers too—this remained a common practice through the 1930s and isn't yet totally extinct—the most notable being "You Naughty, Naughty Men." It was sung by a finger-waving Milly Cavendish to her devotees in the boxes:

> I will never more deceive you
> Or of happiness bereave you,
> But I'll die a maid to grieve you;
> Oh, you naughty, naughty men!

The music was elementary, but it pleased.

Whatever Wheatley's original investment really was, it turned out to be a gold mine. The 3000-seat theatre played to capacity crowds for sixteen months, drawing people back again and yet again to be thrilled (and scandalized) encore.

Wheatley obligingly inserted new production numbers to keep his show in the news. Over a hundred children were featured in a military drill, "Baby Ballet," in mid-1867, and a lush ballroom masquerade excited further comment two months later. By the time it closed to make way for a successor, *The Black Crook* totaled a staggering 474 performances, unheard of for one engagement. Touring companies carried it all over the continent for fifty years, and it was revived eight times in New York alone. When last heard from, in 1929, it was playing Hoboken, New Jersey, scaled down and creaking at the joints but enjoying the services of the young Agnes De Mille as Queen Stalacta.

It is easy to see why *The Black Crook* was such a hit in its day. None of its ingredients—drama, dance, song and spectacle—was a new idea, since each had been, after all, an ingredient used to cook up opera in New York and elsewhere for decades. But opera was in Italian or French, poorly staged if staged at all, and the music was in cultivated—which is to say foreign—style. *The Black Crook,* no less silly than Bellini and even sillier than Meyerbeer, was in English, adroitly put together by that theatre wizard Wheatley. The scenery was eye-catching, the choreography delightful and varied, and at least some of the songs were pure parlor-pianist American. With the addition of the sensational dancing girls, *The Black Crook* was not so much a new idea as an old one that had never been done as well, nor in as "popular" a style. Here was an evening with nothing but divertissement to offer, patter songs and tights instead of cantilena and ruffs. Exactly one hundred and two years later, another musical with a slight story line, "shocking" anatomical revelations, and an unintegrated score would enjoy a success on Broadway as phenomenal as *The Black Crook* had enjoyed in 1866. Even today, the "bookless" musical lives on—as *Hair, The Magic Show* and more, no doubt, to come.

Wheatley followed his bonanza with *The White Fawn* in 1868, adding what was left of *La Biche aux Bois* to a resourceless libretto by one James Mortimer, loaded to the gills with romantic fancies, transformation sequences, animal ballets, and yet more doings of the fairy kingdom. This too was a success, though nothing like the first try. It was time for something new, and the slack was promptly taken up in a few blocks uptown at the Olympic Theatre, where pantomime made its last stand in *Humpty Dumpty.* Spectacle had only scenery going for it, but pantomime had something more enticing, a funny plot. Loosely modeled on the Italian commedia dell'arte, American pantomime was a combination of stylized dumb show and slapstick high jinks in dance and song. Harlequin, Columbine, Pantaloon and such would be transformed by a Mother Goose figure into the stock inhabitants of storybookland, while less inhibited players tumbled around on ladders, rushed in and out of doorways, hid behind screens, and generally cut up. The dialogue was a jumble, largely extemporized, and the music was of minimal interest, adapted from various outside sources. But nobody minded, for the evening (or whatever fraction of it the one-act pantos took up) was intended as a showcase for the particular talents of one or two star comedians.

Humpty Dumpty's star was George L. Fox, one of the few who could keep this dying art form running past Saturday night. All contemporary accounts credit him with supreme talent as a clown, less tough and sassy than lost and innocent. Under his painted smile was the humanity and pathos of a great actor, and his notoriously unbalanced mental condition could only have added to his gifts. Although he closed his career jumping off the stage to harass his public, he was at his height when *Humpty Dumpty* opened in 1868. This virtually plotless trifle realized the story-telling potential of pantomime in collaboration with the splashy excesses of spectacle, though this time the choreography was poor, with no ballet troupe to draw on. It was Fox who made the show (as would Eddie Foy, Ed Wynn, Bobby Clark, and Bert Lahr in similar outings), along with the by this time indispensable fairy grotto, a "Valley of Fertility," a Neapolitan market place in full cry, a "Dell of Ferns," a moonlit skating ballet clipped from Meyerbeer's *Le Prophète,* and an exploding steamboat for the first-act finale. Audiences flocked to the Olympic to catch Fox's act, making *Humpty Dumpty* a bigger hit than *The Black Crook:* 483 performances, several touring companies (successful even without Fox) and numerous revivals. The 1871 version sought to improve on the original with an extra act of novelty turns in the manner of a minstrel show, with comedians, acrobats, children on bicycles, and a cat duet that prompted enthusiastic mewing in the gallery.

In 1873 Fox retired, taking pantomime with him. Lacking an almighty leader, the genus withered, soon to be replaced by a more self-sufficient low-comic medium, burlesque. A kind of adulterated pantomime, burlesque threw out the dumb show altogether but retained the "principal boy" (the hero, played by a girl in tights). Instead of robbing Mother Goose, burlesque spoofed literary works, especially the classics, but the approach was in the same spirit of knockabout comedy and improvisation.

Because it avoided scenic splendor and the stately posturings of the fairy world, burlesque was cheap to produce and racy to attend, with topical references, aggressive one-liners, and high kicks instead of entrechats. The Englishwoman Lydia Thompson took her cue from *The Black Crook* in shoving her bleached blond chorus line to the fore in the first British musical to arrive in New York, *Ixion* (1868), a travesty of Classic Greece (Mars was billed "commander-in-chief, as Ma's usually are"). Lydia always played the hero in her shows and was, for a time, the rage.

Proto-musical comedy really originated in 1874 with *Evangeline,* a burlesque described as an "American opéra bouffe" in a bow to the vogue for Offenbach. Later called an "American extravaganza," it was in fact anything but: gone was the complex decor, the corps de ballet, the dim humanoids of fairyland. *Evangeline* was a takeoff on Longfellow's poem, produced and written by Edward E. Rice and J. Cheever Goodwin, with lyrics by Goodwin and music by the self-taught Rice, aided by a harmony student. The book was not the sort that creates theatre revolutions, and the lyrics were nothing to write home about, but the music was fairly pleasant. If it sounded graceless and dingy compared to what Sullivan, von Suppé, and Offenbach were doing in Europe at the same time, it was at least the first time an American musical sported a score of its own, written for the specific occasion.

Longfellow's picaresque ballad about two separated young lovers who spend their lives searching for each other seemed destined for burlesque. Sprawling, sentimental, and abounding in coincidences, the story gave Rice and Goodwin the chance of their careers. Hewing ever so slightly to the plot source, they dragged their heroine from Acadia to Arizona and Africa, and turned her milk-white cow into a two-man novelty that danced its way into the memory of two generations of theatregoers. In the 1896 revival the cow, along with the chorus line, was one of the few items that had not been discarded (the critic of the *World* referred to the show's "perennial limbs and immutable cow"). Another outstanding feature of the original *Evangeline* that still packed them in in 1896 was the Lone Fisherman, an isolated comic character with no lines—no sounds, even—who appeared and reappeared throughout the show, as at home in Africa as Arizona, adding nothing to the plot but pointless mystery. The public loved it, as they loved the transvestite comic George K. Fortescue in the role of Catherine. He did so well as a maiden lady that he played her for life in revivals and on tour, later to win even greater renown when the Sardou specialist Fanny Davenport was the talk of New York in *Fedora.* Fortescue quickly moved in with a burlesque, *Well-Fed Dora* (1888), that had the town roaring.

Burlesque was in, and like Wheatley with his *White Fawn,* Rice hoped to succeed with a second helping of the same dessert. By now abandoned by Goodwin but holding on tight to his harmony student (Irving Berlin and Noel Coward were to need similar assistance), Rice wrote another complete score for *Hiawatha* (1880), a "new and original American operatic extravaganza." Rice didn't exactly go out of his way to capture the true aroma of the plains, as may be noticed in the title of the show's hit tune "Tea and Toast and Kisses," and Nathaniel Childs' libretto was more New York than Gitche Gumee, but that was no bar to enjoyment. Unfortunately, the poor quality of the show as a whole *was*—and *Hiawatha* vanished after two weeks. Rice did have a high-powered hit in 1884 with *Adonis,* however. Matinee idol Henry E. Dixey sang, danced, cavorted, and showed off his well-turned legs while more and more women picked up the theatre habit, changing forever the character of the country's audiences. Topical lines were updated repeatedly after the premiere, and few were the stage-minded New Yorkers who caught *Adonis* only once.

Spectacle was still a monolithic box office attraction in the seventies and eighties, and still rather messily organized. No less than three colossal adaptations of Jules Verne's *Around the World in Eighty Days* vied for notice in the 1870s, one of them scaling heights of verisimilitude with a trained elephant named Ouina. But spectacles could not supply the one item that was rapidly becoming the potent force in musical entertainment: comedy. Burlesque had it to spare, and wise managers had to concede its all-conquering luster and beat the high grass for good gag writers. Straight farce had already won out as the most popular brand of theatre; the next step was obviously to trick it up with music.

The basic layout of the musical farces in the 1880s was a slim three-act plot that enabled the "combinations," as farce troupes were called, to make the most of their assorted talents. Since burlesque made a point of ridiculing the kind of characters who populated the world of extravaganza, it naturally featured a less "highly placed" dramatis personae.

Farce in turn went one step further into realism, depicting ordinary Americans in everyday settings. Edward Harrigan and Tony Hart wrote and produced the *Mulligan Guard* farces (1879–1885) using the timeless denizens of the urban milieu for ethnic humor, in-jokes, and zippy pacing. Not strictly musicals, the *Mulligan Guard* series depended on dance and song to some degree, and there had to be at least one hit tune calculated to keep the town humming. Nate Salsbury's "laughable and musical farce" *The Brook* (1879) committed its thread of plot to the Five Salsbury Troubadours' "pic-nic" in the country, a sequence of mishaps providing the fun. The dessert basket was found to contain not the expected watermelons but theatrical costumes, giving Salsbury's combination a chance to dress up and strut their specialties.

Evangeline's Edward E. Rice tried his hand at farce with *Pop* in 1883. The transvestite Catherine of *Evangeline,* George K. Fortescue, played a wealthy Southern gentleman this time around but felt limited in trousers and found numerous excuses to slip into dirndls and silk. In true farce tradition, *Pop*'s second act introduced a wildly irrelevant bundle of variety turns: impersonators, vocal solos and duets, and a yodeling troupe. In the middle of the show's run Rice threw in a topical number, "The Dudes and the Dude Princes," an all-girl march inspired by the boulevardiers of New York.

The musical farces virtually never had totally original scores, making do with adaptations and the farceurs' own time-tested favorites. For *The Tourists in the Pullman Palace Car* (1879), for example, an unnamed arranger helped himself to the work of Arthur Sullivan, Robert Planquette, Giuseppe Verdi, Franz von Suppé (whole chunks of *Fatinitza*), and even a *Mulligan Guard* hit, "The Skids Are Out Today." One exception to the rule was Charles Hoyt's *A Trip to Chinatown* (1890), the whopping success of its time with a mostly original score by Percy Gaunt, albeit larded with the usual interpolations. *A Trip to Chinatown* flew to glory with three gigantic pop hits, "The Bowery," "Reuben, Reuben," and "After the Ball," the last two added during the run. All three are remembered today, but "After the Ball" was the great grandfather of Broadway standards. Sad story ballads in waltz time were common enough in the eighties and nineties, but "After the Ball" seems to have struck a responsive chord beyond considerations of fad or fashion:

> After the ball is over,
> After the break of morn,
> After the dancers' leaving,
> After the stars are gone;
> Many a heart is aching
> If you could read them all;
> Many the hopes that have vanished
> After the ball.

Charles K. Harris wrote both words and music, and he was also his own publisher. Though he shared his royalties with J. Aldrich Libby, who sang it in the show, Harris eventually sold ten million copies of the song; some people must have been buying three or four at a time. Harris' firm did so well with this and other songs that he almost singlehandedly founded Tin Pan Alley. In his book, *How to Write a Popular Song,* Harris outlined the rules he lived by:

> Look at newspapers for your story-line.
> Acquaint yourself with the style in vogue.
> Avoid slang.
> Know the copyright laws.

As far as the musical shows of Harris' time were concerned, only the first two ring true.

A Trip to Chinatown followed the with-it tradition of using a big-city setting for fast pacing and up to-the-minute quips. The scene in this case was San Francisco, but it could easily have passed for New York or Chicago. The story pitted young man-about-town Rashley Gay against his pinch-penny uncle Ben; they spent the second act trying to avoid each other in a restaurant, while secondary characters such as Welland

Strong and Willie Grow peppered the proceedings with outrageous stunts and gags.

Hoyt dismissed his play as a "musical trifle," but it was the songs more than the comedy that earned its 650 performances. It stands above its fellow farce comedies on the strength of its music, for the very structure of the medium was too simple and sloppy in style to hold theatregoers for long.

Even without music, the Parisian Georges Feydeau could make farce tell in ways no American could equal. Besides, a new trend toward European comic opera—a new term for a new medium—had already taken wing on this side of the Atlantic and was about to exert a fertile influence on the musical theatre. Critics and ticketbuyers alike were calling for something fresh; it was no longer enough to collect unrelated musical bits and toss them on stage with no more context than a picnic or a train ride. Aided by French opéra bouffes of varying quality, Gilbert and Sullivan were going to force musical comedy up on its feet and start it walking.

2

Comic Opera, Musical Comedy, Cohan and Herbert

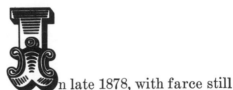

In late 1878, with farce still in vogue, burlesque in its death throes, and musical comedy waiting in the wings, Gilbert and Sullivan's *H.M.S. Pinafore* had its first American performance at the old Boston Museum. Its success was sudden and far-reaching; by the end of the year about one hundred different groups were touring or sustaining long runs, and jaded tastes could choose from a children's *Pinafore,* black *Pinafores*, burlesques of *Pinafore*—even a *Pinafore* in Yiddish. The once and future D'Oyly Carte company crossed the Atlantic to put the stamp of authenticity on the world premiere of *The Pirates of Penzance* in New York in late 1879, with the authors themselves in attendance. The rest is anything but silence.

It was, in fact, the beginning of a rampaging craze for comic opera, though Americans had been introduced to the form as early as 1867, when Offenbach's *The Grand Duchess of Gérolstein* hit New York. But whether performed in French or English, the opéra bouffes of Offenbach, Lecocq, Audran, and Planquette had no chance against Gilbert and Sullivan. For one thing, the hack translations of Gallic wit were as nothing next to Gilbert's spicy patter songs and satiric books, and Offenbach's sparkling, witty music was a mite too charming for the colonies; where Sullivan had heft, Offenbach would only be sprightly. Furthermore, Offenbach's comedies proved risky in any language without a star cast who could really sing. *Pinafore, Iolanthe,* and the rest of G & S not only didn't need stars, they almost didn't need voices. Certainly they relied more on succinct stage presence than the vocal artistry of a Hortense Schneider or a Lucille Tostée, the Parisian and New York Grand Duchesses of Gérolstein, darlings of a day that worshiped singer-comediennes. Lastly, there were more pianos in America at this time than anywhere else in the world. Every middle-class family had its instrument in the parlor, and the neat, easily mastered Sullivan vocal scores were the mainstays of the sing-at-home repertory. Slowly, the public was beginning to appreciate the difference between the motley agglomerations that served farce, burlesque, and extravaganza, and the craftsmanship of an Arthur Sullivan.

By 1881 nearly every American with a more than passing interest in the theatre had seen *Pinafore* and *The Pirates of Penzance* and was eager for more. More duly followed, at the rate of one G & S a year, while producers also imported everything written in Vienna, Paris, and London that wasn't out-and-out opera, fitting them up in English translations run off in haste. Eleven comic operas were performed in New York alone in 1881, one of them by an American, Charles Brown. Entitled *Elfins and Mermaids,* it was so awful that some critics were too embarrassed to write their reviews. Coeval efforts were equally disastrous, as the new medium could only be brought off by a writer with both talent and a feel for comedy. The Philadelphian J. S. Crossey had neither, so his *The First Life Guards at Brighton* (1879) had the distinction of being the first intensely poor American comic opera. Dudley Buck, whose Episcopal church music is still in use today, failed to come up with more than a moderately boring oratorio in his and librettist W. A. Croffut's *Deseret,* a Mormon epic that lasted less than two weeks.

In 1885 *The Mikado* had its first American showing, and Gilbert and Sullivan certified their positions as the undisputed kings of comic opera. Rather than attempt to beat the British champs, American composers and lyricists decided to join them with direct imitations such as Willard Spencer's *The Little Tycoon* (1886), chock-full of patter songs and dithering Japanese comedy, or Woolson Morse and J. Cheever Goodwin's *Wang* (1891), an "operatic burletta" that sailed along for 151 performances on the appeal of its pseudo-Oriental postures.

Viennese comic opera managed to find its niche on Broadway without being widely imitated . . . yet. The Strausses, von Suppé, Genée, and Millöcker all enjoyed some sanction, and smart producers quickly realized that even inadequate comic operas would go over if the composer was foreign and the sets and costumes handsome. Gilbert and Sullivan's public would line up for anything British while waiting for the team's next opus, which explains the popularity of immigrant Edward Solomon, Lillian Russell's second husband. They celebrated their union with *Polly, the Pet of the Regiment* in 1885, produced by *Evangeline*'s Edward E. Rice, who had acquired the Savoyard touch while working with Richard D'Oyly Carte on Solomon's *Billie Taylor* in 1881.

Polly was the show that put Lillian Russell's name in lights; from 1885 till her death in 1922 she was the first lady of the musical theatre, famed more for her golden blond looks than her expert but slightly pallid singing—an important point considering the later division between the legitimate *Rose-Marie* sopranos versus the tough, "heart-of-gold" *Panama Hattie* belters.

Despite the education in musical composition offered America by European shows, shopworn local imitations continued to thrive. Philadelphia made its contribution to the rise of a native comic opera tradition in 1892 with *Princess Bonnie,* by Willard Spencer. His wildly implausible scenario carried Bonnie from Maine to Spain, promoting her from a lighthouse keeper's daughter to a princess of the blood. For some reason best known to New Yorkers, *Princess Bonnie*'s Philadelphia run of 1039 performances dwindled to a mere 40 in Manhattan, but the show clung fast as a staple of the road for twenty years.

The light musical stage held a growing attraction for classically trained composers in the United States, as there had long been in Europe. (Ultimately, this would prove a Promethean boon when men like Kurt Weill and Leonard Bernstein turned their attentions to Broadway.) Opera composer Reginald de Koven scored comic opera librettos for decades, including the madly successful *Robin Hood* (1890), in which de Koven endeared himself to brides everywhere with "Oh, Promise Me," written ten years earlier but unappreciated until Jessie Bartlett Davis warbled it as the minstrel Allan-a-Dale. March king John Philip Sousa penned ten comic operas, only now being revived fresh from the tomb by opera and theatre companies of the 1970s. If Sousa was no symphonist, the emerging colossus named Victor Herbert was, and even the illustrious Bostonian George Whitefield Chadwick tried his hand at comic opera in the disastrous *Tabasco* (1894). Later on, musicals would be largely the province of more primitive musicians, but the comic opera era called for men with a knack for orchestration and full-scale operatic forms.

Still, not every musical show in the late 1880s and 1890s was a comic opera. For the four hundredth anniversary of Columbus' first voyage to America, Carl Pflueger and R. A. Barnett wrote *1492*, a "musical, historical melodrama" which had precious little to offer in the way of melodrama, history, or music.

Part extravaganza, part music hall, it was a giant step backward in the development of the book musical, although its score was beefed up after the opening by additions from Anton Rubinstein and Edward E. Rice, still cribbing his left-hand harmonies from a music major.

Extravaganza lived on, precariously. While the annual number of new productions had been stepped up, most of them were comic operas or burlesques in the comic opera format. The few extravaganzas that paid their way did so only by incorporating the features of comic opera and letting the scenery do the rest, while the French-style ballet that had catalyzed early extravaganza was now permanently retired. A handful of composers set J. Cheever Goodwin's verses for *Alladdin, Jr.* (1895), whose title suggests a burlesque but which was, in fact, one of the more satisfying extravaganzas of its day, with marvelous sets making the most of Peking and the Nile valley. In 1899 *The Man in the Moon* and its flop sequel *The Man in the Moon, Jr.* (at the New York Theatre, too far uptown on Forty-fifth Street) brought the curtain down on extravaganza as such. Except for a concentration on rich decor, the medium was indistinguishable from comic opera.

The term "musical comedy" was coined in England in 1892 for a modest little show, *In Town.* Note that the setting was home (London) rather than the fabled East or brightly uniformed Central Europe, for musical comedy began as comic opera without the ornaments of legend, wishing to be more plausible, with a feel for local mores. The term itself caught on in this country when the British musical comedy *A Gaiety Girl* came over with great réclame in 1894. The *Dramatic Mirror* called it an "indefinable musical and dramatic mélange," but one thing was clear: the score was less an imitation of Sullivan or Offenbach than usual, relying on pop-tune forms of the day such as story ballads, parlor waltzes, and comic-situation rather than rapid-patter songs.

Two years later, Sidney Jones' *The Geisha,* a "Japanese musical play," sought to apply the brisk, up-to-date manner of *A Gaiety Girl* to the still useful Oriental clime. Harry Greenbank passed up the patter but kept his rhymes snappy and cute:

Oh, what will they do with Molly,
With poor little madcap me?
I've got in a mess
In a Japanese dress,
And what will the consequence be?

1900

As the twentieth century drew nearer, more and more English musical comedies visited Broadway until American writers got the hang of it and turned out their own. The German-born Gustave Kerker did such a convincing job on *The Belle of New York* that it totaled 697 performances on Shaftsbury Avenue after only 56 on Thirty-ninth Street. Revived continuously in Britain, it had all the gentle attributes of their home product and so little of the flavor of Manhattan that many Britishers today forget that it was an American show.

Kerker's career is typical of musical theatre trends in his time. He started with a comic opera, *Cadets,* which toured the South in 1879, and Kerker arrived on Broadway with a saga of the Orient, *The Pearl of Pekin,* in 1888. His first solid hit was *Castles in the Air* (1890), followed by three "reviews," as they were spelled then, English-fashion, *In Gay New York* (1896), *All of the Town* (1897), and *Yankee Doodle Dandy* (1898).

The American revue dates from *The Passing Show* in 1894, an attempt to copy the new French vogue for mixed bills of songs and sketches, more or less unified by a general theme, or at any rate a title. Apparently there was an audience for the so-called review who couldn't see going to a music hall for exactly the same sort of entertainment. *The Passing Show* occupied the Casino Theatre, a palace of Moorish gingerbread across from the Metropolitan Opera House; there the smart, urban-aimed revue installed itself in annual editions during the summer months. The species of fare the Casino shows supplied was inadvertently a summing up of all the elements in America's musical theatre heritage: that first *Passing Show,* for example, despite a vaguely Parisian atmosphere, contained acrobatics, topical jests, a "plantation dance," imitations of famous actors, burlesques of recent hits, a short ballet, and something called "Living Pictures." The Tamale Boys were on hand for comedy, seconded by Mabel Stephenson and her "familiar stories about Jonah, Daniel and the bear," while one Gus Pixley leaped to prominence with "his original manner of walking with his head near his heels." In short, this was pure vaudeville, but it pretended to be more sophisticated—and it did have a title.

An even more popular form of variety show was to be found at Weber and Fields' 665-seat Music Hall, opened in 1895 and kept open without a break until 1904. The audiences who flocked to Broadway and Twenty-ninth Street were the same respectable burghers who haunted Tony Pastor's; they felt burlesque was uncouth, but at the same time they resisted the longueurs of comic opera's empyreal probity. Luckily for them, the Music Hall Beauty Chorus struck the happy medium between purity and prurience, and though the comedy was often brutal, it was clean.

Joe Weber and Lew Fields had grown up together and worked out an act while still in their teens. Time was when they would start off with a song that began "Here we are, a jolly pair," but at their Music Hall their antics would take off with Weber's plaintive "Don't poosh me, Myer!" Short and dumpy Weber would appear first, followed by taller, slimmer Fields slicing the air with his cane: "Didn't I telling you, vatch your etiquette?"

Although Weber and Fields' public could look down on

those who were still loyal to burlesque, the Music Hall they attended with such regularity was in fact built around that dying art. The second half of the evening was pure music hall, with various performers doing what they presumably did best, to be joined by the Music Hall Beauty Chorus in the finale. But the first half was always a spoof on the latest hit, musical or otherwise. *The Geisha* was travestied as "The Geezer," *Barbara Frietchie* as "Barbara Fidgety," and *Quo Vadis* surfaced as "Quo Vass Iss?" Even Reginald de Koven's *The Highwayman* got the Weber-Fields treatment as "The Way-High Man."

These parodies were so well known that producers and stars would do almost anything to have their plays assaulted. The Music Hall matinees were on Tuesday instead of the more usual Wednesday so the Weberfields Company, as they called themselves, could visit the show of the moment to give their own version of it the next week, partly from a script and partly improvised. (The cast of the play under examination would then visit the Music Hall on their free Tuesday afternoon for the treat of seeing themselves lampooned.) The bill was repeatedly changed, and customers were further encouraged to return to tune in on such big stars of the day as De Wolf Hopper, Marie Dressler, Willie Collier, and Lillian Russell. The two comedians even approached Met star Lillian Nordica, who somehow got the idea that their offer of three thousand dollars was per performance instead of per week.

It cannot be said that Weber and Fields did much to develop the revue form, for their shows were pure vaudeville plunked down with burlesque. They did popularize so-called Dutch comedy—which both lived on to see revived in *Knickerbocker Holiday* as late as 1938—and sparked many imitators, most notably the Rogers Brothers, Max and Gus, and their series of anarchic musical farces that presaged the Marx Brothers. Weber and Fields' primary contribution was their likable rough comedy, perhaps the most beloved brand of humor in the 1890s:

Weber: A soldier has chust been shot!
Fields: Vhere?
Weber: In the excitement!

By the turn of the century comic opera had finally evolved into musical comedy with no noticeable rise in quality. Under the spell of *A Gaiety Girl,* composers abandoned their aping of Sullivan and Offenbach to reproduce the work of inferior British talents like Lionel Monckton, Ivan Caryll, and Paul Rubens, just as *Hair* many years later brought on a raft of crummy rock scores. The few comic operas that appeared were no prizes, either. But production costs were low—aside from a handful of stars, actors worked for what amounted to honoraria in those pre-union days—and new theatres were raised every year, five in 1903 alone.

Musical shows were so poverty-stricken in the realm of originality that a simpleminded sextet in the British show *Florodora* created a sensation entirely on the basis of the beauty of its six female singers. With thin music by Leslie Stuart and a routine libretto, *Florodora* (not the heroine of the piece, incidentally, but its setting on a Philippine island) played 505 performances on its first run here in 1901 and constantly showed up again through 1920. Broadway luminaries like Diamond Jim Brady booked seats for *Florodora* every night, arriving just before the sextet, "Tell Me, Pretty Maiden" (it was technically a twelve-et, with six men and six women), and departing sated just after.

Like the previously mentioned Gustave Kerker and his compères Gustav Luders and Ludwig Englander, the leading theatre composers of the early 1900s were foreigners passing as American musicians in a business that lacked a genuine American voice. Luders' pièce de résistance, *The Prince of Pilsen* (1903), disclosed little of note in the way of plot, score, or comedy, but its librettist, Frank Pixley, happily assessed its virtues in an interview. To him, a first-rate musical show needed an appeal to "the eye, ear and intelligence of the public," a faraway setting for exciting costumes, a soprano, a tenor, a comedian, and "the bizarre, the unique" (no doubt Pixley's ghost sat in on planning sessions for *Man of La Mancha*). Of *The Prince of Pilsen*'s tale about a Cincinnati brewer mistaken for a prince while traveling in Nice, one critic wrote, "The story is worked out—if it is worked out at all—in the wings." Luders took care to include a sextet, "The American Girl," designed to steal some attention from the one in *Florodora*. It didn't.

The Vienna-born Englander was too filled with memories of the zither and cembalo to pretend he wasn't writing in the Viennese manner, and his tunes were too rudimentary to excite more than passing interest. He did have the presence of mind to write *his* sextet for *The Belle of Bohemia* in 1900, one year before *Florodora* was heard in America. It was Englander who wrote the score for that first Casino review, *The Passing Show,* but his moment of glory came with *The Rich Mr. Hoggenheimer,* a reworking of Ivan Caryll's London trump, *The Girl from Kay's. The Rich Mr. Hoggenheimer* lasted 187 performances, mainly through the efforts of dialect comedian Sam Bernard, who played—as he invariably played—an overbearing Jew. Englander's work on the show pointed out no new paths, but Bernard's did; his emphasis on low comedy within a strictly book-musical format encouraged the growth of shows built around a star comedian. In an almost direct descent from George L. Fox's pantomime *Humpty Dumpty,* the comedy musicals pushed such as Eddie Foy and the team of David Montgomery and Fred Stone to the foreground in a spate of careless but profitable vehicles.

The only touch of freshness on Broadway in those days was found in the books, music, lyrics, and stage direction of George M. Cohan. The songs he wrote for *Little Johnny Jones* (1904)—"Give My Regards to Broadway," "The Yankee Doodle Boy" ("I'm a Yankee Doodle dandy . . ."), "Goodbye, Flo"—boasted an energy and naturalness that grabbed the public on first hearing and seemed capable of sweeping away the cobwebs of *dreivierteltakt* and Hindoo intermezzi.

Englander, Luders, and company could only reach the theatregoing audience, but everyone in the country liked Cohan's music—and everyone could sing it. His lyrics especially were spunky and outgoing, if condescending to the "rubens" in the boondocks. One of the minor *Little Johnny Jones* numbers, "I'm Mighty Glad I'm Living and That's All," is a typical Cohan piece. The tune is simpleminded, but the lyrics carry it off; Cohan knew how to dress hackneyed ideas in a conversational tone, giving his work a lift rare for those times. Unlike most of musical comedy's inhabitants, Cohan's people sang over the footlights as if chatting in the street:

> "This life's a play" said Shakespeare—
> They're the truest words he spoke;
> Mister Shakespeare is a man I wish I'd met.
> For I've seen enough of life to understand that it's a joke;
> It's a joke and no one's guessed the answer yet.
> Why it's all imagination—
> If you'll only stop to think,
> To this positive conclusion you'll arrive:
> We live and then we die,
> And when we die, why it's goodbye,
> So we ought to all be glad that we're alive . . .

As Oscar Hammerstein II put it, "Cohan's genius was to say simply what everybody else was subconsciously feeling."

Forty-five Minutes from Broadway (1906) was Cohan's best work, though the critics were sour about it. They complained of the show's hectic pacing, the intrusive slang, the cheap flag-waving. The New Rochelle Chamber of Commerce objected to the play's setting, which was New Rochelle, and instituted a boycott until it realized that no great harm was being done. *Theatre* magazine called it "rubbish," but the title song and "Mary's a Grand Old Name," "So Long, Mary," and "Stand Up and Fight Like H——" (lyrics patriotically revised in 1918) carried the day. The sheer vitality and Americanness of this archetypal musical comedy was such that the television program *Omnibus* could program it in the mid-fifties without patronizing either the piece or the audience.

Cohan soon became the reigning prince of actor-managers, especially in the musical field, since he was so much in harmony with contemporary audiences while rival producers had only their dowdy rehashes of *A Gaiety Girl* and *Florodora.* But despite his immense popularity with the public, Cohan repelled the critics. Like the anonymous reviewer who took exception to *Evangeline*'s "perennial limbs and immutable cow," Harrison Grey Fiske's *Dramatic Mirror* looked on bewildered: "Precisely why these Cohan concoctions are so popular with the New York public is a mystery. . . . They must be classed, so to speak, as high-grade second-grade productions. Perhaps the true secret of Mr. Cohan's unprecedented success, too permanent for mere theatrical luck, consists of his admirable stagecraft. In the art of presenting musical comedy, Mr. Cohan is apparently without peer."

Other journalists took a harsher stance. Shortly after the premiere of *George Washington, Jr.* (1906), the old *Life* magazine's James S. Metcalfe erupted in print, showing no great love for the musical but a striking respect for its influence on the country: "Mr. Cohan . . . trades on the national regard for the name of George Washington as a dollar-catcher . . . in this character which he has created for himself, he presumably typifies his ideal of American young manhood. He makes him a vulgar, cheap, blatant, ill-mannered, flashily-dressed, insolent smart Aleck . . . the rounds of applause which greet the efforts of this offensive personality must convey to the minds of ignorant boys a depraving ideal for their inspiration and imitation."

Cohan replied to Metcalfe on the front page of his firm's house organ, *The Spot Light,* but he gave a more revealing answer in private to a friend: "I'll never be really happy now until I own a part of Broadway. Just a little part, mind you. The top part."

Musically, there was only one giant in those days, although his work was hardly in the popular idiom and the shows he collaborated on were usually the same dizzy swill displayed in one outdated comic opera after another. Born in Ireland and educated in Germany and Vienna, Victor Herbert had a gift for melody unparalleled in his generation, and as a conservatory-trained cellist and composition student he could bring scoring technique up to a new high level for Broadway. But eleven shows trotted by before he could install himself as a master of his chosen field, and when he did it was via the ancient medium of the extravaganza.

The big hit of 1903 was an adaptation of L. Frank Baum's *The Wizard of Oz,* the author doing his own book and lyrics to the rather flat music of A. Baldwin Sloane and Paul Tietjens. (Oddly enough, Baum's stage version of his children's classic was only approximate compared to *The Wiz*'s more faithful scenario in 1974.) *The Wizard of Oz* earned its huge run of 293 performances on the basis of its lavish scenery, the eccentricities of Montgomery and Stone as the Scarecrow and the Tin Woodman, and a dancing cow named Imogene that gave oldtimers a chance to wax nostalgic over *Evangeline.* Accordingly, a carbon copy was mounted later that year called *Babes in Toyland,* with music by Herbert. In place of the Tin Woodman and the Scarecrow were Little Bo Peep, Contrary Mary, and the rest of that crowd, while a Spider's Forest, the Floral Palace of the Moth Queen, and the Christmas Tree Grove in Fairyland competed with the sights of Oz for New Yorkers' attentions. Since Dorothy and her cow had been blown to Oz in a breathtaking cyclone scene (1974's *The Wiz* had a breathtaking cyclone scene too, but no cow), the babes of the title gained Toyland in a deliberate imitation, billed as an "electric storm at sea and wreck of the galleon." *Babes in Toyland* had a dancing spider instead of a cow, plus a fight to the death between an army of toy soldiers and the babes' wicked uncle Barnaby.

While *The Wizard of Oz* succeeded because of its special effects and two star comedians, *Babes in Toyland* won its 192 performances on the strength of its score. By now aware of a shift in the musical weather, Herbert carefully diluted his European sound with a ragtime bit in "The Song of the Poet," and bettered this with a lengthy ragtime number in *It Happened in Nordland* (1904):

> Bandana Land!
> Oh, it ain't upon the maps;
> It's the land of chicken fighting,
> It's the land of shooting craps . . .

As each new commission came along, Herbert responded with the cream of his talent, but the words he had to work with were still tawdry and old hat for the most part, and the comedy was forever being stuck into the plot at right angles. After the double success of *The Wizard of Oz* and *Babes in Toyland,* it was clear that extravaganza was alive, if unwell; Herbert gave it a fast high with *Little Nemo* (1908), based on Winsor McKay's fantastic art nouveau comic strip. In taking Nemo from the *New York Herald*'s Sunday supplement to the stage, librettist Harry B. Smith missed the light touch of visionary idealism and whimsy that made McKay's adolescent one of the pop heroes of the age, though the spectacle format at least provided a moratorium on the love-crazed shopgirls and cocky juveniles who were infesting musical comedy. *Little Nemo* contained so many songs that the show could have passed for opera, and stage director Herbert Gresham crowned himself king of display with one loud set after another: the Land of the Fairies of St. Valentine, the Weather Factory Office of the Dawn Guard, the cannibal-settled Table D'Hote Islands (with a ragtime chorus for the cannibals, *bien entendu*), a Palace of Patriotism on the Fourth of July, Central Park, a battleship, and, of course, the trademark familiar to the *Herald*'s Sunday readership, Little Nemo's bedroom.

The commercial aspect of the theatre is no small piece of its development. There is a trail of salable properties that career from one medium to another—literature, films, the stage—and this trail takes in some of the theatre's biggest successes as well as some elephantine gaffes. A 1908 staging of *Little Nemo* is not as novel as it sounds, for the strip was already rather theatrical (McKay himself did the show's poster), but it reveals the ease with which musical comedy addressed itself to the news of the day—and, equally, the ease with which it embalmed lively material in case-hardened formula. Perhaps nobody minded when the musical theatre was an innocent fledgling, but later on unwieldy adaptations of major works from other media were to prove a bugbear to critics and public alike.

Veering back and forth between romantic folderol and less hifalutin' comic razzmatazz, Herbert finally found a middle road between the two for his best comic opera collaboration, *Naughty Marietta* (1910), produced by opera impresario Oscar Hammerstein for two of his Manhattan Opera Company's brightest lights, Emma Trentini and Orville Harrold. Rida Johnson Young's book was firm enough for Herbert to build some early book-music integration on, writing songs for specific slots in the story instead of working them in any old way. There were no star comedians in *Naughty Marietta,* just a featured comic in Dutch dialect, for Trentini and Harrold knew what they wanted and took up most of the stage most of the time. Romance had recently entered the picture, courtesy of Viennese pieces like *The Merry Widow* and *The Chocolate Soldier,* and romance there was a-plenty in *Naughty Marietta*. Herbert even tempered the leaden touch of comic opera exaggeration with a colorful evocation of dawn in New Orleans for the obligatory opening chorus. Some foghorn vocalism from the anonymous ensemble was the rule in those days, but only to rev up the audience or help settle latecomers—never were they used as mood pieces or to focus the action. Taking their cue from the French, Englander and Kerker and their coevals wrote throwaway openers that added nothing to the story but time. Gilbert and Sullivan had pioneered in making the first musical item count for something: *Trial by Jury* and *The Sorcerer* start the exposition in their opening choruses, *Pinafore*'s "We Sail the Ocean Blue" has an arresting nautical tang, and in *The Yeomen of the Guard* they brought the curtain up on a solo aria. But not till Herbert did America's composers connect with Sullivan's innovations.

The *Naughty Marietta* score was the most book-coordinated effort of Herbert's career. It had as much variety as the others but held together better, with fewer spare parts and an unusual grasp of characterization. Two comic songs, "Anybody Else But Me" and "It's Pretty Soft for Simon," derived from Simon's personality, though a third number was the more usual catalogue of woman's caprices that were the coin of the comic realm in those days. Check out this prototypical moment in *It Happened in Nordland:*

> Oh, she first appeared in Eden,
> Did the woman in the case,
> Where she made her husband grapple
> With that appetizing apple—
> And we had to leave the place!
> Ev'ry beauty, ev'ry talent,
> It is certain that she had 'em;
> She just smiled a teeny-weeny smile
> And she hypnotized poor Adam!

Herbert's next hit, *Sweethearts* (1913), furnished the test case for ASCAP's (American Society of Composers, Authors, and Publishers) victorious Supreme Court suit to establish royalty payments for public performance, after Herbert caught the Shanley's Restaurant orchestra merrily sawing its way through a *Sweethearts* medley. The decision, written by Justice Oliver Wendell Holmes, was a cornerstone in the rise of pop music as a major American industry.

The composer's personal favorite among his total of forty-two was *Eileen* (1917), a "romantic comic opera" with an exciting, suspenseful libretto by Henry Blossom about lovers and patriots in rebellious Ireland. It had been Herbert's dream to create a genuinely Irish score, and *Eileen* was his masterpiece, meeting *Naughty Marietta* in richness and surpassing it in warmth. Ballads, jigs, comic numbers, and full-throated choruses welled up in such quantity that there was no time for reprises and the audience had its ears full trying to assimilate so much in one evening. Herbert had flirted with the Gaelic sound before at times, but they were genre songs—this was music. This was also a failure, lasting only eight weeks. Only the "big tune," "Thine Alone," had any following, although "The Irish Have a Great Day Tonight" was a superb example of the big Broadway rouser, as Irish as the corner tavern and as aggressive as anything by Cohan.

Herbert was eclipsed before his death in 1924 by younger talents, though his last four shows were all hits. He was way ahead of his contemporaries in scoring sympathetic love plots, but the Viennese imports and American successors to the Viennese style had hit on a more adult approach to romance. Futhermore, the public's response to popular music had shifted slightly during his career. The world of Tin Pan Alley was moving at top speed, garnering new sounds and subsuming them into its morass of moon songs and novelty numbers. "Alexander's Ragtime Band" came out in 1911, the year Herbert wrote "All Your Own Am I" and "In the Golden Long Ago." Only once did he rise above the low common denominator of his public's requirements, in *Eileen,* which had comedy and action but an uncompromisingly integrated score. Herbert had bowed to formula so often that when he leaped ahead of his time he left his audience behind him.

3

Ziegfeld and the Revue

Florenz Ziegfeld got his start in the Midwest managing the sideshow strongman Sandow and—in a lapse of the good theatre sense that would seldom desert him thereafter—"The Dancing Ducks of Denmark" (heat applied to the soles of their webbed feet made them leap around and quack). Following a brief fling in New York he went to Paris, where he met Anna Held, the wasp-waisted singer with the archetypal come-hither look in her eyes. Ziegfeld became her producer as well as her husband, putting her over in a variety of second-rate comic operas like Gustav Luders' *Mam'selle Napoleon* (1903), which one reviewer dubbed a "transplanted rose that turned out to be a particularly large and offensive cabbage."

The Ziegfeld touch was already apparent in *The Parisian Model* (1906): while the chorus girls hymned the convenience of "A Gown for Each Hour of the Day," Held danced in and out in six lavish dresses, making for a rather short day. There was also an approach to nudity in "I'd Like to See a Little More of You"—even simulated nudity was a novelty in 1906 —and for one choreographic sequence the girls were outfitted in bells on their fingers, toes, necklines, and, as one helpful critic put it, "elsewhere."

Back in Paris after *The Parisian Model* closed, Ziegfeld was as taken with the French-style revue as George Lederer had been when he produced *The Passing Show* in 1894. Retaining the digs at urban life that the Parisians adored, and soft-pedaling the near nudity, Ziegfeld presented his own revue in 1907 on the New York Theatre Roof, rechristened the Jardin de Paris for the event and totally done over by Joseph Urban.

Semi-unknown and without a great bank account to draw on, Ziegfeld had to forgo the luxury he was soon to be famous for, but good taste is free and Ziegfeld spent a lot of it. The *Follies of 1907* cost $13,000 in toto, with no stars, limited spectacle, and some quite ordinary songs gathered from here and there in the manner of the early extravaganzas. The *Follies* came into town with no advance fanfare—in fact, the spiffy *Dramatic Mirror* covered it on the vaudeville page. It was a good show, if not earthshakingly different, and it did even better on the road than it had in town, proving that Ziegfeld's first *Follies* couldn't have been as sophisticated as they were eventually to get.

No mere showman but a clever producer with an eye for the next rather than the latest fashion, Ziegfeld stepped up his expenses a bit on the *Follies of 1908*. Purporting to be nothing less than a clever spoof of society from the Garden of Eden to the first night of the *Follies of 1908*, this revue had stars—at least it did after the notices came out. Nora Bayes, Mae Murray, and William Powers won raves, especially for Bayes' "You Will Have to Sing an Irish Song" and "Shine On, Harvest Moon," and the show hit some sort of apex in one sequence for which the chorus girls were costumed as taxicabs.

Now fully bankrolled, Ziegfeld was able to mount the *Fol-*

lies of 1909 in the style to which they would become accustomed. He grew sharper in spotting fresh talent: the 1910 *Follies* had Lillian Lorraine and Fanny Brice, with Bert Williams down from Harlem. The girls, too, continued to be the loveliest creatures ever seen on Broadway, but the composers, lyricists, and sketch writers Ziegfeld hired were hacking out second-rate material until Julian Mitchell was brought in to take charge of the staging. Mitchell had seen battle with Cohan and Herbert; one of the first star directors, it was he, really, who made the 1903 spectacle *The Wizard of Oz* the special pleasure it was, and he was just the man to water the wilting buds of Ziegfeld's flowering art. Together, they brought writers of real talent into the *Follies* camp, and Joseph Urban was secured for the lavish decor that was a given in any Ziegfeld endeavor. Later to design an entire theatre for his pet producer, Urban was one of the most esteemed theatrical artists of his day, heavily influenced by Max Reinhardt and Gordon Craig and way ahead of his colleagues working in New York. Armed with Mitchell and Urban, Ziegfeld's shows were able to achieve the artistic unity that makes a great revue so great, though the *Follies* never had the literate sketches that would so engage the public when *The Little Show* and its stylish progeny rolled in during the thirties.

The Shubert brothers—more about them later—were the first to follow the path Ziegfeld was beating. Recalling that first "review" at the Casino Theatre in 1894, they promptly gave the world *The Passing Show of 1912.* This one harked back to the heyday of burlesque, with parodies of then-current hits (Charles Winninger and Blanche Ring gave their impressions of Lionel and John Barrymore in *The Jest* in the 1919 *Passing Show*), leading slapstick comics like Willie and Eugene Howard and Charlotte Greenwood, and its chorus line, classified by the Shuberts as show girls, mediums, and ponies (Lee's personal favorite).

The Passing Show did well enough to initiate a line of sequels, one a year in late spring. Each would run the summer and then light out for the provinces, "direct from Broadway." The canny Shuberts had learned Ziegfeld's lesson well: hire talented actors, apportion the levity, song, and spectacle evenly, and give the audience something outstanding to gaze at in the realm of feminine charm. By 1914 *The Passing Show* was nudging the *Follies;* it even had its own brand-new star in Marilynn (the spelling changed later) Miller and a bid for prestige in a hopefully arty "Beautiful Persian Garden Scene" in the Maxfield Parrish idiom.

It was easy to see where the revue was headed. Less than ten years away lay the ultimate completion of the form, with full scores by Arthur Schwartz and Howard Dietz instead of donations from various nonadhesive sources, plus performers like the Astaires, Ethel Waters, Clifton Webb, Libby Holman, Fred Allen, and Tamara Geva—style, in short. Well, the *Follies* had the look of style if not the fact, and soon the *Passing Show* began to make diffident bids for sophistication, with at least one song in each revue devoted to the latest town topic. *The Passing Show of 1922* raised eyebrows with a send-up of O'Neill's raunchy *The Hairy Ape,* cast entirely from the girls' chorus, and a ballet performed "in the manner of the Marquis de Sade," while female impersonator Francis Renault went off the deep end in his mannerisms. Unbeknownst to the Shuberts, who assumed they were playing to the gallery, *le tout New York* received the *Passing Show* as a glory of their night life, reveling in its vulgarity and calling it a sort of degraded sophistication.

Joseph Urban's celebrity for his *Follies* designs was not lost on producers ardent to mount their own revues and become Ziegfelds. But decor alone was not enough in revue, even when laid out by Urban—and especially when not: reviewing Jack Norworth's *Odds and Ends of 1917,* Burns Mantle commented, "the scenery is by someone who plays the Joseph Urban harmonies by ear, and is more or less tone deaf."

4

The Birth of Romance

"You Will Remember Vienna"

Even while Victor Herbert was still at his height writing comic operas, the form itself was well into decline. Actually, it looked pretty debilitated all the way back at the turn of the century; the fresher, English-style musical comedies with their relaxing everydayness and brighter comedy aimed the deathblow, and George M. Cohan's patriotic hustle delivered the coup de grace. Comic opera's stock was so low in 1905, the year Franz Lehár's *The Merry Widow* debuted in Vienna, that Henry W. Savage waited until the show literally swept over Western Europe before he dared bring it to Broadway.

But *The Merry Widow* was not exactly a comic opera, even if it was cast in the mold. Its special feature was the deftness and beauty with which the central love plot worked itself out through the evening. Like many another pair of romantic leads, Prince Danilo and Hanna Glawari (renamed Sonia for purposes of glamour) bickered fruitlessly for three acts until they conceded passion's supreme power and surrendered to each other. Lehár gave these debonair sybarites music that was supple and saucy, the first draft of tonal champagne to flow across American footlights.

Savage imported Adrian Ross' London translation of the original German, cast the leads elegantly with Ethel Jackson and Donald Brian, and saw the work through to a sumptuous production on October 21, 1907. This is a landmark date, for neither *The Mikado*'s Yum-Yum and Nanki-Poo nor *The Red Mill*'s Gretchen and Doris (funny name for a man, Doris) nor *Forty-Five Minutes from Broadway*'s Mary and Kid Burns struck the romantic spark as naturally as Sonia and Danilo. The critics cheered, the public was enraptured, and the show ran for a year. Merry Widow picture hats, Merry Widow dresses, even Merry Widow dog leashes became standard articles of fashion, and the show toured the land so extensively that no one who wasn't blind or dead didn't see it.

Of all the songs of that era, the "Merry Widow Waltz" ("I Love You So") best documents the musical's growing prowess at handling a love scene without crashing cymbals, an offstage chorus, or high C's. This waltz, sung as a duet at the end of Act Three, made its first appearance in Act Two, hummed in unison by the lovers as they moved gently around an empty room. The scene was encored nightly by spellbound audiences, of whom few were aware that they were sitting in on the birth of the popular theatre's ability to limn a genuine emotion in terms of the dance. Never before had a romance climaxed so gracefully in a musical show. The stock military drills and step-dances of the past now had to yield the arena to a more personal movement. As of 1907, regimental turns and the fervent nullity of the tap shoe were displaced forever, the first to disappear, the second relegated to the dumpier sorts of musical comedy. The more expressive art of the ballroom dancer would put them into the shadows.

Now that Viennese comic opera was back in view—romantic comic opera; let's call it operetta, though it wasn't at the time—other specimens of the type were rushed to New York in translations commissioned for London productions. While *The Merry Widow* was still running, Oskar Straus' *A Waltz Dream* settled in comfortably with *its* waltz song, "Softly, So Softly" (waltz songs were a must, the signature tune of each individual romance), and 1909 was the year of Leo Fall's American bow with *The Dollar Princess,* a snazzier, less rhapsodic opus than its fellow creatures. Eventually lasting 288 performances, Fall's piece had no spectacular waltz duet to catch the hearts and minds of the public, but it did have a luscius finale featuring the loving couple alone on stage. "No farewell jingle and patter," exulted one critic. "The lovers find awakening, and a golden curtain, like amber-glowing flood of light, enshrines them in its love mysteries."

Straus' *The Heroic Soldier* had all Vienna agog in 1908 because of its plot source, George Bernard Shaw's *Arms and the Man.* Turning the ironic Shavian mouthpieces into comic opera loonies was no easy job, but Bernard Hermansky carefully divested the characters of bite, and the play of its point, substituting the paste and puffery of unrenewed format. Retitled *The Chocolate Soldier,* the show did not equal the sophistication of the *Widow*'s love plot, but was astonishingly profitable here in 1909, the more astonishing because it has faded from the scene (the 1947 revival was a dismal failure) while *The Merry Widow* is still very much with us.

The one dissenting voice in that first chorus of delight was, naturally, Shaw's. He hated it. In fact, he saw it on three separate occasions: "It was so terrible I couldn't bear more than one act at a time!" A few years later, someone was dickering with the playwright over the musical rights to *The Devil's Disciple,* which had been a smash in New York with Richard Mansfield in 1899. Negotiations broke down when Shaw required that the adaptation be a grand opera. The composer preferred to do it as a musical, and told Shaw that no one would want to see a grand opera. "I would not want to see a musical," answered Shaw. End of discussion.

But after those first few Viennese golden eggs, the goose balked. Lehár's *Gypsy Love* collapsed in 1911 after 31 performances, followed by *Eva*'s similar fate in 1912. The hapless Gustav Luders may not have killed himself just because his virtually Viennese *Somewhere Else* flopped so definitively in 1913 (it was generally held that he had), but in any case his career was finished. Romance, however, was not dead; it was just getting started, waiting, as it were, for the right man.

The right man was Belgian-born, German-trained Ivan Caryll, and the right show had already come along in 1911, *The Pink Lady,* one of the consummate entertainments of its time. Based on a French farce called, no doubt presumptuously, *Le Satyre, The Pink Lady* ran an eye-popping 320 times to frequently sold-out houses (unusual in those days), breaking all box office records for the New Amsterdam Theatre, now a run-down movie house at the southwest corner of Broadway and Forty-second Street. The cross-country tour was an unprecedented triumph. Like *The Merry Widow* four years earlier, it was *the* show to see, making the color pink a necessary in every woman's wardrobe. Playing the heroine, Hazel Dawn found time to play the violin as well during the big number, "Beautiful Lady," and Julian Mitchell once again knocked the customers over with special effects, including the full-cast staging of "Donny Did, Donny Didn't" on an elegant double stairway. Approving the show's consistency, the *Boston Herald*'s Philip Hale said, "Here we have a musical comedy that does not depend on the antics of an acrobatic comedian, on clowning or the independent display of brazen-faced show girls."

Caryll went on to *Oh! Oh! Delphine* in 1912, confirming his popularity with a comic song, "Everything's at Home Except Your Wife," and a parrot who shrieked "Oh! Oh! Delphine!" when the action lagged (the parrot did a lot of shrieking). 1914's Caryll entry *The Belle of Bond Street* was the same sort of show (no parrot, it seems) with comedienne Gaby Deslys demonstrating the level of Broadway's concurrent novelty numbers with "Who Paid the Rent for Mrs. Rip Van Winkle?" But Caryll broke out of the *Merry Widow-Pink Lady* rut, reviving extravaganza for 295 performances with *Chin-Chin, or A Modern Aladdin* (1914). The recipe for success in this medium had not changed: lush sets, star comedians (Montgomery and Stone), and a giant hit song, the interpolated "It's a Long Way to Tipperary" by Harry Williams and Jack Judge.

Caryll bypassed the comic opera formula more distinctly in 1918 when he collaborated with Guy Bolton and P. G. Wodehouse on *The Girl Behind the Gun.* Bolton and Wodehouse were already inciting to revolution with their naturalistic plots and lyrics for the Princess shows they wrote with Jerome Kern. This particular item took its cue from the War, running heavily to bistros and uniforms, but it avoided the ermined visions of the upper crust that were overwhelming other musical comedies. Now that the Viennese vogue had run its course, its replacements were to prove more durable, more plentiful, and, at long last, conspicuously indigenous—but everything that followed Lehár had him to thank for the new sincerity at the romantic heart of the musical.

5

The Princess Shows

British musicals were migrating here in large numbers in the post–*Gaiety Girl,* pre–*Merry Widow* days, and it was standard practice to revise the scores, exorcising any predominantly Anglican strain for something closer to home. Jerome Kern's big break came about in this way in 1904 when he was assigned to spruce up *Mr. Wix of Wickham* for female impersonator Julian Eltinge. Alan Dale, among other critics, sat up and took notice: "Who is this Jerome Kern whose music towers in an Eiffel way above the average, hurdy-gurdy accompaniment of the present-day musical comedy?"

Who he wasn't is evidenced by the song titles of his *The Girl from Utah* (1914): "They Didn't Believe Me," "You're Here and I'm Here," "Why Don't They Dance the Polka Any More?," and "Same Sort of Girl." In other words, he was no comic opera hack pimping for hussars, gypsies, and switched babies. A Victor Herbert show of that same year indicates comic opera's dim rapport with the way we were in its song titles: "The Golden Age," "The Springtime of Life," "The Love of the Lorelei."

Meanwhile, F. Ray Comstock, owner of the 299-seat Princess Theatre on Thirty-ninth Street, was looking for a suitable attraction for his low-income-yielding house. A literary agent named Elizabeth Marbury thought a new kind of small-budget musical would go over, and she even had the authors in mind: Kern and Guy Bolton. Within months a short but significant phase was inaugurated at the Princess with *Nobody Home* on April 20, 1915. The wee stage kept matters in trim with an eleven-piece orchestra, a cast of less than twenty and only two sets, thereby eliminating the third-act's-worth of Count Somebody's glittering party.

In eliminating the count and his ballroom, Kern and Bolton naturally junked the aristocratic poses and *faux gestes* of the past. Billed as an "intimate musical" and advertised as a "zippy, fox trotting musical treat," *Nobody Home* was based on Paul Rubens' English show *Mr. Popple of Ippleton.* The plot was no winner, perhaps, but at least there wasn't a glass tiara in every corner nor an obnoxious comedian chopping away at the libretto with cane and putty nose. *Nobody Home* was light and melodious, if without a big song hit, and after the four-month run Marbury and Comstock decided to go another round.

Kern was off having a flop on his own that fall with *Miss Information,* but he returned to the fold in time to pen his fourth score of 1915, *Very Good Eddie.* This one was a whopping hit at 341 performances, even taking into account the Princess' small capacity (the show moved to a larger theatre after five months). The charming "Babes in the Wood" was a favorite at first hearing, with a melody so pure and logical that Kern's harmony could be the simplest imaginable and yet never seem hackneyed. As for the lyrics, they were at long last ready to get down to cases. Good-bye to (naughty)

Marietta's dream melody ("Ah, Sweet Mystery of Life" at last she found it) and hello to 1915:

Dick: Some of the time
I loved a girl from Berlin;
Some of the time
She came from Spain.
And
Italian girls and French I adore—
Elsie: Now that we know who started the war!
Dick: But I love some sort of
Somebody all of the time.*

Bolton based the *Very Good Eddie* book on a bedroom farce, *Over Night,* and stuck close to it, making the most of a simple mix-up involving two couples who accidentally switch partners on a Hudson River honeymoon cruise. Informality ruled the evening; in so small a theatre no nuance was missed, and no one had to belt out a song or bellow a punch line, causing one reviewer to label it a "kitchenette production." Bolton himself said, "It was the first of its kind to rely on situation and character laughs instead of clowning and Weberfieldian cross-talk with which the large-scale musical filled in between the romantic scenes." For the record, there *was* a slapstick comedian, John E. Hazzard as the manic clerk of the Rip Van Winkle Inn, but the two couples supplied most of the evening's jests themselves, so the humor derived causatively from the incidents. We are now on our way to organic.

Very Good Eddie did not represent a gigantic breakthrough—even its intimacy was no novelty, having been tried out first in *Nobody Home*—but it was different. The twelve ladies of the ensemble, described on the posters as the "swagger fashion chorus," wore their dresses down to the ankle, inspiring thanks from Heywood Broun: "One is not called upon to gaze at the knees of the world and weep." Actually,

* "Some Sort of Somebody," rescued from *Miss Information,* had lyrics by comedienne Elsie Janis.

some critics resented the smallness of the show. They liked their musicals big and brawny and they weren't attracted by naturalism in musical comedy books. But the public was much taken with *Very Good Eddie,* displaying an enthusiasm they hadn't for *Nobody Home,* and the Princess shows became a going concern, continuing to emphasize farce in their stories, charm in their songs, and small-town America in their settings. As Bolton put it, "Americans laugh more naturally at a funny hotel clerk or janitor than a crudely drawn cannibal princess."

The cannibal princess was the stock-in-trade of the Herbert shows. Significantly, the Kern–Bolton–P. G. Wodehouse *Oh Boy!* opened in 1917, the year Herbert suffered three flops, *Eileen, Her Regiment,* and *Miss 1917,* a revue that, cyclically enough, was also written by Kern, Bolton, and Wodehouse. Herbert himself predicted that Kern would inherit his mantle, but Kern not only took it over, he took it in as well, retailored for a new age. *Oh Boy!*'s score, for example, contained fewer waltzes than a comic opera, stressing the fox trot and simple 4/4 ballads that were even closer to public sentiment than Cohan's outgoing showstoppers. Kern's music didn't demand sustained applause—it wasn't noisy enough—but it provoked a deep response from its listeners and called for further hearings. Kern was the first American songwriter whose music was true, beautiful, and good, a major gambit in the rise of the romantic musical. He was one of the decisive forces behind *Show Boat* (Oscar Hammerstein II and possibly Edna Ferber being the others), and looking back on his career, one can call him *the* godsend composer in the early years of the artistic musical.

Kern's next show, *Leave It to Jane* (1917), was a Princess-sized affair presented at the slightly larger Longacre Theatre. Again working with Bolton and Wodehouse, the composer produced an energetic score for this prototypical college romp—Big Game and all—based on George Ade's *The College Widow.* More and more critics were realizing that everyday

American settings were not just a fad but a sign of changing times. "The old timers will soon begin to grieve sorely," crowed Alan Dale in the *New York American* after the opening, "as they view the new form of rational musical comedy actually 'getting over' . . . No more is the heroine a lovely princess masquerading as the serving maid, and no more is the scene Ruritania or Monte Carlo. Today is rationally American, and the musical show has taken on a new lease on life."

Ruritania and Monte Carlo were to be the scene for some years to come, actually, and many first-class romantic shows of the forties would delve into a richer, more poetic brand of fantasy, but forward-looking librettists in these early years had a big job in first establishing their brainchildren in America, time present.

It is a modern commonplace that the musicals of this century's second decade had quaint ways of striving for coherence that make them seem even quainter today, but *Leave It to Jane* was revived at the Sheridan Square Playhouse in 1959 with its book and score intact and little cause for giggles in the wrong places. Kern's *Oh, Lady! Lady!* (1918) also came back in 1974, for a sweet revival by Equity Library Theatre. In both cases, the reviewers all felt that Kern's music held up wonderfully well. They were right; it did.

But the Princess shows were not the only items of interest in those days. When Winthrop Ames and an unbilled Lee Shubert brought over the Deutsches Theater of Berlin in 1912 in Max Reinhardt's oriental fantasy *Sumurun,* they were giving rival producers a foretaste of something those hard-bitten realists could all believe in: a passing fad. With its incidental music by Victor Holländer, its subtle decor by Ernst Stern, its speechless pageantry—not a line of dialogue—and its implicit sexuality, *Sumurun* was just the sort of elitist enterprise that thrills the few and bores the many—and provides epochal influences to be taken out of context and larded into next season's shows. The Shuberts pounced on Reinhardt's runway for speechless pageantry of a less uplifting sort in their *Passing Shows,* while the extraordinary unity of Reinhardt's *gesamtkunstwerk* went largely unnoticed. The *Globe* pronounced *Sumurun* "the last word in erotology," whatever that is, and the *Dramatic Mirror* couldn't help observing that "the verb *amare* is conjugated in every form, especially the imperative."

In the 1970s, Lindsay Kemp's *Flowers* and Robert Wilson's *A Letter for Queen Victoria* were exactly comparable to *Sumurun* in their idiosyncratic artistic quests. Like Reinhardt's piece, they were plays in out-of-the-way theatre language, both short-running but talked about, outrageous but intriguing. To the few who saw it, *Sumurun* was extravaganza without spectacle, but if Stern's flat, unadorned sets went universally unimitated at first, Reinhardt's fusion of the fundamental dramatic arts found at least one successor in the British import *Chu Chin Chow* (1917), a "musical tale of the East" given at the Manhattan Opera House. Unwilling to risk *Sumurun*'s fate, *Chu Chin Chow* kept closer to Broadway, or rather the West End, than Berlin, but the narrative did unfold in a Reinhardt-inspired combination of dance, pantomime, far-flung fantasy, and illustrative lighting. Frederick Norton's music had something for everyone, habitués of the concert hall and less exalted haunts alike, and a generous budget disclosed the wonders of Baghdad in a big way. The cast, too, was several cuts above the norm for a musical show, with Florence Reed, Tyrone Power (Senior), Tessa Costa, George Rasely, and even that old matinee idol of *Adonis,* Henry E. Dixey. *Chu Chin Chow* ended up substantially in the black, even if those of its audiences who weren't clued in to the art movement had their hands full trying to keep up with Oscar Ashe's heady book ("Oh, ye who breathe but reek and dust . . . What can YE feel of Passion's gust?").

While Reinhardt, Ziegfeld and the assimilative Shuberts, and the Princess team were launching their innovations, the rest of the Broadway crowd looked to their laurels and churned out more of last decade's fluff. At least one memorable event, however, was *The Red Rose* (1911), a showcase for the interminable fashion parading of Valeska Suratt, who prided herself on her own costume designs. At her command, everybody on stage wore a red rose for the entire evening—in buttonholes, on hats, behind ears, and between teeth—while Suratt danced, changed costumes, and read lines in her unpredictable jumble of accents. Not to be outdone, female impersonator Julian Eltinge rushed into the act scant weeks later with his imitation, *The Fascinating Widow.* In part a throwback to the roughhewn days of burlesque, Eltinge transcended the innate silliness of his profession with his British tact and charm and remained ever popular, the last of the big-time transvestite comedians. Burlesque didn't die with him—it was already dead—but his retirement made it just that much deader.

Even at this early juncture, musical comedy history registers as a conflict between the adventurous, forward-moving creators and the mass of first-, second-, and tenth-rate talents who marked time by appealing to the general public with a conservative policy, combining the best of the elements that they had already seen succeed. In 1909, a generally bum year for American musical comedy, the big Broadway musicals were Viennese imports, *The Chocolate Soldier* and *The Dollar Princess,* with distinctly minor-league contention from the home team via such entries as *The Midnight Sons* and a seafaring dido called *Havana.* Even the great Victor Herbert had two misses and no hits that year, while the strutting Cohan earned but moderate success with *The Man Who Owns Broadway,* in which Cohan's art imitated life less than it imitated earlier specimens of Cohan's art.

1909 was the year the sumptuous New Theatre opened on Central Park West and Sixty-second Street with Julia Marlowe and E. H. Sothern in a loudly disdained production of *Antony and Cleopatra.* The first season of repertory took in Galsworthy, Sheridan, Pinero, and Maeterlinck and proved financially devastating, so perhaps musical comedy's cobblers were wise to stick to their lasts. Certainly they didn't waste time envisioning anything as ambitious as the New Theatre. *The Girl from Rector's, A Boy and a Girl, The Girl and the Wizard* were the rule, and there were no exceptions. An early example of the rah-rah type of college show, *The Fair Co-Ed* had one of Gustav Luders' most underwhelming scores but a rousing libretto by the famed humorist George Ade. Even then, men of some literary standing were starting to be attracted to the form, and if some of them managed to control it and a few even to transform it, most authors learned the hard way that musical comedy libretto writing—the book especially—is one-tenth genius and nine-tenths travail.

The closest thing to novelty in our paradigm slump year, 1909, was John Barrymore's single incursion into the musical end of the theatre with the costume epic *A Stubborn Cinderella.* But the extent to which the medium was willing to feed on itself was demonstrated by a Marie Dressler vehicle of 1910, *Tillie's Nightmare.* In the absence of a genuine song hit, a sentimental ballad of the previous century, "Heaven Will Protect the Working Girl," was brought out of retirement, not to mention the public domain, and A. Baldwin Sloane's and Edgar Smith's score courted tautology with "Life Is Only What You Make It, After All," a not exactly dim reminder of "Life's a Funny Proposition, After All" from *Little Johnny Jones.*

In place of some new slant on presentation, some producers tried new settings for a change of pace, not always skillfully. Karl Hoschna and three librettists failed to make *The Wall St. Girl* pay in 1912, despite a cast led by Blanche Ring, Charles Winninger, and Will Rogers; Lone River, Nevada, furnished the background for Jerome Kern's first complete score, *The Red Petticoat* (1912), with a somewhat *raffiné* chorus of bearded miners and manicure girls (manicure girls out West? Well, why not?). The cinema too came under scrutiny, first in a British import, *The Girl on the Film* (1913), and then by natives in *The Queen of the Movies* (1914). Searching for virgin territory, composer Louis Hirsch took to the air in *Going Up* (1917), one scene set aboard an airplane in flight.

But the slump had to end sometime. Concurrent with Kern, Bolton, and Wodehouse's gentle Princess Theatre revolution came *Watch Your Step* (1914), a "syncopated musical show." Heading the cast were Vernon and Irene Castle, the very essence of debonair youth in the new fox trot, tango, and one-step, while comedian Frank Tinney's subtle monologues set a new style that would flower only in the more sophisticated thirties. The entire score, words and music, was by Irving Berlin in his first full-time venture on Broadway, and his songs did as much to publicize the theory that America could make indigenous sounds in its pop music as Cohan's had ten years before.

Berlin had arrived from Russia as a four-year-old in 1891, quickly becoming as local as a native. Alec Wilder has noted that Berlin's songs reveal a "constant awareness of the world around him: the pulse of the times, the society in which he is functioning." Indeed, from his first exercises in the field, Berlin's tone was not only American but newfangled as well. "Alexander's Ragtime Band" (1911) may not be genuine ragtime, but it was accepted with joy as a prime specimen of the rag sound when the craze for syncopation was at its height. No one was better suited than Berlin to do similar honors for *Watch Your Step,* this modern, dance-oriented revue, and his tunes for it fairly flew onto the ballroom floor. "Play a Simple Melody," with its charming "old-style" ballad superimposed over a brittle rag, was the show's big hit. Going out for a night of dancing was still a newish idea then, and *Watch Your Step* came in at just the right time. Like *Little Nemo, A Trip to Chinatown,* and the later *Leave It to Jane, Watch Your Step* and Berlin's *Yip Yip Yaphank*

(1918), a revue about life in the wartime army, brought another piece of the American cultural jigsaw puzzle to the popular stage, where art could hold the mirror up to nature without insulting anyone, and where music, the *new* music of the times, was the progressive force.

6

The Rise of Operetta

It was O. J. Gude, an advertising designer, who invented the phrase Great White Way in 1901 in homage to the electric steel lights that succeeded the arc lamps and gas of earlier years. New York was in flux, and the theatre district now hovered around Forty-second Street with a few stragglers holding out on Fourteenth. New stars had risen to challenge the established favorites, some of whom came back even stronger and some of whom merely retired or fought a losing war with their waning box office power.

The years of the actor-managers who produced and sometimes wrote their own vehicles, booking their companies for New York runs or long road tours, were superseded by a new breed of producer, sometimes dedicated to the world he created and sometimes just eager for power or money. In 1896 six of the more titanic producers got together for lunch at New York's Holland House. Over dessert, they planned to finish forever the pleasant chaos of actors making their own touring arrangements by forming a monopolistic combine to control all major American theatres. These men ranged from the worldly Charles Frohman to "Honest" Abe Erlanger, a man with real estate rather than theatre in his blood, who one described Broadway opening nighters as "theatre habitués and sons of habitués." Between them they formed the Syndicate, efficient, exacting, Napoleonic. Anyone in the business who tried to deal around them found virtually nothing to deal with: they owned it all. At first, some of the most reputable theatre people tried to oppose them—David Belasco, Richard Mansfield (the first to capitulate when his livelihood was threatened), Joseph Jefferson, Sarah Bernhardt, James O'Neill, Nat C. Goodwin, and especially Minnie Maddern Fiske and her husband Harrison Grey Fiske, publisher of the *Dramatic Mirror*. Despite a court trial (the Syndicate won), no one was able to dare the might of the Trust . . . no one, that is, except the Shuberts.

Working at first out of Syracuse, the three Shubert brothers got a foothold in New York when they leased the Herald Square Theatre in 1900. Sam S. Shubert died young in a grisly train wreck near Chicago, but J. J. and Lee carried on, working their way up with a solid theatre instinct, some incredible good luck, and a platoon of the shoddiest popular hits ever produced out of one office, along with the odd revival of Shakespeare and Ibsen. No melodrama was too hoary, no musical comedy too plotless, no farce too empty of invention if they thought it had a chance. Surprisingly, they succeeded more than failed. The list of their innumerable driveling musicals fills in the gaps of musical comedy history between *Little Johnny Jones* and *Watch Your Step: Chinese Honeymoon, Winsome Winnie, The Babes and the Baron, The Girls of Holland, Mlle. Mischief, The Dancing Duchess, Oh, I Say!*, not to mention *Lady Teazle*, a mildewed transformation of *The School for Scandal* with Lillian Russell and a chorus of eighty-six girls.

It was the Shuberts who revived *The Passing Shows* starting in 1912, but they made one other contribution to the rise of revue even before the first *Follies*. The immense Hippodrome Theatre on Forty-third Street and Sixth Avenue had opened on April 12, 1905, seating over five thousand and calling itself "the largest, safest, and costliest playhouse in the world"; the opening bill was *A Yankee Circus on Mars,* far more circus than either Yankee or Martian. When Lee Shubert stepped into the picture with an extravaganza called *Pioneer Days* in late 1906, the already interested public became true believers overnight, rooting for the cavalry, booing the Indians, ovating the baby elephant Little Hippy and drooling over the magic and mystery of the famous tank into which a hundred baubled chorus girls marched, never to reappear.

Lee produced yearly extravaganzas at the Hippodrome around Labor Day, each one running so long that they had to close while the ledger ink still ran black just to let the next show in. His programs kept extravaganzas alive through 1914, never attempting to key the spectacle to the plot—seldom attempting a plot, in fact. But the Shuberts did have something to boast of in a young Hungarian engineer turned composer named Sigmund Romberg. After years of dainty revue interpolations, Romberg crashed into the big time with *The Blue Paradise* (1915), a revision of a Viennese original. The hybrid score was second-class Danube to the note, but the public adored it. This story of a wealthy businessman who revisits his old haunts and first love had nostalgia to spare, and more comedy than was usual for such events. It was a primeval romantic show, spun of the Viennese cloth with a sense of humor—something its descendants tended to lack—and it managed to be immensely popular even with its embarrassingly substandard, occasionally even subhuman, score.

Romberg threatened to quit the Shubert stables unless they took him off their ceaseless revue and extravaganza projects, and they capitulated with *Maytime* (1917), another adaptation of a European show, but this time Romberg composed an entirely new score for an entirely new libretto. *Maytime* was a lot better than *The Blue Paradise,* but it had very little comedy: with several generations of couples for its three acts, there was no time for extraneous buffoonery. Furthermore, by their very nature the *Maytime* characters took themselves too seriously to be their own comedians the way the close-up farcical Princess people could. *Maytime* was one of the first American operettas, and it proclaimed the vanquishing power of the new format with its warmth, pathos, graciousness, and, above all, the bone-deep potency of cheap romance. Theatregoers could weep freely over the ill-fated love of Ottilie Van Zandt and Richard Wayne, especially since their respective grandchildren brought the sad amour to a happy close.

Romberg's *Maytime* music was a microcosm of fluent melody amid the noisy fleshpots of Broadway, though he could also write at will in the Tin Pan Alley mode for belters and comedians. He also had a snappy dance sense that proved invaluable in all the hodgepodge musical comedies he worked on. Brief, intermittent dance bits were common now in every kind of musical show; full-length ballets were reserved for the more ambitious entertainments, though they went for nothing until Balanchine and De Mille made them an organic part of the plot two decades later. Despite his ease at turning out these natty fox trots and gambados, Romberg detested the whole genre, preferring the full-bosomed waltzes and ballads that so glibly unleashed the vagaries of Vienna on the American stage. However dumb they may seem today, it was Romberg's métier enlightened by Kern's that established the music in music drama, not the zippier proletarian bounce of Irving Berlin.

Maytime was so popular that the Shuberts opened a second Broadway company across the street, and for almost a year the facing marquees of the Shubert and Forty-fourth Street Theatres seemed to be conspiring to bring about a new kind of musical, one with a minimum of comedy, a lot of "high-toned'' music, and an ideal young couple at the forefront, the whole thing discharged so seriously that one just had to Believe—something one never had to worry about in comic opera. Rida Johnson Young's *Maytime* libretto asked—needed—to be taken for real. No, it didn't aspire to dramatic credibility, but it could exert little magic unless its public was willing to lean into it, accept the story as something that happened, will happen, does. It also may have something to do with timing. *Maytime* opened on August 16, 1917—a war year. According to *Maytime*'s star Peggy Wood, *Maytime* was the show most in demand by soldiers departing for overseas.

What Sigmund Romberg was to the Shuberts, Rudolf Friml was to Arthur Hammerstein (Oscar I's son), whose little finger held more good nature than both Shuberts put together. Friml was soon to fall in with the *Maytime* way of doing things. As he explained in the thirties: ''When I write music for the theater, I like books with charm to them. And charm suggests the old things—the finest things that were done long ago. I like a full-blooded libretto with luscious melody, rousing choruses, and romantic passions.'' But in 1912 he was still working out a balance between the coming heroics of the big operettas of the twenties and the prevailing importance of comedy in the plot. Significantly, his first try, *The Firefly,* was billed as a ''comedy opera.'' Otto Hauerbach (later Harbach) had devised a tale of a street singer (tempestuous Emma Trentini) who disguises herself as a boy to follow her beloved on a yachting trip to Bermuda. The requisite happy ending worked itself out at a garden party given by one Mrs. Van Dare, where la Trentini won her man with the high-flying coloratura of a ''concert waltz,'' ''The Dawn of Love.''

This was a plot with plenty of room for fun and games, so Friml and Harbach filled the score with amusing odds and ends, as witness the titles: ''He Says Yes—She Says No,'' ''All the Girlies Call Me Uncle,'' ''Tommy Atkins on a Dress

Parade," "De Trop," and a dizzy dance specialty, "The Latest Thing from Paris." With his classical background, Friml knew how to write for the voice as did few of his colleagues, and Trentini possessed a sweet soprano, although one critic held that she "acted like a jumping jack and talked like a parrot . . . in bastard English." In mixing equal parts of comedy and romance in *The Firefly,* its authors inhibited the love plot from making much of a point; the two leads never even had a duet!

Friml and Harbach stayed with their comedy operas, and though Friml's visions of cadets and dirndls were attempting a takeover, all comic hell broke loose when Ed Wynn was cast in the lead of *Sometime* in 1918. Another of those transcendent clowns who can cut up and cavort at will, script or no script, Wynn was the chief feature of *Sometime,* even with the pert Francine Larrimore as his vis-à-vis and the impertinent Mae West as archvamp Mayme Dean. Friml had concocted a score filled with the music he loved best, but nobody seemed to care. "When Mr. Wynn was on the stage the audience forgot *Sometime,*" was *Theatre* magazine's verdict.

Friml was as accomplished as Romberg at writing genre pieces and up-to-date dance numbers, but unlike Romberg he had no intention of growing with the best of the new shows each year. He spent a few more assignments trying to disentangle himself from the comedy half of musical comedy, finding his niche in the twenties with *Rose-Marie, The Vagabond King,* and *The Three Musketeers*—and he never came out.

7

The Revue Grows Up

When the spring of 1919 rolled around, the sort of musicals holding forth in town included the like of *Somebody's Sweetheart, Listen Lester, Ladies First* (a dinosaur-age spoof of the women's movement), plus shows by Herbert, Cohan, Friml, Romberg, and Kern, and George Gershwin's first score, *La! La! Lucille.* It was time for the standard actor's contract to be renewed, and though the Producing Managers' Association hated having to recognize the six-year-old Actors Equity in the first place, the two sides discussed terms. For management, terms consisted of the status quo: no salaries for rehearsals; actors stranded on the road if a show folded; costumes, drinking cups, and numerous miscellanies charged to their accounts; and no show-cause for dismissal. The actors decided to fight specifically for salary payments for extra performances—and management wouldn't budge.

No one thought the actors would really strike, even most

actors, but on August 6 they voted to walk out and did so, rather suddenly, that night. While most producers spent the evening refunding admissions to ticketholders, actor-managers George M. Cohan and William Brady attempted to give *The Royal Vagabond* and *At 9:45* with themselves and understudies; a stagehands' and musicians' strike put a stop to that. New York's walkout quickly became a national one, lasting exactly a month. Equity's ranks swelled from 2700 to 14,000 in the ensuing days of victory, and its treasury increased eightfold.

The economic impact of the strike would, of course, be far-reaching, but at the time the union's mandates drained off only a little of the producers' profits. Ticket prices were low, but an average-size musical could still pay off in six weeks of good houses, and the bigger shows could employ choruses of fifty without risking life and limb. But there were other considerations. For one thing, Prohibition turned the Great White Way into Bone-Dry Boulevard overnight in 1920. The last hour of that January 16 was an epic of time-passage as bars closed, waiters dressed as pallbearers, and restaurant orchestras played Chopin's funeral march and "Good-by Forever." The sparkle and gaiety of the Broadway area was over; Rector's was gone, and the tense air of the speakeasies and their worldly boredom would be the new sign of the times. Musicals were slow to catch the mood, however. They became even more lighthearted, in fact, as if in self-defense. Straight plays felt the change more keenly: nymphomaniacs, prostitutes, and pretty murderesses cropped up on stage now, with tough, degenerate men for company.

There was also a serious undertone to many plays dealing with the less raffish middle class. The first Pulitzer Prize for drama went to Jesse Lynch Williams' women's liberation comedy, *Why Marry,* in 1918, the second to Eugene O'Neill's vividly realistic *Beyond the Horizon* in 1920. Havens of experimentation like the Provincetown Playhouse, the Neighborhood Playhouse, and the Washington Square Players (soon to regroup as the Theatre Guild) offered a point of departure for the untried prospects of the next generation of playwrights. These years of apprenticeship exploded in a Viking raid on the polite old hat with a rush of productivity in the twenties: *The Emperor Jones, Anna Christie, Lightnin', Rain, The Hairy Ape, The God of Vengeance, The Verge, The Adding Machine, They Knew What They Wanted, What Price Glory?, The Show-Off, Beggar on Horseback, Craig's Wife, The Great God Brown, Porgy, The Silver Cord, Strange Interlude, Dynamo, Street Scene* . . . six of which subsequently became musicals, operas, or what have you.

The musical theatre, however, recoiled from experimentation. The form was working; why push it? A musical couldn't go the way of an *Anna Christie* or a *Craig's Wife,* anyway, because . . . well, it just wouldn't be magic-time any more. Where would the tunes fit in? And the chorus girls? What about funny? No, the most that this musical theatre could manage by way of something different were farces marketing the latest craze or a familiar piece of Americana, like *Going Up* (flying), *Watch Your Step* (dancing), or *The Wall St. Girl* (money).

This topical angle rather found its pulpit in revues, which could devote a five-minute sketch to a newsworthy item or a personality unable to carry a whole show, and the long line of annual revues was in full swing during the postwar boom years. Ziegfeld's series, now officially known as the *Ziegfeld Follies,* were the kingpins in town, while Charles Dillingham perpetuated the Hippodrome epics and the Shuberts overleaped their risqué *Passing Shows* with the same only more so in *Artists and Models,* earning moues of distaste from the critics but giving *Variety*'s reported "seventy-five-percent stag audience" exactly what they came for.

Ziegfeld too, although his *Follies* never stooped as low as the Shubert revues, made nudity and near-nudity regular aids to "glorifying the American girl." While he always had at least two or three stars on the bill, his shows never varied their already successful layout. Like vaudeville, the *Follies* lacked unity; they had formula rather than form.

At least one entrepreneur, however, felt the time was right to sound a different note in the revue. Dangerously avoiding the safety of mass appeal, Britisher John Murray Anderson presented a subtle, centralized evening of songs and sketches on July 15, 1919, at the Greenwich Village Theatre. Produced by "The Bohemians," the *Greenwich Village Follies* had the breadth of literate sophistication, with a visual appeal inspired by the flowering art movement. Anderson staged the show and collaborated on the lyrics, but he had been trained as a designer and his eye for color and line gave his *Follies* a wholeness that even the great Joseph Urban's huge pictures for Ziegfeld seldom possessed. The Greenwich Village Theatre was small, limiting the show's resources but at the same time keeping them at work for subtlety. Composer A. Baldwin Sloane did his best for Anderson with songs like "The Critic's Blues," "My Little Javanese," "I Want a Daddy Who Will Rock Me to Sleep" (a lovely ballad whose verse contained puns on the latest boudoir farces), and "I'm Ashamed to Look the Moon in the Face," striking an ironic tone not often heard in uptown revues. "My Marionette" was accompanied by dancing puppets, perfect for the small scale of the stage, and Ziegfeld's Yama-Yama girl Bessie McCoy had real material to work with in "I'm the Hostess of a Bum Cabaret."

The second edition in 1920 had a change of cast, and if Howard Marsh sounded a note of déjà vu singing "Just Sweet Sixteen" to a chorus of cuties, a zesty cabaret scene evoked the night world of the city with actors got up to represent Manhattan's most frequented haunts. But the tang of the Village eluded Anderson in 1921 when the show moved north to Forty-fourth Street and the low-level audience-targeting of rival attractions proved contagious. The last *Greenwich Village Follies* surfaced at the Winter Garden, home of witless Shubert frolics. Now consonant with others of that ilk, it evaporated forever.

There were also many hodge-podge revues that were not part of a series in those postwar days. These tended to be the cheapest to put on (the Shuberts ran out of theatres filling them up with them), and from 1918 to 1922 the city's night people had their choice of midnight shows headlined by stars who had just finished their evening stints in book musicals a few blocks away. An approach to the dinner theatres of the sixties, they lit up theatre attics—the Century Roof, the New Amsterdam Roof, the Winter Garden Roof—but they subsided when the new "café society" took to the night clubs and speakeasies.

Big names and informality were the keynotes of Raymond Hitchcock's *Hitchy-Koo* revues. The first, in 1917, had Irene Bordoni, Leon Errol, Florenz Ames, and Hitchcock himself, taking the customers into his confidence with impromptu patter. A year later the same cast plus comedienne Ray Dooley busied themselves in an offhand way with material culled from a variety of sources, including a Gershwin song, "You-oo, Just You." But Hitchcock soon awakened to the need for stability in his shapeless routine by hiring one composer to do the whole score. For *Hitchy-Koo 1919,* advertised as "Hitchier than ever in its fun, more Kooey than ever in its music," Hitchcock engaged Cole Porter, just getting out of the comic opera style that proved so disastrous in his first show, *See America First* (1916). *Hitchy-Koo 1919* ran only 56 performances, but it did have Porter's first commercial hit, the sentimentally pallid "Old-Fashioned Garden," one of the few genuinely Kooey numbers Porter ever let himself write. Yet two of the songs, "That Black and White Baby of Mine" and "My Cozy Little Corner of the Ritz," were clear proof that Porter had already found his voice as the satiric chronicler of the cocktail set, although it would take a few popular hits in the smooth, intimate style of "Let's Do It" and "You Do Something to Me" to bring him the recognition he deserved.

Besides Hitchcock, other notables governed similar slight

evenings, reviving their vaudeville specialties and assembling odds and ends around them. Marie Dressler led her *All-Star Gambol* in 1913, and Elsie Janis made a habit of showing up at odd intervals in *Elsie Janis and Her Gang.* The Marx Brothers crucified what small plot there was in *I'll Say She Is* in 1924, and Al Jolson could be counted on to star in a revue or turn a book musical into one with his impassioned clowning and singing.

Comedians really found a home in revues, as the free form gave them room to display their idiosyncrasies without having to barge in on a plot, just as today's comedians work well in musical-variety hours on television, the exact equivalent of the old revue. All that's needed is a winning personality, a solid team of writers, and a mass audience.

After his splash in the *Ziegfeld Follies of 1914,* Ed Wynn returned to the 1915 edition and hid under a table while W. C. Fields was doing his billiards act. Wynn mugged at the audience to steal laughs from Fields, who furiously knocked him out cold with his cue. This was only the beginning, however, for Wynn graduated to his own show in 1920, the *Ed Wynn Carnival,* and a year later Abe Erlanger presented *The Perfect Fool,* "book, music and lyrics by Ed Wynn." The comic carried the entire show for a whopping 256 performances with his crazy inventions, rambling monologues, and grotesque costumes. In 1924 Wynn came back for more in *The Grab Bag.* This time the entertainment had style: instead of skylarking interspersed with a crooning juvenile, a giddy ingenue, and miscellaneous dance numbers, the whole evening was geared to Wynn's perfect foolishness. Even the chorus was picked to second Wynn's antics; at one point a "Russian" octet was dragged on stage to intone that old Russian folk song, "He Eats French Dressing So He Can Wake Up Oily in the Morning," plus "She Might Have Been a School Teacher But She Hadn't Any Class." Every act, every production number carried this all-pervading zaniness. Like the first two years of the *Greenwich Village Follies, The Grab*

Bag had a formal integration other revues didn't even attempt.

In 1919 and 1920 the Princess Theatre mounted two revues that tried to counteract their intimate surroundings instead of exploiting them; both died horrible deaths. Still, the time was right for an uptown revue to provide the wit and glamour of the first two *Greenwich Village Follies*—at least, so thought Irving Berlin and Sam H. Harris. They built the medium-sized Music Box Theatre on Forty-fifth Street as a showcase for a series of brisk, happy musical shows aimed at the au courant following of John Murray Anderson's *Follies,* but with a more substantial production fund. One of the first offerings of the 1921–22 season, the *Music Box Revue* cost $187,613, a staggering amount even with Ziegfeld in town. Hassard Short based his staging on drollery and charm, while Berlin donated a nice collection of ballads and dances, giving the work a sheen—an elegance—that made it that year's novelty. *Theatre* magazine called it "everything that is decorative, dazzling, harmonious, intoxicatingly beautiful in the theatre," and it eventually played 313 performances. It was succeeded by three further editions, each one a happy cross between the bigness of Ziegfeld and the urbanity of Anderson; they also proved the existence of a large audience on the beaten midtown track which did not demand carnality with its comedy.

More directly in the temper of the *Greenwich Village Follies* was the *Grand Street Follies,* which came out in 1922 at the old Neighborhood Playhouse. In this self-styled "Low-brow show for high-grade morons" with "music by the great composers, mostly arranged by Lily M. Hyland," and "book by everybody," satire was the strong point. The tiny stage and cast prohibited imitation of the uptown shows, throwing the prose material into sharp focus; the songs, however, were seldom first-rate, even though Arthur Schwartz and the "in" classical composer Randall Thompson were contributors. The actors were young and full of brio, attacking the mighty with trim caricatures. John Barrymore, Pavlova, the Castles, Chaliapin, Walt Whitman, and, of course, critics, were all under review that first year. Later outings volunteered a look at *The Wild Duck* as Ibsen would have written it in the 1700s; "The South Sea Islands according to Broadway"; and an operatic world premiere, "L'Irlandesa Rosa dell'Abie."

The fifth edition moved north to reach a wider public but kept its tone intact. Two more *Grand Street Follies* blossomed in Winthrop Ames' Booth Theatre in 1928 and 1929 until the Depression shriveled its ticket-buying following. Although the *Grand Street Follies* never had the hit tunes to keep it in the foreground of media consciousness, it remained in its seven years a pleasant antidote to the bankrupt gaiety of musical comedy. Revues die fast, for their topicality is bound to date them, but in their assimilation of materials and their indulgent worldview, these early *Greenwich Village* and *Grand Street Follies* were the direct ancestors of the brilliant revues of the thirties.

Two other producers sought to borrow Ziegfeld's attractions in close approximations. The *Earl Carroll Vanities,* founded in 1923, paralleled the *Ziegfeld Follies* except in the matter of taste. A publicity release at the time of the 1931 edition sums up the case for this corner of theatre history:

> The "picking" of beauties is a ceremony almost as elaborate as the coronation of a foreign potentate. . . . After the ordeal of an Earl Carroll audition a girl feels . . . that she is going to pass the most careful inspection by any other beauty expert in almost the entire world. . . . Mr. Carroll takes the matter of selecting beauties quite seriously . . . his eyes sparkle and his enthusiasm warms when he sees a new specimen nearer to perfection just as does the lapidary or precious stone collector when he discovers a new gem.

Although Burton Lane, Jay Gorney, and Harold Arlen composed for the *Vanities* at various times, the songs were mostly routine and the comedy trivial. Earl Carroll's one contribution to art was Faith Bacon's fan dance in the 1930 edition, which raised the censorship question and a new consideration of thespian morality.

Closer to Ziegfeld in showmanship was his other emulator, George White, a hoofer who turned producer as well for the *Scandals of 1919*. Song and dance were assets in the *Scandals,* not merely obligations, especially when George Gershwin teamed up with B. G. DeSylva and E. Ray Goetz on the songs in 1920. Gershwin wrote all the music for the *Scandals* through 1924, and if most of his first efforts were ordinary, 1920 had the bluesy "On My Mind the Whole Night Long," 1921 brought the subtle "Drifting Along with the Tide," 1922 a serious one-act opera called "Blue Monday" and the jazzy "I'll Build a Stairway to Paradise," and 1924 a long-lived ballad with blue outlines, "Somebody Loves Me."

Since no revue had a plot, no revue ever needed a context song, making the medium a happy hunting ground for the second-rate pop writers who had labor pains with the plot songs in book musicals. Revue scores were a kind of halfway point between the Romberg-Kern-Herbert school and that of the pop writers who occupied the Tin Pan Alley side of Broadway, a gap best bridged by Irving Berlin when he managed to write for New York, Hollywood, and the pop world without having to shift styles.

One team that matched Berlin in this all-purpose efficiency was DeSylva, Brown, and Henderson. Ray Henderson was the musician—conservatory-trained, in fact—and Lew Brown was the lyricist; B. G. DeSylva wrote lyrics, books, sketches, produced shows himself, and was the backbone idea man. The *Scandals* had prospered so nicely that White crossed the footlights to concentrate on managing his operation. He renamed his confection the *George White Scandals* and hired DeSylva, Brown, and Henderson in 1925, when they served a dubious apprenticeship. The 1926 *Scandals,* however, was the best of the lot, with a blockbuster score: "Lucky Day," "Black Bottom," and "The Birth of the Blues" as well as the chummier

"Tweet-Tweet" and "The Girl Is You and the Boy Is Me."

The team wrote their songs organically, all three of them hatching out the germinal idea and sweating it out from there. They had the gift of cluing the phrases in to the pulse of the nation, and whether their ballads were torchy or light, they were up-to-the-minute expressions of universal emotions. The trio particularly excelled in rhythm numbers; there was always a big choreographed segment in their shows built around a new dance sensation, and "Black Bottom" actually started one. "Birth of the Blues" was a hint rather than the real thing, satisfying the great mass of would-be jivers who would have balked at the genuine article. Operating exclusively within the American mainstream, DeSylva, Brown, and Henderson perfected the science of affecting everyone without ever drawing on minority resources.

More *Scandals* followed, lifted out of the common rut only by White's recognition of the importance of a solid musical score, and by his white-haired boys' combination of energy, humor, and wholesomeness. When DeSylva went to Hollywood in 1930, Brown and Henderson wrote alone for White in 1931. One of their ballads, "The Thrill Is Gone," could have been their theme song, for without DeSylva the song lyrics would soon lose that collective address that spiced the earlier songs. Still, Henderson turned out some sparkling tunes: Ethel Merman delivered "Life Is Just a Bowl of Cherries" and "(Ladies and gentlemen) That's Love," Rudy Vallee crooned "This Is the Missus," and Everett Marshall fed New Yorkers' Negro fetish with "That's Why Darkies Were Born." Willie and Eugene Howard supplied the chuckles, aided by hoofer Ray Bolger. *The New York Times'* Brooks Atkinson said, "There is nothing like low comedy to relieve the imposing dullness of a big musical show," perhaps unwittingly signaling Broadway's readiness for something novel in the way of revues.

8

The Twenties (I)

New Voices

Jerome Kern composed his first complete score in 1912 for *The Red Petticoat,* Irving Berlin in 1914 (*Watch Your Step*), Cole Porter in 1916 (*See America First*), and George Gershwin in 1919 (*La! La! Lucille*), but they all bloomed in the twenties. Berlin wrote for the stage only once in that decade—*The Cocoanuts* (1925), George S. Kaufman's spoof of Florida land-grabbing with the Marx Brothers—but Kern, Porter, Gershwin, and the new team of Rodgers and Hart worked exclusively on Broadway, beating new paths in book-music integration and totally reclaiming the national pop music scene.

With the Princess Theatre reforms behind him, Kern still had never had what Broadway calls a major production. He had several immense successes to his credit, had worked with top librettists and often saw his work enhanced by the onstage talent, but except for his three songs in the *Ziegfeld Follies of 1916,* Kern enjoyed no connection with a large-scale, big-name show. It was Ziegfeld who gave him his chance late in 1920 with *Sally,* turning the blond, elfin Marilyn Miller into a star at the same time. With Leon Errol and Walter Catlett, Joseph Urban's glittering decor, and a "Butterfly Ballet" by Victor Herbert, *Sally* had hit written all over it from the first day of rehearsal. Guy Bolton's tale of an orphan who becomes a Ziegfeld girl and marries a millionaire's son was half comedy and half charm, and, enriched by such ditties as "Wild Rose," "Whip-poor-will," the title song, and especially "Look for the Silver Lining," it entranced theatregoers 570 times, becoming one of the most fondly remembered shows of its day. Those long memories may have betrayed *Sally* when it was revived in 1948 with Bambi Linn and Willie Howard and a load of extra Kern songs, for though each tune in the overture got a grateful hand, the show did not go over. "It was Marilyn who really mattered," recalled Guy Bolton years later; "Marilyn who gave to the play a curious enchantment that no reproduction in other lands or other mediums ever captured."

While *Sally* was filling the giant New Amsterdam, Kern did a series of musicals for Charles Dillingham, who like Ziegfeld was keener on assembling top-notch talents to bemingle into a show than on casting and staging a show already written. Working mainly with Anne Caldwell, Kern gave Dillingham one lovely score after another, getting more or less disorganized shows back in return. *Good Morning, Dearie* (1921), for example, was like a nervous peace treaty between the old-style musical comedy and the Princess shows. Not only was there a ball scene, but the love plot tied a costume shopgirl to a wealthy young man, with only a tough mobster and a comic detective to bring the action up to date. Kern's score, however, was a contemporary delight, the charming "Blue Danube Blues" sung in counterpoint to Strauss' waltz but in 4/4 time. Always riding the middle line between the steam-whistle pep of the leg shows and the pageantry of Ruritania, Kern was comfortable with a work such as *Stepping Stones*

(1923), a vehicle for Fred Stone and family that redoubled the death of burlesque by playing "Little Red Riding Hood" straight for its innate joys instead of parody. The joys were so many, in fact, that when father Fred and daughter Dorothy got together on "Wonderful Dad," the audience just didn't know what to do with itself.

Kern was back with Marilyn Miller and working with Otto Harbach and Oscar Hammerstein for the first time on *Sunny* (1925), an attempt to recapture *Sally*'s optimistic glow with Miller as a trapeze artist instead of a dishwasher, and as radiant as ever. With Dillingham's production standards raised to their highest, *Sunny* was the kind of show everyone in New York hoped to write, be in, or see—but it wasn't exactly the organic story told through dance and song that Kern helped pioneer at the Princess. Years later, Hammerstein could look back on the experience with amusement:

> Our job was to tell a story with a cast that had been assembled as if for a revue. Charles Dillingham, the producer, had signed Cliff Edwards, who sang songs and played the ukelele and was known as Ukelele Ike. His contract required that he do his specialty between ten o'clock and ten fifteen! So we had to construct our story in such a way that Ukelele Ike could come out and perform during that time and still not interfere with the continuity. In addition to Marilyn Miller, the star, there was Jack Donahue, a famous dancing comedian, and there was Clifton Webb and Mary Hay, who were a leading dance team of the time, Joseph Cawthorn, a star comedian, Esther Howard, another, Paul Frawley, the leading juvenile. In addition to the orchestra in the pit we had also to take care of George Olsen's Dance Band on the stage. Well, we put it all together and it was a hit.

Like Kern, Cole Porter started on a small scale, but his art, unlike Kern's, had little truck with the open arena of gentle sentiment and good-humored middle-class fantasies. Porter's lyrics frequently went over the heads of the popular audience, and at first he was only appreciated by the few who heard his songs at parties. After years of the European high life and study with Vincent d'Indy in Paris, Porter contributed songs to the successful *Greenwich Village Follies* of 1924 and the Irene Bordoni romp *Paris.* By now, Porter's insouciance and social satire were the hallmarks of his work, and his unceasing scrutiny of love's ups, downs, and outer reaches would travel with him throughout his career. Although sentiment would eventually vie with sophistication in his romantic numbers, the so-called musicomedy *Paris* was nothing but urbanity in 1928. Porter composed eight songs; only five were used, all sung by Irene Bordoni. The salty "Let's Misbehave" was rejected in favor of "Let's Do It," Porter's first lasting song hit, and probably the most suggestive ditty yet heard in the theatre ("Moths, in your rugs, do it—what's the use of mothballs?").

November 27, 1929, ushered in Porter's first score for a genuine musical comedy, the immensely successful *Fifty Million Frenchmen.* Herbert Fields' sprightly book and Norman Bel Geddes' colorful settings attempted to erase all memory of Black Thursday by recreating the jaunty chicté of expatriate Paris, and Porter contrived his best work for the story of a playboy who poses as a penniless guide to win an American filly and a twenty-five-thousand-dollar bet. The songs tended to harp on the more worldly viscissitudes of physical attraction, and some critics found it a little heavy for their taste. While the eminent *dramaturge* George Jean Nathan proclaimed Porter to be "so far ahead of the other boys in New York that there is just no race at all," Richard Watts admitted that "some of us wish that Mr. Porter wouldn't pound at one theme so constantly."

The pounding, as a matter of fact, had only begun, but Porter's subtler traits weren't spotted as easily. His music was remarkably innovative even then, both in terms of song structure and, particularly, the quicksilver chromaticism of his melodies. How different this sound was from the pure, uncorrupted logic and reassuring cadences of a Kern tune. Kern's harmony was seldom striking in those days, avoiding altered chords like the plague. But Kern and Porter were hymning two very different forms of animal life; each man's music was individual, surpassingly attractive and perfectly suited to the sort of stories he worked with.

Porter's distinctive abilities were nowhere better exhibited than in *Fifty Million Frenchmen.* If "I'm in Love," "You've Got That Thing," and "You Do Something to Me" were straight-on statements of romantic bliss, "Please Don't Make Me Be Good" was a joltingly new brand of maiden's prayer, "Find Me a Primitive Man" as libidinous a comedy song as will ever be heard, and "I Worship You" a supreme portrait of the neurotic byways of the haut monde, a scream of agony. If there was ever to be a revolution in theatre music, Porter may be regarded as one of the guardians of the first barricade.

A revolutionary of a different sort was George Gershwin. As author of both words and music, Cole Porter could effect his innovations more completely than Gershwin, who made his statements strictly in musical terms. But Gershwin's statement was a grand one: "to interpret in music," as he put it himself, "the soul of the American people." The interpreting was at first rather oblique, if interpreting it was at all. Gershwin's early songs, written in his teens, have exuberance and dash, but his characteristic sound had yet to evolve and his tunes were no more "American" than those of his contemporaries.

Like Jerome Kern, whom he admired tremendously, Gershwin got his start on Broadway with interpolations, adulterating other composers' scores with his bright ballads and peppy dances. He worked with a variety of lyricists before teaming up with his brother, Ira, for "The Real American Folk Song (Is a rag, a mental jag,)" a significant title considering what George was to do with the destiny of popular music.

Gershwin's dream of fitting the native pop sound into larger forms proved irresistible in the *Scandals of 1922.* The aforementioned "Blue Monday" (words by DeSylva) lacked the maturity that would overrule dissenting opinions on *Porgy and Bess,* but the taste of black jazz was unmistakable—so much so, in fact, that audiences were unprepared for the little opera and shied away. A few critics realized that something big had been set before them, if only half baked; one anonymous reviewer called "Blue Monday" "the first real American opera . . . a human plot of American life." But this was a minority opinion. Most reviewers sided with Darnton of the *World*: "the most dismal, stupid, and incredible blackface sketch that has probably ever been perpetrated." George White realized that more customers would be revolted than intrigued, so "Blue Monday" was withdrawn after opening night and the *Scandals* played on without it. But the show's conductor, Paul Whiteman, liked it and brought it back in later years reorchestrated by Ferde Grofé and retitled *135th Street.*

Jazz and ragtime were under Gershwin's skin by this time, personalizing his idiom to a remarkable degree. Already, the Gershwin trademark was unmissable. "Do It Again" from *The French Doll* (1922), "Innocent Ingenue Baby" from *Our Nell* (1922), and "Nashville Nightingale" in Sam Bernard and William Collier's *Nifties* (1923), all interpolations, stood out from the rest of the Tin Pan Alley output in the same way that Cohan's march time and Kern's ballads outran Victor Herbert and Rudolf Friml.

Gershwin's singular position midway between Tin Pan Alley and the concert rostrum got an early boost when the singer Eva Gautier included a Gershwin set (Kern, Berlin and Walter Donaldson as well) in her recital at Aeolian Hall on November 1, 1923, sandwiched between Hindemith and Schönberg. On July 20, 1925, he made the cover of *Time* magazine, the first American musician to be so treated. Classical composers were old hands at light music by now, of course—but no pop tunesmith had ever written anything like Gershwin's *Rhapsody in Blue* (1924) or Concerto in F (1925). He was by now one of The Street's biggest celebrities, moving in the same rarefied company as Cole Porter but speaking less directly to them than to the public at large. Furthermore,

Ira's lyrics didn't cover the idiosyncratic excesses of the caviar crowd, tending more to the simple ways of the boy-meets-girl bourgeoisie.

The brothers' first hit was *Lady Be Good* (1924), 330 performances' worth of skill and ingenuity about a brother and sister dance team weathering hard times, with Fred and Adele Astaire in the leads, Walter Catlett and Cliff Edwards for high jinks, and Arden and Ohman's duo-piano act cascading Gershwinesque authenticity in the pit. *Lady Be Good* wowed New York with energy, innocence, and syncopation. The score went from strength to strength to strength: "Fascinating Rhythm," "The Half of It, Dearie, Blues," "Little Jazz Bird," "Hang on to Me," and the title song—"tunes that the unmusical and serious-minded will find it hard to get rid of," chortled Stark Young in *The New York Times.*

In the twenties, musical comedy at its buoyant brightest was the Gershwins' forte, but this was the heyday of operetta, so George tried his hand at one in *Song of the Flame* (1925), sharing the musical chores with Herbert Stothart. A spectacular Slavic romance with "mobs, riots, balls and carnivals," *Song of the Flame* used every trick in the operetta handbook to win public favor. It did so, too, 194 times, but Gershwin wasn't at ease with this inflexible form and never repeated the essay. In fact, his next show, with Ira, was another of the slight musical farces they handled so well, what with the wit and hopefulness of Ira's lyrics and the quicksilver drive of Gershwin's tunes. Brooks Atkinson decreed *Oh, Kay!* (1926) "an excellent blending of all the creative arts of entertainment—the arts of staging no less than those of composing and designing," but for many the most creative artiste of the lot was Gertrude Lawrence. After her New York debut with Beatrice Lillie in André Charlot's revues, she was playing her first role in an American book musical as Kay, sister of a bootlegging English lord who uses a gullible Long Island socialite as a front for their rum-running. Abetted by Victor Moore as Shorty McGee—"the difference between a bootlegger and a Federal inspector,'' said Moore at one point, ''is that one of them wears a badge''—Lawrence ran the gamut of wanton mimicry, keeping comedy as her base of operations. She could ride atop a lyric like ''Do, Do, Do (What you've done, done, done before)'' with bemused aplomb, but when the plot yielded romance and the spotlight hovered, she ''wrung the withers of even the most hard-hearted'' (Hammond) with ''Someone to Watch Over Me'' and ''Maybe.'' George had by now acquired the range and facility to handle emotion in adult musical terms, as Ira had lyrically, and their polyrhythmic ''Fidgety Feet'' proved that a pop tune could be complex and accessible at the same time.

Like *Oh, Kay!, Funny Face* (1927) with the Astaires and Victor Moore again and *Rosalie* (1928) with Marilyn Miller were smash hits, triumphs more of casting, staging, comedy, and songwriting than book-music integration. Vinton Freedley and Alex Aarons had produced all the Gershwin shows since *Lady Be Good* except *Song of the Flame,* which as an operetta was rightly Arthur Hammerstein's province. They always caught the friable, heel-kicking tension of the twenties in their shows, and none of their customers felt disoriented by the lack of plot coordination—or even, in the case of *Funny Face,* the lack of plot, period.

The extent to which the musical was still striving to achieve a form was evidenced by the Ziegfeld-produced *Rosalie* in that it ended up part operetta, part musical comedy, and part strutting-star vehicle. Half the music was by Gershwin, half by Sigmund Romberg—but of course a piece that brought the Princess of Romanza to West Point and modeled one of its principals after Charles Lindbergh would think nothing of mating American pop with Middle-European kitsch. Besides, Ziegfeld often preferred diversity to unity anyway, so the Gershwin ''How Long Has This Been Goin' On?'' sang happily along with the Romberg ''Kingdom of Dreams.'' Alexander Woollcott tells it as it was for the record, underlining the twenties' failure to make achievement meet intention:

"Down in the orchestra pit the violins chitter with excitement and the brasses blare. The spotlight turns white with expectation. Fifty beautiful girls in simple peasant costumes of satin and chiffon rush pellmell onto the stage, all squealing simple peasant outcries of 'Here she comes!' Fifty hussars in fatigue uniform of ivory white and tomato bisque march on in columns of four and kneel to express an emotion too strong for words . . . the house holds its breath. And on walks Marilyn Miller."

In 1925, when Kern gave Miller "Who?" and "D'ye Love Me?" in *Sunny,* when Gershwin was stirring up the rabble with *Song of the Flame,* and when the Marx Brothers were subverting Irving Berlin's *Cocoanuts* songs, Richard Rodgers and Lorenz Hart wrote the music and lyrics, respectively, for the *Garrick Gaieties,* a revue sponsored by the Theatre Guild to pay for the tapestries in their new theatre. Produced on a shoestring by Guild apprentices—among them Elisabeth (later Libby) Holman, Sanford Meisner, and Lee Strasberg—the show was in the tradition of the smart little downtown revues, with spoofs of the Lunts in Molnar's *The Guardsman,* of *They Knew What They Wanted* (here entitled "They Didn't Know What They Were Getting"), and of monologist Ruth Draper, plus an "American jazz opera," "The Joy Spreader," inspired by Gilbert Seldes' recent notion that the popular media were valid art forms. The *Gaieties* had originally been scheduled for two charity benefits, but the critical reception was so positive that the Guild closed *The Guardsman* and replaced it with a regular run of the Rodgers-Hart revue.

The reviewers were taken more with the youth and zest of the whole than with the score in particular, noticing little of it other than "Manhattan." George Jean Nathan exercised his notorious tin ear on Rodgers' tunes but did point out the high level of Hart's lyrics. Perhaps the uneven quality of the sketches blinded the critics to the new team's craftsmanship; the *Garrick Gaieties* was, basically, a semiamateur production.

Just as today's young musical writers have a wide choice of forms to choose from, so did the writers of the twenties—and if the music is different, the forms haven't changed all that much (what has changed is how completely they are developed conceptually). Picking examples from the seventies, there are: the snazzy musical comedy (*Sugar, Chicago*); the "nice" musical comedy (*Frank Merriwell, 70, Girls, 70*); the romantic show (*The Rothschilds, Shenandoah*); the nostalgic pastiche (*Grease, Over Here!*); the revue (*Godspell, The Me Nobody Knows*); the novelty act (*The Magic Show, The Wiz*); the spectacle (*Follies, Jesus Christ Superstar*); plus that modish dainty the rock musical (*Purlie* and *Jesus Christ Superstar* again). Except for the rock show, all of the above types were relatively trendy in the twenties, some in decline, some not quite ready to soar. Rodgers and Hart, more than any other team or solo, were to try out most of them, all in the guise of that catch-all phrase "musical comedy," but their first book musical was halfway romantic and halfway snazzy, *Dearest Enemy* (1925).

Variously described as an "operetta with more than a chance flavor of Gilbert and Sullivan," "a befrilled and befurbelowed romance," a "baby-grand opera," and a "deluxe kindergarten," *Dearest Enemy* took its story line from the Revolutionary War. A certain Mrs. Robert Murray apparently dallied with the British General Howe to give harried American forces time to recover in Harlem; with the addition of Mrs. Murray's niece to fall in love with General Howe's aide-de-camp, Herbert Fields had a workable musical comedy book in which to revel in humor and still exploit the charm of period—a book, in other words, to encompass the extremes of snazzy musical comedy and the romantic show in one swell foop. He had some help from the niece, Helen Ford, an Eve for the new race of go-get-'em ingenues who put over wistful ballads as well as suggestive allusions.

Rodgers, Hart, and Fields did well by *Dearest Enemy*'s antique setting, but they were better suited to a modern outlook and seldom strayed into operetta's rarefied realms. Both *The Girl Friend,* about six-day bicycle racing, and the London show *Lido Lady,* likewise inclined to the wide world of sport, were typical Rodgers and Hart fare anno 1926 (Fields only worked on *The Girl Friend*)—sincere but racy, slathering the love plot with Charlestons and flippant charm songs more than sentimental fudge. They were so far ahead of synchronous musical comedy that the second *Garrick Gaieties* (1926) could stand back and lampoon the formula show as "The Rose of Arizona," with the nasal twang of the Brooklyn flapper pealing out in such lines as "Here comes Rose now, with her horse."

The 1910 Marie Dressler vehicle, *Tillie's Nightmare,* gave the inspiration for the team's first breakthrough show, *Peggy-Ann* (1926), again with Helen Ford. By now Rodgers, Hart, and Fields were as well known as Kern, Bolton, and Wodehouse; *Peggy-Ann* was *their* Princess show, blasting the splintery conventions of book-musical staging. The story was simple, vaporous even. Peggy-Ann quarrels with her boy friend and spends the next two hours dreaming, finally waking to make up with her fiancé. The dream, however, was a dexterous succession of surrealist visions—Park Avenue, a department store, a yacht, a raft on the open sea, Havana—and the opening scene didn't come up with a single song for fifteen minutes, with the finale played in near darkness. *Peggy-Ann* ran 333 performances, for critics and public were snowed by the freshness and imagination of the concept. Unlike some inaugural adventures in format, *Peggy-Ann* was adventurous without being extreme. The score, too, was distinctive but wholly diverting, with "A Tree in the Park" for honeymooners and "Where's That Rainbow?" for the smart set. The trio played it safe, however, in *A Connecticut Yankee* (1927). Mark Twain's novel transferred spiffily to Broadway, and if some critics felt that the juxtaposition of Camelot and twenties' slang ("Thou Swell") made for a one-joke show, the customers came running.

Vincent Youmans' career was cut short by tuberculosis when he was still in his prime, so much of his potential was never realized. *No, No, Nanette* (1925), a three-act farce about a Bible publisher involved with three grasping gold diggers, put Youmans on the map for his cheerful tunes, and it didn't harm the lyricists, Otto Harbach and Irving Caesar, either. The show climbed to success in a miniature lifetime of a tryout tour (eleven months in Chicago alone) that made *No, No, Nanette* seem like a revival by the time it arrived in New York. Even in the twenties the road was no longer the great network of theatre towns it had been when the Syndicate held sway, but it was still a profitable avenue for shows not bedded down in the big metropolises. By the fifties the road was gone except for national tours of Broadway hits, but when the seventies brought back the cross-country tour, shows like *Hello, Dolly!, Lorelei, Gigi, Mack and Mabel, Good News,* and revivals of *The Student Prince* and *The Desert Song* chugged along the circuit *before* scheduling New York openings.

Thus *No, No, Nanette.* Its first tryouts were shaky, so producer H. H. Frazee kept it in the Midwest, modifying it until it worked, and opened a London company even before the original cast got to Broadway. Any musical that began with a pert line of flappers gushing and prancing just had to succeed in London, and *No, No, Nanette* ran twice as long in the West End as it did on Forty-sixth Street. With songs like "I Want to Be Happy," "'Where Has My Hubby Gone?' Blues," "I've Confessed to the Breeze," "Too Many Rings Around Rosie (Will never get Rosie a ring)," and of course "Tea for Two," *No, No, Nanette* said as much for the mawkish twitterings of the twenties as will ever be said. The work's alleged timelessness was less in evidence than its nostalgia-pleadings when it came back with a repapered book for a soberingly profitable rerun in 1971.

Even Beatrice Lillie, Charles Winninger, and Helen Broderick couldn't make a hit of Youmans' revue *Oh, Please* (1926), but Herbert Fields' well-constructed script and Youmans' rousing score kept *Hit the Deck* (1927) going for 352 performances. The composer was tiring of vapid farces and embarked on a series of serious and frequently well-integrated shows that were too progressive and sometimes just too disjointed to succeed. *Show Boat* was just around the corner, but as several would-be "Show Boats" proved, a serious musical had to be near perfect to compete with the freaky musical comedies and lush romances of the day.

Unabashed happiness, however, was the keynote of the DeSylva, Brown, and Henderson book shows. Their first musical after the George White revues was *Good News* (1927), a boisterous college romp that treaded but lightly on the toes of higher education, leading Alexander Woollcott to ponder the state of musical comedy librettos: "I confess that I had not precisely expected to attend this season a musical comedy of which the plot would turn on whether Tom Marlowe would pass his astronomy exam, and so be able to go into the big game on Saturday and win for dear old Tait. I had not expected to hear a theatre hushed by Tom's big, manly resolve not to cheat in the exam, but to play fair and square. I certainly had not expected to see a cluster of chorus girls, led by a fair and writhing maiden with implausible hair, lift their approximately assembled voices in soprano fealty to Pi Beta Phi."

Good scores, brisk one-liners, and an abundance of high spirits turned the six DeSylva, Brown, and Henderson shows into consecutive hits without a single miss. George White passed up a 1927 *Scandals* to star Ed Wynn in *Manhattan Mary* for the team, still hawking their sophisticated naïveté, as in the song "Broadway," with its "hard luck tale" and "painted smile."

Always in step with the times, the trio touched on boxing in *Hold Everything* (1928) with Bert Lahr, the country club set in *Follow Through* (1929), and aviation in *Flying High* (1930), again with Bert Lahr, now haunted by his weighty vis-à-vis Kate Smith.

DeSylva having departed the East, Ziegfeld gave Brown and Henderson Mark Hellinger to prop them up for *Hot-Cha!* in 1932, originally titled *Laid in Mexico*. Lahr was a headliner now, to the tune of $2500 a week, and the nightly installments of his feud with co-star Lupe Velez set off more sparks than Buddy Rogers' singing, Eleanor Powell's dancing, or Joseph Urban's settings. If there was a depression on, *Hot-Cha!* didn't seem to notice, possibly because Ziegfeld didn't either. "I look upon the Depression primarily as a lack of confidence," he said at the time. "In 'It's Great to be Alive,' we have the line 'there's just as many flowers, just as many trees.' It's all in the people's minds to a great extent. But people have less money and they spend it more carefully." The next Brown-Henderson entry, *Strike Me Pink* (1933), noticed the Depression only in that its primary investor was Waxey Gordon, an eminent bootlegger.

The fate of Lewis Gensler is indicative of what happens to the second rung of non-conformist tunesmiths. Sometimes ordinary and sometimes distinctive, Gensler never enjoyed the stabilizing axis of a steady lyricist, nor the satisfaction of renown. His adaptation of the ever-augmented repetition that Ravel used for *Bolero* made the production number "Speak Easy" an overpowering experience for audiences at *The Gang's All Here* (1931), and he painted on the same grand canvas in *Ballyhoo of 1932*: in the first-act finale, "Ballyhujah" (lyrics by E. Y. Harburg), a blackfaced Willie Howard embodied radio hard sell, egging the chorus on to pandemonium while two horses laden with beer kegs galloped on treadmills. Nobody was sure what it was all about but they clapped like hell when it was over, inviting more investigations of the national scene from Harburg. One of the first men to use the musical stage for penetrating insights, he drew Depression blood in his "Brother, Can You Spare a Dime?" lyric and then parlayed fantasy into social commentary, most dazzlingly in *Finian's Rainbow* (1947).

Even in the early thirties Harburg was a man with a point of view, something the musical needed badly. The conflux of disparate elements that went into any given evening found a paradigm in *Sons o' Guns,* to pick up one by no means isolated example. This was in 1929, and World War I was considered quaint enough for the nostalgic treatment, so colorful French peasants warbled in and out of the comic action about a playboy private whose sergeant is his ex-valet, a not astronomically novel premise even way back then. The score ran an incongruous gamut, alternating the push of "Let's Merge" and "Red, Hot and Blue Rhythm" with the phoney heart of "C'est Vous Que J'Aime" and the thriftless optimism of "Cross Your Fingers (And make a wish, and maybe your wish will come true-oo)," while the Albertina Rasch Girls had a ballet at the slightest provocation. Part operetta, part extravaganza, but mainly lowdown farce, *Sons o' Guns* was a smash hit even in the bleak days after the stock market crash, but its vagrant style, like that of the Gershwin-Romberg *Rosalie,* failed to fuse its anomalous parts into any particular scheme.

The more homogenized romantic show was better equipped to strike a pose and hold it for two and a half hours. *Irene* (1919) was such a show, a phenomenon of its time. When it closed it held the record as Broadway's longest running musical ever, and seventeen touring companies carried its message to every village and farm, that message apparently being that a shopgirl can find happiness with Prince Charming if she's entrancing, Irish, and sings "Alice Blue Gown." Stupidly enough, the 1973 revival scuttled the feel of the original with a clumsy revision that turned one of the most consistent musicals of its time into one of the most dislocated of *its.*

Meanwhile, in the musical comedy arena, George S. Kaufman and Marc Connelly borrowed straight-play discipline to prepare a somewhat cogent book sending up the business world in *Helen of Troy, New York* (1923), but the score by

Bert Kalmar and Harry Ruby was not the sort that functions for a point-of-view musical; the point was still the chorus girls, and the view aimed from knee to ankle.

Like most songwriters of their time, Kalmar and Ruby were only comfortable writing musical comedies set in New York, which in itself suggests a built-in point of view: the city is fun, the city is wide open, the city has heart. When musical comedy grew up in the forties and had an opinion, it was often just the opposite: the city is rough, the city is a prison, the city is corrupt—a vantage that had already provided the subtext of the romantic shows, from *Show Boat* and *Music in the Air* on up. 1928's flightier version of New York, however, dominated Kalmar and Ruby's *Good Boy,* the story of two hicks at loose ends in Gotham. Urban sprawl was conveyed via Busby Berkeley's treadmills—an innovation then—and the hopscotch of New York life sang out in "Manhattan Walk" and "The Voice of the City." Speaking of structure (forget point of view), Kalmar and Ruby joined up with Kaufman again in 1928 for *Animal Crackers,* with Groucho, Chico, and Harpo Marx doing what they did and Zeppo looking straight and singing the ballads. The show's infectiously loose layout was museumed for posterity in a 1930 film pretty much as it was—including Groucho's airy parody of *Strange Interlude*'s interior monologues—although most of the score was omitted.

Besides the composers, lyricists, and librettists of major and minor note, numerous others worked on the Main Stem, then as now, frequently vacating to less risky vocations after an especially tatty failure or two. In the 1925–26 season, for example—the time of *The Cocoanuts, No, No, Nanette, The Girl Friend, Sunny,* and *The Vagabond King* (lunacy, vapidity, gumption, tenderness, and bombast within a six-block radius at a $4.40 top)—several lesser items fought unsuccessfully for business and died in four or five weeks, unmourned. The flops of that year shared one giant vice with those of today: they just weren't very good. There was a *Hello, Lola* adapted from Booth Tarkington's *Seventeen* with Margaret Sullavan in a tiny role, a *Bringing Up Father* from George McManus' Maggie and Jiggs comic strip, something called *Holka Polka* with onetime Parsifal Orville Harrold and little Patti Harrold as a Czech father and daughter, and a *Florida Girl,* a canker even with the Ritz Brothers and the delectable Vivienne Segal. Perhaps the most patent sensation of death warmed over—no, death raw—was vouchsafed by *The Matinee Girl,* which held out gamely for twenty-four performances (imagine what was folding out of town that season).

There is always room for novelty; an exotic way of doing things was on view in importations from Harlem, at first three or four a year but spiraling to nearly a dozen in 1929. Such opuses as *Liza* (1922), *How Come?* (1923), *The Chocolate Dandies* (1924) with Noble Sissle and Eubie Blake, and *Deep Harlem* (1929) made halfhearted attempts at a story line to tie up the specialty acts, but they were almost all revues, and though they were considered chic and daring, few of them lasted out the first month. *Lucky Sambo* (1925) was an exception, with its tale of Rufus Johnson and Sambo Jenkins conniving at an oil-stock swindle. The authentic jiveassing of the Harlem shows must have seemed shockingly insolent next to the tragic sincerity of nonmusical folk plays such as Paul Green's *In Abraham's Bosom* (1926) and the Heywards' *Porgy* (1927), but then the few successful Negro revues weren't written by blacks anyway. Sissle and Blake's famous *Shuffle Along* so exhausted potential business on 125th Street that its downtown run in 1921 gave out after 27 repetitions. *Dixie to Broadway* (1924) with Florence Mills and Hamtree Harrington was barely profitable at 77 performances, easily outdistanced by two long-runners, Lew Leslie's *Blackbirds of 1928* and *Connie's Hot Chocolates* in 1929. All three were written, produced, and directed by whites, leaving the blacks to supply the Afro-American feel on stage. Jimmy McHugh and Dorothy Fields' score for *Blackbirds* and "Fats" Waller, Harry Brooks, and Andy Razaf's for *Hot Chocolates* aimed at a broad, Northeast urban look at black culture. The former's "Diga Diga Doo" and the latter's "That Jungle Jamboree" gently rippled the stream of race relations, but the McHugh-Fields "I Can't Give You Anything But Love" and the Waller-Brooks-Razaf "Ain't Misbehavin'" evoked a response as universal as "Brother, Can You Spare a Dime?" was to evoke in the thirties. *Blackbirds* was by far the best of the so-called Negro revues, bulging with talent—Adelaide Hall's and Aida Ward's singing, Bill "Bojangles" Robinson's fancy stepping, Tim Moore's Uncle Tom comedy, and the jiving Plantation Orchestra.

The still tentative disciples of *Sumurun* and the art movement were being heard from more and more in the twenties. The success of the Norton-Asche spectacle *Chu Chin Chow* brought forth similar epics in 1919: *The Rose of China* and *Aphrodite,* a "drama of profane love" with music by the opera composer Henri Fevrier, choreography by Michel Fokine, and costumes by Diaghilev's protégé Léon Bakst. An even more voluptuous *Mecca* followed a year later.

The future of musical comedy staging depended on some token advancement at regular intervals, so in 1920 John Murray Anderson gave the lighting crew their head in *What's in a Name,* garnering critics' complaints—in some cases congratulations—that they couldn't see what was happening on stage in all the darkness. An escape from the standard backdrop and wing pieces was the feature of *Johannes Kreisler* (1922), a "fantastic melodrama" in forty-two scenes, some of them played on one half of the stage while the other half was covertly being dressed for the next set. Most musical comedy goers preferred the less sophisticated cornucopias of DeSylva, Brown, and Henderson, however, even when *Arabesque* (1925) starred Bela Lugosi as the passionate sheik of Hammamm seducing Bedouin girls amidst Norman Bel Geddes' striking three-level set. Not surprisingly, the wine had to improve before the bottles could be remodeled; it still lacked body.

9

The Twenties (II)

"The Drum-Drum-Drum of Hoofbeats in the Sand"

After his enormous success with the megaromantic *Maytime,* Sigmund Romberg knew his future lay with operetta. Today a composer can get one show a season at the absolute most (and nobody does), but Broadway was surging in the twenties and Romberg discharged contracts for three or four jobs a season, either dumb musical comedies like *The Melting of Molly* (1918), dumber operettas like *The Magic Melody* (1919), or, dumbest of all, star vehicles like Al Jolson in *Sinbad* (1918), in which all the hit tunes were interpolations by other people.

Then J. J. Shubert enticed Romberg back into the fold with a tempting proposition in 1921. The life of Franz Schubert had been recorded in a European operetta by Heinrich Berté, *Das Dreimäderlhaus* (The Home of Three Girls), using Schubert's own melodies. Dorothy Donnelly was adapting the libretto, and if he liked, Romberg could revise Berté's Schubert for Broadway. Romberg couldn't refuse, and the result of the collaboration became that byword of bargain-basement casting and endless national tours, *Blossom Time*. Its grotesquely fictional plot had Schubert composing the big tune of the B Minor Symphony as a "Song of Love" to his adored Mitzi, then leaving the work "unfinished" when she takes up with his best friend. In the final moments of the show Schubert was seen at his deathbed, schmerzed to pieces and ready for release, but with one hit tune left in him—the *Ave Maria,* no less —which he composes just before kicking off. The original New York Franz Schubert, Bertram Peacock, looked incredibly like the real thing, but there the resemblance to historical past or realistic anytime ended.

Five hundred and ninety-two performances in the original run alone testify to the public's appreciation of this sort of sugar-coated fable, but Romberg was again enmeshed in a series of Shubert potboilers until he had another chance to garnish a romantic theme—this time with his own melodies. The Messrs. were determined to make money on a two-time flop called *Old Heidelberg* . . . would Romberg consider setting the tender affair of a prince and a pretty waitress doomed to part? *Would* he? The "stupendous musical production" called *The Student Prince in Heidelberg* opened at the Jolson Theatre on December 2, 1924, earning raves from the critics and knocking the common people dead. Though Dorothy Donnelly again supplied the libretto, the mildewed fancies of *Blossom Time* were not so apparent here. As Stark Young put it in the *Times,* "the business of an operetta . . . is music," and Romberg had contrived a melodious score. The Shuberts, in a rare moment of profusion, supplied the necessary vocal equipment—Howard Marsh, Ilse Marvenga, Greek Evans, and a male chorus of forty—but as most critics noted, humor was in short supply.

And there it is again—the nemesis of the romantic musical, humor. Operetta's early identity crisis is important in the development of the romantic musical because it had a much harder time with sheer form than plain old musical comedy.

The problem is symmetry: how to equalize the straight parts with the buffoonery, how to satisfy the public's demand for entertainment and yet come up with an elegant libretto. In the twenties the lighter elements jarred stylistically with the gracious ones, and after a while audiences rejected the whole business until theatre craftsmen found ways to make it work in the forties—*Carousel, Song of Norway, Bloomer Girl, The Day Before Spring, Brigadoon.*

Romberg was a power to reckon with in the world of operetta by 1925. The Shuberts had only to check the profit sheets on their touring companies of *Maytime, Blossom Time,* and *The Student Prince* to realize what a friend they had in Romberg. Sure that he had located his niche, the composer produced one of his very best scores in 1926 for Schwab and Mandel, catching the nation's heartbeat in a story of legionnaires, Arabian houris, and haughty French soubrettes embroiled in the passions of the Sahara. With a book by Otto Harbach, Oscar Hammerstein II, and Frank Mandel, *The Desert Song* had more than a smattering of comedy to balance the ardor that swept the stage. The Riff uprisings in Northern Africa had been news scarcely months before, so the setting was ripe for treatment, and the hero, a swashbuckling Riff who masquerades as a sissy when Vivienne Segal's around, was the strong, silent type everyone could admire—and, in his sheik getup, a recognizable trope from the Valentino films. *The Desert Song* racked up 465 performances and played the road forever, one of the few operettas to outlast the eclipse of the form. Most of the lines sound foolish today, but the heroine's approach-avoidance conflict with her ambiguous hero remains a viable theatrical premise, intelligently evolved underneath the Moroccan hoopla.

Never happy out of uniform, Romberg delved into the American past with a Civil War epic, *My Maryland* (1927), then joined up with Gershwin in 1928 for the Ziegfeld-sponsored *Rosalie,* set in West Point. Later that year Romberg enjoyed his longest New York run with the "romantic musical comedy'' *The New Moon.* A chaotic script had made a disaster of the Philadelphia tryout in late 1927 (when co-author Hammerstein was busy with *Show Boat*), but a year-long polishing tour dispensed with the faulty book, much of the score, and most of the immense cast. By the time *The New Moon* pulled into the Imperial Theatre in the fall of 1928, it was ready to triumph.

The story was based on a historical incident involving a pre-Revolutionary Frenchman who founds a republican colony in the Atlantic while en route to Devil's Island for loving the soprano (above his station). The book was satisfyingly long, lush, and ripsnorting, with abundant levity from the secondary lover-comedians, but such book material paled to a shadow when served up with ''Lover, Come Back to Me,'' ''Softly, as in a Morning Sunrise,'' ''The Girl on the Prow,'' ''Stouthearted Men,'' ''One Kiss (one man to save it for),'' and ''Wanting You.'' Look at the titles—what do they say about the Romberg-Friml medium as a whole, especially compared to concurrent musical comedies like *Sally* or *Good News?* Robert Benchley caught the mood of the times splendidly in his *New Moon* review: ''We haven't seen such refayned acting since the days when the Mysterious Stranger turned out to be Prince Boris in disguise. And *then* what merry-making at the inn there was! A toast, a toast to Prince Boris!''

Back when Romberg was trying to extricate himself from Shubert clutches, Rudolf Friml was still fighting off the fetters of heavily comic musicals. In 1924, two months before Romberg's *The Student Prince,* Friml collaborated on the score to *Rose-Marie* with Herbert Stothart, to a libretto by Otto Harbach and Oscar Hammerstein II. This colorful thriller of love and murder in the Canadian Rockies offered an unusual program note in place of the customary song titles: ''The musical numbers of this play are such an integral part of the action that we do not think we should list them as separate episodes.'' A glance at the piano vocal score, however, shows this to be wishful thinking—the songs are certainly separate, but with dialogue between them and cue lines to lead them in they were an early example of Hammerstein's determination to close the gap between musical story lines and the emotions that simmer beneath them.

The *Rose-Marie* score was geared to the *Rose-Marie* book with unusual care for those days, some of the music actually moving the action forward, opera-style. Black Eagle's jealous murder of his rival Hawley in the cabin scene, for example, was told entirely through pantomime, with an orchestral potpourri to interpret the shifts in mood. The finale of Act One was like a slice of . . . no, not life, perhaps, but music drama certainly, with dialogue interspersed with song and a thunderous reprise of the "Indian Love Call," not to mention a high C from the soprano.

More than a few critics welcomed the escapism of *Rose-Marie,* preferring it to the less ponderous but no more vapid musical shows of the day. *Theatre* magazine's Arthur Hornblow considered it "head, shoulders and waist above the customary dribble about Prohibition and Brooklyn." Friml was determined to cater to such tastes, but the word men knew that some measure of humor is needed if a musical show is to succeed. Not surprisingly, it was Stothart who penned the comic-"tainted" songs for Hard-Boiled Herman and Lady Jane in the subplot, while Friml wrote the title song, "Lak Jeem," "Indian Love Call," "Pretty Things," and "The Door of My Dreams." *Rose-Marie* lasted a year and five months at first, and though an end-of-tour revival three years later was a failure in New York, the road and summer stock kept it alive through the fifties, and its music survives today, if fitfully.

Despite *Rose-Marie*'s success, Friml was far more devoted to the freakish bustle and cloakery of romance than to balancing the evening's forces. If the *New York Tribune* could call *Rose-Marie* a "basket of . . . drama and melodrama, musical comedy, grand opera and opéra comique," Friml's

1925 opus, *The Vagabond King,* was a "musical play" and don't you forget it. Virtually without comedy, this was the dernier cri in demented realism, a straight adaptation of Justin McCarthy's *If I Were King,* employing a ton of songs, dances, and incidental music. Dennis King came fresh from his stint as Big Jim Kenyon in *Rose-Marie* to play François Villon, "fitting his pants," as they put it in Texas, the incarnation of bluster and panache. Carolyn Thompson as Villon's vis-à-vis was the indispensable haughty lady, complete with dream vision ("Someday") and pop tune, "Only a Rose (I gi-i-ive you)."

The Vagabond King was a giant hit despite its foghorn libretto, for Friml stood alone in the evocation of romantic derring-do. The less austere Romberg had a more jovial panacea for escapism. Though both men were equals at composing stirring choruses like "The Riff Song" or "The Song of the Vagabonds," Romberg's shows were sprinkled with dialect comedians or funny dances, while *The Vagabond King* and most other Friml opuses had no truck with such Broadway compromises.

Friml went back to musical comedy in 1926 with *The Wild Rose,* working with his *Rose-Marie* librettists Harbach and Hammerstein. Avoiding the huge casts and bulldozing action of the historical romances, *The Wild Rose* pitted an American hero and his wisecracking sidekick against oil speculators and rabblerousers trying to subvert the little kingdom of Borovina, whose princess takes the soprano half of the love songs. As Burns Mantle commented, "It looks at the finish as though they might marry and raise duets," but Friml's music was not up to his best level, so this early attempt to mint a new genre by merging romance with upbeat nonchalance didn't take.

The Three Musketeers (1928), however, was Friml's meat. Since Romberg's *Princess Flavia* had just done well by Anthony Hope's *The Prisoner of Zenda,* Dumas' novel seemed likely competition. Warming to the story's passion and gasconade, Friml concocted one of operettaland's fullest scores. There wasn't even time for an overture; the curtain zipped up on the inevitable tavern scene while latecomers scrambled into their seats. The book and lyrics were the kind that end an era, but Dennis King was again on hand as d'Artagnan, crossing swords with every male in sight and playing his role with "the voice of a canary, the grace of a swallow and the valor of an eagle," according to Percy Hammond. King, Vivienne Segal, and a valiant cast brought Dumas to life amidst Joseph Urban's evocative sets and John Harkrider's splendid costumes, and audiences succumbed to the spell, though it was short on fun ("I did greatly enjoy the first few years of Act I," said Woollcott).

Silly as this may sound, the world of American operetta is one of masks. People are always pretending to be something they're not, something better, superhuman. The Viennese let their princesses masquerade as goosegirls, and of course our own adopted Romberg sent his student prince to Heidelberg to love a lowly waitress. But the later Romberg and Friml shows, and Broadway operetta in general as opposed to European comic opera, dealt with heroism—the clarity of carefree, unreasoning nobility passing every test. Robert and Marianne establish a democracy in the middle of the Atlantic in *The New Moon,* and king-for-a-day François Villon saves Paris from evil Burgundy in *The Vagabond King,* founding a line that stretches (thinly after the twenties) right up to *Man of La Mancha* and *Kean* in the sixties.

In order to support its semifantastic premise, operetta had to sound more imposing than musical comedy. It played a heavy scene—too heavy for the technique of the times, so it came out stilted and unnatural. Still, its message was clear, and its spectators could accept it via the music; the gigantic dimensions that music had to convey finally came through more smoothly in later decades. Operetta never tackled the country-versus-the-city confrontation so endemic to the American worldview because operettas sought out the heroic arena and therefore couldn't be set in the modern era or nearby. When the first operetta *was* so set (*Show Boat*), it didn't deal with heroism and wasn't really an operetta anyway.

Neither Friml nor Romberg had successful imitators. Shows like *Rose-Marie* and *The Desert Song* called for huge casts, acres of sets, and lush costumes (*Rose-Marie*'s "Totem Tom-Tom" outfits cost $2400, a huge expense for just one number). A half-decent musical comedy could scrape by with an ingratiating cast, some chance levity, and a pleasant score, but operettas were big investments, and a half-decent operetta could lose a fortune. Gershwin and Stothart staked their successful claim in *Song of the Flame,* but such lesser composers as Ida Hoyt Chamberlain (*Enchanted Isle*) and Kenyon Scott (*A Noble Rogue*) found the late twenties a pitiless era for romances with less than first-rate music. Even Friml suffered defeat with one of his best scores, *The White Eagle* (1927), a raving adaptation of Edwin Milton Royle's *The Squaw Man.*

The road was still a prime target for past New York hits, so at the Shuberts' behest cheesy companies of *The Student Prince, The Firefly,* et al., traversed the continent, bestrewing it with garlands and mush and finishing in New York for a two-week run while critics fumed at the Shuberts' nerve. It was brother J. J. who thought of creating another *Blossom Time,* first with Offenbach's life and music, *The Love Song* (1925), then with Chopin, *White Lilacs* (1928)—both of them gainful but hardly bonanzas. Some sort of apex would have been reached in *White Lilacs* when J. J. dreamed up a serenade which Chopin would compose and which Odette Myrtil, as George Sand, would play on her violin. Myrtil, who had fiddled on stage in *Countess Maritza* the year before, refused, claiming that George Sand couldn't play the violin.

Jake's reply summed up the operetta epoch for all time. "Who'll know?" he said.

10

Show Boat

The Book Musical Arrives

The late twenties were peak years for Broadway. 1915 had produced 133 shows, 1920 had 144, but 1925 offered 238, and 1927 broke the tape with 268, an astounding total compared to the 1971–72's season's 55 and 1972–73's 50. The musical in particular was doing fine, at least as far as quantity goes. Besides the revues that overran the period with scores by Gershwin, Berlin, Romberg, and company, 1927 alone drew to a close with no less than fifteen smash hits.

But that year's seven moderate successes are more interesting, in a way, for they offer a time-capsule glimpse of twenties musical comedy in the half-world between wonderful and meretricious: *Happy,* concocted by five different people and covering the Hadley College and Southampton, Long Island, set; Romberg's *The Love-Call,* a saga of untamed Arizona with the team of Veloz and Yolanda as "Fiesta Dancers"; *Lucky,* involving Ruby Keeler and Ceylon; *The Night-*

ingale, a "musical romance" on the life of Jenny Lind; *Piggy,* a reworking of *The Rich Mr. Hoggenheimer* with the original star, Sam Bernard, still playing an overbearing Jew; *The Sidewalks of New York* with Ruby Keeler again, this time in a dual role—"Mamie" and "Ruby." There was also *Oh, Earnest,* the first of several musicalizations of *The Importance of Being Earnest,* with one Dimples Riede playing Clarice Chitworth, a character Oscar Wilde would have had trouble placing.

Flops were rarer than hits in those days: 1927 logged only fifteen failures out of thirty-eight productions. Compare that with the tally for 1974: the year closed with only seven musicals on Broadway, including two revivals—*Candide, Grease, The Magic Show, Raisin, Pippin, Over Here!,* and *Where's Charley?,* of which only the first five were to repay their investment (*Over Here!* was a flop and *Where's Charley?* was subsidized by a foundation grant).

The profusion of empty-headed leg shows and collegiate romps aptly suited the era. Prohibition was a bore and gangsterism was on the rise, but everybody had his favorite speakeasy and besides, everybody knew all the gangsters were in Chicago. Furthermore, the country was doing well: the market was booming, workers were earning and spending, and it just seemed natural to go out and have a good time. Musicals were chipper and charming, rabid with happy endings. Tom Marlowe won the Big Game *and* the girl, Rose-Marie la Flamme came back to Jim, and Sally became a Ziegfeld star: art imitated life.

When the real-life Ziegfeld commissioned Joseph Urban to design a theatre for the west side of Sixth Avenue between Fifty-fourth and Fifty-fifth Streets, he was frankly building himself a monument that would stand for the utmost in elegance in exactly the way his shows did. But a playhouse as grand as the Ziegfeld had to be could only open with the grandest show the hand of man could devise. When Jerome Kern and Oscar Hammerstein approached Ziegfeld with a new property they were working on, he knew he had the right hands—but they were holding the wrong property. Kern and his partner had latched on to a sad story of the Mississippi that didn't have a trace of bootleggers, wisecracking flappers, or butter-and-egg men. Not only wasn't this Ziegfeld's type of show, it wasn't anyone's. Novelty was money in the bank, as every producer knew, but only the right kind of novelty—certainly not a grandiose operetta with a real drama at the core and too many subplots for the audience to follow. To Ziegfeld, it didn't even sound like a musical; it was more like five hours of Art that the Theatre Guild might put on.

Somehow or other the authors won him over, but the project took so long to write that Ziegfeld impatiently opened his new theatre with *Rio Rita,* a Wild West frolic that pleased everyone, had a hit title song, ran for a year, and then vanished forever. Meanwhile, the Kern-Hammerstein show worked its way through an extensive tryout tour in Washington, Pittsburgh, and Philadelphia, finally hitting the Ziegfeld in New York on December 27, 1927. Despite his first objections and occasional second thoughts, the producer gave the piece a gorgeous production; it instantly captured both critics and public and made stars of its cast: Norma Terris, Helen Morgan, Howard Marsh, Charles Winninger, Edna May Oliver, Jules Bledsoe, Tess Gardella (Aunt Jemima), Sammy White, and Eva Puck. Ziegfeld didn't get to open his cathedral with *Show Boat,* but his "all-American musical comedy" opened up a much larger arena: theatre in the musical vernacular with the penetration of art.

Show Boat marked a turning point in the history of the musical, possibly the only turning point it ever had. Song and dance had been partners with plot on Broadway ever since *Cherry and Fair Star* in 1824, if not before. Once the medium got over its birth pangs, it achieved form and got very versatile, but it still couldn't tell a legitimate story that wasn't an excuse for jokes, interchangeable love ballads, or a star turn. True, some musicals—Kern's Princess shows or romances like *The Vagabond King,* for example—were based on presumably "well-made" plays and could tell a coherent story, but the musical elements were grafted on with a heavy hand. Situations didn't cry out for songs; songs were written which then required situations, and these situations were dropped into the plot like land mines in a corn field.

At first, Kern and Hammerstein were the only two men not willing to go on with the game. Kern won his spurs by killing off Ruritania and the third act, while Hammerstein had been slowly building up to a show that would fuse all the elements of musical comedy organically—that is, writing the work as a whole, with music defining character and moving the story along instead of intruding on it. When Edna Ferber's novel *Show Boat* was published in 1926, both Hammerstein and Kern felt the time was right to try setting a subject fleshed out with real people rather than the prefabricated ingenues and juveniles they had been, to some extent, serving up on a regular basis. Significantly, *Show Boat* meant a complete break from the snazzy New York show so popular in the twenties, although the two men in their separate careers had had little contact with that sort of entertainment anyway. Perhaps a certain sentimental streak in their personalities kept them away from the razor-edged sophistication that was the trademark of men like the Gershwins, Rodgers and Hart, and Cole Porter. Asked once why he never wrote a sophisticated musical, Hammerstein answered, "You mean one that takes place in a New York penthouse? Mostly because it doesn't interest me."

Ferber was shocked when Kern first suggested taking her novel to the musical stage. Despite his reputation as a composer of distinction, she envisioned an opening chorus of bleached blonde cuties high-kicking on the levee and rhyming "Captain Andy" with "fine and dandy." But Ferber loved the theatre and she finally capitulated—"melted," as she recalled in her first autobiography, "under the bewitching strains of 'Make Believe' and of 'Why Do I Love You?' . . .

And then Jerome Kern appeared in my apartment late one afternoon with a strange look of quiet exultation in his eyes. He sat down at the piano . . . and sang 'Ol' Man River.' The music mounted, mounted, and I give you my word my hair stood on end, the tears came to my eyes, I breathed like a heroine in a melodrama. This was great music. This was music that would outlast Jerome Kern's day and mine."

Years later, Hammerstein's wife, Dorothy, had occasion to correct someone who credited the song to Jerome Kern. "Oscar Hammerstein wrote 'Old Man River,' " she said. "Jerome Kern wrote 'Dum dum dee dee.' " Whether or not the story is apocryphal, the woman was righter than she knew. When Ferber first heard the song, she was probably so moved by its power and beauty that she didn't notice how different Hammerstein's view of the Mississippi was from hers. Oscar Hammerstein did indeed write "Old Man River," and in writing it created a moving, sentimental, and ultimately naïve portrait of what Ferber saw as a titanic force of nature. Here is Ferber's impression of the "swollen and angry stream," early in the book:

> In the ghostly gray dawn the grotesque wreckage of flood-time floated and whirled and jiggled by, seeming to bob a mad obeisance as it passed the show boat which, in its turn, made stately bows from its moorings. There drifted past, in fantastic parade, great trees, uprooted and clutching at the water with stiff dead arms; logs, catapulted with terrific force; animal carcasses dreadful in their passivity; chicken coops; rafts; a piano, its ivory mouth fixed in a death grin . . . a live sheep, bleating as it came, but soon still . . . The Mississippi itself was a tawny tiger, roused, furious, bloodthirsty, lashing out with its great tail, tearing with its cruel claws, and burying its fangs deep in the shore to swallow at a gulp land, houses, trees, cattle—humans, even; and roaring, snarling, howling as it did so.

In both novel and musical the river is a recurrent theme, even more so in the latter as "Old Man River" takes on the character of a leitmotiv. When the story moves on to Chicago, Ferber likens the churning city to the same primal power that divides the American continent:

> . . . this city was only an urban Mississippi. The cobblestones were a river bed. The high grim buildings the river banks. The men, women, horses, trucks, drays, carriages, street cars that surged through those streets; creating new channels where some obstacle blocked their progress; felling whole sections of stone and brick and wood and sweeping over the section, obliterating all trace of its former existence; lifting other huge blocks and sweeping them bodily downstream to deposit them in a new spot; making a boulevard out of what had been a mud swamp—all this . . . was only the Mississippi in another form and environment; ruthless, relentless, Gargantuan, terrible.

Ferber's river is a disruptive force, a monster that devours its dependents. Captain Andy, owner of the show boat and the most likable character in the story, is drowned in an accident two-thirds of the way through the novel—but Hammerstein didn't see it that way. To him, the river was a symbol of home and family, an agent of good will rather than a disinterested natural phenomenon, so Captain Andy is present at the final curtain, henpecked but breathing. On stage, the Mississippi provides the roots of existence without which no one can ever know peace. Away from the *Cotton Blossom,* marriages fail, weak men lose heart and dissipate, fathers desert their daughters, and second-rate actors live off the income of their progeny. Only at home, surrounded by family, can there be happiness.

The novel *Show Boat* is a beautiful book, peopled with tough characters whose lives run a believable course—a few highs and lows, but mostly just day-to-day continuity. The musical *Show Boat* is also beautiful, but in a different way, embodying a different philosophy from Ferber's and marked by constant event, as any three-hour show is bound to be. Hammerstein's strong feelings about the beneficence of rural upbringing in a family setting influenced many of his greatest works—*Music in the Air* and *Allegro* both turn on this theme —and the type of romance that pervades his librettos is very much like that popularized in American movies of the thirties. There, two lovers are separated at the finale (by death, if possible), and the audience feels that nothing else in their lives can ever matter as much as that one perfect affair. This is the ending that Hammerstein and Rodgers chose for their masterpiece, *Carousel*—an ending distinctly less crushing than the one Ferenc Molnar left on the original, *Liliom*.

It would be foolish to discuss the impact of *Show Boat* without taking Kern's music into account, but it was really Hammerstein who pioneered the basic layout of musical comedy that served the genre through its developing maturity and sometimes still turns up today. In simple terms, this is the scene-song scenario: plot action capped by a song to delineate character; blackout; lights up on new set; further plot action; another song; and so on. It may look primitive on paper, but before Hammerstein the songs didn't necessarily connect with the preceding book scenes. Wonderful as the tunes might be, they were noncontextual pieces suitable for any occasion—one size fits all—or any show. In the twenties a song deleted from one show could rebound into the next one, frequently without the slightest change in lyrics. But the practice began breaking down even before *Oklahoma!* and was virtually dead by the fifties.

Oddly enough, some critics resented the growing attempt to write organic music dramas, however comic, instead of more harmless diversions. George Jean Nathan, champion of O'Neill and Saroyan, never tired of complaining about the decline of the quality of beauty in the chorus line. He really raised the roof in the forties when Agnes De Mille hired dancers who were more useful on their toes than in businessmen's laps: "The best musical comedies . . . are those in which sense is reduced to a minimum, the worst, those which aim at rationality. . . . What we want . . . is a return to the old-time absurdity, the old-time refusal to reflect life and reality in any way, the old-time razzle and dazzle and the incredible.''

Only two years prior to 1927, Hammerstein and Kern had been working on just the sort of musical Nathan liked, *Sunny*. Both it and *Show Boat* are vivid memories to those who lived through the era, but the one is the antithesis of the other. *Sunny* was a joyous, chaotic potpourri with a sort of plot; *Show Boat* a single-minded piece with no spare parts, conceived to grow out of itself rather than gather in bits from outside.

The *Show Boat* story covers a lot of territory in time and space: starting in the 1880s and reaching 1927 in the last scene, it moves from Natchez up and down the Mississippi to Chicago and finally back to Natchez. This largeness of scope is emphasized by the timeless feel of the ''Old Man River'' lyrics, a feeling that grows in power on each reappearance. It soon becomes a theme song for the show, used as a constant while the immense plot apparatus shifts gears and ranges over America's recent past. In the space of three hours, the audience has sat in on the lives of several somewhat ordinary people, seen them stir with passions common and uncommon, riding high in prosperity and subsiding in adversity. It has witnessed an American pageant—a river levee with beaux and belles flirting while blacks struggle with cotton bales, the 1893 World's Fair Exhibition with a freak show and cooch dancers, a music hall where suffering talents sing to keep themselves in liquor, and the same levee again, with the belles turned in for flappers and a Charleston instead of a cakewalk. Hammerstein himself said, on the occasion of the 1946 revival, ''there seems to be no way of simplifying this stubborn play. It was born big and it wants to stay that way.''

Show Boat is an epic—an ''all-American'' epic, as Ziegfeld put it—and the spell it casts on an American audience is as much a part of its popularity as the songs. One of the few such musicals to be translated and revived repeatedly in continental Europe, it joins *Annie Get Your Gun, Kiss Me, Kate,*

My Fair Lady, and *Fiddler on the Roof* in trying to please Berliners, Genevans, Viennese on their own terms. But even when cast with real blacks, with singers who can act the dialogue, with idiomatic choreography even, it isn't *Show Boat* any more—to that audience, it's just an American operetta, not as funny as Offenbach, nor as touching as Messager, nor as glamorous as Lehár, nor as lively as Kálmán. On the other hand, European musical comedy has never quite been able to handle a serious story without turning into opera, as the medium has evolved no vernacular style in the way American musicals did. The light classics of the continent are classical in style, however light, sung by legit voices and composed strictly by trained musicians, leaving no middle ground between opera and zither music.

Kern was hardly a slouch among trained musicians, however, and he must have found the *Show Boat* project extremely stimulating. It was he who first read the novel and brought it to Hammerstein, and the care he took in its composition displayed an enormous development over his earlier work. His colleagues considered him the king of the profession, and he could approach the score with a skill far beyond that of his peers. For example, the first six notes of "Cotton Blossom," theme song of the show boat, are an inversion of the first six notes of "Old Man River" played twice as fast, turning the two very different songs into two different views of the same idea. "Cotton Blossom" suggests life as captured on the stage—mercurial, glittering, uproarious. "Old Man River" carries larger connotations of real life—slow, without illusion, only ultimately meaningful.

Kern also took the trouble to cover the years from the 1880s to his present through stylistic development of the musical forms. *Show Boat* is suffused with an entertainment motif, not only in the melodramas played aboard the *Cotton Blossom* but in other types as well; four-part spirituals, ragtime, minstrel olio, story ballads, and lowdown cooch music all give an authentic ring to the genre pieces. Songs like

"Make Believe" and "Life Upon the Wicked Stage" that are musical expressions of plot action are, of course, in Kern's own style, and a comparison of the sort of music he was writing for *Sunny* in 1925 and what he achieved only two years later speaks volumes: "Who?," "D'ye Love Me?" "Two Little Bluebirds," and "Let's Say Goodnight till It's Morning" are amiable nothings when set aside "Can't Help Lovin' Dat Man" or "You Are Love."

But if *Show Boat* is Broadway's first genuine music drama, it is not only because of the score. Hammerstein's libretto isn't just a well-laid-out story, nor, as we have seen, a straightforward adaptation. Like early American plays such as *The Contrast* and *Fashion,* it makes an early American statement, one that the musical would make again and often: that "home and family" business referred to earlier in this chapter—the bounty of roots and a country background, the degradation of city upheaval. *Show Boat*'s climactic scene, in Chicago, finds the mother, Magnolia, singing for her living in a nightclub. Rather than write a pastiche number for her, Kern pulled out "After the Ball," Charles K. Harris' old Tin Pan Alley gigantus used in *A Trip to Chinatown,* just the tearjerker for Magnolia to conquer an unruly New Year's Eve crowd with.

Now the kicker: Hammerstein has Magnolia's long-lost father, Captain Andy, in the audience. The unexpected meeting with her father, who coaches her to victory from his table, plus the built-in nostalgia of the song, gives the scene tremendous impact, besides letting Hammerstein's back-to-one's-roots ethic make its effect without pontification. If Magnolia had to leave home to know misery in strange places, Hammerstein will arrange to have her brought back to her family, in a scene which has no counterpart in the novel.

This is an important point, for many superior musicals are adaptations of stories from other media. It used to be thought that the most adaptable properties were the solid, well-oiled farces, but a three-act, twelve-character comedy littered with songs doesn't usually make much of a musical. For that kind of adaptation to work, the original property has to be "opened up": new scenes and characters are added, a chorus of merry villagers is somehow inveigled into the proceedings, an audience must be convinced that the story *needs* the songs. The essential unity of a one-set comedy ("The living room of the Treadwell apartment in the East Sixties" isn't just a set, it's an American trope) plays against the essential variety of the average musical comedy, if such a thing still exists. The adaptation must not only be skillful to succeed, it must rearrange the original work's physical plant. A play like *Auntie Mame* opened up rather naturally into *Mame* (1966) because it already had a variety of scenes and principals, but William Gibson's two-person *Two for the Seesaw* needed a great deal of imaginative opening up to become a satisfying musical show as *Seesaw* (1973). In the case of *Sherry* (1969), just for example, adding a couple of second-rate ballads and a roller-skating ballet to *The Man Who Came to Dinner* wasn't enough, especially since the dancers couldn't master the fine art of roller skating and tumbled into each other regularly every night until the number was killed in Philadelphia.

Although *Show Boat* was to exert a major influence on the musical theatre in the years that followed, its first success was no more than outstanding. It played 574 performances in New York and toured for seven months (with Irene Dunne as Magnolia), but five other musicals had lasted longer on Broadway: *Irene, A Trip to Chinatown, The Student Prince, Adonis,* and *Blossom Time.* Kern's score was to live a life of its own apart from the play. No other show of its time had as many blockbuster hits (*Show Boat* had six: "Make Believe," "Can't Help Lovin' Dat Man," "You Are Love," "Why Do I Love You?" "Bill," and "Old Man River"—all ballads) and few have since.

Ziegfeld brought *Show Boat* back to town in 1932 with the original principals plus Dennis King and Paul Robeson, and at last the critics were forced to admit its greatness; they had been no more than enthusiastic in 1927. As for the public, the airwaves (and a sort of fledgling cast album on four Columbia twelve-inch 78s with Helen Morgan and Robeson) had familiarized them with the songs to the extent that classic status was gained. A part-silent, part-talkie film in 1929 (with just "Old Man River" and, incredibly, new songs by Billy Rose) added nothing to the work's prestige, but Hammerstein himself did the screenplay for Universal's 1936 version, and he and Kern added three new songs to the score. The form that *Show Boat* has today is largely dictated by the author's revision for the 1946 revival on Broadway.

As Hammerstein admitted, *Show Boat* is big, and its expense is one reason it isn't revived more often. Even in 1946, with no stars in the cast, operating costs were so heavy that the year-long run grossed two million dollars and yet failed to break even. When the Lincoln Center production went on tour in the fall of 1966, audiences failed to show up in sufficient numbers to keep the account books in the black, and *Show Boat* sank halfway through its Philadelphia engagement.

Kern and Hammerstein have been criticized in recent years for *Show Boat*'s failure to characterize blacks realistically, but the fact is they had no intention of separating them from the whites in the story. *Show Boat* is about Americans, not race conflict. Joe and Queenie are as much a part of the saga as the others, perhaps even more so, for they see the immutability of their surroundings in ways the Hawkses and Ravenals can't. Furthermore, while the legitimate theatre had barely begun its documenting of black life (Paul Green's *In Abraham's Bosom* appeared at the tail end of 1926, Dubose and Dorothy Heyward's *Porgy* in late 1927, scant weeks before *Show Boat*), the musical stage had a whole tradition to break away from in the hangers-on from the minstrel shows of the 1850s—a tremendous task considering the popularity of such as Al Jolson (white) and Bert Williams (black).

Oddly enough, there *was* an attempt to bring black music to the stage in a mixed-cast book musical one year prior to

Show Boat. Deep River was advertised as a "native opera with jazz," though it was far from opera and, unlike the black revues of the time, hadn't a note of jazz. In many ways the forerunner of the type of show George Gershwin would write in *Porgy and Bess, Deep River* was the work of playwright Laurence Stallings (who would try again with Arthur Schwartz in *Virginia*), writing book and lyrics; Frank Harling wrote the music. Drawing partly on banjo serenades and spirituals, the score turned to European operetta for the love music, with Creole touches that couldn't save the tunes from sounding like nightclub tangos. Despite the presence of Rose McClendon and two wonderful numbers, "Dis Is de Day" (a "Gumbo Madrigal") and "De Old Clay Road," the show collapsed after 34 performances.

Even with the proliferation of "Negro revues" in the twenties and thirties, the black musical didn't find a continuum on Broadway until the seventies with such shows as *Purlie* and *Raisin.* If *Deep River* and *Show Boat* were breakthroughs for later developments, their black characters are still less authentic than those in *Porgy and Bess* (1935), *Cabin in the Sky* (1940), *Carmen Jones* (1943), and *St. Louis Woman* (1946), where the flavor of black America is keener and more deeply felt. *Show Boat* was a breakthrough, definitely, but for more important reasons. One, it was the first musical to treat a subject with the full compass of the theatre's potential, and two, it was wholly American in concept—not just New York.

11

Of Thee I Sing

The Satire That Didn't Close Saturday Night

A few months before *Show Boat* opened in New York, George S. Kaufman wrote a musical comedy book for producer Edgar Selwyn that pitted the United States against Switzerland in a war over the Swiss cheese tariff. A character outrageously based on Woodrow Wilson's Colonel House spent the evening plotting with an American cheese tycoon to incite the hostilities, and the story closed with the Swiss war ended (we won) but another on the way, this time with the Soviet Union over the caviar tariff. Selwyn was delighted with Kaufman's acerbic satire, and even more delighted when he got George and Ira Gershwin to write the songs. It was clear to everyone involved that the show, *Strike Up the Band,* would succeed. Kaufman had been careful not to overlook romance amid all the irony, and the Gershwins' score was a prize, including the rousing title song and one classic, "The Man I Love" (plus its reprise, "The

Girl I Love''), ousted from both *Lady Be Good* and *Rosalie.*

The late-summer tryout in Long Branch, New Jersey, and Philadelphia drew favorable notices but dwindling audiences; Selwyn finally ran out of money and closed the show. Though excellent satire, Kaufman's book was apparently too grim for a musical comedy, and Selwyn tried to get him to revise it. The author could not bring himself to change what he knew was top-hole material, so he let Selwyn bring in Morrie Ryskind to lighten the plot. When *Strike Up the Band* got to Broadway on January 14, 1930, the cheese had become chocolate, the fighting limited to an immense dream sequence, the parts entirely recast, and the score radically revamped. Gone were all the original ballads, even ''The Man I Love,'' dumped for the third time but already a pop hit on its own. Gone too was Kaufman's savage indictment of the big business of war, especially with the comedy team of Clark and McCullough on the loose. Ryskind changed the sardonic 1927 ending to a happy one for 1930 and added a secondary love plot to be on the safe side; the Gershwins obliged with four new ballads. This time the show pleased the public, even if the point of Kaufman's message had been creamed along with its sting.

In between the two versions of *Strike Up the Band,* the country's economic condition also changed considerably. The stock market had collapsed, unemployment was widespread and rising, and disappointment in Hoover's ''prosperity is just around the corner'' was turning to rage. Kaufman's rage was naturally best expressed in his work, but when he undertook his second political satire he was careful to sugar his barbs as he hadn't before. Morrie Ryskind collaborated with Kaufman from the start this time. They called the show *Tweedle-Dee* and set up a plot which hinged on the Republicans and Democrats vying with each other to develop a new national anthem, finally arriving at almost identical songs. But the first draft had neither romance nor even a significant leading character, so Kaufman and Ryskind threw out the anthem business and hit upon a scheme that could satisfy both audience demands for a love story and Kaufman's demands for a strong statement.

The new scenario pictured neither Republicans nor Democrats specifically. An unnamed party is seen preparing for an election campaign without goals or ideals; they have a candidate but no platform. As Fulton, the newspaper magnate, puts it, "What we need [is] an issue. Something that everybody is interested in, and that doesn't matter a damn. Something the party can stand on." A chambermaid in their smoke-filled room provides the answer. What does she care about more than anything else in the whole world? Money. The politicos reject that and press for her second choice: love. The candidate, Wintergreen, is a bachelor, so he runs for the presidency on a platform of love, sworn to marry the winner of a national beauty contest. Trouble begins when he falls for someone else, jilting the judges' choice, a Southern belle whose French descent ("She's the illegitimate daughter of an illegitimate son of an illegitimate nephew of Napoleon," sings the French ambassador) nearly brings on a war with France. Wintergreen is impeached, and the voting goes against him until his wife runs in to announce that she's pregnant. The Senate can't bring itself to eject an expectant father, since motherhood is if anything more inspiring to the American people than love. The Wintergreens have twins, and everything ends happily.

The Gershwins were again writing the score, Sam H. Harris was the producer—Kaufman the sole backer—and the show was renamed *Of Thee I Sing*. Favorable notices greeted the Boston tryout in December 1931, and in New York only Robert Benchley didn't like what he saw. Actually, the public was more enthusiastic than most critics, who quibbled with the pacing, the tone of the humor, and the choreography. Most of them pointed out the Savoyard feel of the musical (Leonard Bernstein on an "Omnibus" television program in the 1950s compared the first-act finales of *Of Thee I Sing* and *The Mikado*), and the *Post*'s John Mason Brown dubbed it "a new and welcome departure in the world of entertainment . . . a musical comedy which dodges nearly all the clichés of its kind."

Of Thee I Sing was an audience show, and the authors managed to bring their message home without letting up on diversion. Yes, the satire was strong, but contained entirely in comic and musical terms. In place of a conventional opening chorus, "Wintergreen for President" was a torchlight parade with quotations of old campaign rally tunes and Ira's famous couplet, rhyming "man the people choose" with "loves the Irish and the Jews!" Banners and signs filled the air with slogans: "Turn the Reformers Out," "Wintergreen—the Flavor Lasts," "He Kept Us Out of Jail," and "A Vote for Wintergreen Is a Vote for Wintergreen."

Along with the jibes at low-profile committeemen who hold the reins as well as the elections, the most consistent comic business ridiculed the office of Vice-President. As Alexander P. Throttlebottom, Victor Moore brought his zany bumbling to the summit as the country's most prominent Forgotten Man, having to take a visitor's tour of the White House just to get in. William Gaxton was Wintergreen, as suave and hypocritical a leading man the country is ever likely to get ("So here I am, gentlemen—nominated by the people, absolutely my own master, and ready to do any dirty work the committee suggests"). The two men played perfectly together, and Moore seconded Gaxton on a big bass drum in the impudent "Posterity Is Just Around the Corner."

The Gershwins' songs were no small part of the proceedings. *Of Thee I Sing*'s unorthodox subject made it a trailblazer to begin with, but in its musical layout it was one of the formative works of the thirties, not so much for book-music integration as for brilliance of conception. The operatic ensembles for the beauty contest, the inauguration-*cum*-wedding, and the impeachment scene were a far cry from the finale forms of operetta, as Gershwin's tunes were always couched in the vernacular—his own vernacular if no one else's. More than anyone else, George Gershwin hammered the final nail into the coffin of European light music in this country, and furthermore opened up new contours in the layout of musical comedy scores. The ballad "Who Cares?" was first used as the Wintergreens' jaunty reply to reporters asking about the breach of promise suit, and it came off as an upbeat charm song. But later on, when Wintergreen was faced with impeachment, the couple reprised it in a slower tempo; this sincere romantic portrait succeeded with the audience as well as did the riotous comedy scenes. Despite its adult treatment of the musical part of musical comedy, however, *Of Thee I Sing* owed nothing to Kern and Hammerstein: *Show Boat* told one sprawling story through music, whereas *Of Thee I Sing* was a story told around a series of sketches, the whole punctuated by song and dance. Except for the extended sequence of chorus and solos in the scenes named above, *Of Thee I Sing* deliberately made no attempt to utilize the *Show Boat* format, mainly because it was not basically a romantic musical.

Everything worked in *Of Thee I Sing*. It was one of the most profitable shows of its time, enjoying an eight-month national tour with Oscar Shaw, Donald Meek, and Harriet Lake (Ann Sothern), and lasting 441 performances in New York, most of them virtually sold out, a strikingly unusual situation in 1931. Besides the single song sheets, the vocal score was published, once a standard practice but by the thirties a declining luxury since by then people went out to hear music instead of making it at home and the "parlor pianist" had all but vanished. The libretto too was published in book form, selling out seven editions. The increasing awareness that *Of Thee I Sing* might just be more than a better grade of musical show made headline news on May 2, 1932, when the Pulitzer Prize was awarded to Kaufman, Ryskind, and Ira Gershwin (George was not included). With competition from plays such as Philip Barry's *The Animal Kingdom,* Robert E. Sherwood's *Reunion in Vienna,* and, mainly, O'Neill's *Mourning Becomes Electra,* the award seemed ridiculous to many critics. Brooks Atkinson suggested there was "more whim than judgment" in the decision, and Burns Mantle of the *Daily News* wrote, "*Of Thee I Sing* is the most intelligent, the most consistent, the most timely satire of American politics that native theater has yet entertained. But by no conceivable stretch can it be classed as a play in the accepted sense of that term. Strip it of its lyrics and its music and there will be little left of the prize-winner but a half-hour of farcical and satirical sketches." Mantle might have added that a musical that remained a strong work *without* its music and lyrics wouldn't be much of a musical, but the Pulitzer Prize had always gone to plays before, and most people weren't ready to accept the musical form as a vital force in its own right.

One of the few hit musicals of that era not to be filmed, *Of Thee I Sing* impressed Hollywood as being too individual for a mass audience, and an updated revival in 1952 was a dismal failure. Twenty years later commercial television decided the mass audience could handle it, and the CBS network trotted out a gritless *Of Thee I Sing* special with all the afflatus of an atomic-powered hurdy-gurdy.

It was Kaufman's wife who suggested that the further adventures of the Wintergreens and Throttlebottom might make a good sequel, and Sam H. Harris seconded the motion, but Kaufman and Ryskind played *Let 'Em Eat Cake* (1933) for savagery rather than satire. This picture of a blue-shirted revolution overturning the democratic process had all the guts of the first *Strike Up the Band* but little of the fun-poking of *Of Thee I Sing*. The continuity from the earlier Wintergreen story seemed like mere repetition when "Wintergreen for President," "Who Cares?" and the whole-tone scale Supreme Court song were quoted, even if the principals were still Gaxton, Moore, and company.

Furthermore, the Gershwin songs served the context of the book too well to be popular, except for the sole hit, "Mine." George's growth as a composer had reached the highly experimental stage, and for a moment he lost the popular appeal of his melodic gift—although he himself thought *Let 'Em Eat Cake* his best work so far. Most of Ira's lyrics retained their light touch, but even he succumbed to the general bloodthirstiness in "They're Hanging Throttlebottom in the Morning" and "Down With Everything That's Up." As Atkinson put it, the authors' "hatred had triumphed over their sense of humor."

Ultimately, all three of the Kaufman-Gershwin satires did pave the way for musical comedies that were about something, just as *Show Boat* proved the form could hold together as an artistic entity of lyric drama. These two almost concurrent discoveries were the beginnings of America's real musical theatre, tinkered with in the thirties, triumphant in the forties, distilled and varied thereafter. If earlier influences could still be spotted, the finished product was now undeniably native and new-minted. *The Mikado, A Gaiety Girl,* and *The Merry Widow* had taught salient lessons in musical storytelling, certainly, but the form itself—the way the songs and dances were connected to the action, the subjects utilized for the plot, the type of music heard over the footlights—had evolved into a new species.

12

The Thirties (I)

Chicté and Social Conscience

With vaudeville on the wane, with movies just discovering their latest passing fad, sound, and with most book musicals seeming like variety shows with a hint of story line, the revue was a popular form of entertainment in the late twenties but in danger of losing its audience through a lack of the sort of creativity that had sparked it just after the first World War. Along with the messy endeavors of such items as *Bare Facts of 1926, Padlocks of 1927* (with Texas Guinan), *A Night in Spain* (1927), and *A Night in Venice* (1928) there were still the front-line enterpreneurs Ziegfeld and George White and the second-rank Earl Carroll. Amidst the jaded tableaus of skin and familiar buffoonery, Charles Cochran's British revue *This Year of Grace* (1928) was the first day of spring. Like the two *André Charlot Revues* of 1924 and 1926, this elegant affair had first-rate comedy material and the comics to handle it. Beatrice Lillie sang "World Weary" on a bookkeeper's stool and played a channel swimmer erupting from the surf to force her autograph on everyone in sight. Noel Coward wrote the show —music, lyrics, and sketches—and dominated the performance with his urbanity and introverted flamboyance. The *Journal* called his "Dance, Little Lady" a "taut and jazz-strained piece, itched to a frenzy of saxophones as Mr. Coward chants out a deathly song to a girl almost tranced in the vacancy of the hypnotic music. As the rhythm leaps, a group of mannequins shuffles onto the stage, with faces twisted into vapid masks, and presently the girl emerges with them and becomes with them a dummy, treading out the crazy measure in the empty movement of automatons." It was exactly this kind of artful social comment embedded in a song concept that characterized the best of the thirties revues, and which eventually ignited the production blueprints of the book musicals in the forties.

Cochran returned a year later with *Wake Up and Dream,* again with an excellent British cast (plus an American score by Cole Porter), and Lew Leslie's *International Revue* (1930) offered a similar array of foreign abilities led by Gertrude Lawrence. Now it was time for a wholly American effort as urbane and witty as the imports, so Arthur Schwartz and Howard Dietz obliged, with a little help from others, in *The Little Show* (1929). From "Hammacher Schlemmer, I Love You" to "I Guess I'll Have to Change My Plan (I should have realized there'd be another man)," their score reached a wider audience than Porter or Coward while using the same mixture of nonchalance and passion. Fred Allen became a star with his wry, rasping monologues, Clifton Webb danced with prodigious style, and Libby Holman intoned torch songs with a Harlemite throb few other white singers would ever possess. *The Little Show* was truly little, scaled down not for thrift but communication, and the public that had responded to the first *Greenwich Village Follies* found a new home.

If the *Second Little Show* (1930) was a little less satisfying, the *Third Little Show* was no more than a vehicle for Beatrice

Lillie and Ernest Truex. The score was eclectic: Noel Coward donated "Mad Dogs and Englishmen," Herman Hupfeld "When Yuba Plays the Rhumba on the Tuba"; every song was by someone else. Lillie presented a parody of Ruth Draper's dramatic monologues—"In this sketch, ladies and gentlemen, I want you to imagine far too much"—and disinterred Liza Lehmann's "There Are Fairies at the Bottom of Our Garden" from the slagheap of bygone schlock.

Allen, Webb, and Holman were back together in Max Gordon's Schwartz-Dietz show *Three's a Crowd* (1930), which was staged largely for those who esteemed the first *Little Show,* and enjoyed the kind of success that makes producers stop, think . . . and mount imitations. According to Arthur Pollock, *Three's a Crowd* had "a civilized sophistication and a little good, clean-cut, gentlemanly dirt unmarred by vulgarity or exhibitionism," and like *The Little Show,* it had a long run, but both were topped by *The Band Wagon* (1931), another Max Gordon entry. The memories of those who were there persist in maintaining that this was the best of the thirties revues, lighter, faster, smoother. The unsigned *New York Times* review was headed "Beginning a New Era" and concluded that the "suffocating magnificence of formula showmanship will seem more lethal than ever." Gordon had not only retained Schwartz and Dietz but also hired George S. Kaufman to aid Dietz on the sketch material. Albertina Rasch's choreography and Tilly Losch's solo dancing were as new and striking as Broadway dances could be without intimidating, and Albert Johnson's designs included the first revolving stage that showed off for the audience instead of just changing sets. This was put to excellent use in the pictorial narrative of "The Beggar's Waltz" and the "I Love Louisa" merry-go-round.

The *Band Wagon* cast, headed by Fred and Adele Astaire, Helen Broderick, and Frank Morgan, had as much to work with as any revue could offer. Astaire introduced his white tie and tails trademark in "New Sun in the Sky" and was joined by his sister in evening dress, as they greased the floor with jet propulsion in "White Heat," and in a short skirt (to match his knickers) for an "enfant terrible" number, "Hoops." Helen Broderick donned blond braids to twitter "Where Can He Be?" while traipsing from window to window, and Losch glided around on a slanted floor mirroring colored lights for "Dancing in the Dark." The comedy was at its peak in "The Pride of the Claghornes," in which the Colonel (Morgan) threw down his julep and disowned his daughter Breeze (Adele) when it turned out she hadn't gone wrong. "I just can't understand this modern generation," he intoned for the blackout. Percy Hammond said the chorus girls looked "as if they all had mothers," but *The Band Wagon* was no cautious family show. In one sketch, "Pour le Bain," Broderick was a Westchester matron buying bathroom appliances in a too-too cultivated showroom. Sinks and bathtubs examined, she still hadn't seen the . . . uh, final item. The salesman paused, then replied, "Heard melodies are sweet, but those unheard are sweeter."

One year later, in 1932, Max Gordon's third intimate revue came along, again with a special cast and a Schwartz and Dietz score. *Flying Colors* had Webb, Tamara Geva, Patsy Kelly, and Charles Butterworth and a run of 188 performances. It also had "A Shine on Your Shoes," "A Rainy Day," "Louisiana Hayride," "Smokin' Reefers," "Meine Kleine Akrobat," which many thought sounded rather a lot like "I Love Louisa" of the year before, and the even more redundant "Alone Together," which John Mason Brown referred to as "Dancing in the Schwartz." Still, Gordon had instilled the virtues of the small, witty revue in the public mind—first-rate scores, distinctive casting, artistic design and direction, sophisticated humor, and dancing instead of hoofing. Though Ziegfeld and Earl Carroll still offered competition, they were eclipsed by these new trends in the revue format. In fact, Ziegfeld's most potent life-force in the early days of his *Follies* had been Joseph Urban's inspired eye. In 1931 Ziegfeld revived his show after a four-year hiatus, and though it succeeded through the talents of Helen Morgan, Jack Pearl, Harry Richman, and Gladys Glad, Urban was gone and so was the magic.

Billy Rose leaped into the ring that same year with his wife, Fanny Brice, in a "helluva high-toned revue," *Corned Beef and Roses*, which became *Sweet and Low* after a severe critical drubbing in Philadelphia. A third version played as *Billy Rose's Crazy Quilt*, underlining what the second-rate revues seemed to share—a not very organized assortment of run-of-the-mill pop hits (*Sweet and Low* had "Would You Like to Take a Walk?" and "Cheerful Little Earful"), at least two lengthy dance numbers, and tons of low comedy (Phil Barker to the orchestra: "Play 'Old Man River'—and throw yourselves in it!").

The talent on stage was the sole reason for virtually all the nonbook shows, especially comic talent. Beatrice Lillie, Bobby Clark, and Paul McCullough headlined *Walk a Little Faster* in 1932, a better than ordinary show with a Vernon Duke–E. Y. Harburg score. Somewhat in the manner of the Gordon revues, it lacked the ultimate in style and polish. Crooners and belters sang "April in Paris" and "Where Have We Met Before?" while the public recovered from the exertion of watching the clowns in action. Lillie and Clark gave their impression of Tamara Geva and Clifton Webb dancing "Alone Together," and Clark took stage with his impersonation of Joseph Stalin. George White's *Music Hall Varieties* (1932) had Bert Lahr sending up the Debonair Leading Man in "Chanson by Clifton Duckfeet," but most of the sketch material lacked point, even with Lahr's creative clowning. The *Times* review of the *Music Hall Varieties* could well have summed up the big thirties revues altogether: "the material . . . has been tried and played so many times before that the performers don't need much rehearsal to go through with it."

By 1933 the economics of luxury businesses was at an all-time low. Broadway was operating way under par, and even hit shows were struggling to survive. Movies were a cheap resource for the few who could spend money on entertainment, and 1933 brought in only fourteen musical shows. With the Depression on everybody's mind, a growing awareness of the world west of the Hudson began to be felt on Forty-second and Forty-fourth Streets. Then in 1931 columnist Heywood Broun talked a horde of names—including Nunnally Johnson, E. B. White, Peter Arno, Dorothy Parker, Irving Berlin, Dorothy Fields, E. Y. Harburg, Ira Gershwin, Jimmy McHugh, and Vernon Duke among others—to contribute songs and sketches to *Shoot the Works!* in a cooperative venture to supply work for performers and technical staff. Capitalized at six thousand dollars, the enterprise struck Percy Hammond as being "as full of fun as a Socialist picnic," but it managed to attract 87 performances' worth of support. Social comment was going to have to be a little more palatable if it was to pay its way on The Street.

Slightly more palatable social comment was made available in the *Americana* revues, the third and best of which appeared in 1932. Less universal in scope than *The Cradle Will Rock* and *The Threepenny Opera*—both just beyond the horizon then—*New Americana* threw its darts not at Man but at certain men in particular—Jimmy Walker, Al Smith, Herbert Hoover, and John D. Rockefeller. Far less bitter than Blitzstein and Brecht would seem, but not quite as friendly as it might have been, *New Americana* faced the Depression head on with a barrage of tunes to sweeten the pill. Lee Shubert wisely enlisted creators of the calibre of Harold Arlen, Burton Lane, Vernon Duke, and Johnny Mercer to set off J. P. McEvoy's sketches, and E. Y. Harburg and Jay Gorney handed him one of the great social-cultural documents of the decade in the form of a song for a bread-line scene, "Brother, Can You Spare a Dime?" The stage bread line looked real enough, and the situation limned by Harburg's lyrics so true the public had trouble applauding.

But the most palatable social comment imaginable was

vouchsafed the theatregoing public by *As Thousands Cheer* on September 30, 1933. Produced by Sam Harris, directed by Hassard Short, and starring Marilyn Miller, Clifton Webb, Helen Broderick (who "never missed a chance to put poison in the soup"), and Ethel Waters, this revue by Moss Hart and Irving Berlin used an ingenious series of newspaper headlines to fill the evening, taking each new headline as the premise for a sketch or song. FRANKLIN D. ROOSEVELT INAUGURATED TOMORROW showed Herbert and Lou Hoover moving out of the White House—reluctantly. ROTOGRAVURE SECTION featured an old-fashioned Easter Parade as the first-act finale. In METROPOLITAN OPERA OPENS IN OLD-TIME SPLENDOR the Saturday afternoon broadcast of *Rigoletto* was shattered by commercial interruptions, while another sketch viewed ninety-year-old John D. Rockefeller attacking his children when they present him with Radio City as a birthday present. REVOLT IN CUBA pictured the uprising that made a temporary hero of Fulgencio Batista in wild choreographic terms, while Webb and Broderick did a pungent takeoff on Mahatma Gandhi and Aimee Semple McPherson and Waters portrayed Josephine Baker in "Harlem on My Mind." But the crowning moment of *As Thousands Cheer* was "Supper Time," sung for UNKNOWN NEGRO LYNCHED BY FRENZIED MOB. As the man's widow, Waters fidgeted, wept, and sang true while wondering what to tell her children as she set the table for dinner. Waters later said, "If one song could tell the whole tragic story of a people, that was the song."

As Thousands Cheer was foremost an entertainment, and if its 400-performance run attests to its avoidance of the hard sell of *Shoot the Works!*, it did go further into controversy than was the norm for a musical show. As John Mason Brown noted, "I tremble to think of the fate that would await Miss Waters, Miss Miller, Miss Broderick, Mr. Webb, Mr. Berlin, Mr. Hart and Mr. Harris if they had ventured to win laughs of the kind they won so freely Saturday night while living in the shadow of the Kremlin, in Mussolini's Italy, in Hitler's

Germany, in Dollfuss' Austria, or even in the liberal England of George and Mary.''

A unifying theme also entailed the next Schwartz-Dietz revue. *At Home Abroad* (1935) was a world cruise with Beatrice Lillie, Ethel Waters, Eleanor Powell, and Reginald Gardiner, directed and designed by Vincente Minnelli. The producer, however, was not Max Gordon but Lee Shubert. Having captained the unprofitable *New Americana*, he made sure that *At Home Abroad* avoided such rife ports of call as Germany, Ethiopia, Russia, and Spain, all busy making unsavory headlines that year. Instead, the Theatre Guild mounted its ''social revue'' *Parade* with Jimmy Savo, 1935's sole entry of its kind, and its violently pro-left stance almost emptied the Guild Theatre of its first nighters. Notwithstanding Savo's whimsical, touching comedy and Robert Alton's nimble dances, *Parade* attacked with derision instead of humor; its barbs were like bayonets, and it lasted a month. What progress was this when the Guild had won esteem ten years before for its production of John Howard Lawson's *Processional,* a lacerating leftist play with the jazz-manic ambience of an authentic blues combo for interludes and side comments?

Most of the mid-thirties revues continued to skirt major issues with charm songs, star comics, and uptempo finales. There was a posthumous *Ziegfeld Follies* in 1934 produced according to the posters by Mrs. Florenz Ziegfeld (Billie Burke) but actually engineered by the Shuberts, with Fanny Brice and Willie and Eugene Howard. Like later incarnations of revue in the forties and then on television thereafter, the favored American form was a sort of modified vaudeville, sixty per cent humor. ''Only God can make a knee,'' trilled the *Follies'* opening chorus girls, ''and that's where we come in.'' Earl Carroll produced a *Sketch Book* in 1935, George White a *Scandals* in 1936, and Leonard Sillman inaugurated his *New Faces* shows in 1934. This ''intimate revue'' reminded many critics of the *Garrick Gaieties,* especially in the youth of its cast: Imogene Coca, Henry Fonda, Charles Walters, Nancy Hamilton, James Shelton, and O. Z. Whitehead. Two years later Sillman was back, this time with new faces Van Johnson, Ralph Blane, Helen Craig, and one used face, Imogene Coca.

Despite the besetting need for cheering-up shows, political satire was beginning to creep into otherwise harmless divertissements on a regular basis. *Life Begins at 8:40* (1934) included lampoons of Mayor La Guardia (Bert Lahr), Eleanor Roosevelt (Luella Gear), and Jimmy Walker (Ray Bolger). Eddie Dowling's *Thumbs Up!* (1934) offered Bobby Clark as a microphone-hungry judge ignoring a murder trial in favor of a national broadcast audience. Even the *Scandals* (1936) had a black dance team portraying Haile Selassie and two Ethiopian generals, while Willie Howard as Mussolini explained that Italians need *lebensraum* too, "and that's why darkies were born."

If sheer entertainment was the aim of Vincente Minnelli's (sets, costumes, direction) *The Show Is On* (1936), it was a return to the symmetry of the Max Gordon revues, though the score was a grab bag of donations. Beatrice Lillie and Bert Lahr led the evening with pranks of all sorts; Lahr stopped the show with Harold Arlen and E. Y. Harburg's "Song of the Woodman," listing the many uses of wood ("A baby's crib, the poet's chair, the soapbox down at Union Square . . .") while hatcheting away in lumberjack mufti. At odd moments, Lahr would be bombarded with wooden objects from the wings; the entire company gathered backstage to take part. Years later, Lillie commented, "I'd throw boards, brooms, anything I could get my hands on at him. I couldn't wait to see it." Lillie had her moments, too, as the grande dame of the stage in a period piece, "The Reading of the Play." (*Producer:* The play is about a man and a woman. *Lillie:* Too much plot!)

With the European war looming closer and closer, 1937 brought the most lighthearted of the early political revues, *Pins and Needles.* Presented by the International Ladies Garment Workers Union and using only union employees onstage, this amateur effort took over the old Princess Theatre, renamed the Labor Stage for the occasion. The sheet music of Harold J. Rome's thirteen published songs showed a pretty blond garment worker sewing up the backside of a growling banker, a pretty fair summation of the show's tone. The girls in the opening chorus demanded of the boys "Sing Me a Song of Social Significance," and the dancers gave a lesson in "Doin' the Reactionary." Even the love songs caught the militant verve, and a spoof of old-time story ballads recalled the sad tale of Bertha, the sewing machine girl led astray by "a non-union man with a leer."

Not every moment of *Pins and Needles* came out of the headlines, but its best items were related either to the socioeconomic identity of the American working class or the gathering storm in Europe (Chamberlain in a sketch called "Britannia Waives the Rules": "If at first you don't concede, fly, fly again"). The class war was gently nudged in the songs "It's Not Cricket to Picket" (a genteel lady politely trying to disperse demonstrators growing progressively less genteel) and "Chain-Store Daisy" (a Vassar girl forced to find work in Macy's), but the most topical of all was "Four Little Angels of Peace," originally Anthony Eden, Mussolini, Hitler, and an unnamed Japanese statesman. As the months went on, new developments "over there" made line changes necessary, and eventually the song centered on the home front with three brand-new angels of the far right—Senator Robert Reynolds of Virginia, Father Charles Coughlin, and American Nazi Fritz Kuhn. Their act was dubbed "The Harmony Boys of Demagogue Lane."

Pins and Needles had no stars, an orchestra of two pianos (Rome played one himself), and an economical production, but the cast joined Equity (Harry Clark and Irwin Corey left their old jobs forever) and the original plans for weekend presentations turned into an eight-times-a-week schedule for two and a half years—the longest run of a musical show up to then. The original cast went on tour, leaving the successive editions, *Pins and Needles 1940* and *New Pins and Needles,* to hold the New York fort (in a larger theatre), giving the political revue its first successful bastion.

Inspired by *Pins and Needles'* commercial triumph, Max Gordon engaged Harold Rome to do the score for a second such show, this time with a lavish, professional production. The sketches were by Kaufman and Hart and Charles Friedman, and like *Pins and Needles, Sing Out the News* (1938) was pro–New Deal and anti-Fascist, but it made its points in a more artistic milieu, especially in terms of dance. Charles Walters choreographed "Peace and the Diplomat" to show the Goddess of Peace getting the Danse Apache treatment from a corps of cold-hearted officials, while high spirits of the most proletarian kind took over in the joyous "Franklin D. Roosevelt Jones," sung at a christening party in Harlem. The critics were pleased to note that *Sing Out the News* was as lighthearted as Rome's earlier revue had been, but this second show lasted only three months, possibly because *Pins and Needles* was still open and giving it stiff competition. Rome tried again (with Marc Blitzstein and John Latouche, among others) in 1942 with the "social-conscious revue" *Let Freedom Sing,* a vast failure in a time when freedom was singing less and less distinctly all over the globe.

The black revues fared no better in the thirties than they had in the twenties, despite the new place the race had found in book musicals written by whites. Lew Leslie produced another *Blackbirds* in 1930, "glorifying the American Negro." The pattern of pile-driving musical numbers, scat lyrics, and unending tap dancing had lost its novelty: *Blackbirds of 1930* flopped even with Ethel Waters and a good Andy Razaf-Eubie Blake score. Striving for something new, Leslie returned with *Rhapsody in Black* (1931) in a style mired in pretense and good intentions. As the *Herald Tribune*'s Howard Barnes described it, "It dispenses with choruses and in a large measure with the ecstatic shuffling that has marked sepia offerings in the past." Leslie's search for a new idea in black musicals reached the bizarre when he had his Negro choir sing Russian and Jewish songs. A 1939 *Blackbirds* (with Lena Horne) also failed, as did Noble Sissle and Eubie Blake's *Shuffle Along of 1933,* with such authentic musical re-creations of Afro-American life as "Bandana Ways" and "Dustin' Around."

Special note must be made of the "screamlined revue designed for laughing," *Hellzapoppin'* (1938), especially in the light of the growing zeal for either artistic or social qualities in revue material. For although *Hellzapoppin'* ultimately surpassed *Pins and Needles'* record as the longest running musical show on Broadway by three hundred performances, it had no point of view except diversion—and that on the lowest level imaginable. Ole Olsen and Chic Johnson had been touring their madcap free-for-all for decades; Lee Shubert checked them out in Philadelphia and offered to bring them to New York if they could fill a whole evening with their caravanserai. This Olsen and Johnson did. The opening tendered a newsreel of famous men—Mayor La Guardia, President Roosevelt, Mussolini, Hitler—with new speech habits, including animal sounds and, in the case of Hitler, a Jewish accent. Then the two comics drove on stage in a car and trailer contraption for two hours of ceaseless uproar. Besides the tap dancer, close-harmony vocal group, magician, and leggy beauties considered indispensable for the lower forms of revue, numerous gags interrupted the proceedings from the auditorium: a gorilla dragged a woman from her box seat, another woman kept wandering through the aisles calling for Oscar, eventually to be invited on stage and into the wings where she was shot, a ticket scalper hounded customers with the chance to see something better, a nude male rode a horse in the balcony, a sinister clown annoyed promenaders during the intermission, a sideshow Houdini was straitjacketed early in Act One and was seen still struggling with his harness in the lobby as the public departed at eleven o'clock.

Hellzapoppin' was fast and funny, but most of it was just fast, the alleged antidote to the sly, aware commentary of *Americana, Parade, Pins and Needles,* and *Sing Out the News,* the last two being *Hellzapoppin'*s immediate competition. The score was a hodgepodge, and Olsen and Johnson's raucous personalities so unnecessary to the success of the whole that they were replaced by Happy Felton and J. C. Flippen for the last eighteen months of the run with no loss of business.

Almost no fourth estater liked the show. Walter Winchell was the exception, campaigning for it loudly and often, but then *Hellzapoppin'* had no trouble finding an audience. As similar endeavors were to prove in the forties—both Olsen and Johnson sequels or imitative exhibits with other comedians—there was still a public appreciative of lower-class vaudeville that would support it profitably until television wiped it out in the fifties.

13

The Thirties (II)

"Come Out, Rainbow, Wherever You Are!"

The first book musical to continue in the *Show Boat* direction as regards libretto-score integration, native subject matter, and wholeness of style was *Rainbow,* which played the Gallo Theatre for a wan 29 performances in November and December of 1928. The story of a young scout who kills a villainous major in self-defense and flees to California at the height of the Gold Rush to win a bride and a pardon caught the folk character of the American West with a combination of melodrama, romance, and jubilation. Hammerstein was again at the helm, collaborating on the book with Laurence Stallings, who brought a touch of the raunchy, realistic dialogue that had worked so well in his and Maxwell Anderson's more or less antiwar play, *What Price Glory?*. Hammerstein did the lyrics and Vincent Youmans the music, with a heavy use of lusty dance numbers by Busby Berkeley to render the energy of the saloon. A stirring choral number, "On the Golden Trail," both opened and closed the show; in between was a profusion of torch songs, barn dances, virile choruses, and character turns emphasizing the setting rather than the principals (the sole love song, "Who Am I That You Should Care for Me?", was dropped out of town). Despite technical difficulties on opening night—everything from faulty set changes to a leniently bladdered mule—the critics reveled in *Rainbow*'s vitality and grace, pointing out the luminescence of Libby Holman and Charles Ruggles in supporting parts. But Youmans' balladless score was a little too creative and experimental to please the public still humming "Tea for Two" from three years before, Stallings' roughhewn males were a decade ahead of their time (the first-act curtain line, "The son of a bitch shot me," was considered indecent behavior for a musical), and somehow the favorable notices went unregarded. *Rainbow,* the second step forward in the evolution of the modern musical, gave out in less than a month.

Just before the thirties dawned, with the stock market booming and about to explode, the most profitable musical comedies were vapid and overeager, packages rather than conceptions, capable of being written, rehearsed, and opened in a matter of a few months. A run of 150 performances usually meant a success, with production costs averaging between $50,000 and $135,000, a ticket-price top of $4.40, and a weekly operating cost of $6000 to $20,000. (By 1934 the ticket price would drop to $2.75, balcony seats to less than a dollar.) After the Crash, money was harder to raise and experimental shows seemed an impossible risk, just at the time when experiments were ready to be made. But the prime time of the book musical had already begun with *Show Boat,* followed by *Rainbow, Strike Up the Band,* and *Of Thee I Sing.* The new era was born scarred and dented, but it would recover.

In all, the thirties birthed 174 new musical shows. Discounting the 73 revues, there were 101 book musicals, of which no less than 67 were original—that is, not adapted from a previous source. Many of these original works were merely variations on hackneyed themes, but some of them were truly original, utilizing the new concepts in staging and design that infiltrated the serious theatre in the mid-twenties.

At least some of the nonserious book shows weren't marking time. Lacking any connection with the outside world, they nevertheless tightened up the prevailingly loose structure of musical comedy, making them more like artistic entities than vaudevilles. When Alex Aarons and Vinton Freedley played their first hand of the new decade, it was a grand slam, with every element of stagecraft technique in place. *Girl Crazy* (1930) had a peak Gershwin score, a solid book, and a socko cast (Ginger Rogers, Willie Howard, and sudden star Ethel Merman). Though the setting was Arizona, the dialogue was pure New York (Howard communicated fluently with the Indians in Yiddish) and the tunes naturally bore Gershwin's distinctive hallmark, even more distinctive than usual in Merman's "Sam and Delilah," "Boy! What Love Has Done to Me," and "I Got Rhythm," during which she held the "I" for sixteen bars while the orchestra played the melody and the first-night audience lost control of its aplomb.

Unlike the Gershwin brothers, who attended rehearsals and helped in out-of-town revisions, Cole Porter contented himself with song craftsmanship, passing up the formative stages to see the production on opening night. He did make a point of collaborating with the cream of the profession, though. His first thirties opus was *The New Yorkers* (1930), a "sociological musical satire" that aimed its barbs at Park Avenue, Harlem, Reuben's restaurant on Fifty-ninth Street, and, of course, bootlegging. Herbert Fields' book was as tough and savvy as the characters he had to describe, and the cast was truly prominent: Hope Williams, Ann Pennington, Marie Cahill, Oscar "Rags" Ragland, Fred Waring's Pennsylvanians, and the comedy team of Clayton, Jackson, and Durante. This tale of a debutante in love with a gangster pulled no punches. The deb's parents each carried on extramarital affairs shamelessly, aided by Porter's laissez-faire lyrics, spitting out the gamy flavor of New York in every couplet. "Let's Fly Away" disdained it, "I Happen to Like New York" and "Take Me Back to Manhattan" hymned it, and "Love for Sale" both spoofed Friml's tune from *The Vagabond King* and finally set the record straight on prostitutes ("Old love, new love—everything but true love"). As Percy Hammond put it, "When and if we ever get a censorship I will give odds it will frown upon such an honest thing." Honest, indeed. Porter was one of the more apparent heirs to the age of the great unflappable homosexuals, when only the cognoscenti could separate the men from the girls, but he *was* honest in a very few of his lyrics, and in ways that doubtless went right by the uninitiated like Hammond.

Fields was again the librettist for Porter's *Gay Divorce* (1932), but the world of dinner jackets and diamonds took over to such an extent that the show was almost a fantasy. Fred Astaire's first solo outing after Adele's marriage, *Gay Divorce* was a big success all the same. *Anything Goes* (1934), however, was even bigger. The planned tale of a merry shipwreck suddenly lost its appeal when the Morro Castle sank near Asbury Park, drowning one hundred and twenty-five people, so producer Freedley got Howard Lindsay and Russel Crouse to revise the Bolton-Wodehouse script. The new book was finished two days short of the Boston opening, but *Anything Goes* made it anyway, largely on the merits of its cast—Merman, Gaxton, and Moore—and score. The airwaves resisted "I Get a Kick Out of You"—as they had "Love for Sale" except as an instrumental—until Porter changed "I get no kick from cocaine" to "Some like the perfume from Spain." "All Through the Night" was a consummate ballad, "You're the Top" the first (and best) of several Porter catalogue songs, and the title tune did for the thirties what gentlemen purportedly were doing for blondes. Despite its last-minute book, *Anything Goes* was a tonic of its time, even with its flagrant use of standard musical comedy conventions. As John Mason Brown noted, "if it stays for the most part within the time-honored limits of those conventions, it does so only to make clear why it is that time has honored them."

Porter and Moss Hart took a cruise around the world to write another escapist piece, this time *about* escapists. Less ribald than most Porter shows, *Jubilee* (1935) showed a royal family not unlike England's Windsors taking off incognito for frolic and romance. Still unperturbed by the frenzy of out-of-town tinkerings, Porter stood aside while Hart, producers Sam Harris and Max Gordon, director Hassard Short, and choreographer Albertina Rasch saw the ship safely into port. Porter was a specialist in creating material for special performers rather than for special situations, and he wasn't yet furnishing vocal meat to develop the integrity of plot development.

Back again with Vinton Freedley for *Leave It to Me* (1938), Porter was free to write on a large scale and reach a low audience level. Catching the contagious political outlook, book writers Sam and Bella Spewack pitted Victor Moore and Sophie Tucker against the Soviet Union; the Reds won. As Ambassador to the U.S.S.R., Moore did everything he could to be recalled, including kicking a Nazi and shooting a counterrevolutionary in Red Square. When he finally grows to like his post, he advocates a United Nations of Europe—and only then is quickly summoned back home to Kansas.

Porter's biggest thirties success—at 400 performances—was *Dubarry Was a Lady* (1939), which seemed bent on proving that she wasn't and nobody else was either. Porter's score was lewder and more double-entendred than ever before; such ditties as "But in the Morning, No!" "Give Him the Oo-La-La," and "Katie Went to Haiti (But Katie had her Haiti, and practically all Haiti had . . .)" were as high-class as low-down smut could be. Ethel Merman played a nightclub singer, a role originally designed for Mae West, and Bert Lahr played a lovesick washroom attendant as only the gifted Lahr could. In an elaborate dream sequence, he pictured them as Du Barry and King Louis XV, but whether in eighteenth-century France or West Fifty-second Street, he couldn't get the girl. *Dubarry*'s smash success was a high point for the brassy, very New York type of show. The structure of musical comedy had come a long way from the loosely organized vacua of *A Gaiety Girl*, but the sheer entertainment escapist shows like *Dubarry Was a Lady* had changed very little from the leg shows that delighted the predominantly male audiences of the turn of the century; ultimately, they were still leg shows. If the sounds and settings were pure native, the chorus girls owed a lot to Lydia Thompson, the with-it lyrics were indebted to the Mulligan Guard songs, and the star comic's preeminence to pantomimist George L. Fox.

Merman, however, was a new idea. The characters she played, like those of Mae West in straight plays and movies, would never have done for Lillian Russell or Marilyn Miller. Tough, big-hearted, more riveting than glamorous, this new-ish archetype put the kibosh on the old-time comedy songs about woman's instability and materialism which had been so much a part of the scene through the first two decades of the century. Merman had help: similar roles were tailored for such as June Havoc, Audrey Christie, Nanette Fabray, and Celeste Holm, and after them, musical comedy heroines didn't have to be wispy to carry a show.

At the opposite pole, Jerome Kern's shows let gentle ballads and sweet affections take up the slack left by the remnants of twenties operetta. After the supreme triumph of *Show Boat*, Kern went on refining both his art and the medium as a whole. In *Sweet Adeline* (1929) he and Oscar Hammerstein contrived a nostalgic romance for Helen Morgan, but *The Cat and the Fiddle* (1931), libretto by Otto Harbach, was a smooth wedding of operetta form and contemporary tempos. The lovers were a Rumanian musician (Georges Metaxa) and an American pop singer–composer (Bettina Hall) in Brussels, surrounded by local color and music both jazzy and legit. According to Gilbert Gabriel, "Broadway [had] not heard lovelier music in all its life."

Back again with Hammerstein for *Music in the Air* (1932), Kern wrote another modern operetta, this time avoiding the low comedy and the interloping ballet sequences that still plagued the sentimental shows. As in *Show Boat* and *The Cat and the Fiddle,* underscoring was used to a marked degree, sometimes playing under whole scenes, making the songs seem like a continuing chain of lyrical expression. Using very little plot, Hammerstein enlarged on his favorite theme, rural purity versus urban decadence. A Bavarian village teacher with a head for pop tunes travels to Munich with the girl next door to sell "I've Told Every Little Star." In the big city, the teacher gets involved with an operetta queen, the girl with a debonair composer, even getting her big break by starring in his latest opus, *Tingle Tangle.* Via an unexpected twist, she goes out there a nobody and comes back a nobody, having flopped resoundingly with the public. The composer's ensuing harangue about the dedication of stage pros was a rare moment of strength and realism in an otherwise gentle tale that could picture Munich in 1932 without a single Nazi. Kern and Hammerstein staged their piece themselves, quite nicely, and Joseph Urban's matchless sets added the literal magic. Atkinson's first night report opened with "At last the musical drama has been emancipated. . . . What *The Cat and the Fiddle* began last season Mr. Kern and Mr. Hammerstein have now completed by composing a fable that flows naturally out of a full-brimming score." Even George Jean Nathan, who couldn't tell one tune from another without consulting a program, always recalled *Music in the Air* in later years when the serious aspirations of the forties musicals were wearing him down.

As the years passed and musical shows gained headway in realism, Kern continued to compose for a statelier medium. *Roberta* (1933), book and lyrics by Otto Harbach, was as hugely successful as Kern's preceding shows had been but tended to avoid the light-opera-ish underscoring of book material and had a noticeably zippier score, not to mention the dizzy comedy of Bob Hope to balance the straighter presences of Tamara, Ray Middleton, and veteran Fay Templeton. Once again, Kern's music towered over all competition in expressiveness and warmth. But if "Smoke Gets in Your Eyes" and "Yesterdays" are two of the finest popular songs of their time, "The Touch of Your Hand"—like *Show Boat*'s "You Are Love"—was almost too fine, less popular song than demoralized opera. Kern sometimes repented when his inspiration resulted in one of these hybrids, but he was reaching for a higher plane of expression in musical comedy composing, one which would limn character within the framework of popular-song form.

Kern's last Broadway show was one of the last of the decade, *Very Warm for May* (1939). Hammerstein was the librettist, and the story was the "c'mon-kids-let's-put-on-our-own-show-right-here!" sort already tried by Rodgers and Hart in *Babes in Arms,* among others. The youngsters included Vera-Ellen, Hiram Sherman, June Allyson, and Don Loper, the more practiced troupers Eve Arden, Jack Whiting, and Donald Brian (New York's original Prince Danilo), but their various subplots were not worked out coherently enough to please the critics. Max Gordon and Vincente Minnelli gave the work a handsome production, however, and Kern's score was an amazing amalgam of past and present. The hit tune "All the Things You Are" and that lost classic "In the Heart of the Dark" are as forward-looking and artistic as anything else of their time, while "That Lucky Fellow (Who gets you)" could almost have been written in 1925.

After *Very Warm for May*'s 59 performances Kern returned to Hollywood. His only remaining work for Broadway was "Nobody Else But Me," the one new number in the 1946 revival of *Show Boat.* His contemporary Irving Berlin went on for many years after, but worked in films more than Kern and on Broadway far less. Besides *As Thousands Cheer,* Berlin's only thirties show was *Face the Music* (1932), and like his revue, this book musical was one of the first of its species to recognize the time and space it occupied. *Of Thee I Sing*'s producer, Sam Harris, and co-author Moss Hart were in charge, but this time the political travesty was more direct. If William Gaxton's President Wintergreen had been a mildly devious replica of Jimmy Walker, *Face the Music* named names, focusing on specifics of Manhattan life rather than national problems. The first scene was an Automat at dinnertime, with Astors, Woolworths, and Barbara Hutton eating at the only place they could afford. The Palace Theatre was said to be offering Ethel Barrymore, Albert Einstein, Aimee Semple McPherson, Eddie Cantor, Al Jolson, Tony the Talking Horse, and lunch—all for five cents. With the Four Hundred on their knees alongside the working class, only a policeman had enough money to invest in a musical. Hart was careful not to mention Walker, but as his administration had just been rent by its worst scandal in the findings of the Seabury commission on corruption, everyone knew the basis for the plot when a "little-tin-box" type of police sergeant financed *The Rhinestone Girl* to get rid of the loot he had accumulated in bribes. (What better way to lose money than backing a musical comedy?) *Face the Music*'s first-act finale was *The Rhinestone Girl*'s big mirror number, with a second row of dancing girls aping the first in place of real mirrors. Though the investigation eventually caught up with the principals, the show was no sugar pill even after *Of Thee I Sing*. Unlike the hard metal and right-on brittleness of Gershwin's music for the Kaufman-Hart satires, Berlin's for *Face the Music* complemented the jibes with his smooth, sentimental style, proving that satires don't need satirical scores in order to work. Even if "Manhattan Madness" exploited the vital frenzy of city life, "Soft Lights and Sweet Music" and "Let's Have Another Cup of Coffee" gave a respite from venality and hard times, making *Face the Music* both relaxing and pointed at once.

After the smash success of *A Connecticut Yankee* in 1927, Richard Rodgers and Lorenz Hart stuck close to musical comedy while operetta, revue, and three-act farces like *No! No! Nanette* swirled around them. But *Chee-Chee,* the third Rodgers and Hart show of 1928, was something different. Casting an eye at a similar note in *Rose-Marie*'s program, the authors (Fields did the book) announced that "the musical numbers, some of them very short, are so interwoven with the story that it would be confusing for audiences to peruse a complete list." *Chee-Chee,* like *Rose-Marie,* was no opera, but the show did pull away successfully from the even balance of full-length numbers and storytelling book material taking polite turns with each other that had been set up since comic opera days. The authors managed their trick well, but their subject matter was so gruesome that few theatregoers were able to respond favorably. Fields' book about the son of the Grand Eunuch who wants out of the family business made rather a lot of capital out of castration, a ticklish subject for a whole evening's jests. The reviews were highly mixed, from St. John Ervine's critique in the *World,* headed "Nasty! Nasty!" to Robert Benchley's rave in *Life.* Daring of any kind does not always please the first time around and *Chee-Chee* expired after only 31 performances.

Rodgers and Hart learned their lesson; at least they waited a while before trying anything new. Now without Fields, they embarked on a series of commercial musical comedies, all more or less successful. *Spring Is Here* (1929) was a slight boys-and-girls-together farce, *Heads Up!* (1929) dealt with the yachting set, *Simple Simon* (1930) had Ed Wynn dreaming up a fairyland of storybook characters, in the midst of which Ruth Etting warbled "Ten Cents a Dance" in a set representing the walled city of Dullna, apparently not distressing Cinderella, Little Boy Blue, and others of that fraternity with the hard-bitten realities of the outside world.

With Herbert Fields, the team took a step up with a satire on Hollywood, *America's Sweetheart* (1931), one year after Kaufman and Hart's burlesque of starlets and moguls, *Once in a Lifetime.* Topicality in this case was more adroitly handled in the score than the book—just as the other foremost songwriters of the time could set the tone for a show in the musical numbers better than could the book writers struggling with the demands of structure and methodology. In 1931 Rodgers and Hart went to the Coast themselves, working through 1935 on six films, two of which experimented with what Hart called "rhythmic dialogue"—lyrics that stood alone without music, carrying the plot forward without pausing for orchestral accompaniment. *Love Me Tonight* (1932) was their masterpiece, perhaps the consummate movie musical of the early thirties, in no small measure because of Rouben Mamoulian's inspired direction. Strangely, the unique uses found for integration of story and score utilized in *Love Me Tonight* never found their way into a Rodgers and Hart stage musical. In fact, their next Broadway show turned out less a musical comedy than a circus: *Jumbo* (1935) was a $340,000 Hippodrome colossus produced by Billy Rose in the style to which the Hippodrome had once been accustomed. The thin Romeo and Juliet story line offered romance to the son and daughter of feuding circus owners, punctuated by acrobatics, equestrian acts, aerial dances, sideshow turns—even a girl shot out of a cannon. The ghost of extravaganza must have hovered happily in the air when the elephant, Big Rosie, did her stint in the title role, but Ben Hecht and Charles MacArthur's book did little to incorporate late developments in libretto writing into the hoary spectacle format. Burns Mantle gave *Jumbo* three and a half stars in the *Daily News* but called the story "something that MacArthur and Hecht must have spent all of half a day jotting down on scraps of paper."

Just as *Jumbo* was circus, *On Your Toes* (1938) was ballet, but this time the special material was carefully integrated. Rodgers and Hart wrote their own book for the first time, with George Abbott, encompassing both popular and elitist dance forms in the tale of a hoofer who abandons vaudeville for classical realms. This Gershwin counterpart mixed his dance styles with devastating results in the first-act finale,

"La Princesse Zenobia," but hit just the right middle line in the second-act "Slaughter on Tenth Avenue." The choreography was by George Balanchine, not yet the arch-eminent king of the ballet world but still a novel choice to stage musical comedy dances, and most of his steps were handled by real-life hoofer Ray Bolger and real-life ballerina Tamara Geva, who had carried the torch of semiclassical dance in *Three's a Crowd* and *Flying Colors* earlier in the decade.

Much has been made of "Slaughter on Tenth Avenue" 's importance as a book-integrated ballet, but it was, in fact, a ballet-within-a-play, a set piece danced "on the stage of the Cosmopolitan Opera House"—*not* a part of the story told in choreographic terms. Only toward the ballet's end did plot collide with set piece when the hoofer learned that two gangsters were planning to gun him down from a box in the theatre at the end of the number. Exhausted, terrified, he must keep dancing to save his life until help comes, and thus a ballet sequence in *On Your Toes* turned into the *On Your Toes* plot. The audience had to follow the final moments of the show exclusively in terms of dance, and for a moment it was hard to tell where the "dancing" left off and the dancing began.

On Your Toes created a big stir in 1936, running 315 performances. It was just the right time for dance to come into its own in the musical, especially after Albertina Rasch and Charles Weidman paved the way for ballet, the first in the Schwartz-Dietz revues, the latter in *New Americana* and *As Thousands Cheer*. Most important, the films of Fred Astaire and Ginger Rogers had already used dance as a force of storytelling in *The Gay Divorcée* (1934), *Top Hat* (1935), and especially in the "Never Gonna Dance" scene in the Kern-Fields *Swing Time* (1936).

Even with the Ballet Russe playing the Met in the same season, *On Your Toes* didn't get a single bad notice. Brooks Atkinson applauded "the uniformity of its viewpoint," Robert Coleman the libretto's "new high in originality and smartness.'' It went over to London in 1937 (with Jack Whiting and Vera Zorina) at a time when few American musicals crossed the ocean, but the 1954 Broadway revival disappointed the same critics who applauded it years before. Atkinson now thought the book ''labored and mechanical and verbose,'' though he still found the work as a whole ''original and exhilarating.'' Even with Balanchine recreating his original choreography, the revival folded in a few weeks.

The only aspect of *Babes in Arms* (1937) that could be considered new was its cast, some of whom were but halfway through their teens, but *I'd Rather Be Right* (1937) succumbed brilliantly to the prevailing political air with an evening-long spoof of President Franklin Delano Roosevelt. With Sam Harris producing yet another diplomat's holiday, Eleanor was gracefully spared, but the Kaufman-Hart book brought in the entire cabinet, names and all, with Secretary of the Treasury Morgenthau crooning ''A Baby Bond for Baby'' on one of Roosevelt's fireside chats.

Almost the entire show was a dream in which the President tries to balance the budget one Fourth of July in Central Park so the juvenile and ingenue can derive economic stability and get married, but this slight story line was secondary to the succession of high jinks and japes at the foibles of American government, especially those of the New Deal. A federal theatre unit materializes and performs a lavish Straussian fanfaronade, ''Spring in Vienna'' (changed to ''Spring in Milwaukee'' in May 1938), that would have made Lee Shubert twinkle. Shovels on high, the ''P.W.A.'' shows up—ten of the country's leading industrialists, crowing because they no longer have to pay Roosevelt's crippling taxes. Secretary of State Cordell Hull attempts to adjourn the cabinet meeting so they can take in the latest Marx Brothers movie, and Roosevelt's onetime opponent Alfred E. Landon is now Roosevelt's mother's butler, grinning broadly as he refuses to tell how he balanced the budget as governor of Kansas: ''It's true I didn't photograph well, nor did I have that smile. And I will frankly admit that I was lousy on the radio. But Mr. Roosevelt, I balanced my budget! So as we say in Kansas, Mr. Roosevelt —try that on your ukelele!''

Then, now, and forever, there is nothing like a star turn to stimulate business, and Harris had the genius idea of hiring his ex-partner George M. Cohan for the lead. Cohan had won critical huzzahs for his wise underplaying as Nat Miller in O'Neill's *Ah, Wilderness!* in 1933, but *I'd Rather Be Right* was his first musical role since his own *The Merry Malones* in 1927, and the last role but one of his remarkable life. As Roosevelt, he made every second count. In an eleven o'clock song called ''Off the Record'' he rattled off patter, swung his cane, and pranced in his kangaroo-step trademark, adding such theatrical zest to the material that the critics bent over backwards not to notice how thin the second act was or how sketchy the structure. *Time* felt Rodgers' music was lax in setting a tone for the piece, but Burns Mantle dubbed it ''one of the most important musical plays of this generation.'' With the earlier Kaufman-Hart-Harris political shows under their belts, critics and public could accept political travesty calmly and merely discuss its merits qua musical comedy, especially as the satire was more warm than heated.

The call of operetta was as loud as ever, but it had a more than faintly manic overtone in the thirties. The aggregate runs of Sigmund Romberg's five thirties musicals added up to less than the original engagement of his last twenties show, *The New Moon.* Working mainly with Hammerstein and Harbach, Romberg just couldn't seem to make the form tell the way it once had. Perhaps it was the Depression, perhaps the glut of similar entertainments from Hollywood—no longer silent upon a peak in Darien—or perhaps the younger audiences didn't respond to brigands and laundresses the way their parents had. After a middling success and two outright duds in the *Desert Song–New Moon* mold, Romberg pulled an about-face and adapted to the times with *May Wine* (1935), his one hit of the decade. Hammerstein did the lyrics, Frank

Mandel the book, and if their setting was Vienna, their subject was—lo and behold—Freudian psychoanalysis. As Brooks Atkinson noted, "the excrescences and stock appurtenances of the musical form" were suppressed, even to the exclusion of the chorus, leaving Romberg without his surefire stout-hearted men's ensemble. But once having rid the musical of the need to make no sense whatever, Hammerstein wasn't about to lose his stranglehold on sloppy storytelling.

For his part, Rudolf Friml was really in a bind. He had finally escaped musical comedy for all time only to find that audiences grew impatient with unremittingly serious romances. Unlike Romberg, whose last show was produced posthumously in 1954, he refused to move with the evolution of pop music, stubbornly composing two grand operettas in 1930 and 1934 that ran 21 and 29 performances respectively. Though he lived on into the seventies, he never had another show on Broadway.

The rest of the operetta world did what it could, fitfully and with varying results. Johann Strauss' *Die Fledermaus* came back translated as *A Wonderful Night* in 1929, with Archie Leach (Cary Grant) lip syncing Eisenstein's songs while a tenor sang for him crouching behind the furniture. Two other Viennese pieces were smash hits in spectacular productions at the Center Theatre: *The Great Waltz* (1934), a concoction of Strauss' life and melodies, and the Benatzky-Stolz *White Horse Inn* (1936). But Lehár's *Fredericka* died the death in 1937, Grace Moore couldn't make a success of Fall's *Dubarry* in 1932, and Yvonne Printemps had similar troubles with Noel Coward's *Conversation Piece* two years later. The Victor Herbert mother lode, dependable for numerous revivals in the twenties, wasn't mined once in the whole decade, while the young Frederick Loewe made an inauspicious Broadway debut in 1938 setting Earle Crooker's lyrics for *Great Lady,* a romance with heavy overtones of bedroom farce. This attempt to combine the sleazy elements of popular musical comedy with the leaden display of operetta was a disaster, even with

Norma Terris, Irene Bordoni, Helen Ford, and Dorothy Kirsten in the cast. The chorus boasted three future ballet stars—Alicia Alonzo, Nora Kaye, and Jerome Robbins—with André Eglevsky the premier danseur, but William Dollar's arty choreography wasn't integrated and stuck out like a sore thumb.

An interesting experimental operetta followed Vienna and the Austrian Tyrol into the Center Theatre in 1937. Laurence Stallings and Owen Davis did the book, Arthur Schwartz the music, and Al Stillman and Stallings the lyrics for *Virginia,* a saga of pre-Revolutionary American theatre. Like its Center Theatre predecessors, *Virginia* was extravagantly mounted, but like Stallings' previous excursions into America's past, *Deep River* and *Rainbow,* it just didn't work. Critics found it overwritten and stodgy, perhaps because Schwartz' training in the deft Max Gordon revues held him back from the extroverted writing that Romberg and Friml had mastered. *Virginia* was a huge, polite bomb.

Schwartz was still very much Dietz' partner when he composed his first (and Dietz' second) book musical, *Revenge with Music* (1934). This adaptation of Pedro Antonio de Alarcón's little novel *The Three-Cornered Hat* landed somewhere between operetta and the artier sorts of musical comedy, with a score so beautiful that it almost kept the lumpy book moving. The mid-thirties were still prime time for lush European romances, but only when their authors were able to create a realistic modern ambience, as Kern and Hammerstein did in *The Cat and the Fiddle.* Whereas an English audience could savor the delights of, say, Coward's *Conversation Piece* for years on end, wearing out their sets of original cast 78s (West End hits had had cast albums since the twenties, including American imports such as *Lady Be Good* and *Sunny*) and then clamoring for a revival, the New York critics and public found unrenewed operetta too mawkish or flimsy to praise. Critic John Anderson called *Conversation Piece* "lace handkerchief theater," while *The Great Waltz* was "the town's most brilliant parade going, I suspect, nowhere." Robert Garland too disdained *Conversation Piece* ("mannered and immaterial") as well as *The Great Waltz* ("a big, beautiful bore that chases itself around in circles"). Anderson and Garland had plenty of company. True, *The Great Waltz* and some few others of its kind attracted customers, and Shubert tours still infested the hinterland with Romberg and Friml, but men of vision began to feel the need to retailor the operetta style for a modern age rather than simply adulterate it with sheiks, flappers, and jarring one-line gags.

Dietz and Schwartz came closer to the mark in 1937 with *Between the Devil,* sophisticated as Cole Porter but not nearly so wicked. By no means unaware of the need for experimentation, Dietz proposed that the Shuberts hand over one good-sized theatre for trying out new ideas. As he explained it, "the theater would become a school and stars would be teachers." The Shuberts were making too much money with old-hat nothings to agree, so Dietz and his colleagues had to perform their experiments in the commercial theatre, a fact which kept many experiments minimal and some off the boards entirely.

Vincent Youmans' thirties career was a sad one. 1930 brought *Smiles,* a Ziegfeld disaster with Fred and Adele Astaire, Marilyn Miller, "Time on My Hands," and no book. 1932 brought *Through the Years,* an adaptation of *Smilin' Through* that unfortunately stayed faithful to the bathos of the original. Youmans, like many of the more creative composers, was caught between the romantic bonanzas of the twenties and the more demanding audiences of the thirties.

Youmans' one great thirties success—and his last score—was not solely his. *Humpty-Dumpty* miscarried badly when it first opened in Pittsburgh in the fall of 1932. A show-within-a-show spoofing America's historical past, it died in five days only to rise again because its authors were also its producers. Buddy DeSylva and Lawrence Schwab threw out their concept and revamped the entertainment to include a love plot and a few new songs by Richard Whiting and Herb Brown Nacio (later changed to Nacio Herb Brown for some reason). A new title wrapped it all up, and *Take a Chance* was a smash in New York as an old-fashioned musical comedy that neither made nor satisfied elitist demands. But slapdash as it was bound to be, *Take a Chance* had a good balance of forces. It also had a classroom example of the "big number" that catalyzes the evening and becomes synonomous in the public mind with the show itself, "Eadie Was a Lady." Mentioned in every review, plugged on the airwaves by various singers, sung in the theatre to a rapturous hush while wives nudged dozing husbands, the big number was an old, old idea and still going strong. Decades later, some shows would capitalize too much on this with their title songs, leaving the audience bewildered and frustrated when the big number proved petite, but *Take a Chance* managed it more spontaneously. The teary story ballad of the nineties had now become a cynical narrative of point-blank, boozy whoring, stopping the show every night in Ethel Merman's galvanizing performance. The public delighted in each new verse about the lady who "had class with a capital K" and who, in DeSylva's lyric, "did things in a ladylike way":

> In her cups she'd get her local eggs crossed,
> Picked the ones that seldom paid—
> But you'd never catch her with her legs crossed
> In the wagon after a raid . . .

George Jean Nathan thought it the best song ever written for a musical.

14

Porgy and Bess

Genre Criticism

The growing confrontation between the expressive new pop sound of Kern, Rodgers, Gershwin, Porter, Youmans, Schwartz, and Vernon Duke and the potentialities of libretto writing—a confrontation made inevitable after *Show Boat*—came to a climax in the thirties. The awareness of daily life that marked a few of that decade's shows was only the beginning of a growing trend toward realism in the musicals that followed. Less and less would producers sign up stars to arrange on a stage like cake trimmings, for the triumph of *Show Boat, Of Thee I Sing, Face the Music,* and *Music in the Air* was one of material, not just performances. No one will ever be sure just how much of everybody's favorite show, *Sally,* was *Sally* and how much Marilyn Miller, but these new dreadnoughts were winning favor more for the art of the creative artists than that of the recreative artistes.

Kaufman and Hart made their contribution in bringing musical comedy books up to the level of their legit comedies.

The Gershwins, Dietz and Schwartz, and Rodgers and Hart all collaborated with them on musicals conceived as continuous narratives with an overall point of view rather than star vehicles and on-and-off vaudeville shtick. But it was Hammerstein and Kern who forced the evolution of the integrated book musical, particularly in their basic fusion of text and dialogue into scene entities of musical-dramatic exposition, broken up only by set changes or dance numbers. Eventually, the integration of dance into the superstructure in the forties and the revamped stage mechanics of the fifties and sixties made the progression even more fluent, and though Kern died in 1946, Hammerstein had already undertaken a second, more intense pilgrimage with Richard Rodgers that would fulfill another stage of musical comedy maturity.

Not only *Show Boat* in 1927 but *Sweet Adeline* in 1929 and *Music in the Air* in 1932 made the Kern-Hammerstein duo the ideal choice for musical comedy that would be popular and uplifting at the same time. No wonder the Theatre Guild turned to them when Al Jolson wanted to star in an adaptation of Dorothy and DuBose Heyward's play *Porgy,* based on Heyward's novel of life among the Gullah blacks of Charleston. Kern and Hammerstein were interested; so was Heyward. But even before *Porgy* appeared on October 11, 1927, George Gershwin had written to Heyward suggesting they turn his book into an opera. At first Mrs. Heyward's stage project got in the way, but once *Porgy* reached the stage in Cleon Throckmorton's painstakingly eye-witnessed designs and Rouben Mamoulian's atmospheric direction, Gershwin was positive that this romance between a middle-aged cripple and a drug-addicted whore would be just the work to move him from the light popular stage into the world of artistic genius. Eventually Kern, Hammerstein, and Jolson bowed out of the picture, and Gershwin and Heyward set to work.

Gershwin called *Porgy and Bess* a "folk opera," and he did much of his ground work in Charleston and on the barrier islands off the coast. Not a note of the score is a quotation of folk material, but the personality and contours of the vocal lines are based on models Gershwin heard while staying with the Heywards. Heyward wrote all the lyrics to Act One, then collaborated with Ira Gershwin on the other two acts. The Theatre Guild again produced, Mamoulian again directed, and Alexander Smallens led the forty-two-man orchestra (Gershwin had done his own scoring for the first time). Capitalized at $70,000, *Porgy and Bess* had its world premiere on its Boston tryout on September 30, 1935 (a private concert of the entire four-hour score had been held in Carnegie Hall in New York a few days before). There was none of the frantic rewriting that attend most out-of-town engagements, but some cuts were made to tighten the action, including Jazzbo Brown's opening piano blues with its scat-singing chorus, seldom heard since.

Thunderous applause greeted the first night in New York at the Alvin Theatre on October 10, but few of the critics were truly enthusiastic. Both the dramatic and musical press turned out, the theatre men by far the more favorably impressed with the piece—but then music critics are usually the last to accept anything new. Virgil Thomson, fresh from his success with that *locus classicus* of Mother Goose sophistication, *Four Saints in Three Acts,* called *Porgy and Bess* "crooked folklore and halfway opera." Winthrop Sargeant likewise demurred, and Olin Downes of the *Times* claimed that the style of composition "is at one moment of opera and another of operetta or sheer Broadway entertainment." Inches away on the page lay Brooks Atkinson's critique, an unqualified rave. Atkinson felt that the musical *Porgy* had the soul and vitality the straight *Porgy* had lacked: "Gershwin has found a personal voice that was inarticulate in the original play. The fear and pain go deeper in *Porgy and Bess* than they did in the penny plain *Porgy.*"

It had been the same in Boston. Drama critic Elliot Norton admired it; his counterpart at the music desk called it "incidental music." Frankly, neither the music nor the drama critics were ready for this titanic work. The theatre people responded to "I Got Plenty of Nothin' " and "Summertime" but were ill-equipped to deal with "Bess, You Is My Woman Now" or the wake scene with its throbbing spirituals, first dirgelike ("Gone, Gone, Gone"), then nervous ("Overflow"), followed by the extraordinarily Negroid "My Man's Gone Now." In fact, they were totally unprepared for any music that developed the plot with expansive lyricism, using a wide vocal compass, symphonic scoring, and a blatant lack of the familiar brush rhythm and bleating brass section of pit bands. They were not too young to remember the trained voices of operetta, but Victor Herbert's waltz songs and ripping good comedy numbers were no preparation for "What You Want wid Bess?" or "They Pass by Singin',"—two perfect examples of a song type that sets mood and establishes character and yet doesn't ask the plot to sit this one out while the audience forgets its troubles and taps its toes.

Atkinson did object to the actors' singing all the everyday, in-between lines: "Why do composers vex it so? 'Sister, you goin' to the picnic?' 'No, I guess not.' Now, why in heaven's name must two characters in an opera clear their throats before they can exchange that sort of information?" The music press, on the other hand, for years had been distastefully eyeing Gershwin's "cheap" melding of the classical sound with the pop idiom. This was their chance to put a stop to that sort of thing for all time. But music critics, past and present, are notorious for their lack of abilities. Most of them—not all, but most—simply do not know music, either as a trade or as an art; they not only don't know what's good, they don't even know what they like.

Thomson's modish-sounding crack about "crooked folklore" really raises one's eyebrows, as he had had an opera on Broadway with an all-black cast just the year before, that same *Four Saints in Three Acts.* Produced by the Friends and Enemies of Modern Music, *Four Saints* was undeniably an opera ("an opera to be sung," the program helpfully put it for those who weren't sure), unlike *Porgy and Bess,* whose classification is still under debate. Although Gertrude Stein's poesy was a prime example of Late Abstruse and Thomson's charming music not the kind to be hummed on first hearing, the production seemed to some a junction-point of Negro vaudeville, surrealist farce, and urban chicté. Chic it certainly was, surrealist not much, but neither farce nor vaudeville and most definitely not Negro.

In the end, *Porgy and Bess'* original New York run was only 125 performances, half of them with a reduced cast. A tour started in Philadelphia, moved to Chicago, and abruptly closed in Washington, leaving the project in the red. But the rest of the story is a lesson in how the public learns to accept and finally welcome an unfamiliar species of musical through the popularity of its songs. Prominent singers adopted them on radio and in clubs, and RCA Victor released selections on four twelve-inch 78s with Met stars Lawrence Tibbett and Helen Jepson backed by the original conductor, chorus, and orchestra. Meanwhile, it had not deserted the stage, turning up in San Francisco and Los Angeles for six weeks in 1938. Then came Cheryl Crawford's triumphant 1942 New York revival, with the recitative played as spoken dialogue and with prominent recantations from both Thomson and Downes.

It had been easy to debunk *Porgy and Bess* in 1935. Nobody knew where it would lead to, but it sure sounded like a weird idea, and it wasn't even the work of a "real" composer. But if nothing succeeds like success, it's also the second time you meet that matters, and any musical score of some complexity that doesn't repeat itself a lot needs exposure before it comes across. Most theatregoers aren't trained musicians—they need repeated hearings to pick up on a tune. No really good score ever sounds as good the first time as it does the second or third, and not until the *Porgy* score had extra chances to ingratiate itself did it actually arrive.

By the forties *Porgy and Bess* was able to pay its own way in the theatre. George Gershwin was dead, which only added to the *Porgy* legend, and the folk-inspired music was becoming folklore on its own. Copenhagen produced it in 1943, Zurich and Moscow (the Stanislavsky Players, no less) in 1945, Stockholm in 1949. Blevins Davis and Robert Breen mounted it in Dallas in 1952, and it was this production that made history crisscrossing the globe for years. Its New York stand at the Ziegfeld Theatre with Leontyne Price, Le Verne Hutcherson, and Cab Calloway was treated almost in awe, and the opera's status as a classic was further upheld by constant City Center revivals through the fifties and sixties. A big-budget Hollywood movie came along in 1959, cementing the work's place in the consciousness of the nation.

Aside from enriching Broadway's stockpile of enduring works, Gershwin did exactly what he had planned to do as early as 1922 in his *Scandals* one-acter "Blue Monday," and what he continued to do in Rhapsody in Blue, Concerto in F, *An American in Paris,* the three preludes for piano, and occasionally in musical comedy songs such as "The Man I Love" and "Someone to Watch Over Me": to compose music in the native idiom that would stand up to scrutiny as significant and lasting. In a way, only *Porgy and Bess* works in this regard, for the orchestral works are weak in construction, more like potpourris than symphonic forms, and the musical comedy songs are, ultimately, just unusually insightful pop tunes. But *Porgy and Bess* succeeds on its own terms. It is indeed a "folk opera," mined from an American subculture and imbued with authentic geographical flavor—St. Michael's Church, Kittiwah Island, the blackfish banks. Heyward's novel *Porgy* is one of the strongest statements ever made about the black race in this country. Throughout the short book, the Charleston whites suspect, cajole, threaten, or ignore the Gullah Negroes; at one point a plainclothes detective sums up all of Catfish Row as "one murder and a happy-dust riot already this summer," and the blacks play the game too, faking Uncle Tom bewilderment whenever a Buckra enters their domain. But left to themselves, Heyward's characters inhabit their own kingdom, with its laws, its superstitions, its moral code, its justice. All this was carried through faithfully in the first stage version, and Gershwin's music made it ring.

Some critics, searching for a reason for their inability to fathom a new medium, jumped on the popular quality of the "big tunes," claiming that they didn't jibe with the rest of the score. Repeated hearings of the whole work, however, throw this aside. Big tunes always stand out—that's what makes them big. The songs fit in snugly with the "busy music"—dialogues and choruses in between the famous titles—partly through the use of identifying motives for certain characters and for other elements in the work. For example, the distinctive harmonic progression of Porgy's "I Got Plenty of Nothin' " turns up again in his crap game prayer, "Oh, Little Stars." Sportin' Life also has his motive, so does the love plot, so does Catfish Row, and one violent tympani theme could pass for a "fate motive" in a story so closely connected with Zola's predestinate naturalism. Then too, the songs really flow out of the action as never before 1935 in musical comedy, because the adaptation was so secure. Most of the song cues can be found in Heyward's novel, and except for the ecstatic finale in which Porgy rides off to find Bess (as in the play), the opera follows the novel closely.

Quite apart from artistic considerations, *Porgy and Bess* made a significant contribution to Negro theatre as well. Like most of the best black revues, *Porgy and Bess* was written by whites, but it was all the same the first musical to present the black nation as a fact rather than a fancy, an un-Harlemized sanctum of Southerners ethnocentrically close to their African antecedents (the coincidences of vocabulary between African dialects and Charleston's Gullahs is startling). If anyone understood the distinct qualities of American black music it was Gershwin, who once stole the show from the champion "shouter" at a spiritual get-together. For his part, Heyward got as close to the inscrutable world of the ghetto as anyone of his race ever could. His third-person narration was neither glorifying nor cold-blooded, but interested, loving, honest, and poetic. Similarly, *Porgy and Bess,* an opera deliberately composed for the commercial theatre, hasn't a trace of the commercial theatre's glitz.

The Gershwins and Heyward were doubtless influenced to some extent by the incalculable extra weight granted the *Show Boat* text by Kern's songs, interludes, and underscorings. In one sense, the *Porgy and Bess* authors came up with the first Broadway musical with a completely integrated libretto, but then that's precisely what an opera is. The large cast and orchestra made the piece an expensive proposition, limiting its exposure; this, plus its racial subject and (to many) inaccessibly artistic reaches kept it from affecting the mainstream of American theatre in turn. There were never any *Porgy and Bess* imitations, even after it proved an economic success in the forties. The next black musical of note was the quite different *Cabin in the Sky* (1940), a ritualized good-versus-evil fantasy distilled through the by then sophisticated art of Broadway hoopla. In fact, the sole successful Negro shows in the five years between *Porgy and Bess* and *Cabin in the Sky* were two jive guyings of Gilbert and Sullivan, *The Swing Mikado* and *The Hot Mikado,* both in 1939. Later that year came *Swingin' the Dream* (from *A Midsummer Night's Dream*), with a racially integrated cast including Ruth Ford, Dorothy McGuire, Butterfly McQueen, Louis Armstrong, and Benny Goodman. Agnes De Mille devised ballet for the white folks, Herbert White jitterbug for the blacks. A basically disorganized effort, it failed in a wash of artistic intentions while the two Harlem *Mikado*s were commercial hits.

15

The Thirties (III)

Social Conscience, No Glamour

Even within the ranks of the commercial composers and librettists, risks were taken in the thirties that contributed to the future of the "aware" musical. Among the revues, *As Thousands Cheer* gently suggested social concern with a load of superior stagecraft, *Shoot the Works!* pestered amateurishly, *Parade* came too early in rage, and *Pins and Needles* hit the right combination of good timing and good, clean side-taking. Sam Harris got Kaufman and Hart to push the political book musical into being with *Of Thee I Sing,* the authors tempering their brainchild with lessons learned from *Strike Up the Band,* but waxed too angry in *Let 'Em Eat Cake.* Then Harris, Hart, and Irving Berlin showed them how to do it on a municipal level in *Face the Music* with its ingenuous pop-tune orientation. Only one level of socioeconomic satire had yet to arrive: the truth.

It was Kurt Weill and Bertolt Brecht, Weill and Maxwell Anderson, and Marc Blitzstein who finally thrust the musical theatre into its soapbox stage. The German pair came first. Their *Threepenny Opera* had its first New York hearing in 1933, five years after a sensational premiere at a little cabaret theatre in Berlin, and our first nighters were disgusted. In taking the characters and plot from William Pepusch and John Gay's ballad opera of 1728, *The Beggar's Opera,* Brecht pictured the corruption and self-centered zeal of society, our society. His indictment of capitalist morality was unequaled for savagery in a Broadway musical offering till *Chicago* forty years later, and Weill's music, like Gershwin's for *Let 'Em Eat Cake,* was angular and percussive, scored for a nasty combo rather than the usual pit band. 1933 was altogether too early for a musical show of such uncompromising vision; the critics would have none of it. Percy Hammond called it "a mummy grinning on a dung hill," Richard Lockridge "sugar-coated communism," Gilbert Gabriel a "dreary enigma." Even the astute John Mason Brown found the libretto "the most appallingly stupid . . . which any production that benefits from music has been cursed with in recent years."

By the time the monthly *Stage* magazine came out, *The Threepenny Opera* had played the last of its twelve performances, but Hiram Motherwell complained in a *Stage* article of the daily reviewers' "willful blindness." Truth to tell, most of the critics had been taken with Weill's distinctive sound, and the *Times* man Lewis Nichols had thought the piece "worth the seeing." But clearly, social commentary could not succeed if the comments were too harsh. It was easier for the revues to balance their tougher sketches with sentiment and glitter, for the unity of a variety show is a less palpable thing than that for a book show, which has to hold together more strictly from scene to scene. In *Threepenny Opera*'s case, continuity was supplied by the self-oriented rationalizing of the London underworld, a risky unity even for New York's sophisticated audiences.

Weill himself came to town in 1935 to write incidental music for Max Reinhardt's biblical pageant, *The Eternal Road.*

Times had changed since *Sumurun*'s tepid reception, but then *The Eternal Road* was no *Sumurun*. An Old Testament epic that sprawled all over the Manhattan Opera House, it cost $540,000 to produce and was undoubtedly the biggest "play" Broadway had ever seen. Opening night on January 7, 1937, lasted till three a.m., but critics wrote their mostly rave notices after seeing only the first half of the show. With the third and fourth acts quietly dropped as of the second night, *The Eternal Road* gave 153 performances to packed houses, dispensing tips to directors, designers, and even a few producers who took it in time and again. Art, like satire, didn't necessarily close on Saturday night: it was all a matter of how—and when—it was done. A revival of *Sumurun* in 1937 might well have been the rage of the season.

Weill's music for *The Eternal Road* was well received, but his first American musical seemed an unsuitable project for an alien: Paul Green's "play with music" *Johnny Johnson,* "a fable of ancient and modern times," produced by the left-wing Group Theatre in 1936. *The Eternal Road* had been delayed by financial and production difficulties, so Weill's second American commission was actually his first to be heard. Green's antiwar libretto told the story of an innocent idealist, a creative man (he earns his living as a stonecutter) whose romance with a small-town belle is interrupted by World War I, in which he enlists. Willing but unable to kill, Johnny invades Allied headquarters with laughing gas and almost brings the fighting to a halt, but he is arrested, the war continues, and Johnny ends up in a lunatic asylum. His ideals somehow intact, he organizes the inmates in a miniature league of nations and is finally released to make his way as a toymaker. In the show's final scene he accidentally runs into his onetime fiancée, now married to his onetime rival. Ironically, they are on their way to a Preparedness rally, and Johnny is left alone on stage with his tray of toys, wandering off as he sings that one day mankind will "work and strive . . . the better way to find."

Directed by Lee Strasberg and cast with such future stars as John Garfield, Elia Kazan, Albert Dekker, Sanford Meisner, Luther Adler, and Morris Carnovsky, *Johnny Johnson* was a musical born of the legitimate theatre, for of the production team only Weill had ever worked on a musical before. The story was almost but never quite surrealistic, and although there was comedy, it was not the sort Broadway was used to. Green and the Group Theatre had something to say, and they used every means at their disposal to say it: on his way to Europe, Johnny is sung to by the Statue of Liberty, heard but not seen; a German sniper who hides in a hollow Christ figure is befriended—loved—by Johnny and finally sent back to the enemy with a message of peace; the first chorus showed Johnny's fellow citizens firmly isolationist, but news of Congress' declaration of war finds them singing the opposite sentiments to the same music.

Bertolt Brecht knew that songs lightened the audience's burden at an ideological drama, so his plays are littered with lyrics to ingratiate his dogma. When the Nazis came to power, their exhibition of decadent art included a gramophone playing Lotte Lenya's recording of the Moritat ("The Ballad of Mack the Knife") from *The Threepenny Opera,* but the room was eventually closed because the public was enjoying the music too much. It was just this brilliant work with Brecht that made Weill an unlikely choice for *Johnny Johnson.* For one thing, his personal style was at odds with the American sound—perfect for Brecht's Berliners masquerading as London gangsters, yes; perfect also for the dry, preachy methodism of the "epic theatre." But Green's book was not as self-controlled and direct as Brecht's texts invariably were; this was a hybrid item, a "play with music." Then too, how would Weill's sardonic bassoons and cymbal stingers adapt to the distinctly American characters Green had created—especially his devastatingly innocent and sincere protagonist?

As it happened, Weill's music complemented *Johnny Johnson* surprisingly well. The German had the ability to incorporate his talent into the superstructure of each new collaborative project, a rare talent in the popular arts, where people usually prefer to stick to their specialty. Only five years later he would give Moss Hart and Ira Gershwin a glittering, uptempo Broadway "tuner" in *Lady in the Dark* when flash and glamour were required. But now, in 1936, he gave *Johnny Johnson* pretty much the sort of music it needed—character numbers like the ironic "Psychiatry Song" or "Captain Valentine's Tango" (what Brechtian titles, however!), a cowboy pastiche for "The Rio Grande," pop ballads for "Mon Ami, My Friend" and "O, Heart of Love." There were atmospheric choruses for the war scenes and novel solutions to all the genre pieces. Tying the whole score together with a recurring theme for Johnny, Weill gave it voice with Green's lyrics only at the very end of the story when the hero fades off into the night.

Although *Johnny Johnson* was not a commercial success, the critics responded positively to it. Some were reminded of Georg Büchner's play *Woyzeck* and the opera Alban Berg made of it, some of Charlie Chaplin's silent film *Shoulder Arms*. The *Tribune*'s Richard Watts, Jr., found it a "disturbing and often hilarious medley of caricature, satire, musical comedy, melodrama, farce, social polemic and parable." The *Times* thought it "an original and deeply moving work;" Robert Benchley called it "exciting and imaginative . . . something really big, even if it does have flaws." Once convened together at the end of the 1936–37 season, the Critics Circle voted *Johnny Johnson* runner-up as the best play of the year. But any musical that is part melodrama and part satire, as Watts pointed out, is in trouble. Weill's music strikes a consistent tone, but Green's book and lyrics are a little out of sync as regards style, and two New York revivals in 1956 and 1971 lasted a few days each.

Weill's early collaborations with serious dramatists in Germany left him with no desire to write a tired-businessman type of show. In 1938 he hooked up with Maxwell Anderson, already the author of *Elizabeth the Queen, Valley Forge,*

Winterset, The Wingless Victory, and *High Tor,* among others. Anderson had never written either book or lyrics for a musical, and Weill's particular acoustic was still somewhat ahead of what the average theatre buff expected, but somehow they and Joshua Logan contrived a commercial success with a story of old Nieuw Amsterdam and the appropriation of its democratic process by Pegleg Pieter Stuyvesant. *Knickerbocker Holiday* had none of *Johnny Johnson*'s quasi-fantasy, nor *The Threepenny Opera*'s gruesome sermons or raffish dramatis personae. It did have an unhackneyed historical background, a happy-ending romance, an inspiringly versatile score including one of the theatre's great mottos, "September Song," and a salty star turn by Walter Huston, simulated peg leg and all, "in the grand manner with a homely brand of native wit."

As entertainment, *Knickerbocker Holiday* had difficulty assimilating Anderson's dramaturgy into the bounds of musical comedy, but then Anderson had no mere entertainment up his sleeve. He made use of the setting to draw a parallel with the hows and whys of fascism, characterizing the American spirit in his young hero, a freethinking gadfly who can't take orders, and pitting him against the tyrant Stuyvesant. Noting Anderson's difficulties in working in the song cues, Atkinson lauded his use of the popular stage for a heavy statement: "Under the conventional pattern of musical comedy making, Mr. Anderson has some general observations to make—about democracy as government by amateurs, which is superior to the practised corruption of professionals, and about the anarchic spirit of the true American." *Knickerbocker Holiday* wasn't the first musical comedy to deal with politics, of course, but its predecessors merely poked fun at our own government. This one warned of the dangers of certain rival ideologies, and the Americans-as-individuals theme was less self-congratulation than a call to arms.

Unlike Weill, the Philadelphian Marc Blitzstein wrote words as well as music, but his subject matter was if anything more obviously leftist than the librettos Weill worked with. The two had a dissonant, sardonic musical idiom in common, but Blitzstein lacked the melodic facility to put his work over to a large audience, whereas Weill's scores would concede a blockbuster pop hit like "September Song" or "Speak Low," not to mention underground classics like "It Never Was You" or "Here I'll Stay," purveyed by elegant cabaret diseurs. Not a single Blitzstein tune ever caught on in the pop market, although his first show, *The Cradle Will Rock,* was the first Broadway musical to sport an original cast album.

This *Cradle Will Rock* was a symbolic rallying cry addressed to the workers of the world. With its all too obvious villains (Mister Mister, Mrs., Junior, and Sister Mister) and equally opaque hero Larry Foreman, with its Brechtian prostitute and machine age artists Yasha and Dauber, *The Cradle Will Rock* was a wild choice for the Federal Theatre Project of the WPA, but Orson Welles and John Houseman were determined to see the work to the stage. The first public preview was planned for June 16, 1937, only two weeks after the tragic CIO march on Republic Steel in Chicago. But Washington suddenly found itself unwilling to sponsor so frankly subversive a show and had the Maxine Elliott Theatre padlocked. Here follows what must be the most distinctive opening night in the history of the musical: rather than give up, Welles, Houseman, Blitzstein, cast, crew, ticketholders, passersby, and a piano moved a few blocks uptown to the Venice (later the Century) Theatre. Actors Equity and the musicians' union forbade their members to appear on stage or in the pit, reflecting the *non serviam* opportunism of the very people Blitzstein expected to reach—but nothing could stop the actors from buying seats in the auditorium to play their parts where they sat or in the aisles. The composer accompanied the show from memory at the so suitably gutted piano onstage, with some aid from an accordion in the balcony, while lighting director Abe Feder lit the action with one wrathful, roving spotlight.

It was quite an affair, outrageous, tense, sweaty, defiant, the wrecked piano symbolizing what Blitzstein had done to the orthodox format of the light musical theatre. Before the performance, Houseman came out with Welles to describe what the sets and staging would have looked like, adding to the feel of an Event. In his memoirs Houseman recalls explaining that "ours was a gesture of artistic, not political defiance," and so it doubtless was. But it is hard to consider a performance of *The Cradle Will Rock* as anything but a political act, artistic though it certainly is. The late thirties were parlous times for radical movements, but musical comedy—and the legit theatre as well—was then beginning to grasp what a weapon it had in entertainment. *Of Thee I Sing* in 1931 or even the earlier *Strike Up the Band* in 1927 seemed like ahead-of-their-time advances of the light musical stage, but *The Cradle Will Rock* was bound to be written, *had* to be performed, in 1937. Compared to *Pins and Needles,* whose creators were politically in Blitzstein's camp, *The Cradle Will Rock* is a new dimension in which art is the means and a brave new world the end. While Blitzstein's way with dramatic structure was nerve-ending powerful and his use of pop song archetypes adroit, his music has scant melodic appeal to those who would be revolted by his viewpoint in the first place.

After 19 showings at the Venice, *The Cradle Will Rock* played a few Sunday nights and then nested on Broadway at a $1.65 top for 108 performances at the Windsor and Mercury Theatres, Blitzstein still alone at the piano. Now the critics entered the picture, admiring the author's singlemindedness but not relishing the savagery of his concept. Irving Kolodin called it a "modern immorality play," but to Atkinson it was the "most versatile artistic triumph of the politically insurgent theater." The work still has its backers, although subsequent revivals have failed to establish this "play in music" as anything but dialectic.

The Federal Theatre's other projects drew less publicity, but in these days of unsubsidized art it is of use to note what the Roosevelt administration supported in the way of theatre. One of the two productions was *Swing It,* an all-black entry about a Harlem River showboat, like the earlier black shows half revue, half book show. The other was Lehman Engel and Theresa Helburn's *A Hero Is Born,* a knight and damsel burlesque that failed to charm its fifty audiences because of miscasting.

With star comedian vehicles still thriving in the thirties (they'd be thriving today if the star comedians weren't all in movies or television), it was perhaps inevitable that somebody would get around to treating Fascist Europe the way *Of Thee I Sing* treated Washington. Howard Lindsay and Russel Crouse's book for *Hooray for What* (1937) took world armament and germ warfare for its subjects, but the evening's real subject was Ed Wynn—his lisp, his bizarre inventions, his screwy costumes, and, on this outing, his secret formula for a lethal gas. As a horticulturist trying to kill off the world's worms (dancing worms, "because they like to go into the big apple"), Wynn provided the loose structure and let's-wing-it optimism of the twenties shows, exactly the sort of thing people like Kaufman and Hart had eliminated in their work. *Hooray for What* aimed only to divert—although there was a striking, ironic "Hero Ballet" by Agnes De Mille—and the satire consisted in knockabout farce and Wynn's fast one-liners ("This gas will revive the dead. I've got a big offer from the Republican party").

Unlike Gershwin's integrated scores for his political shows, Harold Arlen and E. Y. Harburg's *Hooray for What* songs were totally in the pop tune mold, avoiding the operatic ensembles and context songs that would never catch on out of the theatre. This was only Arlen's second book musical and his third full-length score; he had yet to reach his prime, when he would cross the line from pop singles into the world of the art song ("Right as the Rain," "I Had Myself a True Love," "A Sleepin' Bee," and "Cocoanut Sweet," for example). But Harburg was already on the road to the socioeconomic satire of *Finian's Rainbow* and *Flahooley.* The conception of the show was his, and if the reviewers gave the palm to Wynn, it was really Harburg who set the tone for the sly topicality of the libretto. *Hooray for What* wasn't the first musical with dignitaries from the League of Nations in its cast list, but it helped to set up a much needed middle ground between the high-level spoofs like *Of Thee I Sing* and *Knickerbocker Holiday*—not to mention the uncompromising anticommercial attempts like *Parade* and *The Cradle Will Rock*—and the often pointless boy-girl-song-dance-and-comedy charades. Such halfway pieces as *Hooray for What,* neither truly novel nor yet truly old hat, would prove a useful starting point for the forties, when musical comedy began to experiment with form and subject matter in happily unusual ways.

Intermission

"Hoping That Your Eyes Won't Misinform You"

Speak, pictures. Speak: sets, costumes, proscenium masks, chorus groupings, contours of dance patterns, savvy comediennes cutting loose down front, ingenue and juvenile O.D.ing on charm, ballads, and up tunes, Brechtian frenzy or forties folk play or eternally ditsy show-biz club sandwiches of gags and sentiment. All speak to us, show and tell.

Show Boat comes first, the original great musical, here looking rather dated—but then it has been nearly fifty years. Ziegfeld correctly dubbed the Kern-Hammerstein operetta-turning-into-musical play "all-American," and lavished an unstinting production on it, reveling in the scenes that took him back to his midway-and-music-hall days in Chicago. But Ziegfeld, like most others in 1927, underrated it. Not till he revived it in 1932 with the best of the premiere players and some improved new casting did the

Show Boat

epic make its cumulative effect. Then, finally, *Show Boat* overwhelmed.

Kern was the giant of his profession and *Show Boat* was his giant score. But Hammerstein, the giant of the word men, was not yet totally emancipated, and, thematic depth notwithstanding, there are flaws in his book. Even in 1927 it was generally conceded that the second act kind of crawls along (and Act I is no dog race, either). Furthermore, some of the comedy is less intrinsic than painted in as if by number. As Captain Andy Hawks, Charles Winninger did what he would have done anyway; at least the casting was perfect. You can take the man out of vaudeville, but you can't take vaudeville out of the man: here's Winninger knocking them dead aboard the *Cotton Blossom.* The two scruffy mountain men in the box at the upper left have just disrupted the show, *The Parson's Bride,* and

As Thousands Cheer

scared off the actors; Captain Andy shows the crowd what would have happened next for a slambang blackout finish. Note Captain Andy's wife, Parthy Ann, in that same box—Edna May Oliver, looking (as she was born to look) insatiably dour.

While *Show Boat* pioneered the new idea of penetrating music drama in the pop idiom, others sought sophistication and style, especially in revues. Irving Berlin's *As Thousands Cheer* songs mostly upheld the unreconstructed pop-tune status quo for 1933, but they gave a nice background for Moss Hart's social comments. Next to topical world-viewing, the great thirties revues loved classy stars, and no one had more class than Marilyn Miller. Here she is, backed up by Albert Johnson's set and Varady's costumes, dolled up and ready to caper with the archetypes of the Sunday supplement for Berlin's "The Funnies." The tune was dull and the lyrics insipid, but Miller put it over. Her specific

Porgy and Bess

talent was dancing; she *could* sing, more or less, but her range was limited to one high, loud note —an F, apparently. Arrangers always had to make sure that the big ballad in a Miller show was pitched so as to match its climactic note with hers. (Miller and her sore thumb of a high F came back in *Chicago,* played by a transvestite. Think about that for a minute.)

In 1935 *Porgy and Bess* demonstrated how profoundly vernacular music could illuminate a drama, aided to the utmost by Rouben Mamoulian's stunning conception of folk-play plastique. Later to direct *Oklahoma!, Carousel,* and *Lost in the Stars* in the forties, he connected the early experiments of the art movement with the triumphs of "whole idea" director/choreographers like Champion, Fosse, and Bennett—Mamoulian made stage America look righter than any other director of his time. Above, Act II, Scene 4—the hurricane, with Crown (Warren Coleman) challenging God to a test of strength as Todd Duncan and Anne Brown huddle together in the foreground at left.

One Touch of Venus

Meanwhile, in the realms of pure musical comedy, plots c. 1943 were still finding room for a secondary comedienne like Paula Laurence as a secretary in *One Touch of Venus,* singing the suggestive title song and "Very, Very, Very" so the sex war could continue and man and wife could know where they stood. Laurence and her *commères* stood front and center, usually "in one," which means you could hear the scenery screeching into place behind the traveler curtain when the lady wasn't belting out tag rhymes about how roguish women had become since the days of *The Madcap Duchess* and *The Lady of the Slipper*. Notice the surrealist art: Laurence's boss, John Boles, was an aficionado.

Musical comedy choreography arrived almost before the shows themselves did, triggered by Charles Weidman, Agnes De Mille, and such, but *On the Town* in 1944 integrated dance into the entire evening. Jerome Robbins' ballets didn't exactly baptize choreography for Broadway, but he can be said to have held the confirmation class. His *High Button Shoes* had a zany period dash, and *Look Ma, I'm Dancin'!* was rich in ballet burlesque, but *On the Town* was modern art, in tone and outline and feel.

George Abbott, Betty Comden, and Adolph Green called their heroine Miss Turnstiles instead of Miss Subways, but their setting was still the true New York, bobbing and skipping and sometimes in a great lonely hush, yet always magnetic. Sono Osato was Miss Turnstiles, singled out of the crowd for her media-approved ordinariness, yet brought to life in her private vision of fleeting success, choreographed with adoring suitors, fellow New Yorkers, and a suave radio announcer.

Robbins' supreme presentation may be *Fiddler on the Roof,* but back in *On the Town* he caught the antiglamorous attraction of the city without

On the Town

On the Town

ever seeming to gild or candify. Here's "The Imaginary Coney Island," with Osato and Fred Harrison as the Great Lover—the metaphorical common man reaching out to the eternally feminine in jukebox city. Some applause, too, for Oliver Smith's designs, among the most characterful of their decade.

The forties were the heyday of the romantic show—the heyday as well of Oscar Hammerstein, who redoubled *Show Boat*'s "there's no place like a country home" message in *Allegro.* If the romantic show did not already exist, Agnes De Mille would have had to invent it; as it was, she was there in time to put her stamp on romantic-show movement in *Oklahoma!* and *Carousel,* branching out to settle musical comedy's hash in *One Touch of Venus* and *Bloomer Girl.*

Richard Rodgers later insisted that *Allegro*'s message devolved not on a town-versus-country debate but on "the corrupting effect of big institutions," yet De Mille's staging pleaded a strong case against the city, regardless of what Rodgers thinks he and his partner wrote. The big institution in this case was a spiffy hospital for wealthy

Allegro

hypochondriacs, and in this final scene the hero, Dr. Joseph Taylor, Jr., abandons the *soigné* types (left) for the folk (right) while his dead mother and grandmother egg him on in the background and Lisa Kirk, nurse, moves to join him (in the picture, it *should* be Lisa Kirk; one has to admit it doesn't really look like her). A show with strong thematic substance requires pointed direction, not musical comedy hoopla; *Allegro,* properly, represented an apex of brilliant material brought home in a brilliant production.

Spiraling economics should have revived interest in the charming little shows like *Leave It to Jane* and *You Never Know,* but by the fifties they were nearly extinct. Here's a typical moment from the 1951 adaptation of Booth Tarkington's *Seventeen,* a little show, nothing but sunny nostalgia. The stage business here is the

Seventeen

first meeting of Willie Baxter and summer visitor Lola Pratt; the locale is Indianapolis, "the largest city in the world not on navigable water," in 1907; the ingenue is Ann Crowley; the dog is Flopit; the juvenile is Kenneth Nelson, who was expected to grin engagingly or to mope, depending. His Willie Baxter was prototypical little-show winsomeness and pluck, tending to the far side of credibility, but more than two decades later he sang Cole Porter's "I Worship You" in the London revue *Cole* with such elegant, deviant, tortured precision that you have to stand up and give actors credit for being more interesting than people.

Little shows were usually musical comedies, seldom romantic; for that kind of weight you need bulk, although the gentle *She Loves Me* seemed to span both worlds. Concurrently with

Seventeen, Rodgers and Hammerstein gave the world their last fine musical play, *The King and I,* with all the pageantry and dramatic heft such endeavors use so tellingly. A tense moment: the King's slave Tuptim (Doretta Morrow) loves another, so the King (Yul Brynner) figures to whip her in front of the straitlaced, sympathetic Mrs. Anna (Gertrude Lawrence). It was hair-raising theater, certainly, but more than that, Hammerstein used the confrontation to climax the life-and-death battle between Eastern feudalism and Western democracy. What the world needs now is subtexts (and more Jo Mielziner scenery).

Speaking of personalities like Lawrence and Miller, what ever happened to the leading man? Since the twenties there have been few, except for comedians like Bert Lahr and Bobby Clark and a lusty baritone or two. Richard Kiley joined the elite ranks in 1965, playing Cervantes/Don Quixote in *Man of La Mancha,* but before that he was bucking the female-star system, as

The King and I

Redhead

in 1959's *Redhead,* a vehicle for Gwen Verdon. In between Bob Fosse's feline dances the plot was encouraged to take a turn or two, and here Kiley sings "My Girl Is Just Enough Woman for Me," so we know that the love story is neatly chugging along. But this was musical comedy, not a romance, and nobody took the affair seriously. Besides, how could Kiley possibly latch hold of Verdon when she was so busy doing cartwheels, flying her entrechats, and having dream ballets?

Verdon remains the last of the big-time box-office draws in the musical comedy world, though she didn't get a first-class show till *Chicago*. Her detractors like to remind you of her undernourished vocal equipment, but even her admirers may not be aware of her consummate acting ability. Listen, on the *Chicago* cast recording, to her longish spiel at the start of "Roxie," especially the bit about ugly guys taking her out to

Chicago

show her off—"ugly guys like to do that," she smirks over the vamp of her more or less title song-type number. That kind of strutting iniquity is too frank for most musical comedy performers. Liza Minnelli couldn't make it work when she took over for Verdon in August 1975 (on only six days' rehearsal, admittedly)—but then Verdon is Fosse's signet and Fosse doesn't package serene romances. He could probably sell the horror film *Night of the Living Dead* as a musical; in a way, he already has.

The *Chicago* snapshot records the "press conference rag," "We Both Reached for the Gun," with lawyer Billy Flynn (Jerry Orbach) manipulating dummy Roxie (Verdon), not to mention the ladies and gentlemen of the press. Mary Sunshine (Michael O'Haughey) is one of each, the aforementioned transvestite Marilyn Miller with the power to help clear a guilty murderess. That's "she" behind Verdon and Orbach; to the audience, the orchestra players were also

visible directly above the actors, planted on a great cylinder in the center of the stage. Tony Walton's spectacular designs don't come through in photos, unfortunately. Elevator, turntable, neon lights, logo scrim, and that backdrop of a newspaper front page cut in the shape of the United States all had to be seen live.

Chicago could never be as effective without grandiose showmanship because that's what it was about, and the same goes for *Follies*. The sad thing about the two big shows of the modern era is that they almost certainly won't be revived on that scale again, and yet they just can't make their point with less. A particularly minute touring company of *Follies* brought this home while plaguing the countryside in 1972. Michael Bennett's originally bulging "Who's That Woman?" routine now looked like a sister act, and the pit orchestra sounded like two harps, someone's old flute, and the drum-and-woodblock brigade of the local nursery school.

16

The Forties (I)

"Use Your Imagination"

The musical theatre entered its finest era in the forties. Elementary lessons in form and stagecraft had been learned; it remained only to utilize them for dramatic penetration. To some, these last few years before *Oklahoma!* in 1943 represent the final hours of the musical's infancy, leading in clear steps to the great Rodgers and Hammerstein triumph and exultantly moving on from there. But the first half of the forties had more than *Oklahoma!* to prove its maturity. Some of the big ones even preceded it, for *Oklahoma!* was less a culmination in itself than a reassurance that this culmination had already come about.

While Hammerstein and Kern pioneered the development of the plot musical, Porter, the Gershwins, and Rodgers and Hart found a new level of expression for theatre songs. But it was mainly the last two who pushed the genre question. After raiding the comic opera library for *Dearest Enemy,* experimenting in *Peggy-Ann* and *Chee-Chee,* or marking time with unadulterated musical comedy, the team furnished the late thirties with a final solution to the operetta problem in *I Married an Angel* (1938). A reworking of a Hungarian play, this spiffy effort managed to present a romance side by side with sophistication and yet seem all of a piece. The dancing was legitimate ballet, again by George Balanchine, and there was so much of it that the book (by Rodgers, Hart, and director Joshua Logan) only had room for nine songs and one reprise. Logan's staging—his first for a musical—was brilliant, Jo Mielziner's sets befittingly elaborate, the cast large and talented: Vivienne Segal, Dennis King, Walter Slezak, Audrey Christie, Charles Walters, and the Angel, Vera Zorina. The show took place in modern-day Budapest and incredibly enough was an unabashed fantasy: a jilted count swears off romance, vowing to marry only an angel . . . and one promptly flies through his window. The difficulties of life with a perfect girl who can only tell the truth provided much of the fun, especially when juxtaposed with Segal's and Christie's worldly sarcasm. One tasty number, "At the Roxy Music Hall," had these two giving their all as a Rockette chorus line of two, with Zorina rising like Venus from the sea to perform an expressionistic pas de deux with something that had no head (Slezak got to be a sea monster). Every review was a rave. If old-time romance could seem so new-minted, the future of operetta was assured—no longer as operetta per se but in a regenerated form based on wit and excellence of stagecraft.

Now moving in big strides, Rodgers and Hart could return to musical comedy with the confidence of guaranteed winners. *The Boys from Syracuse* (1938) was Shakespeare's *The Comedy of Errors* transplanted to Broadway, Ancient Greece, but the team's ability to transcend the demands of a commercial enterprise with artistry was an example to others on The Street. Such noteworthy ballads as "Falling in Love with Love," "The Shortest Day of the Year," and the expansively chromatic "You Have Cast Your Shadow on the Sea" heightened the sincerity of the love plots without ripping the tender fabric of profitable showmanship. George Abbott's book and direction were right as well as racy, with choice sprinklings of burlesque (both the old-fashioned Weberfields kind and the sleazier sorts), and Balanchine was on hand yet again to exalt musical comedy choreography, but the key to it all was the score. Rodgers and Hart could write context numbers as well as anyone (the detailed plot exposition was unthreaded entirely in song, seldom attempted again until the recent *Goodtime Charley*), but their way with a sensitive love song made their shows less gaudy and ephemeral than most others. Hart rivaled Porter, and no one rivaled them, in portraying adult emotions in AABA pop tune structure, yet Hart's complex rhyme schemes seemed as natural as June and moon. Just as *Of Thee I Sing*'s audiences enjoyed the satire but loved that touching reprise of "Who Cares?" Rodgers and Hart's public would quickly forget the comedy but treasure the ballads for years.

Then the forties dawned, and novelist John O'Hara invited the team to work with him in making a musical out of his *New Yorker* series of letters from a small-time nightclub emcee to a friend, all signed Pal Joey. Now it was not a question of genre, but range, for *Pal Joey* (1940) was pure musical comedy peopled with the high and low life of Chicago's North Side—an adulterous socialite, her amoral emcee, the flotsam and jetsam of the nightclub set, even a pair of blackmailers. The wonder was not that the *Pal Joey* characters were so unlikely for a musical but that they were depicted so honestly. Most critics were taken aback by the rough element that dominated the story, but they had to admit that the authors and director George Abbott had done a smashing job. 1929 had been too early for the raunchy gold rushers of *Rainbow,* but *Pal Joey,* though still avant-garde, managed to put itself over for an eleven-month run.

A first-rate musical comedy score is not just a collection of good tunes and lyrics, of course—there must be an identifying purpose behind them, setting mood, tone, character. Much has been made of the need to smooth out the creases between text and songs, but there was an even greater need for dramatization through words and music. Rodgers was the home town boy, sincere and unaffected, Hart the city slicker, but that very contrast was what made them so appealing. If their earlier shows—except *Peggy-Ann* and *Chee-Chee*—fitted into a workmanlike frame, their shows after the Hollywood years in the early thirties demonstrated a sharp nose for interesting story premises and new ways to rev up the show shop motor.

Thus *Pal Joey*. Despite their reservations about the subject (*Variety* called it "in some respects a quite unpleasant evening because of the complete lack of sympathy for our heel of a hero"), audiences could respond to the show because its treatment of the story was so *right*. The production numbers were used as amusing takeoffs on the whole world of dingy nightclub rites, but the first-act finale, "Joey Looks into the Future," was a remarkable communication of the antihero's conscious and unconscious dream pictures in Robert Alton's choreography and Gene Kelly's dancing.

The potential for trying allegedly outrageous subjects on the musical stage was opening up, and the forties would see all sorts of successful experiments on such themes as race relations, marriage problems, and psychoanalysis. By the time *Pal Joey* came back in 1952 with Vivienne Segal from the original, Harold Lang, and re-staging by Alton, no one was shocked, and the revival was even more successful than the original had been—542 performances in 1952 over 374 in 1940.

Cabin in the Sky opened exactly two months before *Pal Joey*, a vastly different type of musical with equally far-reaching influence. An all-black "musical fantasy," *Cabin in the Sky* took no cues from *Porgy and Bess,* as it was neither an opera nor a realistic, microcosmic slice of life. It owed nothing in its black orientation to either *Deep River* or *Show Boat,* much less to the formless Harlem revues. Somewhat in the style of Marc Connelly's folk play, *The Green Pastures,*

Lyn Root's script pitted The Lawd's General against Lucifer, Jr., for the soul of Little Joe Jackson, a shiftless backslider with a pious, loving wife, Petunia, who finally redeems him and squeezes him into heaven through a chink in the pearly gates. George Balanchine staged the entire production, Boris Aronson's sets and costumes supplied the necessary mixture of fancy and innocence, and the distinguished cast—Ethel Waters, Dooley Wilson, Todd Duncan, Rex Ingram—brought metaphor to life in the action. The Russian-born Vernon Duke was writing his first book musical after a decade of revues for comediennes such as Fanny Brice and Beatrice Lillie, yet his music seemed to close with the Negro idiom without needing the jazzy elements Gershwin always used, and John Latouche's excellent lyrics combined effortless poetry with the fried chicken and gravy of folklore. Even with the wild African dancing of Katherine Dunham, temptress for the devil's side, the show had dignity and grace, tapping new resources of subject matter as well as new ways to present them.

Only a moderate success, *Cabin* was the first major black book musical. It spawned no immediate successors but did launch Katherine Dunham on a series of black revues and one weighty book show, *Carib Song* (1945). In 1946 Dunham did the choreography for *Windy City,* an offbeat urban fable that somehow never got to New York. Isolated in its short Chicago run, it had no chance to share its riches, which were considerable, particularly in a ballet thrown around, above, and below the steel columns of an elevated railway. Musical comedy dancing was already becoming more than a few frisky intervals in the plot, and such leaders as Agnes De Mille, Robert Alton, Jack Cole, Jerome Robbins, Helen Tamiris, Michael Kidd, Carl Randall, Hanya Holm, and Charles Walters were to be considered prime movers in the form a given musical was to take.

Three years after *Cabin in the Sky* came another black show, Oscar Hammerstein's *Carmen Jones,* an exemplary lesson in how to mount a foreign work in strictly indigenous terms. The source, needless to say, was Bizet's *Carmen,* transplanted from Seville to the American South. World War II was on then, so the cigarette girls worked in a parachute factory, Don José was Joe, an Army corporal, the toreador Escamillo a prizefighter, Husky Miller. Hammerstein stuck like a wonder paste to the Meilhac-Halévy libretto, using spoken dialogue as Bizet had intended but which only recently has replaced Ernest Guiraud's recitative in some of the world's opera houses. There wasn't a trace of the folklorist in Hammerstein's approach, nor the wonderful twilight world of the racial psyche that had sparked *Cabin in the Sky,* but like *Cabin*'s, his blacks weren't Broadway Jim Crows either. Hammerstein always resisted the slangy urban carnivals of musical comedy, and the confrontation between his type of show—the romantic musical, as it were—and the racy glories of Cole Porter and company came to a head in this decade. The one type aspired where the other catered; one was insightful, the other merely slick. Yet both were, ultimately, entertainments, and both could fail as easily as succeed. *Carmen Jones* succeeded, immensely, and not as a gimmick, either. Bizet's score was only slightly shortened, his scoring faithfully scaled down for a Broadway pit by Robert Russell Bennett, and Hammerstein's lyrics bore out his integrity in every line. The opera *Carmen* is a masterwork; Hammerstein called it "the perfect wedding of story and music." The musical *Carmen Jones* is hardly less so.

That perfect wedding of story and music was achieved again in *Oklahoma!* (1943), so well that it is still held up as the first paragon of the form. Certainly, few musicals are more popular in this country, even today, though its unorthodox approach to musical comedy made it an outlandish proposition at the time. It was based on a not very successful folk play by Lynn Riggs, *Green Grow the Lilacs,* absurdly inapposite material for musical comedy adaptation. The famous in-crowd report from New Haven of "no girls, no gags, no chance" is misleading, however, for its out-of-town audiences liked it—how could an audience not like *Oklahoma!*?—and there was very little revising needed during the four weeks of tryout. Still, no one could be sure how it would go in New York; after all, it *was* about these farmers and these cowmen, right?

As the show's choreographer, Agnes De Mille, tells it, "the first night was by no means sold out . . . the curtain went up on a woman churning butter; a very fine baritone came on stage singing the closest thing to lieder our theater has produced. He sang exquisitely with his whole heart about what a morning in our Southwest is like. At the end, people gave an audible sigh and looked at one another—this had seldom happened before. It was music. They sat right back and opened their hearts. The show rolled."

Except for Wilella Waldorf of the *New York Post,* whose track record was outrageous anyway, all the critics raved. Lewis Nichols of the *Times* called it a "folk operetta"; Burns Mantle, George Freedley, and Joseph Wood Krutch compared it to *Show Boat* and *Porgy and Bess.* Mantle phrased it best when he wrote, "it is held to the native idea and kept sufficiently clean to give it standing in the western country from which it springs . . . *Oklahoma!* is different—beautifully different."

Well, it was different, although the authors, De Mille, and director Mamoulian brought it together so smoothly that most people didn't notice just how different until they thought about it later. Unlike the artistic musicals that would make their points through unusual staging techniques—*On the Town* with its narrative choreography or *Allegro* with its bare stage and Greek chorus—*Oklahoma!* was a fresh use of a familiar medium, not an offshoot, nor a new idea, but very solidly constructed and beautifully, sparingly produced. All right, it had a dream ballet and a murder (in self-defense) and the chorus didn't come on till halfway through Act One and even then the ladies of the ensemble weren't wearing anything like tights. Plus it all took place out in the sticks. But none of that was new, for *I Married an Angel* and *Pal Joey* each had a dream ballet, fine ones, and *Lady in the Dark* had three, albeit with song as well as dance. *Rose-Marie, The Vagabond King,* and *Porgy and Bess* had murders. Even Noel Coward's bittersweet little *Bittersweet* had a murder. As for the chorus' delayed entrance, that may have been daring at the time of *Peggy-Ann,* but this was seventeen years later, and chorus girls had been covering their knees in every period show ever produced. Furthermore, rural settings were no novelty. True, such Western gambols as *Girl Crazy, Rio Rita,* and *Hold On to Your Hats* spiked their bucolia with New York's latest answers, but lots of musicals had hymned the genuine boondocks before and nobody shuddered. Granted, the well-known music and lyrics are marvelous. Hammerstein's sunny words and Rodgers folk-inflected tunes disguise a cunning craftsmanship and set a tone for the story, one after the other, whether belying the flippant surface of the "People Will Say We're in Love" rhymes or exposing the ugly underside of the villain Jud Fry in "Lonely Room." Lastly, De Mille's extraordinary ballet at the end of Act One develops the action psychologically, and the use of the secondary characters Ado Annie and Will Parker lends some useful comedy to the proceedings. Agreed. What then, is so special about *Oklahoma!*?

Ah, but. In laying out their adaptation of Riggs' play, Rodgers and Hammerstein did the above-mentioned slightly unusual things in a very unusual way: organically. Like *Show Boat,* but better than *Show Boat, Oklahoma!* told its American grass roots tale in the language of the fruited plain, lighter in tone than *Green Grow the Lilacs,* with dream ballet, murder, and chorus of farmers and cowmen all playing exactly their parts in the story, and no more or less. The seams of musical comedy craftsmanship didn't show this time because this one wasn't a patchwork in the way that nearly all musicals had been before. As De Mille says, it rolled. From the twittering prelude and "Oh, What a Beautiful Mornin' " right through to that joyous reprise of the title song for a finale, the story flowed in one straight line. It never bored. It never tried too hard or traded glitz for glow. It rolled.

Now that they proved the existence of an ideal musical comedy format, one that never compromised with lazy audiences and yet somehow never failed to entertain, Rodgers and Hammerstein aspired a little higher and produced their masterpiece in 1945, *Carousel.* It remained their personal favorite of nine shows, one movie, and one television "spectacular," and although its original New York run of 890 performances places it way behind *Oklahoma!*'s 2212, it has supplanted the earlier work in public appreciation. When the United States sent two musicals to play the Brussels World's Fair in 1959, the chosen ones were *Carousel* and the later *Wonderful Town,* a bright, jazzy musical comedy set in New York. The pairing is a statement of sorts, for these two embody the two basic kinds of musical, the uptempo city show and the sentimental romance, of which *Carousel* is one of the most cherished examples. There is a depth of feeling to its ballads that is lacking in *Oklahoma!*—properly lacking, for *Oklahoma!* is a happy show with a few scary moments while *Carousel* is tragic throughout. Though the score is once again not just lovely but pertinent, it works harder than the *Oklahoma!* score does. The scene in which "If I Loved You" first appears is an extended sequence of dialogue, musical underscoring, songlets to characterize the two principals, and finally the big tune. If "This Was a Real Nice Clambake" and "Blow High, Blow Low" are not earthshakingly nonconformist in the rouser department, "The Highest Judge of All" is a singularly powerful song for a Broadway baritone, even one who is about to assist in an armed robbery.

"The business of an operetta is music," Stark Young had said in 1924. That's doubtless why operettas didn't have to make much sense, at least in 1924. But *Carousel* proved that operettas—read romantic musicals in the forties—could make sense if their business was not purely music but music that distilled personality, the specific personality of the story that inspired it. What better way to define the male lead, Billy Bigelow, than in a long solo scene, as moody and tender as his search for meaning in life? Character arias were the backbone of opera construction for centuries, and any half-decent music dramatist knows the audience has to learn just what's going on in the principals' minds. But in order to reveal some depth of character, musicals had to forgo the AABA pop song form and move into something less one-dimensional than, say, Gaylord Ravenal's "Who Cares If My Boat Goes Upstream?" (*Show Boat*) or Captain Paul's "You Are My Woman" (*East Wind*), both products of the early Hammerstein. Billy's famous Soliloquy, Julie's "What's the Use of Wonderin'?" Carrie's "Mister Snow," and Snow's "Geraniums in the Winder" aren't just songs, they are songs *about* the people who sing them. If *Carousel*'s enduring popularity can be attributed in some degree to America's weakness for sentimental romance—even one . . . no, *especially* one . . . in which the heroine ends up a widow surviving on the knowledge that someone loved her once—it also has to do with how well that romance is delineated through the music, a great deal to do. The business of an operetta is music.

The production team was the same for *Oklahoma!* and *Carousel* (Mamoulian directing, De Mille choreographing, the Theatre Guild overseeing it all), and both were cast with unknowns—Alfred Drake, Joan Roberts, Celeste Holm, and Howard da Silva in the first, John Raitt and Jan Clayton in the second. *Oklahoma!*'s plot unfolded naturalistically over a period of a few weeks, while *Carousel* took fifteen years and roamed into fantasy for its final scenes, putting the dead hero in purgatory and then bringing him back to earth to redeem himself through his widow and daughter. Hammerstein's message is clear, as in *Show Boat:* home, family, love. In the thirties the brazen clamor of urban musical comedies edged out the dream world of home truths, but the creative forties often turned to fantasy to make their point.

Neither *Carmen Jones* nor *Oklahoma!* nor the first act of *Carousel* is realistic. No musical can be, in a way, if only because real people don't sing and dance. But art isn't life, it's form. Once that hurdle was conquered, musicals could be art, and form was a strong point of the forties. As early as 1941 Moss Hart, Kurt Weill, and Ira Gershwin merrily toppled the form problem in a two-act comedy with a full score that wasn't even a musical, *Lady in the Dark*. Hart's book about a liberated but troubled woman who achieves true liberation under psychoanalysis called for one song, "My Ship," and three complex dream sequences, each a one-act opera in prime musical comedy language. Brilliant stagecraft exploited the contrast between the day-to-day scenes and the three garish fantasies: Hattie Carnegie designed costumes for the magazine office, Irene Sharaff those for the dreams, while Harry Horner's sets produced solid walls and office furniture for the real world, revolving stages and tricky paraphernalia for the imaginary one.

Those three little operas are the stuff of which theatre history is made. To distinguish the heroine's subconscious visions from her daily life, the authors dealt exclusively in song and dance—and what songs! Weill's music was by then all-American, agile and hot and sassy, while Gershwin's lyrics remain a model for generations to study. They ranged from the sybaritic jive of the haut-monde Glamour Dream to the nostalgic platitudes of the Wedding Dream, thence to the witty jamboree of the Circus Dream, in which Ethel Merman's *Take a Chance* bombshell, "Eadie Was a Lady," was obliterated by superior material in "Jenny," the saga of the woman "who *would* make up her mind."

The Lady of the title called for someone awfully special, who could play a successful magazine editor, a high-school girl, the toast of Manhattan, and the star attraction of her own "gargantuan three-ring circus" all in the same evening. In Gertrude Lawrence the authors had their Lady, at $3500 a week plus a three-month summer vacation. Lawrence was a decent actress, an uneven though marvelous singer, and an okay dancer, but boy, did she have talent. To this day her performance is a landmark, and it was Lawrence who made *Lady in the Dark* one of the first musicals—or whatever it is—to sell out consistently through its run.

Weill scored an even bigger success two years later with a more or less garden variety musical comedy, *One Touch of Venus* (1943). This was the era of fantasy, so no one was terribly shattered when a statue of the love goddess came to life and complicated Manhattan for a bit. Agnes De Mille's ballet "Forty Minutes for Lunch" was a momentous breakthrough in recording the feel of metropolitan life in choreographic terms, a useful endeavor since most musical comedies favor urban settings anyway. Venus was Mary Martin, a star ever since her naïve striptease to "My Heart Belongs to Daddy" in *Leave It to Me*'s Urkutsk railroad station. With Martin, Kenny Baker, John Boles, Paula Laurence, Teddy Hart, and Harry Clark, the show had familiar faces from radio, films, and the stage to hold things together between entrechats. Ogden Nash's lyrics sought out that synthesis of wit and colloquialisms that lit up his verses, but the spell of romantic fantasy caught the public far more than the levity. They left the theatre humming "Speak Low," not comedy songs.

Among the newer voices, Harold Arlen continued to be the most individual. Harold Rome had yet to write his first book show and Lerner and Loewe had one tacky flop behind them (*What's Up*) while Jule Styne and Frank Loesser had still to sing at all when Arlen collaborated with E. Y. Harburg on the score to *Bloomer Girl* (1944), one of the classier sorts of musical comedy that gave its wartime public the escapism of period sets and costumes but the grim *memento mori* of a Civil War ballet by De Mille, known as "The Harvest According'' on its own. Celeste Holm played a hoopskirt tycoon's daughter who joins forces with her suffragette aunt to wear the militant emblem, bloomers. There was a great deal of patriotic nostalgia in this show—the primeval uproar of the women's movement, the North-South debate, the Underground Railroad, the small-town bourgeoisie exhibiting themselves in procession after church with appropriate side comments from Holm, and a presentation of *Uncle Tom's Cabin* made vivid with Arlen-Harburg songs. The whole score was first-rate musical comedy, individual and inner-purposed, making lyrical points even in the ballads.

Bloomer Girl helped force the trend started by *Oklahoma!* toward musicals set in America's historical past. Chafing at having had to sit through *Bloomer Girl*'s two Agnes De Mille ballets (and the dance-heavy *Carousel* was promised for later that season), George Jean Nathan suggested a musical based on Chicago's Haymarket Riots of 1886 and frothed at the ingenue tactics of *Bloomer Girl*'s Joan McCracken: ''Someone should . . . confide to her that making with the eyes, arching her posticous bulge, girlishly tossing her head about like a badminton quill, and comporting herself assiduously like a coy lambkin does not quite contribute to the impression that she is another Yvonne Printemps.''

Between these highs came lows as poor as anything in the reckless, spendthrift twenties—*The Time, the Place and the Girl* (1942, 13 performances), a reworking of a 1906 show about a sanitarium beset by a schoolgirl invasion and a measles quarantine, or *Dream With Music* (1944, 28 performances) in which a dwarf made an elaborate attempt to seduce Vera Zorina while Aladdin, Sinbad, and assorted houris chose between Balanchine's Eastern *tours jetés* and the tap routines of Henry Le Tang. But every season has its unthinkable flops, and the average for the better-than-average shows was definitely on the upswing. In the area of musical comedy, Arthur Schwartz and Dorothy Fields had to buck the New York World's Fair with *Stars in Your Eyes* (1939), originally intended to mock the growing radicalism of Hollywood (originally entitled, in fact, *Swing to the Left*). But the director, Joshua Logan, didn't think all that satire would go in a big budget musical. Out went the fifth-column jokes, the pointed songs, the carefully planned-out book. All that remained was the movie lot of Monotone Pictures and the cast, Ethel Merman as a temperamental movie star, Jimmy Durante as the studio troubleshooter, Richard Carlson as a roiled-up writer, Mildred Natwick as Dorothy Parker called something else, and Tamara Toumanova as (what else?) a ballerina. Merman and Durante supplied the vigor lacking in the hashed-up book, and lyricist Fields gave The Merm comedy songs as impudent and hip as the old-time heroine's numbers were coy and wistful:

> A new chauffeur on Monday,
> He drives me all day Monday,
> I take a taxi Sunday—
> A lady needs a change!

Speaking of Merman-type lyrics, Cole Porter was the songwriter best suited to her style, rapidly becoming *the* style for musical comedy in the forties. After playing Dubarry for him in 1939, Merman stepped right into *Panama Hattie* a year later, using her clarion charm to play a whore and not give offense, except to the daughter of the man Hattie hoped to marry by the curtain's fall. Things looked tough at first, but when push came to shove, Merman and little Joan Carroll lifted their voices in "Let's Be Buddies" and there wasn't a dry seat in the house.

After *Panama Hattie*'s 501 performances, Merman was ready to play a less convivial hooker in *Sadie Thompson* (1944), the Duke-Dietz-Mamoulian adaptation of *Rain,* but some far from serene rehearsals finished with June Havoc in the role, giving one of the outstanding performances of the decade . . . and closing after seven and a half weeks. Poor Vernon Duke kept writing wonderfully creative music for a succession of shows with book troubles; even his nonbook shows *Two's Company* (1952) and *The Littlest Revue* (1956) failed.

But nothing could stop Porter, at least not in the early forties. *Let's Face It!* (1941) touched lightly on the armed forces in its Herbert and Dorothy Fields book about bored women chasing servicemen from a nearby camp. Danny Kaye left *Lady in the Dark* to wield his talent for rapid-fire patter and childlike hysteria, while Eve Arden, Vivian Vance, and Mary Jane Walsh dropped one-liners from the corners of their mouths like movie gangsters. *Something for the Boys* (1943) was a real wartime show boasting one of Porter's most winning scores, more pop tunish than contextual and rather less cynical than usual for him. *Let's Face It!* was still too with-it for words—"I Hate You, Darling," "You Irritate Me So," "Let's Not Talk About Love"—but *Something for the Boys* struck a more ingenuous note in "I'm in Love with a Soldier Boy," "Could It Be You?" "When My Baby Goes to Town," and "Hey, Good Lookin'." Even the torch song "He's a Right Guy" didn't sound half as blowsy as *Red, Hot and Blue*'s "Down in the Depths (On the ninetieth floor)" or *Panama Hattie*'s "Make It Another Old-Fashioned, Please."

With *Mexican Hayride,* Porter slipped a little in consistency of style. Out of the forgotten recesses of the past the lurid call of operetta intruded into a racy Bobby Clark–June Havoc vehicle with the very legit soprano of Corinna Mura singing trills, portamenti, and high notes in "Sing to Me, Guitar" and "Carlotta" so ravishingly that the audience must have thought it had blundered into the Met. Listening to the cast album Decca made of the show is a lesson in how many varieties of theatre music can turn up in one smash hit musical: "What a Crazy Way to Spend Sunday" is a flat genre piece for the chorus, "Girls (To the right of me, girls to the left of me)" is a hoary-leading-man-with-cane-and-ladies-of-the-ensemble-wiggling-behind-him number, "Count Your Blessings" a prime example of late Tennessee barn dance, "Abracadabra'' and ''There Must Be Someone for Me'' standard comedy songs about sex/love, and Mura's two arias sound like *Son of The Desert Song.* To top it all, the big ballad, ''I Love You''—a Cole Porter ballad, remember—mentions the April breeze, the golden dawn, daffodils, and birds on the wing. Of course, Porter intended it as a parody, but the music sounds awfully sincere.

Before he teamed up with Hammerstein, Rodgers did one last new show with Hart, *By Jupiter* (1942). They did their own book, casting Ray Bolger as the milquetoast husband of amazon Benay Venuta and going for a whole evening of reversed-sex jokes. Some of the critics protested, but the public ate it up because, as before, the team wrote so distinctively and freshly that even a run-of-the-mill musical seemed great. The last Rodgers and Hart show was a revival of *A Connecticut Yankee* in 1943. Despite updating and some new songs, the second go-round was less of a smash, even with the luscious Vivienne Segal as murderous Morgan le Fay.

But while the book show was in its heyday, the revue had literally vanished, replaced by cheap evenings of vaudeville. *Hellzapoppin*'s phenomenal profits called for sequels—*Sons o' Fun* (1941) and *Laffing Room Only* (1944), both with Olsen and Johnson milking their formula for slapstick, mayhem, and supersonic pacing, again with great success. Variety shows were in, hastily thrown together under a title; gone was the tradition of smart revues with top-drawer casts, songs, and sketches. Ed Wynn headlined *Boys and Girls Together* (1940), Lou Holtz and Willie Howard *Priorities of 1942,* while something called *Laugh Time* (1943) pushed variety to its limits, containing Ethel Waters, Frank Fay, Bert Wheeler, the dance team of Buck and Bubbles, and a dog act. Each performer in these shows had a specific slot or two for his specialties gathered from here and there. All that was lacking was unity, rhythm, and artistic enterprise of any kind, yet the above three were successful, for there was no other kind of revue in town.

Some feeling of wholeness was supplied by *This Is the Army* in 1942, Irving Berlin's all-soldier revue and his first Broadway opus since *Louisiana Purchase* (1940), a neat travesty of the Huey Long school of politics with Gaxton and Moore, Vera Zorina and Irene Bordoni ("Latins Know How," she sang, and she ought to know). Berlin had always been big on flag-waving, and in the tense days of World War II *This Is the Army* must have been an exhilarating experience. The cast of three hundred had good material to play, and New Yorkers seemed to enjoy the jingoistic outlook even when one of the ballads was sung by a pilot who mentioned the dropping of bombs almost in passing. But one had to admit being thrilled when the finale filled the stage with uniformed men crossing their bayonets as they prepared to march off to war.

Berlin and Harold Arlen among others donated songs to Michael Todd's bump-and-grind revue *Star and Garter* (1942), as disorganized as the other vaudevilles of its time but at least blessed with veteran burlesquers Bobby Clark and Gypsy Rose Lee. Better organization but lack of sinew kept *Sing Out, Sweet Land* (1944) from making much of a stir. Elie Siegmeister and Walter Kerr's "salute to American folk and popular music" started with the Pilgrims and journeyed rather ponderously through the national panorama, enlivened only by Burl Ives' and Alfred Drake's balladeering and some evocative ensemble dancing.

It took a real showman to hit the apex of the uncoordinated revue. Billy Rose spent $350,000 on *Seven Lively Arts,* on the premise that collecting the "best" of each of them would result in enthralling theatre. A champagne-splattered opening night at the Ziegfeld revealed a great deal too much: Beatrice Lillie and Bert Lahr for yoks, Benny Goodman for jazz, Doc Rockwell for stand-up comedy, Delores Gray and William Tabbert for old-fashioned Cole Porter show tunes, Alicia Markova and Anton Dolin for a new ballet (by Dolin) to music by Igor Stravinsky, and chorus girls for what chorus girls do. Norman Bel Geddes designed some superb sets, May Shaw and Valentina likewise superb costumes; Robert Shaw drilled the chorus, Maurice Abravenal conducted, Hassard Short directed. It should have been wonderful but it never quite jelled, partly because much of the material, especially the sketches by Kaufman, Hart, and Ben Hecht, was second-rate, although Stravinsky's "Scènes de Ballet" scored a triumph. Porter's stuff was definitely not up to his standard. It did contain "Ev'ry Time We Say Goodbye" and "Only Another Boy and Girl," but the patter songs fell flat and "Is It the Girl? (Or is it the gown?)" must be one of the strangest songs ever written by anybody. *Seven Lively Arts* lasted 182 performances, too short a run to recoup Rose's enormous investment. It looked as though the artistic revue were in big trouble—and nobody even owned a television set.

17

Follow the Girls

Spangle Time

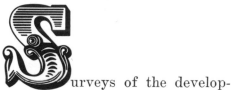

Surveys of the development of an art medium tend to jump from one high point to another, with occasional mention of the false starts, new ideas, and progressive experiments in between.

But too often no representation is given in cultural histories to the trash that makes the world go 'round. Since the main business of theatre is entertainment—sometimes among other things and sometimes just for its own sake—any musical that managed to entertain bears some witness to the identity of the medium as a whole. Aside from the classics (apparent and undercover) are the big shows of this, last, or next season that make a big splash, run for years . . . and vanish so permanently they might well never have existed. What ever happened to *Little Jessie James* (1923) by Harry Archer and Harlan Thompson? An amiable farce about nothing in particular (despite its descriptive title), it lasted 453 performances in New York, an incredible total for the period. It even had Miriam

Hopkins in a featured part and a big hit song ("I Love You"). What of *Sons o' Guns,* 1929's smash hit? What of *Star and Garter* and *Sons o' Fun,* colossi of the forties? Neither one had what might be called superior scores, but the public came running. Admittedly, an entertaining musical that tells an adult story like, say, *The Most Happy Fella,* or one that functions with a great deal of personality like *Guys and Dolls,* or one that showcases a favorite star like *Annie Get Your Gun* has a distinct edge over the show that just entertains period, especially if it does so with less than top-hole score.

On April 8, 1944, the musical comedy *Follow the Girls* opened at the Century Theatre. It wasn't a star vehicle, although one of its cast subsequently became a household word, nor were many established talents on its creative team. Dave Wolper and Albert Borde produced it, Guy Bolton, Eddie Davis, and Fred Thompson did the book, Phil Charig the music, Dan Shapiro and Milton Pascal the lyrics—except for Bolton, all virtually unknown. In the cast were Gertrude Niesen, a popular radio vocalist, Jackie Gleason, Irina Baronova, and William Tabbert. The show received mixed notices but it caught on somehow, and though Niesen's "I Wanna Get Married" had a little play for a while, nothing in the score could be called a hit. Decca had been recording hit shows by then as a matter of course; *This Is the Army, Oklahoma!, Carmen Jones, Mexican Hayride,* the *Connecticut Yankee* revival, and *One Touch of Venus* all came out in the two years preceding *Follow the Girls,* but there was no cast album this time. Yet when *Follow the Girls* closed in 1946, it was the second longest running book musical in Broadway history, topped only by *Oklahoma!,* then entering its fourth continuous year.

Shows were running longer by the second World War. The biggest successes of the twenties barely passed the 500 mark—*The Vagabond King* at 511, *Sunny* at 517, *Good News* at 551, and *The Student Prince* the champion at 608. The hits of the thirties leaned to smaller engagements (except the revues *Hellzapoppin'* and *Pins and Needles,* both over 1000), and for decades the longest running shows were all straight plays or comedies. The fabulous record set by *Irene* at 670 was to stand until *Oklahoma!*, but the late forties brought the average up, with 734 for *Call Me Mister,* 792 for *Where's Charley?,* and 860 for *Song of Norway. Follow the Girls* was surpassed almost immediately by *Carousel,* while *Kiss Me, Kate, Annie Get Your Gun,* and *South Pacific* at the end of the decade closed after passing the 1000 mark.

But these shows were classics, cast albumed, toured for years, sent abroad, and revived forever (the one exception is *Call Me Mister,* doomed to obsolesence by its topical nature and lack of plot). *Follow the Girls,* however, is a puzzle. Despised by many as vulgar and tedious, it was a prime example of the "audience show," one that gets gales of laughter and applause at each performance no matter what the cognoscenti think. Of course, *Carousel* pleased its audience too, but *Carousel* is now part of our heritage while *Follow the Girls* has disappeared, doubtless forever. It was the type of musical that inhabits a low rung in the gap between the occasional artistic endeavors, written and produced mainly by strange names, a sometime thing tending to the garish, paying for the space it occupies with an intent to soothe the ticket buyers, keep the theatres open, and make money. Often it survives a critical drubbing to find a public, although it has gotten harder and harder to do that today. Such shows are still with us, in such instances as *Golden Rainbow* (1968), *Illya, Darling* (1967), and *Over Here!* (1974), all more or less attached to names above the title. *Golden Rainbow* was a hit with Steve Lawrence and Eydie Gorme, *Illya, Darling* a flop with Melina Mercouri; the Andrews Sisters kept *Over Here!* floating for nine months, though it failed to return its investment even with its skeleton cast and cheesy production.

Most shows date at least somewhat, and a show as purely forties as *Follow the Girls* was—wartime forties, specifically—must be paleolithic by now, but the blueprint for this type of show hasn't changed very much. *Follow the Girls* is as good an example as any to demonstrate just how a poor musical works, and no one could describe it better than the admittedly banana-eared George Jean Nathan. In his annual review of the Broadway season, *The Theatre Book of the Year,* he dispensed with critique and simply described what went on scene by scene:

> 8:40 p.m.—Opening: The chorus boys dressed as soldiers, sailors and marines singing the stock introductory number whose lyric consists largely of popular names in the news: Katharine Cornell, Lunt and Fontanne, Frank Sinatra, Walter Winchell, et al. Enter the fat comedian in civilian clothes who wants to enter the canteen to see the strip-teaser whom he loves. He is refused admission and is informed that only soldiers and sailors may enter. A sailor approaches and tells him that his uniform has a zipper attachment. After cavorting about the stage for several minutes, indicating pleased meditation, the fat comic rips off the sailor's uniform. Blackout.
>
> 9 p.m.—Inside the canteen, with the girls dressed in enough spangles to outfit a circus. The tenor sings a song, "The grass is always green where you are, the sky is always blue where you are." The fat comic reappears, curves his right hand over his head and ejaculates, "What the hell!" Follow two hoofers who negotiate a fast dance, the woman partner singing a ditty called "You Don't Dance" and the male partner, at the conclusion of the hoofing, drolly kicking her in the seat.
>
> 9:15 p.m.—The chorus reappears in more spangles and is followed by the entrance of Bubbles, the strip-teaser, who delivers a number called "Strip Flips Hip," duly accompanied by the hip flips. The fat comic curves his right hand over his head and ejaculates, "What the hell!" Enter a regal brunette. The strip-teaser tells her to go about her business. "I am my own mistress!" haughtily retorts the regal one. "That must be wonderful for you for a change!" snaps back the stripper.
>
> 9:25 p.m.—Two male and one female hoofer perform a hard-shoe number, the meanwhile delivering a ditty, "Thanks for a Lousy Evening." Re-enter Bubbles, the stripper, backed by the chorus in still more spangles, and followed by the fat comic, who curves his hand over his head and ejaculates, "What the hell!" "When I was in burlesque," observes Bubbles, "they yelled 'Lights off' and I thought they said 'Tights off'." Then

a song by the fat comic to Bubbles: "You're perf, you're magnif, you're wonderf, you're grand."

9:32 p.m.—"Here comes Anna Viskinova, the greatest ballet dancer in the world!" "She's beautiful!" "She's the toast of the town!" "You'll all adore her!" Enter Irina Baronova, of the Russian ballet, who is made to execute, of all things, a stock Marche Militaire.

9:42 p.m.—The girls come on in five times the number of spangles they have worn before, parade around, and exit. Bubbles reappears in a purple light and moans a paraphrase of "Body and Soul" called "Twelve O'Clock and All's Well."

9:48 p.m.—A hoofer shuffles before a curtain while the scene is being shifted. The fat comic appears, curves his hand over his head and ejaculates, "What the hell!" Blackout.

9:50 p.m.—Scene: the trophy room. The chorus girls come on in even more spangles. The fat comic mentions the Virgin Islands. The tenor in love with the ballet dancer says wittily, "I have an idea that the virginity of the natives is somewhat overestimated." He follows with a reprise, "The grass is always green where you are, the sky is always blue where you are." At its conclusion, he observes that he thinks the regal brunette is a suspicious character. "She is a witch," he allows. "You mean bitch," exclaims the ballet dancer.

10 p.m.—The ballet dancer does another turn in a red dress, the number naturally being called "Flamingo Dance."

10:10 p.m.—Bubbles and the entire company, in spangles, appear after the three hoofers before noted have negotiated another dance, ending with one male kicking the other in the seat. The fat comic curves his hand over his head and ejaculates, "What the hell!" "Follow the Girls," loudly sings the ensemble. Curtain.

Act II. 10:20 p.m.—The girls enter clad in enough spangles to outfit ten circuses. The scene being a flower garden, the tenor, backed by the sailors, sings a song about John Paul Jones. Another dance by the hoofers, at the conclusion of which the female member for a change kicks one of the males in the seat. The fat comic curves his hand over his head and ejaculates, "What the hell!" The tenor and ballet dancer come on arm in arm. The tenor reprises, "The grass is always green where you are, the sky is always blue where you are."

10:35 p.m.—A room in a house. In order to keep his rival from marrying the strip-teaser, the fat comic gives him a

Mickey Finn and tells him he is on a boat and that the sea is very rough. Convincing himself, the fat comic rushes to the bathroom to vomit. On come the two hoofers who squirt seltzer bottles at the rival to persuade him that he is drowning. Blackout.

10:45 p.m.—The show-girls, spangled to the ears, walk on in the rôles of bridesmaids. Bubbles (Gertrude Niesen) sings a saucy number, "I Wanna Get Married," which, humorously delivered, provides some surcease, even though one verse has to do with the singer's purchase of a bureau and the wish that some man may share her drawers.

10:50 p.m.—Another dance by the ballet dancer, followed by a couple of ballroom dancers with the male partner swinging the female around on his shoulders (the ballroom they come from must be peculiar). The regal brunette then reappears. The fat comic learns that she is a German spy, thus freeing from suspicion the ballet dancer. Several plants in the audience hiss the brunette, whereupon she walks to the footlights and drolly hisses the audience. The fat comic curves his hand over his head and ejaculates, "What the hell!" (He has previously donned a WAVE's blue skirt, leading an elderly officer to mistake him for a woman and to make a date with him.)

11 p.m.—The chorus now again issues forth in more spangles than have been seen on the stage in the last fifty years combined. The fat comic and Bubbles, aided by two of the comedy hoofers, sing a song, "A Tree That Grows in Brooklyn," which scintillatingly includes allusions to Flatbush, Jamaica and Canarsie. The hoofers go into another dance, terminating with one kicking another in the seat.

11:10 p.m.—The entire bespangled company gathers at the footlights and lifts its voices, "The grass is always green where you are, the sky is always blue where you are." The fat comic puts his arms around Bubbles; the tenor puts his arm around the ballet dancer; the hoofers again kick one another in the seats; and the fat comic curves his hand over his head and ejaculates, "What the hell!" Curtain.

The public, albeit sober, thought it was swell.

18

On the Town

"Why Be Afraid to Dance?"

The biggest hits of the forties were mainly musical plays or romantic shows, but there was no lack of musical comedy. Certainly, it has the format that most people find easiest to enjoy—fast, funny, dancey, and lilting, a bit of fancy here, a bit of shtick there, a hip urban setting (or at least a slick tone to the dialogue, whatever the setting), a big noisy overture—very reassuring, that—a big noisy chorus, and possibly, though not necessarily, a big noisy woman belting out comedy songs to keep things hopping.

The most admired musicals aren't exclusively of that type, however. Counting by performance totals of the original runs, only ten of the top twenty book shows, and only three of the top ten, are musical comedies as such. The others are either larger in scope like *Fiddler on the Roof* or romantic musicals like *Man of La Mancha*. These shows and others like them stay with the public longer than musical comedy, for their draw on the senses is keener, less diverting than cerebral, and their showmanship less flimsy than gripping. *Follow the Girls* is a prize sample of the gimcrack musical comedy of the lower orders, but really gifted creators can make a dazzling show out of essentially the same materials; before the forties, aces like Porter, the Gershwins, Rodgers and Hart, and their various book writers (not omitting the gentler-styled Kern, Bolton, and Wodehouse) enjoyed repeated successes with the format. The only differences between a *Follow the Girls* and a *Guys and Dolls* are talent, good taste, and a point of view.

But not only must the material itself be sharp, it must be produced well to go over. An inferior director can turn a great show into a flop, and in this area musical comedy had a benefactor in George Abbott. Sometimes writing the book, sometimes producing, but mostly directing *and* editing the book, he has put his stamp on the way comic musicals happen—blackout punch lines, crossovers, and all. Although his early tries in the field were with Rodgers and Hart in the thirties, after *Pal Joey* in 1940 he spent ten years working with less established (sometimes virtually anonymous) writers, and his first post-*Pal Joey* show, *Best Foot Forward* (1941), was cast with teenagers like Nancy Walker, June Allyson, and Maureen Cannon. The Army draft may have been the reason for hanging the story line on prom weekend at a boy's prep school, but as Abbott was to prove throughout his career, musicals don't need strong plots if they have a good score, a funny script, and solid directorial leadership.

Abbott could have his flops, though. *Beat the Band* (1942) devoted its two and a half hours to the underground of jive and hepcats, with an orchestra in the pit and a student combo on stage. David Lichine's choreography climaxed in Act Two with a blaring jitterbug number, "The Steam Is on the Beam," but the book was hopeless, Atkinson thought the score "less like music than the clearing of a throat," and Abbott himself called it "the poorest job of directing and producing that I ever did." Even Abbott couldn't save *Beggar's Holiday*

(1946) when called in to doctor it during its chaotic tryout. John Latouche's updating of *The Beggar's Opera* was not as vicious as *The Threepenny Opera,* and its interracial romance was considered a significant step toward mature love stories, but Duke Ellington's music did not adapt well to the demands of musical comedy. It struck its own stance rather than that of the show, and the ballads tended to plod rather than expand. Still, *Beggar's Holiday* did make a brave stab at integrating current pop musical trends into formal stage use, while *Beat the Band* merely put a few bits of "white heat" on display.

Barefoot Boy with Cheek (1947), an adaptation of Max Shulman's wacky college stories, was an unfortunate illustration of what can go wrong in the Abbott-style format. Campus satire was glued rather obviously to the mongoloid football hero ("the legendary Eino Fflliikkiinnenn"), the venal frat brothers of Alpha Cholera, the stick-in-the-mud sociology prof, and the haughty sorority girl (Noblesse Oblige) twenty years after *Good News* had done it better (and twenty-seven years before the *Good News* revival would do it worse with a ghastly rewritten book). Nancy Walker extracted the comic possibilities in Yetta Samovar, the campus radical, but her material was so rotten it was like pulling teeth. Nathan claimed *Barefoot Boy with Cheek* presented undergraduate life as "a cross between imbecility and St. Vitus disease," but he could have been describing the more remiss musical comedies in general, making up in energy what they lack in foundation.

On the other hand, *High Button Shoes* (1947) showed how far Abbott could go with good material—or, better, how far good material could go under the protection of a wise director. Set in 1913, *High Button Shoes* had a good score by Jule Styne and Sammy Cahn, wonderful performers, and tremendous choreography in its corner plus a little mild nostalgia. As a real estate con man, Phil Silvers radiated the sure savvy of his baggy-pants apprenticeship in burlesque, Nanette Fabray sparkled with charm, and Jerome Robbins concocted a wildly farcical seaside ballet derived from Mack Sennett that is still talked of today. Its memory shone extra brightly in 1974 when *Mack and Mabel* offered Gower Champion's Sennett pastiche, but more of that later.

A lead comic like Silvers is always a good start for a slick musical comedy, but even a star turn needs a book and score to back it up, and *Look Ma, I'm Dancin'* (1948) tended to slip when Nancy Walker wasn't spoofing the ballet world. *Where's Charley?,* however, had the benefit of Brandon Thomas' well-made farce *Charley's Aunt* to derive from as well as Ray Bolger's inspired transvestite clowning.

The best thing about the form of these Abbott shows is their adaptability. The theatre must pay its way to survive, of course, but it needn't be a ruthlessly commercial show factory either. In fact, the best Abbott show of the decade seemed fresh and daring even while drawing heavily on established practices. Like so many other musical comedies, *On the Town* (1944) had a *very* slender plot line, no stars, and an unheralded production team. But it happened to be based on a ballet, a short piece called "Fancy Free," laid out by Jerome Robbins to Leonard Bernstein's music. Their sketch of three sailors on shore leave impressing three girls in a bar caught the jittery rhythm of New York in both music and movement, and the juicy collaboration of content and form was carried through brilliantly when opened up into a full evening. Betty Comden and Adolph Green supplied book and lyrics that were carefree without being scatterbrained, tracking romance in the simple terms of everyday speech, while Bernstein's tunes glowed with the freedom that trained musicianship brings to pop music.

On the Town's biggest treat, however, was its dancing. Agnes De Mille had weaned Broadwayites on the new look of theatre choreography (with a little help from the thirties), but her work came off as set pieces plunked down in the middle of the story. Sometimes they developed naturally out of the context, as with Laurey's lengthy dream in *Oklahoma!*, but more often they capped the action, cutting into it from a different medium, as in *Bloomer Girl*'s Civil War ballet. Since *On the Town*'s microscopic story line had room for all the development it could get, what could be more natural than to extend the narration through dance, the original source of the play? Robbins created his best work for Broadway in "Miss Turnstiles," the public life of this month's poster girl; in a pas de deux after "Lonely Town"; in a raucous production number for Times Square; in a travesty on nightclub routines; and in two different views of the Coney Island mystique. Bernstein rose to the occasion momentously, hiding his strict formalism under the vitality of his urban-textured ballet music. What with Kurt Weill writing out his own orchestrations and dance arrangements for *One Touch of Venus* the year before, musical comedy was suddenly in command of a surge of "legit" sound; the full score of such works was no longer a string of songs handed over to others for scoring, dance interpolations, and incidental music. Just as George Gershwin brought the complexion of pop music to classical forms, now Bernstein brought classical craft to pop music. Two of the *One Touch of Venus* ballets were recorded in Decca's cast album, an unusual omen; of *On the Town*'s two recordings, the RCA Victor gave equal time and billing to Bernstein's dance music, a sign of the public's acceptance of the dance portions of musical comedy as being—as needing to be—more than chance potpourris.

Besides setting a new standard for the integration of dance into the drama, *On the Town* was also a landmark show for not just being set in New York but caught up in it. The dizzy chasing around after Miss Turnstiles wasn't only vigorous—it was Manhattan-vigorous, atmospheric without literalizing, outgoing and lowdown the way Times Square used to be, when a clip joint could be amusingly parodied. New York isn't a very nice place any more, and a musical show that portrays it realistically, as *Seesaw* did in 1973, can't help but offend somewhat. But in 1944, ration cards notwithstanding, New York was chummier and certainly far less dangerous, so the authors and Abbott and Robbins could only delight with their re-creation of one crazy day around town. The critics overworked the word "fresh" and sprained their thesauruses devising encomiums for the cast—cabdriver Nancy Walker, anthropologist Comden and sailor Green, and la Turnstiles herself, Sono Osato.

On the Town's format is a special one, fraught with pitfalls, but the forties were full of beans and some later musicals used dance almost as heavily as *On the Town,* though with less acumen in slipping it into the plot. Comden, Green, Robbins, and Abbott tackled the twenties in another dancing urban show, *Billion Dollar Baby* (1945), but not everyone responded to the satire or the distinctive leading lady, Joan McCracken, and Morton Gould's music just didn't jell. Even *On the Town*'s enthusiastically embarked national tour collapsed on its first date, in Chicago, though in an admittedly inferior production. As some very New York shows were to prove, parish entertainments have trouble out of the parish.

19

The Forties (II)

"Here's to Your Illusions"

E. Y. Harburg once said, "I don't believe the theatre is a place for photographic reproduction. That's why I'm attracted to fantasy, to things with a poetic quality. Through fantasy, I feel that a musical can say things with greater effectiveness about life. It's great for pricking balloons, for exploding shibboleths. Of course I want to send people out of the theatre with the glow of having a good time, but I also think the purpose of a musical is to make people think."

Somewhere below, the shade of George Jean Nathan is raging and cringing, but Harburg's librettos enjoyed the kind of success that turns an idea into a viable commodity, the idea being that a razzmatazz musical comedy didn't have to be mere entertainment yet could entertain flawlessly. Unlike another thoughtful librettist, Hammerstein, Harburg shied away from romantic realms, emphasizing comedy to get his message across. His masterpiece arrived on January 10, 1947, *Finian's*

Rainbow, a fantasy grounded in reality with social commentary that connected with the up-front works of the thirties. Half the chorus were blacks, sharecroppers being railroaded by a bigoted Southern senator ("But before I yield up our glorious South—and her sister commonwealth the U.S.A.—I will lay down my life. I will go further than that—I'll filibuster. Back, you crackpots, and forward, America. Forward to the hallowed principles of our forefathers! Forward to yesterday!"). Into their midst comes a blarney-filled Irishman with a pot of gold stolen from the leprechauns to be planted in American soil. He hopes it will multiply like the gold in Fort Knox and make everybody millionaires ("But are there no poor in America," asks his daughter, "no ill-housed, no ill-clad?" "Of course," he replies—"but they're the best ill-housed and best ill-clad in the whole world.").

The *Finian's Rainbow* book by Harburg and Fred Saidy was a gem, funny in itself rather than dependent on the specialties of a Bert Lahr or Bobby Clark. There were no names above the title, but Ella Logan, David Wayne, and Donald Richards all made their marks (Finian himself was the so-right-for-the-part Irish comedian Albert Sharpe), and Burton Lane's music sported an amazing amount of smash hits—"How Are Things in Glocca Morra?" "If This Isn't Love," "Something Sort of Grandish," "Old Devil Moon," and "Look to the Rainbow." Harburg's lyrics made the most of his socioeconomic satire in songs like "Necessity," "When the Idle Poor Become the Idle Rich," and a giant spiritual for the first-act finale, "That Great Come-and-Get-it-Day":

> I'll get my gal that calico gown;
> I'll get my mule that acre of groun';
> 'Cause word has come
> From Gabriel's horn:
> The earth beneath your plow is a-buddin'
> And now it's yourn!

Now that musical comedy dances were expected to uphold the consistency of a show's individual tone, Michael Kidd obliged with a zany picture of the American dream of affluence in "When the Idle Poor" and a Gaelic free-for-all for "Look to the Rainbow," but *Finian's Rainbow* made a spectacular place for itself in the matter of race relations. This had already been a feature of *Deep River* and *Beggar's Holiday,* but never before for the mass audience of an allegedly escapist musical comedy. One scene, almost a self-contained sketch on stereotypes, showed a black college student paying his tuition money by butlering for the bigoted senator. He is instructed in the fine points of shuffling and julep serving, but when the senator gets some bad news and calls for a Bromo Seltzer, the new butler goes into his Uncle Tom routine and the lights fade on the villain crawling in desperation toward his Bromo, which is forever out of reach in the hand of the snail-paced, yawk-yawking servant.

Four years later Harburg and Saidy tried fantasy–*cum*–socioeconomic satire again with *Flahooley,* but the conception was foiled by faulty cohesion of forces. The Peruvian vocal phenomenon, Yma Sumac, was the nominal star, singing three and a half octaves' worth of special material composed in an unknown but deranged-sounding tongue and remote Aztec style that could never coexist with Sammy Fain's charming pop tunes. Sumac played an Arabian princess who brings her busted Aladdin's lamp to America for repair at the toy factory of B. G. Bigelow (Ernest Truex). Bigelow's fair-haired boy has devised a laughing doll whose unprecedented popularity causes economic disaster and national panic, killing off the genie (Irwin Corey) who had popped out of Sumac's lamp. Barbara Cook's sincerity brought him back to life, and Sumac paired off incongruously with Truex, but it was a case of an integrated score with a clumsy book to integrate with. This was a sad loss, as Harburg's lyrics had something special to share with the public. In the opening scene, the Bill and Cora Baird marionettes—that's right, puppets—advised the audience not to take on so about the hectic vagaries of society:

Man, man, silly man,
Full of human folly!
Why be Grable fan,
Ku Klux Klan,
When you can
Be Kukla, Fran
And Ollie?

"Come out of the woodwork, brother," they chortled, "and join the brotherhood of man!" With Senator Joseph McCarthy leading the brotherhood in a witch hunt at home and Korea adding to the trouble abroad, no wonder Harburg had a hard time selling economic satire in 1951.

Fantasy was also the strong suit of Frederick Loewe and Alan Jay Lerner at the time. They had bombed out with *What's Up* (1943), a lackluster frolic about soldiers loose in a girl's school, but *The Day Before Spring* (1945) was a sophisticated romantic musical set at a college reunion and featuring a foiled adulterous elopement decorated with Anthony Tudor's ballets and one rather jarring moment when the heroine received advice from Plato, Voltaire, and Freud. Two years later, two months away from *Finian's Rainbow,* came *Brigadoon,* like it a fantasy but unlike it a romantic show twelve stations removed from musical comedy. There was a relaxed earthiness from two secondary characters, but the bulk of the show was a heady Scotch mist about an archaic village that appears but one day in each century, stumbled upon by two world-weary Americans. Robert Lewis' direction pointed up the alluring ingenuousness of the simple life as compared to the disillusioning, boozy New York rat race, making *Brigadoon* at least that little bit more than a contemporary operetta. But then, the whole affair was invested with an unusually strong productions on all counts. The casting was excellent, all unknowns as so often in the forties for economics had not yet made the signing of the star's contract all that important an announcement at backers' auditions. Oliver Smith's sets were gothic and colorful by turns, and De Mille's atmospheric dances her best till then, with James Mitchell's sword dance in the wedding scene a thrilling tour de force and Lidija Franklin's funeral solo pitched at an artistic level far above what the Ziegfeld Theatre was used to.

The fast colored society of St. Louis in 1898 formed the subject of a lively show with period costumes but modern flair, *St. Louis Woman* (1946). Passing up *Cabin in the Sky*'s fantasy-folklore and *Carmen Jones'* gutsy music drama, *St. Louis Woman* was sui generis, three acts instead of the usual two, dazzlingly beautiful to see, cast from the front ranks of black comedian-singer-dancers (as Butterfly, Pearl Bailey made up for approximate dancing with dead-on ad libbing), and scored by Harold Arlen and Johnny Mercer as if pop songs had posterity to answer to instead of the top ten. Mercer's lyrics flowed out conversationally with an uncanny ear for the spoken language; even the song titles speak true: "Anyplace I Hang My Hat Is Home," "Come Rain or Come Shine," "I Wonder What Became of Me?" "Lil' Augie Is a Natural Man," "Sleep Peaceful, Mr. Used-to-Be," and "Leavin' Time." (Just a few blocks uptown the long-running *Are You With It?*, with a carnival background, pleasantly upheld hollow convention with "Here I Go Again," "This Is My Beloved," and "Just Beyond the Rainbow.") Though he was still working for a mass audience in Hollywood, Harold Arlen now combined universal melodic appeal with heightened compositional techniques in his Broadway scores, achieving an immense range of expression in "I Had Myself a True Love" without making it sound like an undressed aria. The song is an aria, in fact, rich in its vocalism, soaring, wide open, and yet as natural as a street vendor's cries. Book problems brought *St. Louis Woman* down after only 113 performances, but many who saw it speak of it as a super show with a tang all its own.

Far removed from *St. Louis Woman*'s earthy amoralizing was *Lute Song* (1946), a "love story with music" adapted by Sidney Howard and Will Irwin from an ancient Chinese classic, *Pa-Pa-Ki.* This tale of a faithful wife who searches for her scholar husband only to find him remarried against his will was intended to be a spectacle of high style but seemed more like an out-of-whack vehicle for faithful wife Mary Martin and even more for Robert Edmond Jones' stunning sets and costumes. John Houseman and Yeichi Nimura's staging emphasized the ritualistic dignity of Chinese theatre, but the evening got its biggest lift from the graceful score of Raymond Scott and Bernard Hanighen, a string of numbers that purposely stood outside the story, defining the reserved ethos of the production rather than specific characters or situations. Hanighen's poetic lyrics sometimes strayed into an awkward, vaporous netherworld, but they strived for a poetry to enhance the show's low-key chinoiserie ("While the stars steal on China like a sigh . . .").

But if Harburg exploited musical fantasies to conceal a message in entertaining wrappings, some authors just exploited fantasy. *Toplitzky of Notre Dame* (1946) somehow got an angel into Our Lady's football team, while *Happy as Larry* (1950) gave Burgess Meredith the once-in-a-lifetime chance to play his own twice-married grandfather for a grand total of three performances. The common or garden forties musical could get away with a great deal while the public crowded into theatres for diversion, but a fantasy must be securely defined in tone to suspend all that disbelief. As Nathan pointed out, the cast of *Happy as Larry* seemed helplessly undecided as to "whether they were supposed to be appearing . . . in burlesque melodrama or in a Christmas pantomime at Drury Lane."

Even as the more or less fantastic shows proliferated, realistic musicals with noticeably American themes developed the *Show Boat–Oklahoma!* tradition, while such fluff as *The Girl from Nantucket* (1945) and *Louisiana Lady* (1947) apparently chose their locales after examining the local costumer's trunk. Rodgers and Hammerstein followed up their two period adaptations with a third "musical play," as they quite honestly assessed them, this one an original in modern dress. *Allegro* (1947), directed as well as choreographed by Agnes De Mille, was a unique production: no sets, just backwall projections, and a large cast including a Greek chorus that commented on the action in song and speech. Heralded by a persistent tantara of publicity, and overshadowed as it was bound to be coming after *Oklahoma!* and *Carousel, Allegro* struck some theatregoers as trivial and pretentious; others considered it the supreme achievement of the era. Certainly, its simple story and avoidance of show factory pandemonium were enough to disappoint those who liked their musicals splashy and bombastic.

Allegro presented the first forty years of a doctor who has to choose between material success in Chicago and the quiet rewards of home-town practice—an easy decision in a Hammerstein libretto, where the cards are dealt against the big city in every hand. As in *Show Boat,* nothing works out when you desert your roots: the doctor's city clients are all wealthy hypochrondriacs, denying him the fulfillment of his vocation, and his grasping wife cheats on him with a more sympathetic colleague. Jo Mielziner's subtle lighting effects were a noteworthy contribution to theatre history, and if De Mille's abstract staging was too mannered for some tastes, she absorbed *Allegro*'s mood splendidly in her mass groupings, enpicturing the charged tensions of the urban rat race in a frenzied dance for the title song and in a cocktail party scene with all the guests crushed together on a platform singing nonsense syllables at each other.

Originally intended to take Joseph Taylor, Jr., through his life, *Allegro* settled for childhood, med school, early marriage to the girl next door, crisis in Chicago, and anagnorisis in the final scene, where he rejects his new post as physician-in-chief of a new hospital pavilion and decides to return home to "people I understand." Though the story unfolded chronologically, the constant use of the omniscient chorus made it almost surreal, some musical numbers turning into little cantatas for soloists and ensemble. Without the reassuring status quo of scenery, *Allegro* had to make its points in the immediacy of action: when little Joey first learned to walk he was unseen, the moment covered by his mother, his grandmother, and the chorus gazing out joyfully into the theatre at his first struggling steps, cheering him on in "One Foot, Other Foot." Later, in Act Two, when his shattered marriage and lifeless career crushed Doctor Taylor, his dead mother appeared behind him singing "Come Home":

> You will find a world of honest friends who miss you,
> You will shake the hands of men whose hands are strong.
> And when all their wives and kids run up and kiss you,
> You will know that you are back where you belong . . .

Then, in the finale, when Taylor rejected one bright future for a far brighter one, his mother and grandmother came out with the same elation as they had when he learned to walk, and the chorus reprised "One Foot, Other Foot" in a sincere outburst of the kind Broadway sees but seldom.

Therein lies the difficulty—one of them, at any rate—for musical comedy finds its audience most readily when the leap of the evening is toward a rousing last chorus of "There's No Business Like Show Business" or, sentimentally, the haphazard drivel of "Look for the Silver Lining"—when, in other words, you don't have to *believe.* There are potent exceptions, of course, like that monolithic final hymning of "The Impossible Dream" in *Man of La Mancha.* But that show was not a moralistic work like *Allegro;* it was *easier* to believe.

Not everyone was ready in 1947 for this junction of artless plot with arty production, and *Allegro* lasted only 315 performances (and lost money because of its gigantic cast), but oddly enough, the critics responded to it far more than the public. Howard Barnes: "a consummate theatrical achievement and an electrifying entertainment"; Richard Watts, Jr.: "another landmark in pushing back the frontier of the American musical drama"; George Freedley: "a masterpiece which surpassed [*Oklahoma!* and *Carousel*] by far in its conception''; Atkinson: ''the staging has the eloquent simplicity of genuine art . . . it has made history on Broadway.''

Alas, genuine art that lasts but ten months has a hard time making a permanent impression, and though its optimistic message has long been a staple of American cinema good and bad, and its advanced lessons in staging were eventually learned in the sixties, *Allegro* has for all practical purposes vanished from the scene. Hammerstein was contemplating a revival with a new second act just before he died; now its future, if any, is left to others.

The team returned to more conventional storytelling in *South Pacific* (1949), acting as their own producers and employing stars in their shows for the first time, Mary Martin and Ezio Pinza. But the plot, adapted from James Michener's short stories about the Pacific islands before and during World War II, was still out of the norm for a musical. The Martin-Pinza romance united a race-conscious young Navy nurse from Little Rock with an aging French planter who has two mulatto children, and the even more outspoken secondary love story brought together a Tonkinese girl and a Navy lieutenant who underlined this hopeless, rapturous fling with an adult, un–musical-comedy assessment of the way the world looks on such matters, in ''Carefully Taught'' (''to hate all the people your relatives hate . . .'').

The occupation of an alien world by American seabees provided a natural background for comedy, a strategic feature of a book-strong show with virtually no dancing. Joshua Logan's fluid direction eliminated the fifteen-second breaks for set changes that sap the arching vitality of a theatrical evening. *Lady in the Dark* managed it with superimposed dream sequences, *Knickerbocker Holiday* with the use of a single set (with two tiny insets), the George Abbott musical comedies with crossovers in front of a traveler curtain, and *Allegro* had no sets to change. But Jo Mielziner designed *South Pacific*'s drops and wing pieces for flow: as one scene ended, the next was already beginning. The show was an entity, a continuous stream of play and music avoiding the artificial contrivances of the musical form the way a straight play does, yet enjoying the heightened expression of lyricism. Uncontaminated entertainment, it thoroughly deserved its prizes: Tonys, Donaldsons, the Critics' Circle award for best musical, and the 1950 Pulitzer Prize for drama.

After the smash success of his sole adventure in the realm of urban musical comedy, albeit via fantasy, in *One Touch of Venus,* Kurt Weill suffered a bad turn with a baffling operetta about Benvenuto Cellini, *The Firebrand of Florence* (1945). Casting Weill's wife, Lotte Lenya, opposite the eternal Pop-off, Melville Cooper, made for a tenuous assimilation of warring styles, and Weill re-embraced a local setting two years later with a complete departure from his previous work, a "folk play with music" based on Elmer Rice's 1929 hit, *Street Scene.* The action took place on "the sidewalk in front of a sandstone tenement house in New York City," following the comings and goings of the occupants and their neighbors. In the blistering heat of summer, a woman nears the end of her pregnancy, a schoolgirl receives an art school scholarship the day before her family is evicted, a jitterbugging couple tear up the sidewalk in a hot pas de deux, a young couple trapped by poverty break off their engagement, and the girl's mother and her lover are murdered by the outraged husband, leaving the play to close on yet another blistering summer day. In *Theatre Arts,* Rosamund Gilder called *Street Scene* "a symphony of the city with its strands of love and yearning and violence woven into the pattern of daily drudgery. [Weill's] music reflects . . . the ebb and flow of anonymous existence."

Street Scene's Zolaesque realism raised eyebrows in 1929 as a three-act play: in 1947 it was no less startling as a musical, or as Weill aptly put it, "a real Broadway opera." Langston Hughes' lyrics vivified the humanity of Rice's shocker, torturedly eloquent in "Lonely House," "Somehow I Never Could Believe," and "What Good Would the Moon Be?"

while the composer worked almost exclusively in operatic forms, insisting that "Broadway represents the living theater in this country, and an American opera, as I imagined it, should be a part of the living theater." He never lost touch with the vernacular sound, but even so, the *Street Scene* score has a passion and a poetry that raised it above the level of even high-class Broadway and into genuine artistic reaches. Little was left of Rice's book (adapted by Rice himself); music took over; music could do that now.

Love Life (1948), a Weill-Lerner collaboration, was perhaps the most American musical comedy of the late forties, for its form was a variety show of past American theatrical species and its subject was American marriage. Carrying an unaging Sam and Susan Cooper from 1791 to 1948, *Love Life* was a cavalcade of vaudeville turns—crooners, madrigalists, minstrel combinations, barbershop quartets, a magician, a trapeze act, pantomimists—all utilized to greater or less effect in a social satire, while the marriage itself was destroyed by such forces of social "progress" as industrialism, women's rights, and middle-class materialism. *Love Life* didn't subdue its freewheeling entertainment sharply enough for the commentary to come through, at least for some tastes, though it was better received than *Park Avenue* (1946), a satire on the divorce craze rooted firmly in present-day New York.

Weill abandoned his adopted country as the setting for his last work on Broadway, joining up with Maxwell Anderson for the "musical tragedy" *Lost in the Stars* (1949), a powerful adaptation of Alan Paton's South African novel *Cry the Beloved Country.* By then the great white father of arty Negro epics, Rouben Mamoulian directed for grandeur, bringing out the larger implications of the eternal white-black conflict. Parts of Anderson's libretto were perhaps too melodramatic, but his and Weill's score was well-nigh faultless, far less "operatic" than *Street Scene* and without a trace of pseudo-African claptrap in the orchestration—a significant achievement in a business where the composer often relinquishes his own voice for pastiche or local color. Though the man in The Street will tell you that anything billed as a musical tragedy cannot run, *Lost in the Stars* paid the rent for thirty-four weeks, admittedly in one of musical comedy's worst seasons ever: one decent and five deathly revues, two out-and-out operas, six stock musical comedies, three of them disasters, and *Lost in the Stars*.

Before his death in 1950, Weill completed a one-act opera using American folk songs, *Down in the Valley,* and left unfinished a Huckleberry Finn musical he and Anderson were working on. Oddly enough, his present high status is based largely on his worst Broadway flop, *The Threepenny Opera,* which was finally revived downtown on Christopher Street in a translation by Marc Blitzstein, filling the 299-seat Theatre de Lys for six years. Justly admired for his soaring conception of music's place in musical theater, Weill refused to be typed as a composer of American operas. In his own words, "it's my opinion that we can and will develop a musical-dramatic form in this country, but I don't think it will be called 'opera,' or that it will grow out of the opera which has become a thing separate from the commercial theatre. It will develop from, and remain part of, the American theatre—'Broadway' theatre, if you like."

One of the two operas that 1949–50 season was *The Consul,* an extraordinarily powerful drama of people trapped behind the Iron Curtain trying to crawl out to freedom under a barrage of red tape and bureaucratic indifference. Hailed by critics and public, *The Consul* was the work of Gian Carlo Menotti, a man who composes operas rather than musical comedies or plays and who bears no connection to the stream of American theatre history but for the fact that several of his operas were first given on Broadway. The other opera was Marc Blitzstein's *Regina.* This one was at least the product of an American theatre man, but the unapproachable Blitzstein was still inspired to write tunes even sharp theatregoers had trouble absorbing. His subject was a likely one for native music theatre, Lillian Hellman's *The Little Foxes,* and his treatment was forthright and arresting, but whereas musically *Porgy and Bess* and *Street Scene* have a place in a developing Broadway tradition, both *The Consul* and to some extent *Regina* stand apart from the musical vernacular—which is all to the good for their own success but leaves them on the outskirts of the national theatre milieu. Though they both proved again that through-composed music drama is viable for Broadway, they themselves belong on the legitimate lyric stage of an opera house, which is exactly where both of them have since resided.

America past and present was still a workable subject for musical comedy purview as the decade closed, but most entries—such as a dowdy adaptation of Washington Irving, *Sleepy Hollow* (1948)—cannot be said to have added much to Broadway's chronicle of national mores. *Arms and the Girl* (1950) was a Theatre Guild type of musical comedy, i.e., classy (it was produced by the Theatre Guild, in fact) during which Revolutionary War heroine Nanette Fabray scouted and spied (and got "bundled" with Hessian deserter Georges Guétary) for our side until General Washington begged her to cease and desist. Pearl Bailey supplied the sass, John Conte looked dashing, and Morton Gould's music was lovely, but *Arms and the Girl* was pure frolic, not insightful comment. *Texas Li'l Darlin'* (1949) offered some satire on the "ma fraynds" genre of grass roots politician, but it was a hit only by default. Politicians on the federal level were barely touched on in a show about the first woman president of the United States, *As the Girls Go* (1948), no satire but a vehicle for Bobby Clark as the first male first lady. With Ed Wynn in Hollywood and Bert Lahr temporarily out of the picture, Clark was king of comedy, rivaled only by the much younger Phil Silvers. Singing, dancing, girl-chasing, and generally cutting up, Clark was that breed of performer who carries second-rate material to glory, leaving it to founder and dissolve after his last performance.

Irving Berlin and Robert E. Sherwood cast an eye at the Pulitzer-Bennett newspaper circulation feud c. 1885 in *Miss Liberty* (1949), but even with two bright young faces, Allyn McLerie and Mary McCarty, even with a snappy Policeman's Ball number by Jerome Robbins, even with—or possibly because of—Berlin's papal setting of Emma Lazarus' Statue of Liberty pedestal inscription ("Give Me Your Tired, Your Poor"), it was just another brightly hued musical. *Gentlemen Prefer Blondes* (1949) had the twenties to roar about as well as Carol Channing's adroit incarnation of Lorelei Lee, but Anita Loos' satiric prose didn't travel all that distinctively into another medium, and when it surfaced again in 1974 as *Lorelei* it looked really hopeless.

Far more durable material was provided by two outstanding musicals of the late forties, both of which resisted the artistic developments discussed earlier in this chapter, *Annie Get Your Gun* (1946) and *Kiss Me, Kate* (1948). Both had insanely high entertainment value. *Annie* offered Irving Berlin's best-ever collection of pop tunes, a rock-solid book by Herbert and Dorothy Fields rooted in standard format, joyous staging by Joshua Logan and Helen Tamiris, and, for every one of the show's 1147 performances, Ethel Merman as Annie Oakley. *Kiss Me, Kate* was equally well grounded in production, especially in Hanya Holm's gamut-running choreography—elegant solos, a blissful tarantella, a blazing jitterbug—but it was far more sophisticated than the rural *Annie,* subtler, more adult, more roguish. It too had a best score, Cole Porter's in this case, a dazzling array of smart fancies and Shakespearian infusion for its play-within-a-play adaptation of *The Taming of the Shrew,* as smoothly integrated as anything short of Rodgers and Hammerstein. Both *Annie* and *Kate* are part of musical comedy heritage, staples of summer stock and spring revivals at the New York City Center in its fifties–sixties heyday. They have also entered the "light opera'' repertory in Europe, parading forever their balance of robust (*Annie*) and risqué (*Kate*) humor and cheap sentiment, not to mention the culture shock of Porter's transcendent setting of Shakespeare's ''I Am Ashamed That Women Are So Simple'' speech.

It was in the late forties that the dormant revue of the thirties came back to life. *Call Me Mister* (1946) was the turning point, a unified medley of the years in and just out of uniform. Some aspects of Army life were spoofed in Harold Rome's songs and Arnold Auerbach and Arnold B. Horwitt's sketches, but the serious moments made a more vivid impression: Lawrence Winters making a touching tribute to President Roosevelt from the black point of view, or recalling the glory of the all-Negro ''Red Ball Express'' just before being turned down for a job because of a whites-only policy, and two ballads, ''When We Meet Again'' and ''(You've always been) Along with Me'' recalling the separation of man and wife so much a part of the war years. Now that the fighting was over, *Call Me Mister* would recall it without scaring away customers or waving a hysterical flag—and there was always Betty Garrett bumping her way through a rejection of Latin American rhythm, ''South America, Take It Away,'' to plug the show on the airwaves. Not counting crap like *Hellzapoppin'* or *Sons o' Fun* or the largely pantomimic French import *La Plume de Ma Tante, Call Me Mister*'s 734 performances are still the record for a big Broadway revue (that is, discounting the amateur *Pins and Needles* at the tiny Labor Stage), and its success reminded producers what profits could be had from adult, well-crafted revues in place of last-minute variety shows like *Hilarities* (1948) or *Ken Murray's Blackouts* (1949).

Lend an Ear (1948) was an intimate gem of a revue that first bobbled up at Carnegie Tech and a summer theatre in Cohasset, Massachusetts. Charles Gaynor's songs and sketches sized up psychiatry, the silver screen, and grand opera, peaking in a devastating burlesque of twenties musicals, ''The Gladiola Girl.'' So cunning in their mockery were Carol Channing and Yvonne Adair that they went directly into leads in *Gentlemen Prefer Blondes.* In fact, 1948 was a vintage year for revues, for besides *Lend an Ear* and a second little show, *Small Wonder,* there was *Make Mine Manhattan,* a "crowded entertainment of bubbling youth," according to *Variety,* but more exactly a comedy-oriented evening with a few production numbers devoted to the idyllic aspects of city life. Sid Caesar and David Burns were the comedians of the moment, daffiest in a send-up of *Allegro* with Caesar as a bungling dentist instead of an idealistic doctor. 1948 did have its potpourris with little axis other than a catch-all title—*Caribbean Carnival,* and *Angel in the Wings* with Grace and Paul Hartman and Elaine Stritch—but there was also, on a higher level, a Schwartz and Dietz show, *Inside U.S.A.,* with views of Pittsburgh, Churchill Downs, the San Francisco waterfront, Miami Beach, a Wisconsin state fair, and New Orleans at Mardi Gras time. The quality of the whole was not up to thirties par, but there was top-level comedy from Beatrice Lillie and Jack Haley and exciting dancing from Valerie Bettis.

Neither revue nor yet musical was *Ballet Ballads* (1948), three one-act "dance plays" with music by Jerome Moross and scenario and lyrics by John Latouche. There was no dialogue, just songs and continuous movement in the style of Weill and Brecht's *The Seven Deadly Sins,* each piece different from the next. "Susanna and the Elders" was rural Americana, "Willie the Weeper" urban surreal, "The Eccentricities of Davey Crockett" folk tale panorama. Though *Ballet Ballads* might well belong more to dance history than the theatre, Moross and Latouche were making a point for Broadway—the same point Robbins made in *On the Town* and would repeat in *West Side Story:* dance in musical comedy did not have to be contained in three or four compact set pieces but could wander in and out of the directional plan—of the concept—as needed, collaborating with the story instead of trailing along behind. The idea did not take root until the late fifties, when choreographers became directors as a matter of course, and not till after Moross and Latouche brought their message home in a *gesamtkunstwerk* musical comedy that shared its virtues equally among drama, song, and dance, *The Golden Apple.*

20

Operetta, the Corpse That Refused to Die

Although Hammerstein and Kern did bring their 1927 masterpiece back for a triumphant (and costly) revival in 1946, the other big romantic shows of the past were not merely dead but downright skeletonic, at least in New York. The gold mine road had more or less gone dry, and summer stock wasn't to take up the slack till the fifties, flowering in tents and barns with seasons of *The Desert Song* and *Rose-Marie* mixed in with *Best Foot Forward* or *Annie Get Your Gun.*

However, on a national level, operetta was not entirely gone. In the forties, American theatre was still New York theatre. New playwrights had not arrived till they arrived there, such bold experiments as were attempted were attempted there (then toured about to bring the rest of the country up to date), and actors and directors and producers—the theatre business—dwelled there. But outside of New York, backwaters looked fondly toward the past. In California, always a haven for extremists of any stripe, including reactionary, the Civic Light Opera of San Francisco and Los Angeles produced a yearly repertory of Herbert, Romberg, Friml, Kern, and Youmans. Not content with heirlooms, its impresario Edwin Lester searched for people who were willing to write new works in the old style. In this manner he presented a number of disasters but also one of the few new operettas of the forties that prospered—in New York as well—*Song of Norway* (1944).

Songed up by Robert Wright and George Forrest, *Song of Norway* devolved on a favorite Shubert Brothers formula—the biography of a composer told through his own music and bearing about as much resemblance to his real life as J. J. Shubert did to Eleanor Roosevelt. Tricked up with a relentless load of Balanchine choreography, replete with song titles like "Strange Music," "Bon Vivant," and "Freddy and His Fiddle," and starring Irra Petina as a self-indulgent opera diva (perfect casting), *Song of Norway* was Edvard Grieg just as *Blossom Time* of the twenties had been Franz Schubert and *The Great Waltz* a decade later had been Johann Strauss—that is, a fanfaronading blancmange of unrelieved fantasy. New Yorkers adored *Song of Norway;* it enjoyed one of the year's longest engagements, 860 performances, suggesting to some producers that operetta might not be so dead after all.

Accordingly, a number of different possibilities were explored by way of bringing the ancient method back into style. An updated version of *The Red Mill* from California was a hit in New York in 1945, and another Herbert show, *Sweethearts,* came back in 1947 as a vehicle for Bobby Clark; it too succeeded. Both productions coasted on strong comedy while avoiding camp: when the buffoons were offstage, the creaky love plots went their way as originally written, depending on the appeal of the music to get by.

But it was a risky business. An assortment of collaborators bombed out in 1945, demolishing Chopin's life and music with *Polonaise;* neither John Latouche's lyrics nor Jan Kiepura and Marta Eggerth at the top of their lungs could save that one. Lester revived Herbert's *The Fortune Teller* (remember, it dates back to 1898) as *Gypsy Lady* (1945), spruced up with music from other Herbert shows and a new libretto; this too went down the drain. *Polonaise* took itself too seriously, while *Gypsy Lady* aimed for a tongue-in-cheek approach and only ended up with a primeval pass at bad camp. But that same year, 1945, brought the sole nonhybrid, sincere, original operetta of the decade that prospered, *Up in Central Park.* Herbert and Dorothy Fields' book dealt neatly with Tammany Hall corruption in the days of Boss Tweed, and Sigmund Romberg stretched his adaptability to the utmost in composing an utterly charming score that gave new strength to an essentially outmoded structure, but then the Fieldses were too urbane to write an old-hat operetta book and Dorothy's lyrics were properly sentimental without sounding ridiculous. The final touch was supplied by Helen Tamiris in a skating ballet modeled on Currier & Ives prints. At 504 performances, *Up in Central Park* was outdistanced by *Song of Norway* but made for a vastly more together evening.

Aside from these few hits, operetta was mainly misses in the forties. Lehár's *The Land of Smiles* failed in 1946 even with Richard Tauber singing "Dein ist mein ganzes Herz" (in English, when he remembered), Oscar Straus' *The Chocolate Soldier* did likewise a year later, and poor Romberg suffered defeat with *My Romance* in 1948. The summit of reactionary producing was reached with *Music in My Heart* (1947), a "romantic musical play" serving up Tchaikovsky's music with an episode of his life involving him—with an unlikely enthusiasm, shall we say?—with an opera singer, one Desirée Artot. An odious ballet opened the show, bewildering the audience, and an impassioned parting closed it. In between were such fresh song ideas as "Unrequited Love," "While There's a Song to Sing," "Am I Enchanted?" and the indispensable "Song of the Troika." The extent to which comedy was still considered necessary in such endeavors regardless of how it fit into the framework is seen in the casting of the delectable Vivienne

Segal as well as borscht belt comedian Jan Murray in featured roles, but nothing could save an operetta whose second scene was located in the Café Samovar.

Not until the fifties did the inventory of operetta adapt to modern times, and it did so, as musical comedy had already done, by combining the too strongly differentiated planes of humor and romance into an organic whole. To survive, operetta had to dump Popoff the bilious blusterer, Lady Jane the archetypal man-chaser, the hero and heroine who sang ecstatically but read lines like ailing trees, the anonymous merry villagers with no purpose other than to make noise, the untouchable corps de ballet with their tutus and epaulettes—all the obtuse regalia that could serve no function other than the single function they served. Now the leading characters had to sing *and* dance and carry their share of the comedy; now the chorus had to give some reasonable account of their presence on stage.

At first it didn't seem feasible—at least, no one had tried it in New York. Not until the final hours of 1953 did it happen, in the "musical Arabian night," *Kismet.* In Alfred Drake, Broadway had a leading man who could do everything with aplomb, perhaps the first since Dennis King brought Big Jim Kenyon, François Villon, and d'Artagnan to life in the twenties. In Doretta Morrow and Richard Kiley it had an ingenue and juvenile who looked great, sang sweetly, and didn't seem as if they'd break if you pushed them; in Henry Calvin a droll villain who actually counted in the workings of the plot mechanics; and most unusual of all, it had in Joan Diener a legit soprano with sex appeal and comic timing. There was disarmingly erotic choreography by Jack Cole, book direction by Albert Marre that respected romance but instilled the values of solid pacing, and Lemuel Ayers' stupendous sets and costumes. Furthermore, the busy story of a beggar who attains position, riches, la Diener for himself, and the handsome Caliph for his daughter all in one frantic day in old Baghdad was a substantial plot to hang the set pieces on. It had to work.

It did. But no production, however glorious, can carry hopelessly inferior material, and this time the gods were favorable. Wright and Forrest shook off their *Song of Norway* and *Gypsy Lady* cooings to collate first-rate Borodin tunes with up-to-date lyrics, and the book by Charles Lederer and Luther Davis (based on Edward Knoblock's 1911 Otis Skinner hit) was amusing and cogent. The *Kismet* score played the stylistic field, from the cloud cuckooland of "And This Is My Beloved" to the lusty pre-rock beat of "Rahadlakum," but the juggling transitions from Broadway double entendres to high-note rhapsodies were accomplished with finesse in the same season that Romberg's posthumous *The Girl in Pink Tights* attempted the same type of assimilation less successfully. Then, shortly thereafter, what must have been the last gasp of old-time operetta was heard for four performances in 1954. *Hit the Trail* was set in Virginia City, Nevada, during the mining boom of the eighties and starred the apparently undiscourageable Irra Petina. As John Chapman explained it, "the prima donna doesn't know whether to marry a banker or a gambler. Well . . . who ever did?"

The explanation for the flurry of operetta production in the forties is simply that the popular demand for the romantic musical was as strong as ever and some authors hadn't yet realized that the form of the romantic musical had changed. To an extent, shows such as *Carousel* and *Brigadoon* were the better grade of reconstructed operetta—removed from reality, set in the past or the distance, inclined to sentimentalizing, and, most importantly, dependent on powerful scores to support their message. The old way of doing that kind of show was just too silly to survive. Hammerstein, Kern, Harbach, and the others had developed beyond recognition, outmoding the work of their youth, and even the scrappier musical comedies were expected to hold together somewhat in terms of structure. Any show that called for hussars, pert waitresses, and crusty grand dukes was automatically cutting off most of the available consumers.

Almost all musical shows of whatever type turn on romance, but the love plots in, say, *Panama Hattie* or *By Jupiter* or even *Oklahoma!* are conceived in different terms than are those in *Carousel* or *Brigadoon.* It isn't a question of the amount of comedy, either, for *Brigadoon* and *Carousel* both have a full measure of humor from their secondary characters. No, it's what psychology terms *gestalt,* the whole idea, and in the case of the romantic musicals it is predicated on an intrinsically more *musical* structure, one that must provide the story with a tonal identity in a way that musical comedy pop tunes simply can't. The gestalt of the romantic musical springs from the Viennese school of Johann Strauss, Leo Fall, and Franz Lehár. Without their groundwork, *Carousel* might have sounded a lot like *The Boys from Syracuse*—affecting but not penetrating—and *Show Boat* would never have left the dock.

Most immediately, *The Merry Widow* forced the trend and twenties operetta developed it, but by the forties it had progressed to a point where it bore little trace of its origins. Distinctly overshadowed by the jauntier musical comedy since then, it hangs on year after year, and reached a culmination in 1974 with *A Little Night Music.* In short, though the forties were the great day of the romantic musical, they sounded the knell of operetta, which ultimately proved to be merely a clumsier way of doing the same thing.

21

The Fifties (I)

"Free Trade and a Misty Moon"

People who were around then tend to think of the forties as a golden age of the musical. If *Carousel* or *Brigadoon* isn't their all-time favorite, *Lady in the Dark* is, or *Kiss Me, Kate* or *Finian's Rainbow*. The truth is that the imaginative shows of that decade did have fewer successors in the fifties. Fantasy and romance were on the downswing, but even so, uptempo musical comedy trailed considerably behind, leaving the whole arena of the musical without artistic leadership. Of course, critics everywhere were proclaiming the decline of American play writing, but critics often do that—Merrill Denison in *Theatre Arts* magazine, for example: "Both as to quality and quantity, the period under review was the thinnest known in the metropolitan theatre for so many years that only an elder playgoer could produce a parallel from his own experience . . . current theatrical criticism is even worse than making bricks without straw, for it is the critic's dilemma to find himself without clay as well." And that was way back in 1933.

They were getting angry again in 1950. The war years had brought a thoughtful new drama to the New York stage, and the postwar seasons had Arthur Miller, Tennessee Williams (William Inge came along in early 1950), and some striking first tries such as *Home of the Brave, Mister Roberts, Trio,* and *A Sound of Hunting.* But by 1950 rising costs made laudable noncommercial ventures rarer than ever. As the straight theatre took on a more and more commercial identity, the musical theatre turned equally less creative, pirating the experiments of the forties, depending to an embarrassing extent on adaptations from books or plays, reveling in cliché to wow an undemanding public. One utterly typical fifties musical comedy, *Ankles Aweigh* (1955), was so mired in formula that it could top its limited riches with Betty and Jean Kean hymning the hows and whys of "An Eleven O'Clock Song," apparently unaware that an eleven o'clock song that trite could only turn up in something like *Ankles Aweigh.*

The first big hit of the new decade was *Call Me Madam* (1950), now justly neglected but at the time a hot ticket because of its star, Ethel Merman. Irving Berlin's pop tunes were extremely popular, however abstemiously oriented to their context, and the Howard Lindsay–Russel Crouse book provided Merman with dandy one-liners but utilized embarrassingly little resource in tying up the strands of formal convention. Apparently, an original musical needn't be all that original. The song cues were so obvious you could hear them in New Jersey, and the situation of a Perle Mesta–type ambassadress mucking about in a mythical European duchy marketed cracks about Margaret Truman's singing and our government's long Democratic regime rather than pungent satire.

But one month later came *Guys and Dolls,* a "musical fable of Broadway" based on Damon Runyon's stories about the gamblers, showgirls, cops, and big- and small-time hustlers who inhabit the environs of Duffy Square. Jo Swerling and Abe Burrows' book preserved Runyon's "friendly spirit without any show-shop hokum," (Atkinson), and Frank Loesser's music and lyrics went to wondrous extremes to define the character of the piece. Two years before, his *Where's Charley?* plot numbers were well crafted but on the dull side. In *Guys and Dolls* "unhummable" melodies like "Fugue for Tinhorns," "Marry the Man Today," "The Oldest Established" (permanent floating crap game in New York) and "My Time of Day" delighted the public, who found it needed only a hearing or two of the cast album to master Loesser's individual sound. As Burrows noted, "nothing is in there that doesn't belong. . . . We didn't concern ourselves with reprising songs for no reason at all . . . everything fits. That must be what makes it a hit."

Well, not quite. George S. Kaufman's pointed direction and Michael Kidd's energetic dances helped. The cast put in its oar, particularly those handling the raffish element: Vivian Blaine's Miss Adelaide, Sam Levene's Nathan Detroit, Robert Alda's Sky Masterson, Stubby Kaye's Nicely-Nicely Johnson, Tom Pedi's Harry the Horse, B. S. Pully's Big Jule. The atmosphere of Runyon came through without patronizing; simply put, the show had a lot of personality.

Personality is what most good musicals have, in fact, if nothing else, but rather a lot of musicals seemed willing to get by on as little as possible. Even Cole Porter, whose shows always had flair, produced a somewhat earthbound piece for an adaptation of the Amphitryon legend, *Out of This World* (1950), with Charlotte Greenwood reviving her trademark high kick as a husband-hunting Juno. The Parisian *Can-Can* (1953) had a funny Abe Burrows book without a trace of Paris in it, although Jo Mielziner's evocative sets, Kidd's choreography, and Lilo gave the show some definition. Porter felt out the Gallic accent with "Allez-vous-en" and "Never Give Anything Away," and if "I Love Paris" sounds Russian, so do many Parisian street songs. But while Porter could still pen a distinctive ballad in his own style, "I Am in Love," *Can-Can* was a rather rudimentary show, and it's odd that the extraordinary *Kiss Me, Kate* is only five years older.

Porter's last Broadway production was *Silk Stockings* (1955), a reworking of the Garbo film *Ninotchka* that started out as a sophisticated light comedy but arrived in town after a protracted tryout as a loud professional hack job with a score way below par.

Of the reigning masters like Porter, Arthur Schwartz too had problems with the general level of the two musicals he worked on in the early fifties, though he was still at the height of his powers. *A Tree Grows in Brooklyn* (1951), with lyrics by Dorothy Fields, was billed as a musical play but was more like "musical comedy versus the romantic musical." It had one of the era's finest scores, but the dialogue never decided whether it was working for a comic show or a work of art. George Abbott and Betty Smith's book from Smith's rich, episodic novel of life among the Irish in turn-of-the-century Williamsburg was strong when dealing with the love story but overweighted with humor when Shirley Booth took stage as the endearing, sluttish Aunt Cissie. Schwartz and Fields gave the show superb material in both areas, serious and comic, and used the chorus for atmosphere instead of cheap nostalgia. The opening of Act Two was an impromptu street dance set off by the appearance of an old-clothes man. Encouraged by the noise, two little girls started to jig, the rag man joined them, and soon the stage was covered with people shrugging off their troubles with a reel and some washline philosophy:

You wear 'em, you soil 'em,
You soak 'em, you boil 'em,
You dry 'em and iron 'em,
Laugh in 'em, cry in 'em,
Live in 'em, die in 'em.
That's how it goes!

But the contrasting halves of the show warred uncontrollably with each other, the sad marriage of Katie and Johnny Nolan with its moving ballads versus Aunt Cissie's uproarious carryings on—one to be taken seriously, the other guffawed at. But the Nolans never laughed; their hopeless poverty and blighted romance sank them deeper and deeper into serious drama while the Cissie half of the show distracted the public without actually having a storyline to draw them on. Something a novel can be that a play absolutely mustn't is static (all right, there are exceptions like *Waiting for Godot,* but still). The Cissie subplot essentially went nowhere, but the audience leaned into it because of Booth's personal magnetism, leaving the play without its necessary conflict.

But the critics loved it, the landmark score was popular, and *A Tree Grows in Brooklyn* managed to last out eight months. Its failure to establish itself in the repertory of classic musicals is saddening, for the artfulness with which it recalled time and place was of the highest order, and Herbert Ross' choreography hammered another nail in the coffin of extraneous entertainment-factory footwork. His prize piece was a nightmarish Halloween ballet that coincided with the well-meaning but spineless hero's hour of self-recognition, expressing both his self-loathing and self-destructiveness in terms of dance. Having in Johnny Johnston a hero who could step as well as sing, Ross was able to fill the stage with dramatic images—jeering trick-or-treaters, hoodlums, a rape victim who makes erotic overtures to Nolan, his old friends turning on him. Even Mielziner's backdrop of the Brooklyn Bridge disengaged to unravel its cables grotesquely overhead, and the music added to the horror with invidious distortions of Schwartz' tunes. It was strong stuff, a telling force within the plot structure instead of a mere set piece.

By the Beautiful Sea (1954), the second Schwartz-Fields period show, aspired less highly and was unquestionably Shirley Booth's evening. From the standpoint of genre, it was purest middle-of-the-road mid-fifties musical comedy: realistic as opposed to fantastic, two standard love plots (Booth and legit baritone Wilbur Evans at center stage, ingenue Carol Leigh and juvenile Richard France down at the footlights for set changes), loads of comedy (from Booth and a wisecracking maid, Mae Barnes), lively dances for lift rather than message, colorful sets (Coney Island, 1907), a charming score with a few hopeful pop hits (hopes were dashed), and a plot that circumnavigated for two and a half hours and ended happily. Whether set on the Boardwalk, in seventeenth-century Belgium invaded by Spaniards (*Carnival in Flanders,* 1953), or in modern-day Amish country (*Plain and Fancy,* 1955), the general tone of mid-fifties musicals was pretty much the same, even if the Belgians were invaded by John Raitt and the Amish had to make do with a pair of blasé New Yorkers.

Novelty was often a substitute for imagination in the early fifties, novelties coming cheap and imagination apparently not forthcoming at all. *Top Banana* (1951) had Phil Silvers and a pride of burlesque comics Floogle Streeting in idiomatic style, *Wish You Were Here* (1952) had a swimming pool and a basketball court, *The Girl in Pink Tights* (1954) was about *The Black Crook,* that so-called first musical (ha!). None of these shows was terribly special, but *Wish You Were Here* must be the only musical to last 598 performances after almost unanimously bad notices. Director Joshua Logan continued to tinker with it after the first night, and as it improved, Eddie Fisher's 78 single of the title song began to show up with astounding frequency on the radio waves. A sort of bolero torch number, "Wish You Were Here" practically owned the country during the summer of 1952, and with show tunes, familiarity breeds not contempt but business, and the public came running. Admittedly, Logan had salvaged the show, but the charm of the original, Arthur Kober's comedy *Having Wonderful Time,* vanished in the wake of musical comedy overstatement. The director was already king; in the sixties he would be God. "It appeared to be Mr. Logan's evening," reported Burns Mantle. "Broadway's most successful man of the theater had lopped off all outmoded excrescences, including the idea of human beings."

Novelty was also the calling card of *House of Flowers* (1954), a West Indian gambol about life in a bordello. Another adaptation, this time from a short story by Truman Capote,

House of Flowers did have personality, from the police whistle and steel drums of its overture through Oliver Messel's gorgeous designs and Herbert Ross' erotic choreography to the ingratiating presence of Pearl Bailey. Unfortunately, the show had virtually no book (by Capote), and, most unfortunately, Harold Arlen lavished on it a score of incomparable virtuosity, wasting such gems as "A Sleepin' Bee," "I Never Has Seen Snow," and the title song on a play-without-a-play.

Some top-notch "fun" shows in this period haven't been forgotten in the intervening years. Possibly the best of the lot was *Wonderful Town* (1953), the second New York show with a Bernstein-Comden-Green score, Abbott direction, and at least some Robbins choreography (he . . . uh, assisted Donald Saddler during the Boston tryout). If *On the Town* was as big as Manhattan and up-to-the-minute as possible, *Wonderful Town* concentrated on Greenwich Village in the thirties—without a trace of heart-on-sleeve nostalgia. Bernstein turned on to the beat of bohemia, opening the show with a clanging orchestral vamp modeled on a piano riff Eddie Duchin might have fondled, closing it with the jazzy "Wrong Note Rag," meanwhile fitting both conga and bop into the musical layout. Rosalind Russell, who had sung in the third *Garrick Gaieties,* sang again as the wiser older sister, protecting Edie Adams from assorted wolves while trying to launch a career in the big town. The score was vivacious theatre music, chock-full of grand tunes, reaching a new level of tonal painting in "Conversation Piece," a quintet of ill-assorted people trying to have a party. Brass snarls and terse dialogue led off, the ingenue had a little song, then a loud faux pas exploded in musical hysteria. Even in the fifties the form was still collecting new subtleties.

The Pajama Game (1954) had less point than *Wonderful Town,* for it offered neither the élan of period nor as well crafted a score nor much of a second-act book, but it played 1063 performances on pacing, a spunky cast, and a lot of rousing, quirky dance numbers by Bob Fosse—not a touch of

De Mille anywhere in sight. Richard Adler and Jerry Ross' score had a strong pop affiliation; "Hey There" was the "Wish You Were Here" of 1954 in terms of exposure. "There Once Was a Man," "Steam Heat," "Hernando's Hideaway," "Once a Year Day," and "I'm Not at All in Love" sounded rather naïve next to, say, *Can-Can* or *Wonderful Town* of the year before, but then that's probably why they seemed so fresh.

Like *Wonderful Town, The Pajama Game* had an opening number that struck exactly the right tone for what followed on stage. *The Pajama Game* was about union troubles in a garment factory, so "Racing with the Clock" was a frenzied double chorus for the workers panting through their time-clock schedule. *Wonderful Town*—another Abbott show, remember—took off with "Christopher Street," a Cook's tour of the Village with song and dance framing spoken vignettes to introduce the minor characters—Apopolis the devious landlord, Violet the call girl, out-of-season football player The Wreck, Lonigan the cop—all backed up by the charivari of Sheridan Square. In its pre-Broadway tryout, without this number, the show wasn't working, for audiences need guidance in preparing themselves for the style of a show. Years later the hysterical *A Funny Thing Happened on the Way to the Forum* (Abbott again) fell flat out of town with a graceful opening, "Love Is in the Air"; not until the boisterous "Comedy Tonight" replaced it did the whole show play.

The Pajama Game production team returned in 1955 with the same genre of musical comedy, *Damn Yankees,* this one about baseball, and it too ran for two and a half years. If good romantic shows tend to vary the procedure a trifle, good musical comedies hew more closely to established convention, but as long as it was an Abbott show with a good score and cast upholding said convention, the crowds lined up for miles. Actually, baseball is a definitely unconventional (read suicidal) subject for musical theatre, and business was slow until the posters of Gwen Verdon in uniform, cap, and mitt were changed to Verdon in tights.

Like Lillian Russell, Marilyn Miller, Ethel Merman, and Mary Martin, Verdon became a star of such magnetism that after *Damn Yankees* shows were tailored to her extraordinary talents, and it didn't hurt that her then-husband Bob Fosse was a brilliant choreographer, either. *Damn Yankees'* Faustian plot really utilized baseball instead of diddling it for a few laughs, suggesting that a musical can tackle any subject, no matter how allegedly risky, as long as the creative team comes up with ace material. Then too, Abbott was sharp at casting; for someone with a very individual directing style, he worked (at least in the fifties) almost exclusively with actors who had their own very individual personalities—Merman in *Call Me Madam,* Booth in *A Tree Grows in Brooklyn,* Russell in *Wonderful Town,* Eddie Foy, Jr., in *The Pajama Game,* and the ineffable Verdon in *Damn Yankees.*

Musical comedy not only overshadowed the romantic shows in the fifties, it also cold-shouldered the American subjects popular in the forties. One exception was *Seventeen* (1951), Broadway's second adaptation of Booth Tarkington's novel, an idyllic, understated show that attempted to mirror the Hoosier author's picture of a high school summer vacation in the days when Indianapolis was a small town. Far less pushy than *Hello, Lola* had been in 1926, *Seventeen* avoided Tarkington's ironic tone to zoom in on the drug-store loafing and front-porch sparking of the Midwestern past with a rare avoidance of pretension or neurotic gaiety. The evening was rich with Twainlike archetypes of growing up: rehearsing a speech and stealing father's dress suit to impress a visiting belle, losing the spotlight to a college man with a roadster, ecstatically planning an elopement to paradise. Sally Benson's book purveyed the same sort of rustic charm that worked so well for the *Meet Me in St. Louis* movie, and the usual mixture of comedy and romance worked out well here as it hadn't in the much grander and more artistic *A Tree Grows in Brooklyn.*

But the ticketbuyers' increasing refusal to settle for less than splashy dynamos was nosing out sweet little shows like *Seventeen,* and the only other small-scale book musical of the early fifties was *The Boy Friend* (1954), a British burlesque of the twenties that gave seventeen-year-old Julie Andrews her big break. Minuscule casts and no scenery, however, proved useful for the revue, a risky endeavor now that television gave it away for free in everyone's living room. A number of bright off-Broadway revues with casts of five or six were to gather steam later in the decade, but for the time being the revue had to survive on the main stem, even such special-interest pieces as *Hayride* (1954), an affable country-and-Western concert with such matinee favorites as Cousin Joe Memphis, the Coon Creek Girls, and Zag, the Ozark Mountain Boy.

Of the notable revues of the early fifties, only *New Faces of 1952* succeeded with a smallish cast, its seventeen debutants forming their own backup for ensemble numbers. Leonard Sillman presented a noteworthy array of talent—Paul Lynde, Eartha Kitt, Ronny Graham, Alice Ghostley, Carol Lawrence, Robert Clary—and that old *Greenwich Village Follies* brain, John Murray Anderson, directed and designed to a fare-thee-well, but the material by a host of collaborators was what really made it go. There were send-ups of Tennessee Williams, of pop singer Johnny Ray, and of Menotti's horror opera, *The Medium;* wonderful songs like "Boston Beguine" and "Penny Candy" that developed their own contexts; and an emcee, Virginia de Luce, repeatedly hushed by someone in the wings when she tried to sing "He Takes Me Off His Income Tax" while introducing the sketches. Subsequently filmed and shown on television's "Play of the Week," this *New Faces* was the last one that really clicked. Though the 1956 edition had Maggie Smith, Inga Swenson, John Reardon, Jane Connell, and

Virginia Martin, its material was far less impressive, while the 1962 and 1968 *New Faces* were fast flops.

Of the bigger revues, *Two on the Aisle* (1951) with Bert Lahr and Delores Gray was a final look at the headline variety shows of the past; *Theatre Arts* called it an "authentic flashback to the nearly forgotten formula." *Two on the Aisle*'s topical jests were more quaint than acidulous, unlike those in *John Murray Anderson's Almanac* (1953), a bouncy hit built around stellar talents rather than stars—Hermione Gingold, Polly Bergen, Orson Bean, Kay Medford, Carleton Carpenter, Billy de Wolfe, Harry Belafonte. Perhaps the evolution of dance theatre on Broadway inspired Anderson to revive the little ballet-opera "The Nightingale and the Rose" (from *The Greenwich Village Follies of 1922*) in a palmy moment of his *Almanac*. Two years earlier, Bette Davis illustrated the inherent perils of the star revue by dancing and singing inexpertly in *Two's Company* (1952). "Just turn me loose on Broadway," she warbled hopefully in her opening spot, and the customers were thinking exactly the same thing. By the time Vernon Duke's heavenly ballads turned up, no one was in the mood.

Though romantic musicals were getting fewer and farther between, they held up their end of things better than the jazzy shows. Rodgers and Hammerstein presented Broadway with their fifth musical play, *The King and I* (1951), again with a name above the title. This was to be Gertrude Lawrence's last job, her first book musical since *Lady in the Dark* ten years before; the role of a Welsh schoolteacher at the court of Siam was less volcanic than Liza Elliott, less an accomplishment on its own than a radiant touching part of a working whole. Some critics hailed the authors for continuing to produce unhackneyed musicals, while others felt *The King and I* was processed in the Rodgers and Hammerstein kiln. But the central relationship between Lawrence's proper, hoopskirted schoolmarm and Yul Brynner's barbaric king was something new to the musical, a romance that was technically no romance at all. "The intangibility of their strange union," said the authors, "was a challenge to us . . . we could not write songs which said 'I love you' or even 'I love him.' We were dealing with two characters who could indulge themselves only in oblique expressions of their feelings for each other, since they themselves do not realize exactly what these feelings mean." There was a subtle magic about this show, almost a feeling of fantasy—in the way Jo Mielziner's settings and Irene Sharaff's costumes pictured the exotic land, in the way the Siamese extras spoke in pantomime while the pit woodwinds chattered for them, and especially in Jerome Robbins' ballet "The Small House of Uncle Thomas," Harriet Beecher Stowe's classic of American slavery as dramatized by one of the king's slaves. Silk screens, masks, "foreign" ballet music, and the most ritualized choreography since *Lute Song* made the extended scene a touchstone of creativity in theatre dance. Unfortunately, the high quality that Rodgers and Hammerstein brought to the serious musical was not exploited in their first musical comedy, *Me and Juliet* (1953), an enjoyable backstage story. With its load of dancing, *Me and Juliet* hit the expressionist school of musicals with a barrage of parody that failed to reach the public, though the show as a whole was smartly crafted.

The King and I arrived in a fairly busy season—ten new book shows, five of them successes—but the following 1951–52 season volunteered only four new book musicals, two of them romantic shows. *Three Wishes for Jamie* (1952) was a California import based on a Christopher Award novel (Jamie's three wishes were for travel, the girl of his dreams, and a son who speaks Gaelic, and he got them—it was that kind of musical). In Anne Jeffreys and John Raitt it had singers to justify the impressive range of Ralph Blane's captivating score, and in Bert Wheeler's blarney it had the comedy angle sewed up, but the book leaned too far to homely Irish susceptibility on one hand and Broadway gags on the other. Loewe and Lerner's *Paint Your Wagon* (1951), a saga of the Gold Rush, was actually a rather earthy show, with three superb De Mille dances and a book-light second act; its beautiful score sold records and sheet music long after the original company had disbanded. Both these shows were box office failures at 91 and 289 performances respectively, for though a poor score can keep a musical from success, a good, even an excellent, score cannot save it alone.

The Opera-for-Broadway lobby hadn't given up: Charles Friedman did to *Aïda* what Hammerstein had done for *Carmen,* convincing no one, with *My Darlin' Aïda* (1952), and yet another Menotti opera, *The Saint of Bleecker Street* (1954) played the great Broadway Theatre to critical acclaim in the last truly active season until the sixties: eleven new book shows, one revival, and the one opera.

Original cast albums were a thriving business back then, slight investments bringing fast returns, so Decca (which more or less originated the trend), Columbia, RCA Victor, and Capitol vied for recording rights, ultimately immortalizing every book show of the 1954–55 season (with the sole exception of the four-performance blunder, *Hit the Trail*). Such items as *Ankles Aweigh* and *Seventh Heaven* didn't exactly get to glut the market, but *House of Flowers, Damn Yankees, Peter Pan,* and *Fanny* endure to merchant the authentic tonal ambience of mid-fifties composition, orchestration, and performance variables, vastly at odds with the aural gestalt of the present day. *Peter Pan* (1954) was a Christmas pantomime of the kind still popular in England (Tommy Steele headlined a London *Hans Andersen* in 1974 that incorporated Frank Loesser's 1952 movie score). James M. Barrie's enchanting warhorse, a New York vehicle for Maude Adams, Marilyn Miller, and Eve Le Gallienne since 1905, acquired four songs by Leonard Bernstein for the 1950 Jean Arthur–Boris Karloff production and achieved ultimate completion as a full-fledged musical for Mary Martin and Cyril Ritchard in 1954. Jerome Robbins' ingenious staging and choreography supported the star turns with a fanciful all-around concept, a rare instance of total fantasy in the realistic fifties.

Fanny (1954) was undoubtedly the prize of the season, a spectacular adaptation of Marcel Pagnol's plays of life on the Marseilles waterfront. Harold Rome penned the most ambitious score of his career, an almost operatic host of character songs, duets, and trios totally beyond the ken of *Wish You Were Here*'s hoydenish summer campers. The love plot between a young girl and the boy who loves her back but loves the sea more ended up secondary to Ezio Pinza as the boy's father and Walter Slezak as the older man who marries Fanny during her pregnancy, but at least *Fanny* was unusually artistic in its musical layout. A theatre score was usually twelve to fifteen songs with a few late reprises of the intended hits to fix them in the public's memory. But *Fanny* had twenty-three separate numbers; the repeated material wasn't just restated but developed to encourage the story line as it wavered back and forth among the principles, strengthening the bond between drama and song, making them fertilely dependent on each other. Technically, *Fanny* was thus tilling the musical play soil already farmed by Rodgers and Hammerstein. But in its wealth of melody and its strong musical delineating if not its gag-ridden book, *Fanny* came as close to liberated music theatre as a fifties musical could get without being opera.

22

The Golden Apple

"Steppingstones of Our Dead Selves"

T*he Golden Apple* started out as a musical comedy for Broadway, commissioned by Cheryl Crawford. Jerome Moross was writing the music, John Latouche the libretto—those two of the *Ballet Ballads,* which hadn't run too long in 1948 but which made such a stir in theatre circles with their intriguing collaboration of song and dance and drama. Their new work was to be a retelling of the *Iliad* and the *Odyssey,* updated to America. "It was to be no adaptation of Homeric grandeurs," Latouche later recalled, "but a comic reflection of classical influence on the way we think nowadays. Therefore any myths we might use were to arise out of our native songs, dances, jokes, and ideas."

It sounded daring and wonderful, and more than that, perceptive, drawing on indigenous sources to create a panoramic theatre piece. *Love Life* had sort of done that, but *Love Life* was episodic in its storytelling and uneven in its entertainment. Latouche's scenario was more of a linear narrative, beginning with the return of the "boys in blue" from the Spanish-American War. Ulysses is the local hero returning to his wife, Penelope, Helen is the local farmer's daughter—"always willin'," as the boys sing it—and Paris is a traveling salesman from the big city. Homer's golden apple was retained, but the three goddesses who vied for it became familiar leaders of small-town society, and the setting was now Angel's Roost in the state of Washington in 1900, with Homer's twenty-year span halved to ten. It all seemed to promise what Broadway was in dire need of: a new idea in musical comedy.

But when Moross and Latouche finished their musical comedy, it turned out they had written an opera—a full-length ballet ballad, really—two acts and two and a half hours of continuous singing and dancing. Suddenly, a work written for Broadway seemed too elitist for the common throng—at least so said the big producers. They loved the score, loved the premise, but felt the thing just wouldn't go in New York.

In the end, it was the farsighted founders of the Phoenix Theatre on the Lower East Side who gave *The Golden Apple* its hearing. T. Edward Hambleton and Norris Houghton were looking for something different in the way of musicals for the tail end of their season of Sidney Howard, Shakespeare, and Chekhov, and William and Jean Eckart catalytically thought up a scenery plot on a shoestring budget, the whole production costing only $60,000. The premiere was March 11, 1954, and the show moved uptown to the Alvin a month later, for the critics had fallen all over themselves raving about it. John McClain called it "a milestone in the American musical theater," Robert Coleman "the most original and imaginative work of its kind to blaze across the theatrical horizon in many a moon . . . a magnificent achievement." Of the original cast, only Kaye Ballard went on to stardom, but the others bear names familiar to theatre folk: Stephen Douglass, Priscilla Gillette, Bibi Osterwald, Portia Nelson, Jonathan Lucas, Jack Whiting, and Jerry Stiller in a small part.

Quite aside from the invention and taste of the production,

aside even from Hanya Holm's tour de force in laying out myriad dances to leap in and out of the story (Paris never opened his mouth at all, miming his part in ballet), aside furthermore from the incredibly high quality of Moross' music and Latouche's lyrics, *The Golden Apple* was a seminal work for Broadway in that it was something deeper than the plot balancing on its nimble surface. Avoiding the pulpits of portentous symbolism, the authors made a statement about America, an America changed from a seacoast and frontier with homey stability to an industrial complex of mass structures, corrupt and power hungry, damaged and seductive. Telling their fable through the eyes of Ulysses, they portrayed him as a man in search of a stable value system in a protean world, a vigorous and wise man who has the option of self-determination. The conflict was his struggle, and this musical was a play.

According to Latouche, "lyric theatre has a definite place in the dramatic orbit." According to Mozart, according to Wagner, according to Verdi. There is no reason why a musical can't be a work of art, especially when it overthrows the conventions of format, but there have been precious few successful attempts. *Porgy and Bess* qualifies, no doubt, but its heavy melodrama puts it in the category of verismo opera, which is great as far as it goes. *The Golden Apple* is something else—a comedy, for one thing, a fantasy for another, two levels removed from reality and two levels closer to the truth—born wholly of the sound of America, absorbing and yet declining the spirit of bourgeois theatregoing. It teaches rather than pets its audience: "This is how it could be done!"

The opening, for example. Convention, or rather the simple fact of economics (Stein's first law of Broadway manufacture: "a flop is a flop is a flop"), dictates that the first number set the public up for what is to follow. Not so here. After a brief fanfaric prelude, the curtain rises on the Eckarts' famous expressionistic apple tree made of bright green rectangles. There is no opening number per se; the musical has already begun.

The Trojan War was fought on the Phoenix stage in the city of Rhododendron, where Paris has taken Helen in his balloon. Now, the 1900–1910 decade was a dizzy one for the United States, with the mechanics of civilization dragging the land into the modern era, and the Angel's Roost boys, come to Rhododendron to bring Helen back, are uncomfortably awed at their first glimpse of the New World. They're all for turning back, but our protagonist, Ulysses, sees an outlet for his energies never offered him in Angel's Roost. He is hypnotized:

> See them buildings push the sky up!
> See them streets and railroads glisten
> Never knew a town to fly up
> So almighty fast as this'n.

The war is played out as a boxing match, Ulysses vs. Paris, and Ulysses wins. Helen is sent home and the home-town boys plan to celebrate with a night out. But Rhododendron's mayor, Hector, a Jimmy Walkerish song-and-dance man in spats, striped trousers, morning coat, and top hat, readies his side to get even. "The city itself will be our stratagem," he declares, with its temptations of wealth, fame, security, liquor, knowledge, sex, and power—"every soul alive has his fee."

Then, in a series of music hall turns, Ulysses' wanderings take him through the pitfalls of modern times as one by one his men are knocked off and vanish. Each villainous aspect of Rhododendron was designed to be played by one of the Angel's Roost characters, and though Ulysses does not recognize them, there is a momentary unconscious reaction in him, as if he had already faced this tentacled urban cacophony every day of his life without knowing it as such. One by one they track him, each in a set piece of musical pastiche that digs into the national tapestry of song styles. First Madame Calypso, the scandalous social arbiter, then Mr. Scylla and Mr. Charybdis, stockbrokers (in a bumptious duet modeled on "Positively Mr. Gallagher, Absolutely Mr. Shean"). "Want to be an empire builder?" sings Mayor Hector. "Want to play the game of games? Drachma, dollar, ducat, guilder—one big fact with different names." Next to harry the boys is a siren pulled in on a platform laden with flowers and a gaudy palm tree to croon a Hawaiian specialty, "Goona-Goona," followed by a cheerful lady scientist with "Gadget X" to fly us to the stars.

Finally comes Circe, appearing in a flash like a giant *Police Gazette* cover atop the city skyline. Latouche planned her to be played by Ulysses' wife, Penelope, for she represents his chance at complete domination: "in order to secure this he must give up what is most tender and most alive in himself." In a last gleeful melee the citizens of Rhododendron encircle Ulysses and Circe while Hector gives Paris a knife to kill the two remaining intruders from Angel's Roost. Holm's choreography rose to classical heights in this scene, translating the chaotic clarity of a drunken bender from unconscious reception to wakeful prescience with figures weaving in and out of shadows to fight over the rematerialized golden apple. Ulysses retrieves it just as Achilles, his last companion from home, intercepts Paris' blow, and finally alone in the black alleyway, Ulysses questions his role in life. He satisfies himself that life, death, love, faith, and hope are what they are—life is life's answer, and man's aspirations all exist together "in the unspoken wisdom of the living heart." Tossing away the golden apple, Ulysses returns home to a furious, bewildered Penelope, who reluctantly agrees to give him another chance.

The reunion between Ulysses and Penelope was a tricky moment to bring off. The producers were afraid to use Moross and Latouche's complex soprano-baritone duet, so they made one concession to formula with a reprise of the couple's love song, "It's the Going Home Together," though Moross' final chords sound more like sardonically raised eyebrows than blue-skies-and-bluebirds time. (Incredibly, *somebody* wanted to plug Helen's seductive "Lazy Afternoon" for the finale.) When *The Golden Apple* was revived off-Broadway in 1962, the original duet was put back in and proved its superiority.

Ground-breaking works like *The Golden Apple* don't always succeed in a big way, and the original run at the Phoenix and the Alvin lasted only 125 performances despite unanimously favorable reviews. If it were an opera in the usual sense of that term, with "high-toned" music inaccessible to the mainstream of Broadway customers, one could shrug off its short run as a delusion of venue. But *The Golden Apple,* creative and farsighted as its music was in concept, was composed in a kind of megadimensioned musical comedy style, with a raft of light, appealing melody. True, the part writing is legit, as in *Porgy and Bess* and *Street Scene;* only trained musicians could get through Penelope's or Ulysses' music. Also true, Penelope's "Windflowers," sung during her husband's ten-year absence, is of art song status, spun out in ethereal, long lines, a popular song that outwits the confines of popular music. But the whole two-and-a-half-hour experience is of hearing the best of what the popular theatre can support musically, number after number flowing neatly into self, instead of a series of songs linked arbitrarily.

The lesson is not that musical comedy could be opera, nor that opera could be fun, but that the musical comedy form could say something of interest while exploiting its technical apparatus artistically. Remember this about opera: except in very uncommon environments like East Berlin's Komische Oper where Walter Felsenstein rehearsed his production indefinitely (sometimes for eight or ten months) until they were finished theatre pieces in every respect, opera is poor theatre —not opera as written, but opera as performed in the world's repertory houses great and small. As F. M. Pugell pointed out in *Theatre Arts* when *The Golden Apple* won the Drama Critics Circle Award as the best musical of the year, "No Broadway producer could turn up his nose at an audience for a straight play if that audience could understand only every third word . . . why then should it be different in opera?" Besides the language problem, besides the diction problem for an opera done in the language of its audience, there remains the inescapable fact that opera is almost never rehearsed enough. Familiar works are often thrown on stage with stars who jet in on the day of the performance, whereas a musical gets five weeks of rehearsals followed by four to eight weeks of previews and polishing. This is one distinction that musical comedy has over its supposedly superior relative, opera: it has the option to be powerful theatre on a regular basis.

Seven months after *The Golden Apple,* the Phoenix courageously mounted another audacious work, *Sandhog* (1954), by Earl Robinson and Waldo Salt. Billed as a "ballad," this one was really more of an opera, for its music was that of the concert hall crossed with the energy of American song. *Sandhog* had spoken dialogue, like *Street Scene;* it also made more use of the chorus than ever before in a musical, with extraordinary part writing of the highest level. This tale of the building of the first tunnel under the Hudson River in the 1880s also had a fundamental endowment of social significance, but the burdened tread of the common man—"it's sweat that makes the world go 'round," sang a quartet of sandhogs—was beautifully portrayed, never overworked or pulpiteered. *Theatre Arts* called it "the most fulfilled example of the musical play since *Carousel.*" 1954 was a tough time for a piece of this weight, for this was the era of crash-bang, see-no-evil musical comedy—and maybe theatregoers were aware of how much more than sweat goes into making the world go 'round . . . technology for one thing, and capital for another. Still, whether or not one accepted the authors' point of view, they created a stirring work of art, fully borne out in the Phoenix production, especially Howard Bay's single set that took in everything from a tenement alleyway to the diabolic pits below the river. Perhaps one day *Sandhog* will come into its own in a major revival; until then it remains a glorious statistic.

In an exclusively musical sense, these two Phoenix shows were not the first instances of sophisticated composing for Broadway. There had already been serious composers plying an elitist trade in commercial precincts—Gershwin with *Porgy and Bess,* Weill with *Street Scene* and *Lost in the Stars,* Bernstein for the *On the Town* dance music and later for *Candide* and *West Side Story,* and more recently Stephen Sondheim, whose scores, however accessible to the masses, are in sophistication and subtlety pitched above their pop connections. Theatre music has reached a point where the vernacular idiom is no limit to artistic expression. Furthermore, the apparent breakdown in communication between opera composers and *their* public, who rush home from the latest premiere to wash out their ears with recordings of *Tosca* and *Lohengrin,* has taken much of the satisfaction out of watching the opera repertory grow.

Along with the emergence of serious composition for Broadway came an examination of the national identity, both developments dating from the forties but more successful artistically thereafter. *The Golden Apple* took on middle America, *Sandhog* the ethnic melting pot; both added to our self-knowledge. *Sandhog*'s wake scene of multilingual mourning for a man killed in the tunnel is the cry of all men drudging wretchedly at the bottom of the socioeconomic hole, as articulate as anything in music. *The Golden Apple*'s climax, in which the hero forsook his power struggle for a stable home life, carries the same message Hollywood has been broadcasting since it started talking, most notably perhaps in films by Frank Capra and John Ford. Both Phoenix shows pleaded strong cases against the city, that hell for modern myth, but as the *Sandhog* quartet admitted, "Hell was built by sandhogs and a sandhog's life is . . . well, it's not so bad. After a bit you almost get to like it."

23

The Fifties (II)

Stereo Era

Even counting excellent City Center revivals of *The King and I, Carmen Jones,* and *Kiss Me, Kate* for short limited engagements, the 1955–56 season was a small one for the musical, with but six book shows and two revues (Marc Blitzstein's *Reuben, Reuben* didn't even wing it past its Boston tryout). The legitimate theatre was in better shape, playing host to Jean Anouilh, Jean Giraudoux, Samuel Beckett, and Sean O'Casey (not to mention Christopher Marlowe) from abroad, and enjoying such homegrown efforts as *The Diary of Anne Frank, Time Limit!, A Hatful of Rain, Middle of the Night, A Roomful of Roses, A View From the Bridge,* and *The Matchmaker.*

Up-and-at-'em musical comedy wasn't even holding its own that year. Carol Channing came and went almost overnight with a messy satire of the silent screen, *The Vamp* (1955), and *Mr. Wonderful* offered Sammy Davis, Jr.'s, nightclub act anointed with a thread of silly plot. After their brush with the format in *Me and Juliet,* Rodgers and Hammerstein billed *Pipe Dream* as a musical play, but it was actually more of a dour musical comedy. Using John Steinbeck's raffish Southern California demimonde was a good idea; casting onetime Brünnhilde Helen Traubel as a bordello madam possibly was not.

Excepting the three-week *Shangri-La,* whose gigantic glass mountain shattered with a gigantic whimper on opening night, the romantic musical did itself proud that spring with Loewe and Lerner's *My Fair Lady* and Frank Loesser's *The Most Happy Fella,* two beautiful shows that triumphed via two completely different methods. Take structure, for example. Based as it was on Shaw's *Pygmalion, My Fair Lady* had a well-made foundation to open up, which Lerner did simply by adding in what the playwright originally had occurring off stage, like showing Doolittle in his natural element on Tottenham Court Road and the flower market at Covent Garden. *The Most Happy Fella* also had a solid source to draw on, Sidney Howard's 1924 Pultizer Prize play, *They Knew What They Wanted.* Howard's tale of a middle-aged winegrower (a bootlegger, in fact) who sends his foreman's picture to entice a mail-order bride was substantially unchanged, though the foreman lost the socialist sympathies he held in the original. But if *My Fair Lady* used the Hammerstein scene-song set up, *The Most Happy Fella* was more complexly laid out, with twice as many songs as usual and a surprising amount of what can only be called recitative. To those who suggested that he had written an opera, Loesser just shrugged: "Actually, all it has is a great frequency of songs. It's a musical with music." So much music, in fact, that Columbia took three discs to record it.

Or take the style of musical characterization. *My Fair Lady*'s songs are classy theatre music, neither highbrow nor "orchestral," witty rather than sardonic, well-bred and easy to love. Always writing within the American sphere, Loewe has a way of slipping a little atmosphere into his tunes. "Almost Like Being in Love" was as 1947 Broadway as anything could be, but some of the other *Brigadoon* songs carry a noticeable Highland aroma, while the Western *Paint Your Wagon*'s "They Call the Wind Maria" and "I'm on My Way" sound as if they were composed on the banjo. But *The Most Happy Fella* didn't have a time and place to establish, as *My Fair Lady* did Edwardian England; besides, Loesser's personal style was more casual than Loewe's, more fluent in accosting the man in the street. For *The Most Happy Fella* he gave hit paraders like "Standin' on the Corner" and "Big D" to the livelier folk, but more personal outpourings for his principals. "How Beautiful the Days" and "Somebody, Somewhere" were pitched at an emotional level more profound than that of most theatre music, and seldom does a musical get to implant characterization as formidably as in the foreman's mysterious, long-lined "Joey, Joey," a stunning incarnation of restless hedonism.

Or take the use of generic elements, the paraphernalia that leaven the outer edges of a big show. These were the days when musicals had overtures as a rule, hopefully festive to assure the audience that a good time would be had by all. *My Fair Lady*'s overture was the standard potpourri—a bustling comic operetta setting of "You Did It," a once-over-grandly of "On the Street Where You Live," the shimmering "I Could Have Danced All Night," a fanfare, and out. *The Most Happy Fella,* however, offered no pre-curtain medley but a succinct prelude of themes that summed up the drama, connected with the hero, his love for his bride, and his willingness to accept her as she is. Then too, in the use of minor characters, *My Fair Lady* just employed the usual chorus of extras, raggle-taggle proletariat in the flower market and aristocrats at Ascot and the Embassy Ball. Loesser's show was studded with minor characters forming a palpable community—even the ensemble was called "the neighbors and all the neighbors' neighbors" in the program. In updating and depoliticizing *They Knew What They Wanted,* Loesser strengthened it by extending his musical range. *My Fair Lady* did that only in the impromptu dance that broke out after Liza's first progress in "The Rain in Spain," which Wolcott Gibbs called "just about the most brilliantly successful scene I remember seeing in a musical comedy."

Ultimately, both shows have entered the repertory of enduring works, though *My Fair Lady* overshadowed not only *The Most Happy Fella* but all the musicals of the decade, so immense was its success (its cast album is the biggest all-time seller in the field). *The Most Happy Fella,* a musical comedy raised to greatness with a romantic show's advanced musical foundation, has claim to more riveting subject matter, perhaps, but for sheer perfection of material and high-class production technique, not to mention Rex Harrison and Julie Andrews, *My Fair Lady* is one of the supreme works of the medium.

As the fifties progressed, musical comedy continued to overpower the romantic shows, and the revue all but disappeared. There was a *Ziegfeld Follies* in 1957, a pale imitation of the old days with Beatrice Lillie, sixteen different authors, and an ominous air of déjà vu as early as the opening number, "Bring on the Girls."

Where book shows were concerned, bringing on both girls and boys in cardiacally unrestrained jubilation had become obligatory: the little musical is dead, long live the production number. Of the old guard only Rodgers was left. Irving Berlin was still alive, but his plans to adapt James Michener's *Sayonara* with Joshua Logan fell through and he wasn't heard from until the sixties, while Hammerstein was engaged with his partner in creating polished, unremarkable musical plays, leaving the splashier shows to younger men such as Harold Arlen and Jule Styne. There were still new roads for Rodgers and Hammerstein to pave in their field if they so chose, but they frankly didn't in their television fling with *Cinderella* in 1957, or in *Flower Drum Song* (1958) or *The Sound of Music* (1959). All the parts worked fine and the music and lyrics were still appealing, but the musical dramatization was not as well advantaged as it had been in their first five tries. Other authors were taking Hammerstein's procedure into new areas of story treatment, whereas *Flower Drum Song* was merely Chinese-American and *The Sound of Music* blond.

Arlen had two musicals in the late fifties, *Jamaica* (1957), with Harburg lyrics, and *Saratoga* (1959), based on Edna Ferber's *Saratoga Trunk. Jamaica* was a hit, fast and funny, with intricate ballads like "Cocoanut Sweet" and "Take It Slow, Joe" that are too good for most people to pick up on the first time around. Lena Horne and Ricardo Montalban played opposite each other, she so light and he so dark that no one seemed to notice they weren't of the same race, so Broadway waited until Sammy Davis, Jr., and Paula Wayne loved in *Golden Boy* in 1964 to make a fuss. Harburg's satirical touch never really took over in *Jamaica*'s story of an island beauty who craves urban sophistication, except in a few lyrics ribbing the computer age ("Push the Button") and the fickle transitions of fame ("Napoleon's a pastry . . ."). *Saratoga* was not a hit, though Ferber's picture of the cool adventurer and the gorgeous courtesan who unite platonically for fortune hunting and wind up in each other's arms is a standard American fable.

Jule Styne, working with Comden and Green, had a smash in *Bells Are Ringing* (1956), a conventional show made wonderful by Judy Holliday's tour de force as an answering-service girl who interferes in the lives of her clients. But the trio was way below peak form for *Say, Darling* (1958), a "comedy about a musical" accompanied by two onstage pianos instead of a pit band. This backstage show said less about the business of getting a musical on than *Me and Juliet,* but it did have Robert Morse's ingenious imitation of Hal Prince.

Among theatre composers Leonard Bernstein was the giant of the decade; for sheer talent, nobody even came close. With the gleaming transfusions of *On the Town* and *Wonderful Town* behind him, Bernstein floored the overdrive with two somewhat concurrent projects that remain object lessons in musicality even today, *Candide* (1956) and *West Side Story* (1957). Content dictates form: the former was a "comic operetta," the latter a romantic musical, the first such to occupy a city slum. A few of the rejected *Candide* melodies found their way into *West Side Story,* but no two scores could be less alike in feeling, the one arch, witty, razor-sharp—pinched, even—the other restless, blunt, violent, lyrical.

As it happened, *Candide*'s heavy parts brought it down, for though its cast and physical production were excellent, half of Lillian Hellman's book, of Richard Wilbur's lyrics (with two by Bernstein, two by Wilbur and John Latouche, and one each by Hellman and Dorothy Parker) and of Bernstein's music redoubled Voltaire's irony while the other half took itself seriously. The novel *Candide* is brief and deftly simple, but by the time the five authors finished their work there was a problem of tone. Instead of sustaining the satiric point of view, they crosscut it with sincerity; even Voltaire's rather casual final line was turned into a princely finale for double chorus, "Make Our Garden Grow," one of the most eloquent pieces ever sung on Broadway but a curious climax for a witty and provocative musical that had the guts to bill itself as a comic operetta.

Though *Candide* ran only three months, Columbia's cast album was a best seller, and since so few had seen it but everyone knew about it, the show soon passed into legend. Rumors of revivals circulated for years. There was a concert performance at Philharmonic Hall, and a national tour was headed for New York in the early seventies but foundered in Washington, D.C. Finally, the Chelsea Theater Center in Brooklyn mounted it in 1973, with an entirely new book by Hugh Wheeler, some new lyrics by Stephen Sondheim, a small, youthful cast (most of the original Broadway players were pushing their dotage), and a unique arena-style staging (with some of the audience perched on stools right in the midst of it), all masterminded by Hal Prince. A smash in Brooklyn and then on Broadway, this new piece may have been Voltaire's *Candide,* but it wasn't Bernstein's. His and Hershy Kay's distinctive orchestrations were filtered down (by Kay himself) for a scrawny sixteen-piece band, six numbers were cut, and the score was handed over to actors who could sing . . . just. Worst of all, the new book was right in tone but not as funny as Hellman's original, though Wheeler had just penned one of the wittiest books any musical has ever had for *A Little Night Music.* Prince's runaround staging was prankish and delightful, and the experience of being surrounded by gladsome actors cavorting in a gladsome piece doubtless accounts for a great deal, but this new *Candide* was a trifling, synthetic musical comedy where the first attempt was a flawed masterpiece.

West Side Story also has a touch of legend about it, for though it holds classic status as a breakthrough music drama, it wasn't until the movie reached a national audience that the work gained wide acceptance. The show was by no means a failure, but no bonanza except, artistically, for those who saw past the updated Romeo and Juliet business and watched Jerome Robbins' uncannily right conception unfolding. Running a tightrope between literalism and dreamworld, Robbins adapted his *On the Town* trajectory for more serious purposes. Few of the critics knew what was happening (few critics do), but Atkinson proved an exception: "Everything in *West Side Story* . . . contributes to the total impression of wildness, ecstasy and anguish . . . the ballets convey the things that [book writer Arthur] Laurents is inhibited from saying because the characters are so inarticulate." Atkinson even gave credit to Jean Rosenthal's lighting, most noticeable in *West Side Story* since so much of it was dance and so much of (modern) dance is lighting.

Nowadays anyone can hum "Tonight" or "Maria" or "Somewhere," but back in 1957, sitting in the darkened Winter Garden, many patrons' reaction to the Bernstein-Sondheim score was interested but chagrined: Where was the tune? The best theatre music—it has this in common with opera and symphony—does not necessarily register the first time, because a work of art, however compact, usually needs a little reflection before it can be grasped. Today's less cultivated theatregoer complains that show tunes are no longer hummable. Well, they aren't—the first time around. Aside from the fact that the succession of second-act reprises so endemic to the structure of forties musicals had vanished by the late sixties, the theatre music of today is more advanced in harmony, form, and melodic outline than it used to be. It was already advanced when Bernstein wrote *Candide* and *West Side Story,* and few were able to collect the full extent of what they were hearing. There is an immediate emotional response, of course, but seldom total comprehension. Good music is not necessarily simple music, and great art can be an awesome thing.

The fundamentally American show of the forties had not wholly vacated the Broadway orbit. December 19, 1957, brought *The Music Man,* an extremely Midwestern musical comedy by the Iowan Meredith Willson employing some fresh conceptions of song form within the framework of a play that took root in the Hawkeye State instead of just taking place there. The opening number was scraped out in the rhythmic dialogue Rodgers and Hart had fiddled with in Hollywood (in *Love Me Tonight* and *Hallelujah, I'm a Bum*), four minutes of salesmen talking shop to the sales-pitch beat of a moving train; another song was doled out metrically over a series of old-fashioned piano scales. Willson didn't ignore the pop tune. The hero's "Seventy-Six Trombones" and the heroine's "Goodnight, My Someone" (two versions of the same melody) assumed the standard positions, as did "Till There Was You," but the genre pieces and character songs were noticeably unconventional. The heroine's love song, "My White Knight," rambled on conversationally, following a train of thought rather than a hokey pattern, and Willson festooned the entire event with barbershop quartets, a joyful polka called "Shipoopi," and a lulling boogie "left hand" ostinato for "Marian the Librarian." The author wore his heart on his sleeve, no question about it, but he still contrived to poke some gentle fun at provincial life as it could only be lived in the corn belt. Walter Kerr hailed *The Music Man*'s "eternally infectious footwork . . . the rich and racy gaiety that erupts in an innocent world," and there was nothing but highest praise for Robert Preston as the blasé con man who loses his heart in River City and for Barbara Cook as the maiden librarian who finds it for him. Drama—music drama—had already established itself at the core of the romantic shows. Now (and about time, too) musical comedy was in the process of bracing itself with singers, dancers, and singer/dancers who didn't just read lines but could act a role.

New Girl in Town (1957) came along at the right time to instill the values of solid drama under the enamel of showstopping whoop-de-do. Based on O'Neill's *Anna Christie* and set on the old New York waterfront with a prostitute for a heroine, *New Girl in Town* was billed as a "musical play," Rodgers and Hammerstein style, but its lighter sections let the propulsion of musical comedy replace the culture-myth tapestries of the predecessors, midwifed as it was (book and direction) by George Abbott. As Anna, Gwen Verdon had a lot more to do than just dance. In fact, in the first flush of the planning stage she wasn't going to dance at all, but the exigencies of creating a smash out of town sometimes compromises a work's intent, and the role ended up as a tour de force of musical-comedy dancing and singing as well as musical-play acting. Bob Merrill's attractive score hewed to the lighter and lyrical sides of O'Neill's scenario, but included one stunning solo for Anna when she first meets her unknowing, credulous father, "On the Farm," as ironic and acid a theatre song as was then to be heard, tearing into the "God made the country" myth with a rude, offhand vehemence.

Merrill's next work was another O'Neill adaptation, *Take Me Along,* this one from the playwright's warm family comedy *Ah, Wilderness!* Well cast with Walter Pidgeon, Jackie Gleason, Eileen Herlie, Una Merkel, and Robert Morse as the teenager aquiver with the self-importance of growing up, *Take Me Along* was careful not to dilute O'Neill's worldview, peaking with a "Beardsley Ballet" in which Morse's adolescent fantasies ran amuck after a first tentative binge in the town saloon. Painted whores with dice for breasts, George Sand, Salome, and sloe-eyed vamps out of Tagore congregated on stage in a lusty spoof of old-time prurience. In *Theatre Arts,* Jack Balch said, "I can't remember seeing a more plastic externalization of a boy's longing and ache as he begins to visualize the sweetness and torture that girls are. It is good O'Neill—and an O'Neill who has come a long way, from the horse and buggy to the jet-propelled age of the theatre."

That new generation of songwriters in the twenties and thirties made their reputations first for the quality of their songs as songs, only gradually developing a scope for music and lyrics that bear an artistic burden. For example, Richard Rodgers earned his flight wings early on composing "Yours Sincerely" and "My Heart Stood Still" but rose to eminence in the forties with "What's the Use of Wonderin'," a superior tune that primarily works in a specific time and place, defining why Julie sticks with Billy even when their marriage is clearly going awry.

But by the fifties musicals were more instinctively dramatic than they had been in the Rodgers and Hart days, and the new voices could start right in with theatre songs, what with a familiar tradition pointing the way. Such a team was Jerry Bock and Sheldon Harnick. For the flimsy boxing background of *The Body Beautiful* (1958) they wrought a somewhat all-purpose string of pop tunes, but only a year later they were ready to give the far more solid *Fiorello!* the definition a superior book musical requires. George Abbott and Jerome Weidman's chronicle of La Guardia's political career was a serious show about fifteen years of New York mayors—"Gentleman" Jimmy Walker, then La Guardia, then Walker again, with La Guardia shown being sworn in once more during the curtain calls. Of Bock and Harnick's thirteen songs, all were enjoyable, some outstanding, but they clearly fed off and illuminated the plot. There was one moment of glamour in a campaign song-*cum*-Charleston, "Gentleman Jimmy," a nifty tap number by girls in cut-off dinner jackets and top hats—this in blinding contrast to Fiorello's campaign song "The Name's La Guardia," no set piece by sappy showgirls but a part of the set-to-music story with the would-be mayor pleading his issues on the streets of ethnic neighborhoods.

Fiorello! was an ensemble show, with a cast unknown to the general public. Tom Bosley seemed more like the "Little Flower" than La Guardia himself (he had to be with only two and a half hours to be in), Ellen Hanley sang "When Did I Fall in Love?" with heartrending appeal, Patricia Wilson and Nathaniel Frey made their points like people instead of comics, and Howard da Silva's kingpin of the smoke-filled room was a humdinger, especially in the satiric "Politics and Poker" ("Shuffle up the cards and find the joker"). Almost every critic mentioned "Little Tin Box," a soft-shoe retelling of the Seabury hearings, and suddenly it was a whole twenty-six years of maturing after *Face the Music* covered much of the same business as pure musical comedy. Like *Of Thee I Sing,* with which it has virtually nothing in common, *Fiorello!* won the Pulitzer Prize.

Musicals that are about something get better all the time, whether romantic shows or otherwise, while strictly-for-fun musical comedy in the fifties was only coasting, albeit in some cases with great glee. Al Capp's Dogpatchers came to life in *Li'l Abner* (1956), born to dance Michael Kidd's rambunctious production numbers, while Don Marquis' archy and mehitabel were treated to an offbeat evening, *Shinbone Alley* (1957), extended from an inventive one-act opera by George Kleinsinger and Joe Darion. Both shows were veristic in concept while dealing with fantastic characters (*Shinbone Alley* was nothing but animals); the one real fantasy of the period was *Rumple* (1957). Irrepressible Eddie Foy, Jr., and captivating Barbara Perry were comic-strip regulars threatened with extinction unless they could help their creator out of his mental block. A nice enough show with a little too much whimsey for its own good, *Rumple* suffered mixed reviews (Atkinson: "elaborately dull"; Chapman: "handsome and gently nutty") and shuttered in six weeks.

There were as well, as there always are, star vehicles. Ethel Merman kept *Happy Hunting* (1956) open for a year, both through her signature gusto and the mild notoriety of her onstage tiffs with Fernando Lamas. Gwen Verdon was equally essential to the fortunes of *Redhead* (1958), a murder mystery set in Victorian London that pushed dancing as if it were going out of style (it did, but not till the mid-sixties; by the seventies it was back in fashion again), but this was showshop production-number time, not dance theatre. Tony Randall made his musical comedy debut in *Oh, Captain!* (1958), playing the role Jack Buchanan did in the Schwartz-Dietz *Between the Devil,* a proper English sea captain with a proper wife who keeps a French mistress in Paris for an improper second ménage. Stuffy at home, a tyrant on the channel, and a rampaging apache in Montmartre, Randall embodied the distinctive performer who can carry a show without having a distinctive specialty, like Merman's voice or Verdon's legs. Nancy Walker, an unequaled comedienne and a smashing singer to boot, played an impedient rookie policewoman in *Copper and Brass* (1957), alas briefly, as she was shortchanged in the quality of the show itself.

The proportion of adaptations to "new" stories was about half and half in the late fifties, though the 1957–58 season (the time of *West Side Story, The Music Man,* and one stuporous flop, *Portofino*) had eight original books; only *Oh, Captain!* borrowed old clothes for the ball. Of course, a musical that isn't based on anything doesn't have to be all that original. Jean and Walter Kerr trapped the ghoul of formula in their book for *Goldilocks* (1958), actually a rather jolly retrospective of the American cinema in the days when it still operated out of the New York suburbs. The characters were thrice-familiar: Don Ameche played a nasty director obsessed with creating the next Biblical epic, and Elaine Stritch was the definitive sarcastic lady as a musical comedy star who loves to hate Ameche and finally just loves him. Margaret Hamilton and Nathaniel Frey were Ameche's chortling bad companions, Russel Nype the unflappable socialite who loses Stritch but wins the ballads, and Pat Stanley reserved the ingenue's right to be a deluge of cute. The critics were less than ravished with the passé blueprint, however well it was filled in, and *Goldilocks* closed as soon as it ran out of theatre parties. Social historians examine our mass media for definitions of America's self-image, and the celluloid dream factory, silent or vocal, is a likely subject for musical comedy, yet it is seldom drafted for comic or serious purposes. Back in 1931, Rodgers, Hart, and Fields spoofed Hollywood in *America's Sweetheart* (just before Rodgers and Hart went there to work for four years), and *Goldilocks* was certainly an advance on *The Vamp* or George S. Kaufman's crestfalling *Hollywood Pinafore* (1945), but since then only *The Apple Tree* (1966), *Fade-Out, Fade-In* (1964) and *Mack and Mabel* (1974) have joined the group.

After *The Music Man,* regional Americana didn't fare so well, Broadway lagging far behind in microscoping slivers of national identity. In 1958 the American Indian broke a tradition reaching back to *Rose-Marie* and *Rio Rita* of being associated with beads, teepees, and high blood pressure on the musical stage, but even if it did take place on a reservation in Montana, *Whoop-Up* was so Broadway schlock that only a massacre would have evened the score. *Happy Town* (1959), another funeral, dealt with Back-a-Heap, a Texas village in an uproar because it didn't have a single millionaire; the deal was fatal.

The urban arena came under scrutiny in two shows that did without the usual panoply of dithering choruses and gala sets that the big-city musicals used as a rule. *Simply Heavenly*

(1957) was the first black show of the modern era written by blacks, and if Langston Hughes' lyrics were a letdown after his *Street Scene* poetry, at least his book and David Martin's music embodied the neat-gin and scrabbling-for-rent idyll of Harlem life. *The Nervous Set* (1959) was equally attuned to the beat generation (What ever happened to Jack Kerouac—besides death?) with beards and bongo drums, but it was thwarted by low-level material.

The value of diversion for its own sake stood behind *Once Upon a Mattress* (1959), a sportive retelling of "The Princess and the Pea" that brought Carol Burnett to the fore and was perhaps the only musical ever to tour Manhattan, stalked as it was from theatre to theatre by other shows' prior bookings. Born at the Phoenix, cradle of the avant-garde *Sandhog* and *The Golden Apple, Once Upon a Mattress* was clearly intended for the uptown crowd. The evening commenced with a lute-strumming minstrel balladeering the familiar story while three dancers gently mimed the tale behind him in semidarkness. His song ended, the minstrel felt bound to admit that it hadn't happened *quite* like that, and the lights came up on an ecstatic burlesque—the mollycoddled prince, his domineering mother and henpecked-to-dumbness father, the soft-shoeing jester, the court wizard complete with moth-eaten parlor tricks, and of course, Burnett as Winnifred the Woebegone, swimming the moat, getting drunk, lifting weights and yodeling at a ball, and spending that famous sleepless night on her twenty mattresses. If George Abbott's staging held a little too fast to the custom he helped establish back in the forties, it was generous with comedy. Richard's daughter Mary Rodgers' music and Marshall Barer's lyrics were wonderfully beguiling, while William and Jean Eckart's designs and Joe Layton's choreography suggested the middle ages without resorting to tiresome parodies. In fact, the whole show avoided contaminating the medieval drift of the subject with garish Broadwayisms, but had a bright, neither-here-nor-there air all its own.

The hard lot of superromantic musicals that weren't as marvelous as *My Fair Lady* was getting harder, as witness the well-intentioned adaptation of Jane Austen's *Pride and Prejudice, First Impressions* (1959)—sumptuously appointed, liltingly scored, respectfully transcribed to the stage by Abe Burrows, and personably cast with Polly Bergen, Farley Granger, and Hermione Gingold (it was a good year for ruthless mothers, for besides Gingold's Mrs. Bennett there were Jane White's Queen in *Once Upon a Mattress* and Ethel Merman's Mama Rose in *Gypsy,* all within two blocks of each other). As adaptations go, it was an infuriating one for Janeites, passing up the original's pyrotechnical ironies for cautious politesse, and Gingold's matchmaking mother bullhorned out to the mothers in the audience, but as romantic musicals go, *First Impressions* was certainly pleasant enough, if short on sparkle. In any case, as romantic musicals go, *First Impressions* went, after 92 performances, leaving its admirers to mutter about the decline of taste in the theatregoing public.

Meanwhile, on the national scene, television fell under the Broadway influence with revivals of past successes and new items for the small screen cast in the hoary mold. "Your Hit Parade" seldom offered a show tune, but the pop music business was still plugged in to Broadway in the fifties, and the musical portions of TV programs helped connect Manhattan's theatre district to the rest of the nation. Ed Sullivan's Sunday variety hour often featured a scene or two from the latest musical; his first night, when the program was called "The Talk of the Town," presented Rodgers and Hammerstein themselves performing songs from *South Pacific.* The 1954 Mary Martin *Peter Pan* was videotaped shortly after it closed, while such shows as *Dearest Enemy, Babes in Toyland, Lady in the Dark* (with Ann Sothern), *Annie Get Your Gun* (Mary Martin and John Raitt), and *Bloomer Girl* (Barbara Cook) were televised during the fifties, bowdlerized and cut for time slots but ambassadors nonetheless of what Broadway meant to the hinterland, not to mention such outposts as Bayonne and Rego Park. Ethel Merman and Rosalind Russell even got a second chance at their roles in *Panama Hattie* and *Wonderful Town,* while a *Kiss Me, Kate* "spectacular" brought back the two original stars and the bulk of the original show.

The musical is one of our native art forms, and television, our native media leveler, could never resist the musical, even running up its own adaptations of, for example, Maxwell Anderson's *High Tor* for Julie Andrews and Bing Crosby (with a Schwartz-Anderson score) or a *Marco Polo* (music courtesy of Rimski-Korsakov, *Blossom Time* and *Kismet* fashion) for Broadway regulars Alfred Drake and Doretta Morrow. Even Burr Tillstrom's Kukla, Fran, and Ollie occasionally resorted to full-length (for them) musicals such as *St. George and the Dragon* and *The Mikado.* This activity lessened in the sixties —though the Stephen Sondheim–James Goldman "Stage 67" *Evening Primrose* was an outstanding *cri du coeur* of creativity in 1966—and now is almost dead, except in Carol Burnett's Saturday night burlesques in Rodgers and Hammerstein style.

Closer to The Street, but just barely, was the off-Broadway world. This stratum of small, smaller, and downright pygmy theatres (plus a few old barns on lower Second Avenue left over from the heyday of the Jewish theatre) around town are generally thought to be hotbeds of daring experimentation. This was true of the legitimate drama going back to the Provincetown Playhouse and the Washington Square Players in the early twenties, but it seldom applies to the musical. Discounting the screwy gallimaufries of off-off-Broadway, which beg to be discounted, the little off-Broadway musicals weren't daring or experimental, just little. Played in theatres seating two hundred or less, limited to small casts and almost no scenery, accompanied by piano, drums, and the occasional clarinet, the off-Broadway musical was a pallid cover slide of the uptown show, frail in conception, sometimes frailer in execution. Most interestingly, though they were cheaper to mount, their chances of success were frighteningly small.

There have been long runs, of course. *The Fantasticks* is going into its fifteenth year as of this writing, and such other standouts as *The Threepenny Opera* and *Godspell* must be accounted for, but in those tiny theatres a good week's business will seat as many people as a Broadway house accommodates in one night. With this one-to-eight ratio, *The Fantasticks* has only been running about two years now, not an exceptionally long stay by today's standards. On the other hand, the cul-de-sacs of *The Fantasticks'* children's show conceits would be lost in a big house.

Frequently a haven for old plays, off-Broadway also took a second look at old musicals during this time, not doing well with the big shows. Most Broadway musicals don't work scaled-down, especially if they were conceived to . . . well, take up room. The drum and piano treatment is an awful letdown, to begin with; one of the thrills of musical comedy is the sound of the orchestra. Until the revival of the big bands in the seventies, Broadway was the last stronghold of that massed sonority that so galvanizes the public, and the off-Broadway revivals of *House of Flowers, The Golden Apple,* and *Cabin in the Sky* among others were scuttling their own tradition. In the 1957–58 season, a *Boy Friend* revival did well at the Cherry Lane Theatre, for *The Boy Friend* was small in the first place. But *On the Town* isn't that small; not surprisingly, it lasted eight performances at the Carnegie Hall Playhouse in *its* revival a year later.

Of truly original material off-Broadway there was little sign. The favorite sort of show was an adaptation of a British comedy: *The Importance of Being Earnest* turned into *Earnest in Love* (1960), *The Rivals* into *All in Love* (1961), *A Midsummer Night's Dream* into *Babes in the Wood* (1965), all amiable enough but hardly individual. The sixties brought two different versions of Dion Boucicault's *The Streets of New York,* a *Man with a Load of Mischief* from Ashley Dukes' old warhorse, *Autumn's Here* from "The Legend of Sleepy Hollow," even a revue with sketches from a juvenile humor magazine, *The Mad Show:* revivals and adaptations. And of course there were the spoofs. Rick Besoyan's tiny *Little Mary Sunshine* (1959) demolished the mounties and maidens of operetta with forces one-tenth the size of the originals via deft pastiche and some tactful overstatement. Who could ever forget Eileen Brennan's Little Mary, with that maniacal smile? She looked like a petit-four in heat. The picture is completed by a deathly series of intimate revues, more topical than not and frequently showcasing vivacious talents who happily went on to more congenial affairs. At least in the fifties, what little daring and experimentation there was occurred north of Fourteenth Street.

24

Juno, Gypsy, Mata Hari

Entertainment without Compromise

The Broadway career of Marc Blitzstein through the forties took in one social polemic (*The Cradle Will Rock*) and one opera (*Regina*). The third work for the commercial plateau by this highly noncommercial creator never actually got to Broadway, closing in Boston after two weeks. *Reuben, Reuben* (1955) was one night of contemporary life on Manhattan's Lower East Side as populated by such varied singing-acting talents as Eddie Albert, Evelyn Lear, Kaye Ballard, George Gaynes, and Sondra Lee, and like Blitzstein's other pieces it was hogtied by its author's refusal to water his enormous gifts with a "hummable" tune. Actually, any tune is hummable, from Mozart to Berg, but theatregoers find some more hummable than others, and nobody in Boston was humming *Reuben, Reuben*'s "Mystery of the Flesh" or "Monday Morning Blues."

But Blitzstein undoubtedly felt, along with Kurt Weill, that Broadway was the heart of America's theatre, and what was he writing if not theatre pieces? *Juno* (1959), based on Sean O'Casey's *Juno and the Paycock,* told a tragic working-class family saga superimposed on Dublin's time of "the troubles" in 1921. Blitzstein collaborated this time around. Joseph Stein did the book, Blitzstein the music and lyrics, adhering more closely to the traditional look of a musical than he had in *Reuben, Reuben,* not the least because Agnes De Mille staged the musical numbers. Generically, *Juno* was an adult music drama stuffed to the gills with integrity, using musical comedy forms rather than an operatic layout. O'Casey's play is a powerful tragedy, bitter, ironic, human; *Juno* was equally powerful, tragic, and human through its music.

The evening opened with one of the best first five minutes any musical ever had, with its Dubliners singing a jaunty, stirring "We're Alive" in the face of adversity, until an Irish youth fleeing the British is shot down in the street. As his body was borne away, a group of keening women set up a descant for a second chorus of "We're Alive," now dragging its heels in a death march until the spirit of rebellion brought it back up to a shattering climax. The same song also closed the show with similar sting, but the harsh story was too unremitting for most people and the characterful music was not the sort that assaults the memory of nonmusicians. Casting Shirley Booth and Melvyn Douglas in the leading roles was a wise move, though, for if neither is a singer, both were skilled at "playing" a song to its core. *Juno* didn't last long, unfortunately, mainly because its refusal to cater scared away its audiences.

This does not mean that only sunny musicals can succeed, however. *Gypsy* (1959), by Jule Styne, Stephen Sondheim, and Arthur Laurents, was the *Oklahoma!* of the modern era, enforcing the belief that musical comedy, already integrated as to music and drama and already liberated to deal with adult emotions or social messages or poetic themes, could supply these, remain true to itself, and still be a smash. *Gypsy*'s patrons weren't responding to a spry uptempo show like, say, *The Pajama Game.* Yes, *Gypsy* was uptempo. It moved fast and had a lot of dancing—but no set-piece production numbers in the *Pajama Game* sense. Most importantly, though *The Pajama Game* did tell a story, it wasn't really about anything (and was about even less when the 1973 revival placed black Barbara McNair opposite white Hal Linden and then dismissed the whole business in one revised line of dialogue). *Gypsy,* which covered the early years of Gypsy Rose Lee, her sister June Havoc, and their domineering mother, *was* about something, about accepting unpleasant truths about oneself, accepting oneself as a product of one's parents—accepting one's parents, ultimately, as one's new children.

Like *Juno, Gypsy* let the musical dramatization rest in the realm of the popular song form. Styne has the universal appeal that Blitzstein lacked, and his collaborators and director Jerome Robbins must have been nagging at him to break new ground for himself in composition subtleties. Early on in the show, Gypsy's mother, Rose, sang "Some People," a brisk, pushy song about getting out of the house and into the limelight, a number with rather more profile than the Rose, Ethel Merman, was used to. It is a compliment both to Merman and the *Gypsy* script and score that she came across as a singing actress instead of a singer with a surefire eleven o'clock number and a baritone in her arms. For the first time in her foreground career, Merman had a part. Selling her father on getting out with the kids into vaudeville, Rose sums up her whole life so far in a few pithy lyrics—"knitting sweaters and sitting still" and "living life in a living room."

This is what musical comedy can do that drama can't, and what opera thinks it might but doesn't because operagoers are seldom able to catch the words: set up a full dramatic enterprise in a few deft moments of song. Almost in passing, Rose speaks of "all the sights that I gotta see yet, all the places I gotta play," and this is her tragedy, the spine of the show.

Starting out too late, she has no chance at the stage and will attempt to live a career through her children: "all the places *I* gotta play."

Now, after one chorus of "Some People," Rose proceeds to a middle section describing a dream she had, built on a four-note theme that will be heard again in *Gypsy,* always attached to Rose's neurotic projections. It is both the first measure of the spectacular overture and the last of the show proper. With sparse use of rhyme and discordant music (some of it related to the main part of the song), this "trio," as musicians would call it, conjured up personality instead of ovations—but it got the ovations too. The business of an operetta (remember Stark Young?) was no longer music in 1959. It was music drama.

Gypsy's score was on a high level throughout, but it peaked in its last five minutes in a song—no, a freight train of song parts—called "Rose's Turn." Using some new themes but basically built on musical *and* verbal ideas already presented, "Rose's Turn" was no eleven o'clock number but the capstone of the conflict, Rose's vaudeville turn for an empty house, but also Rose's turn to understand what has happened to her. It was followed by a brief spoken scene with her daughter in which young Gypsy came to her own understanding of the problem: the mother who should have been the daughter, the daughter who in a way has now become the mother. *Gypsy,* a proved audience show, is utopian musical theatre, devoid of the standard compromises with convention. It was a triumph in its time, for Merman, for her vis-à-vis Jack Klugman, for Styne and Sondheim and Arthur Laurents, for Robbins, for producers Leland Hayward and David Merrick, though the authors and Robbins were definitely the muscle on this one. Great works of art should hold up with time, and *Gypsy*'s 1974 London production and subsequent American tour and New York stand was another triumph, again for the show itself and anew for Angela Lansbury's glory of a Rose.

The 1967–68 season's winter was a trying one for Merrick: he had three musicals on the road, all in trouble. One of them he closed in Washington; neither of the two he brought in succeeded. One, *How Now, Dow Jones?* was a brainless Wall Street contraption (good title, though), the other a charming but book-troubled adaptation of *The Happy Time* called likewise. The out-of-town casualty, *Mata Hari,* was bedeviled by serious production problems, but the show as written was an impressive one, an ambitious antiwar but not propagandistic piece about how society condones official, white-collar bestialities for God and country but hunts down individual examples of freedom and beauty. Like *Gypsy, Mata Hari* bypassed show-shop formula. Like *Gypsy, Mata Hari* was a musical play of substance, not without its humorous moments but with the integrity of purpose. Unlike *Gypsy, Mata Hari* failed, because it was simply not well produced.

This World War I romance between a French intelligence officer and an enigmatic beauty suspected of spying for the Germans was at least well cast. The stunning Marisa Mell with her deep voice and untraceable accent was the perfect Mata Hari, Pernell Roberts a natural choice for Lafarge, the "family" man with unexploited longings who lives by mottos of home, church, and state. Jerome Coopersmith's literate book moved fluently from Paris and Madrid to the front lines and back, while Edward Thomas and Martin Charnin's superb dramatic score reaped consistent images in keeping with the libretto's premise—the martinet who lives by the rulebook falls irretrievably in love with the free woman who knows no laws, then must destroy her or see his assumed set of values crumble. Mata Hari's songs slithered with ambiguity: "Everyone Has Something to Hide," "The Choice Is Yours"; Lafarge's scenes were tense with the need for provable convictions ("Is this fact? This is fact!" was his opening shot) until, disturbed by the open sensuality of love, his safe world dissolved.

Mata Hari was a big show, bursting with crowd scenes and color, working within a heightened, almost cinematic format but without the extraneous doodads that mark the border between gossamer and art. If the nicest shows came in the forties, the artistic trophies came more frequently later. Those that present a text beneath the story—not just serious musicals like *Street Scene,* not just shows with surpassing scores like *House of Flowers,* not just shows with a point of view like *The Cradle Will Rock,* nor shows with grown-up satire like *Of Thee I Sing*—are the rich vein of the musical's history: *Show Boat, Allegro, Finian's Rainbow, The Golden Apple, Gypsy, Anyone Can Whistle, Fiddler on the Roof, Mata Hari, Follies, Chicago.* As Lafarge said angrily to his beautiful devil, "Wake up, my dear. You're not in your dream world now where everything turns out well in the end." End of adolescence.

25

The Sixties (I)

"Getting It Together Is the Whole Trick"

As the slim seasons of the late fifties thickened up again, from a record low of six book shows in 1956–57 to eleven in 1960–61 and fourteen in 1964–65, musical comedy retained its preeminence, at least in sheer numbers, over the romantic show. In the legitimate theatre, nonprofit repertory institutions began to mushroom all over the nation, turning, as off-Broadway had done in its younger days, to established and ancient playwrights during a doldrums of new drama, while off-Broadway and the infant off-off-Broadway explored new ideas. The economics of a big main-line musical were more impossible than ever, production costs reaching an average of $500,000 in the early sixties, while the deterioration of the theatre district—not so much the physical plant as the street people who frequented it—added another obstacle for casual theatregoers.

Of the grand old men of the business, most survived and were working but few were getting produced. Richard Rodgers was a notable exception, even writing his own lyrics now that Hammerstein was dead. *No Strings* (1962) brought Rodgers back to his youthful nonconformist days, a serious story about a white novelist and a black model meeting, loving, and parting in Paris. Samuel Taylor's book concentrated on the principals, slipping a bit when aimed at the hedonists of Europe's resort trail, but Joe Layton's fluid staging and David Hays' visual effects kept the show fleet and original. There was no pit band: the seven musicians tootled nonchalantly in and around the action on stage as if part of the celebration. Excellently enacted by Diahann Carroll and Richard Kiley, the bulk of *No Strings* was a touching love story freed from the limitations of the usual set-heavy musical and without a vestige of ditz.

Rodgers had apparently reassumed the tradition he started with Hart in *Peggy-Ann, Chee-Chee,* and *Pal Joey* of bringing the customers up to his level, a tradition he seemed to have forgotten in the last few shows with Hammerstein. Alas, *No Strings* was his last glimmer of nonconformity—to date, at least; from the bold David of broken icons, Rodgers had turned into a Goliath of priestly convention. Working with lyricist Stephen Sondheim on *Do I Hear a Waltz?* (1965), Rodgers lit on Arthur Laurents' bittersweet *The Time of the Cuckoo,* excising most of the bitter. Sondheim's awesome verbal abilities, exploding into high gear in *Gypsy,* were held in check by his fatherly collaborator, who was also the producer of the show. What Rodgers said, went—and what went out included one of the most sophisticated lyrics ever planned for a musical comedy, "We're Gonna Be All Right." Sung by a married couple on the rocks, as ultimately performed it was a cute, optimistic piece with a tune that sounded like the Rodgers of the thirties rather than the maximal composer of musical plays, but the deleted original verses had the sting of truth:

> I was told
> Just be faithful and never scold.

Sounded easy, so
I was sold—
I've been miserable since.

I was taught,
When a prince and a dragon fought,
That the dragon was always caught—
Now I don't even wince . . .
When it eats the prince . . .

Most of the holdover authors from the early years were content with fluttery musical comedies. Schwartz and Dietz made a fabulous comeback with their score to *The Gay Life* (1961), but a rocky book bedeviled what could have been one of the prize adornments of the era. Their last work together was *Jennie* (1963), a lifeless excuse for Mary Martin to play Laurette Taylor. Irving Berlin returned in 1962 for the first time since *Call Me Madam* in another ever-so-slightly political show, *Mr. President*. Expected to compose the kind of songs "they're not writing any more," Berlin made it only too clear why, in a parade of dispirited pop tune carcasses, all the more embarrassing because of their lack of theatre orientation. E. Y. Harburg's sole sixties venture was a reworking of *Lysistrata* with Offenbach tunes, *The Happiest Girl in the World* (1961). Cyril Ritchard and wonderful Janice Rule were amusing antagonists as Pluto and Diana, but the show's best quality was still Harburg's use of fantasy in a down-to-earth way for, as always, satirical point.

Foreign importations such as *Irma La Douce* (1960), *Oliver!* (1963), and *Half a Sixpence* (1965) made a place for themselves without changing anyone's opinion of British musicals much (*Irma* was technically French, but it was seen here in Peter Brook's London production with the ever-British Elizabeth Seal, Keith Michell, and Clive Revill). Meanwhile, that chipper old import Noel Coward wrote, directed, and designed the poster for *Sail Away* (1961), though he ceded the lead to Elaine Stritch. This shipboard romp was designed expressly for Broadway, but Broadway found it wanting, and unceremoniously rejected also *The Girl Who Came to Supper* (1963), Coward's and Harry Kurnitz' adaptation of Terence Rattigan's *The Sleeping Prince,* operetta to the core.

For some reason, Coward didn't adapt his play *Blithe Spirit* himself, but he directed Hugh Martin and Timothy Gray's musical version, *High Spirits* (1964), keeping the ghostly triangle plot in battle trim. Martin had led the vanguard of theatre composers alive to new music in *Best Foot Forward* and *Look Ma, I'm Dancin'*. Now he could span a wide range of sounds in a cohesive whole, giving Beatrice Lillie's Madame Arcati comedy spots, Tammy Grimes' heavenly Elvira insinuating rhythm numbers, and Edward Woodward's Charles Condomine a super forties-flavored plaint, "I Know Your Heart (By heart)."

Loewe and Lerner entered the sixties having to live up to *My Fair Lady;* they nearly did in *Camelot* (1960). A heavy layer of sentiment obscured the work's heroic nature, but strong public response was a vote for the romantic show and an easy message at a time when such parcels were down to one or two a year. There were those who assumed that *Camelot*'s story about a king trying to impose democracy on a barbaric feudal state paralleled John Kennedy's New Frontier, but, more importantly, Loewe and Lerner's powerful concatenation of legend and realism could hold the stage at a time when loud musical comedies like *The Unsinkable Molly Brown* and *Do Re Mi* were the businessman's favorites. *Camelot* had class. Richard Burton, Julie Andrews, and sorceress M'el Dowd were dramatis personae in spades, and director Moss Hart subjected the book to more last-minute polishing than a new invention. Lerner's script certainly mangled the dimension of irony that T. H. White gave to *The Once and Future King,* Lerner's Arthurian source, but it did have the luxury of a first-class score.

Camelot's fantastic side ran rampant in *On a Clear Day You Can See Forever* (1965), which Lerner wrote with Burton

Lane. Having to engage reincarnation on his first Broadway show in eighteen years, Lane proved himself anything but a reactionary, imbuing this romantic-show-within-a-musical-comedy with the energy of contemporary sound. On the other hand, Frank Loesser's *Greenwillow* (1960) was a netherworldic show with a netherworldic score, a complete turnabout from the natty pop feeling of "Once in Love with Amy" or the elevated ambit of the *Most Happy Fella* songs. Not strictly a fantasy, *Greenwillow* was set in a sleepy backwater, a place where people have calls to wander, baptize baby calves, and indulge in earthy emotions without resorting to barn dances to express their folk feeling. B. J. Chute's world-of-its-own novel was faithfully translated into musical theatre under George Roy Hill's direction, and her disarming rural society was brilliantly served by Loesser's score. Few musicals can boast a juvenile and ingenue with the presence of *Greenwillow*'s Anthony Perkins and Ellen McCown, not to mention its two opposing country vicars, one blissful and one dour, but it was Loesser's music and lyrics that towered above all in setting and holding to a dramatic conception, working within folk-song types for mood yet transcending them for characterization. *Greenwillow*'s score may well have had too much quality for its own good, in fact, for Broadway disdained it, leaving Loesser to come back with a glib, ordinary string of songs for *How to Succeed in Business Without Really Trying* (1961). This very funny satire on the business world was so well put together that it won the Pultizer Prize, but it was hardly that special an endeavor. True, it did have Robert Morse's beau ideal of a lovable rogue and Bob Fosse's madly determinate dances, but on the whole, *How to Succeed* was the last word in fifties convention, brightly played and perfectly synchronized.

Other familiar names were also mining more or less familiar terrain. Comden and Green solidified their partnership with Jule Styne in several high-powered musical comedies, giving Nancy Walker one of her few chances to play a hit and redoubling her with Phil Silvers in *Do Re Mi* (1960), proving that the old-style comedian-as-king musicals were scintillant forever as long as the comedy was an integral part of the story. *Subways Are for Sleeping* (1961), an offbeat look at Manhattan's lost and lonely, went in for charm, but *Fade-Out, Fade-In* (1963) restored the trio to socko comedy. This was the first successful musical satire of Hollywood since *Stars in Your Eyes* in 1939, for Comden and Green's book tendered a little light commentary behind their Cinderella send-up of a star-struck usherette put under contract by mistake in the thirties.

Comden and Green had worked in Hollywood themselves, and it had been no labor of love. They retained a wry appreciation of how the film industry works, so distorted and unreal that they had little exaggerating to do in their scenario: the ill-educated, impulsive, despotic mogul; the nepotism (*six* nephews); the matinee idol enslaved to the studio by his gambling debts; the well-spoken black who turns into Stepin Fetchit for the camera; the has-been silent stars demoted to extras; the asinine gossip columnist (". . . far-off Vienna, that beautiful country which gave us Maurice Chevalier"); and, especially, the hope that Hollywood dangled before the nation: it could happen to you:

> So don't give up, all you short or fat or tall girls—
> Democracy says fame can come to all girls . . .

Fade-Out, Fade-In was a star show, and in Carol Burnett the authors had a comedienne who could take pratfalls or make animal noises without losing audience sympathy as the girl next door in search of happiness—which at first seemed to be fame, riches, and glamour. But no. As American films kept reminding girls who sat enthralled in the Depression's movie palaces, happiness was, ultimately, love.

Riches and glamour, however, were definitely the goal of *I Can Get It for You Wholesale*'s antihero Harry Bogen in 1962. Jerome Weidman's book, adapted from his novel, ripped with honest embarrassment into the Depression-era garment district, ending up a notably serious musical with funny parts rather than a musical comedy. A hustler's sordid rise and fall made for articulate social drama, so popular with playwrights of the thirties, but the resources of the musical stage were able to push open the parlor walls with a disturbing Brechtian number, "What Are They Doing to Us Now?" for the abused working masses. Lillian Roth made an imposing comeback as Bogen's Jewish mother—a role played this time for pathos and nobility rather than cheap ethnic jokes.

Now, it so happens that the Jewish audience forms a substantial chunk of New York's theatregoing population, but it tends to be reactionary in its tastes. A show like *I Can Get It for You Wholesale,* lacking the familiar cues and Yiddishisms ingrained in television comedy, unnerves them with hard realism when all they ask is sentiment and shtick. Even with an absurd happy ending tacked on to the grim final scene between mother and son as performed out of town, this musical was too far ahead of its own public, giving them only Harold Rome's excellent score and Barbra Streisand in a featured role to keep them warmed up.

Far sweeter to Jewish—and everyone's—taste was *Funny Girl* (1964). Set in the same era as the Rome-Weidman piece and this time starring Streisand, *Funny Girl* was show-biz legend at its best, underlyingly serious but prepossessingly uptempo at the same time. Streisand was perfect for this recreation of Fanny Brice's Ziegfeld heyday, and Jule Styne, working with lyricist Bob Merrill, created the second artistic score of his career, with a pair of musically sophisticated ballads in "The Music That Makes Me Dance" and "Who Are You Now?" Looking back, it is easy to see why *Funny Girl* prospered when *I Can Get It for You Wholesale* didn't. They shared a less than ebullient outlook on life, but *Funny Girl* didn't ask its audience to believe that people—some people, at least—were self-seeking and vicious. The garment district probably teems with evil, now as then, but this particular pill is not one that goes down easily. *Pal Joey*'s heel couldn't scare anybody: he was an entertainer, and everybody knows how weird *they* are. Besides, *Pal Joey* was set in foreign lands (Chicago). In tackling a similar subject closer to home, *I Can Get It for You Wholesale* had a hard time pleasing its ethnic relations, who prefer Jewish shows in which the characters are, if American, neurotic but lovable (*A Family Affair,* 1962), or if alien, idealistic and high-spirited (*Milk and Honey,* 1961).

Of the younger songwriting talents—rare enough in the early sixties but not as rare as talented book writers of whatever age—Charles Strouse and Lee Adams turned out the sleeper hit of 1960 in *Bye Bye Birdie,* a colorful look at middle-American youth at the height of the rock and roll era. The adults definitely won out in Michael Stewart's script, however. Dick Van Dyke and Chita Rivera were the front couple, Kay Medford was Van Dyke's pushy mother, and representing situation-comedy small-town America was Paul Lynde in the role he does best, a persecuted, wisecracking father. The show was both directed and choreographed by Gower Champion, who added no small luster to the presentation. Dancing was still an endemic piece of the musical comedy action then, much more than later, and it was a natural step for enterprising choreographers to take whole shows under their wing. (De Mille had staged every minute of *Allegro* in 1947, with Robbins, Fosse, and Jack Cole following suit soon after, though the idea goes back to Julian Mitchell and his strong leadership of musical shows for Ziegfeld and Victor Herbert.)

Champion worked similar wonders with *Carnival* (1961), using only one set but vast ingenuity on this adaptation of a gossamer 1953 movie, *Lili.* Faced with the challenge of having to equal *Lili*'s "High-Lili, High-Lo," Bob Merrill rose to the occasion with the equally sweet and witless "Love Makes the World Go 'Round." The next Champion show, *Hello, Dolly!*

(1963), was a slick and salty blockbuster with very little feeling in it, but perhaps heart is something the audience requires only of a romantic show. Jerry Herman did contrive a sincere ballad late in the evening, "It Only Takes a Moment," but the love plot was so secondary to Carol Channing's personal antics that it was too late for anyone to be much moved. Still, as an example of how to stage a brassy show—and how to sit back and enjoy one—*Hello, Dolly!* was an exemplary lesson, for its tricks blended consistently with each other, whether Oliver Smith's dapper black-and-white period mock-ups or, lo and behold (let's hear it for *Sumurun*), the runway on which Dolly and her waiters sauntered into posterity.

Of those music-and-word teams unwilling to be subsumed in a Champion package, Jerry Bock and Sheldon Harnick were summa cum laude in the writing of integrated theatre scores. *Tenderloin* (1960) starred Shakespearean Maurice Evans as a crusading minister at war with Manhattan's red-light district in the 1890s with a sly use of old-time music, even a three-verse story-ballad, "Artificial Flowers." The opening number was especially effective, an exponential proof positive that musicals weren't going to limit themselves to "fourth-wall" literalism any more: a few representatives of the underworld spoke from limbo on their own brand of upward mobility, followed by a short sermon from the preacher backed by his hymn-singing flock, then at last the work's true hymn, "Little Old New York (Is plenty good enough for me)," sung by the Tenderloin in full cry—prostitutes, swells, bought cops. It was the nasties who gave *Tenderloin* its atmosphere, and they who closed the story, moving on to wide open "Little Old Detroit."

Bock and Harnick gave the romantic musical a celestial break in *She Loves Me* (1963), a subdued European valentine liberated from the leaden gush of operetta; a little show, a gem. Working with producer Harold Prince, the team was not under pressure to produce high-voltage smashes, for Prince was—still is—willing to take risks. *She Loves Me*'s tale about parfumerie clerks—particularly two who fight with each other and end up in a clinch—was mounted with style and grace; not a trace of assembly-line crowd-pleasing tactics.

Granted Prince's earnest aspirations—*New Girl in Town, West Side Story, Fiorello!*—he should have been due for a tremendous bomb about then. Ironically, the next Bock-Harnick-Prince show was Broadway's longest-running musical ever, *Fiddler on the Roof* (1964). It is tempting to compare *Fiddler* to *Dolly,* runner-up in the long-run sweepstakes, but there is no comparison. *Fiddler* is a concept show, anchored in a subcultural way of life (the village Anatevka) and illustrating how its narrow but explicit requirements—"Tradition," as the opening number explains it—govern every function of existence. On the other hand, *Dolly* had no concept; few pure musical comedies do. It was a freewheeling jamboree beribboned to best advantage by volcanic showmanship. *Fiddler* had showmanship, too, thanks to Jerome Robbins' organic command, but in *Fiddler* everything that happened developed out of its tradition theme. *Dolly*'s action was hinged on a plot kicker, which was thrown out by Dolly herself to her public right at the outset: How will she snare wealthy Horace Vandergelder? *Fiddler* had no such device; it almost didn't even have a plot. But that show breathed! Robbins, Bock, Harnick, and book writer Joseph Stein presented a slice of Russian-Jewish village life, with a highly developed sense of background: the rabbi, the matchmaker, the pipe-smoking policeman, the local Aryan muzhiks, before whom danced Tevya the dairy farmer, his wife, Golde, and their marriageable daughters. Even the chorus members were identified in "Tradition" according to their slot in Anatevka's pecking order.

The folkloric zest of Sholom Aleichem's original stories was rekindled for *Fiddler* in all things—dialogue, dance, and song, whether in Tevya's little interior monologues or in the lengthy dream he unraveled to convince Golde that her late grandmother wants their eldest girl to marry her sweetheart rather than a wealthy aging suitor. Even Boris Aronson's backdrop was Eastern European expressionistic à la Chagall. The summit of stage imagery was the real-life, wordless fiddler who helped Tevya open and close the show, literalizing that "tradition" of the total concept. In Tevya, Zero Mostel had the role of his life, but *Fiddler* was no vehicle and remained a full-brimming evening in the years after Mostel vacated the scene. Similarly, though Robbins' staging was the nucleus of the original production, *Fiddler* has flourished in Europe (as *Anatevka*) in all sorts of productions, including one at East Berlin's celebrated opera-as-drama emporium the Komische Oper, complete with interpolated Yiddish songs. Ultimately, the material is what counts.

A decade newer than Bock and Harnick, Harvey Schmidt and Tom Jones left their tiny *Fantasticks* puttering happily down on Sullivan Street to bring their simplicity and directness to Broadway in *110 in the Shade* (1963), about a con man rainmaker who brings a diffident spinster out of herself. Agnes De Mille was again on hand to abstract the wide open prairie in her choreography, and Hershy Kay's remarkable orchestrations used the hollow fourths and fifths that always seem to suggest Indian country to American musicians (it's also useful in Appalachian contexts). Similar atmospheric devices were the property of Richard Adler in his Africanesque songs for *Kwamina* (1961), a few of which did encase the feel of the veld and, quite properly, a touch of calypso.

The main concern for composers in the sixties—along with enlarging the scope of theatre music—was finding a new language and structure for librettos, new-style words for new-style music. If the actor-managers of Cohan's day were replaced by producers of taste in the thirties—like Sam H. Harris and Max Gordon—and by smart packagers in the fifties, prime movers in the sound department such as Frank Loesser, Jerry Bock, and John Kander would have to seek out men of vision to help them build the better mousetrap.

Another prime mover, Stephen Sondheim, was now setting

his own lyrics instead of handing them over to Bernstein, Styne, or Rodgers. In his first solo outing he had balanced the maniacal pacing and burlesque whirligig of *A Funny Thing Happened on the Way to the Forum* (1962) with inventive, stylish comedy songs and lilting ballads to provide breathing spaces for George Abbott's breakneck farce. Bert Shevelove and Larry Gelbart's Plautus-derived book had demanded not character or plot songs so much as melodic lift, but Arthur Laurents' three-act script for *Anyone Can Whistle* (1964) called forth a tour de force of definition and story-line numbers. Cast for sharpness with actors rather than singers (Angela Lansbury, Lee Remick, and Harry Guardino), *Anyone Can Whistle* lasted only a week in New York, but its subrealistic satire on our society made it a landmark show, ahead of its time, yes, but more significantly a ruthless mirror held up to America's way of doing things. There's a lot of room for examinations of the national conformity-versus-iconoclasm battle and of our need for sacred cows. Whitney Bolton said in the *Morning Telegraph,* "If *Anyone Can Whistle* is a success, the American musical theater will have advanced itself and prepared the way for further freedom from now old and worn techniques of points of view. . . . It is a bright first step toward a more enlightened and cerebral musical theater [that] can say something about its times and the mores of those times."

Spiraling production costs were making big-name stars almost indispensable in the sixties, especially in the matter of attracting theatre parties. Unfortunately, this led to a greater supply of star vehicles emphasizing the star turn and losing sight of the integrity of the material itself. Vehicles don't tend to aspire artistically. The authors have to cater to the star, for one thing, and the audience too expects to see its favorite doing what it did before. To surprise them is to invite disaster.

But there are always exceptions. Ethel Merman had been vehicle-trapped before *Gypsy* came along, yet *Gypsy* was a show with a star rather than a star's show. Sometimes you can have the cake and eat it too, but more often vehicles turn out like those for Lucille Ball in *Wildcat* (1960), Tammy Grimes in *The Unsinkable Molly Brown* (1960), Vivien Leigh and Jean-Pierre Aumont in *Tovarich* (1963), or Ray Bolger in *All American* (1962)—all amiable shows, certainly, but so built around a personality that they lacked any of their own. *Hello, Dolly!* was a vehicle many times over, showcasing one prima donna after another in New York when Channing took it on tour. When Pearl Bailey stepped in, Merrick had the show entirely re-cast with blacks. Bailey herself was a smash, even if Jerry Herman's strict format songs were uncomfortably staid for her compared to the loose, curvy Harold Arlen numbers she had delivered in *St. Louis Woman* and *House of Flowers* or her two lazy comedy tunes from *Arms and the Girl.* But *Hello, Dolly!* was indestructible by then, and the embarrassingly substandard production backing Pearlie Mae became that season's hot ticket. What consistency the piece had was demolished by its inferior new cast, yet the critics, led by Clive Barnes ("my sensitive white liberal conscience was offended at the idea of a non-integrated Negro show [but . . .]", drooled over the wreckage of a decent book musical like Cole Porterites at their first Cotton Club revue. Worse luck, the fatal pall of starism continued to hang heavy over *Dolly* when Merman assumed the role originally intended for her. But a star doesn't guarantee success: even Judy Holliday couldn't keep *Hot Spot* (1963) running, or Bert Lahr *Foxy* (1964). Conversely, the unknown Libi Staiger gave a performance of shattering immensity as the young Sophie Tucker in *Sophie* (1963), and the show lasted a week. You never can tell.

While there's nothing like star billing to grease the slide to a substantial run, not all shows with stars depend solely on that one performance to make it through an evening. Dramatists Clifford Odets (who died while working on the show) and William Gibson reached back to Odets' 1937 hit, *Golden Boy*

(1964), updating the story of the young boxer who tries to pull himself up in the socioeconomic strata with his fists. In the title role was Sammy Davis, Jr., necessitating a racial instead of merely ethnic (Italian in 1937) subcultural point of view, and succeeding like gangbusters. The musical *Golden Boy* was life-large, for it sometimes seemed that Davis was playing himself, adding that much more to the tragedy of the outsider who can never fit in . . . and isn't all that sure that he wants to. Now, at last, Strouse and Adams broke away from their past habits with a jazzy, saxophonic pop score, brilliantly instrumented by Ralph Burns, that pointed up *Golden Boy*'s naturalistic atmosphere.

Another leading-role show of the era was far less realistic but equally pointed. *Flora, the Red Menace* (1965) looked in on the Depression by way of Lester Atwell's novel *Love Is Just Around the Corner,* like it expressing the belief that institutions and movements are harmful to the independent mind, the institution being a Fifth Avenue department store and the movement being the Communist party. *Flora* the musical took a more optimistic stance than its source, however, with a score suffused with youthful energy. In John Kander and Fred Ebb's music and lyrics, 1935 was the best more than the worst of times: valedictorian Flora led her art school classmates in a right-on march, "Unafraid," sang "All I Need Is One Good Break" while filling out a job application (for no job), and even when fired could summon up the jubilation of "Sing Happy," which started out ironically but quickly succumbed to the general feeling of hope. Only nineteen in 1965, Liza Minnelli made her Broadway debut as Flora, embodying to perfection the outrageous happiness of being young and talented and moving up in the world that *Flora* was all about.

The Great Depression has become something of a modern myth for American writers but has received scant attention from the musical. With the same gusto as *Wonderful Town, Flora, the Red Menace* focused on the brighter side of Manhattan in the thirties, but stands out for its satiric broadside at the party workers, not excluding the grosser sorts of people attracted to programs of self-denial and conspiracy. "Sign Here," sang Comrade Harry, Flora's love interest, selling her on "the rights of man" and "free milk for kids," but of course in musical comedy the good guys wise up in time.

Flora exercised the ability of the musical to call up the ethos of an era through the use of archetypes that are as much a part of America as our foreign policy or our social developments (as would a later Kander-Ebb show, *Chicago,* and far more tellingly). A common practice of Hollywood movies in the thirties was to juxtapose two characters with diverse backgrounds to show how anyone can fall in love with anyone else in democratic America—bank clerks and heiresses, showgirls and princes. *Fade-Out, Fade-In*'s send-up of the movies invented titles like "The Fiddler and the Fighter" and "The Farmer and the Fan Dancer"; accordingly, *Flora* offered its unlikely duo amidst bread lines and knock-knock jokes, a Major Bowes cowboy, and an obsessed party worker, Comrade Ada. Love conquered all in a loony spoof on native tropes, James Cresson in his Stetson and mile-wide grin, Mary Louise Wilson in her moth-eaten overcoat: the Oklahoma plains meets Union Square, the Cowboy and the Bombthrower. It's a long way back to *Let 'Em Eat Cake* and *its* way of dealing with revolutionary movements, a long way and too little representation in the musical.

Speaking of depressions, the romantic show was still suffering one in the early sixties, victimized more than musical comedy by production costs. This made things rather tight for specialists in the field. Wright and Forrest had a disaster with *Anya* (1965), based on *Anastasia* and set to Rachmaninoff's music (at least it wasn't about his life), but the pair wrote a dramatic original score for *Kean* in 1961, from Jean-Paul Sartre's being-and-nothingness view of an actor's dual existence, the stage versus reality. If musical vehicles center on leading ladies or male comedians like Lahr and Bolger, singing actor Alfred Drake was a conspicuous exception. He had much meat to bite into as Edmund Kean, the consummate actor who seems to live only on stage, chiding Shakespeare for omitting to write the part he craves most—his own.

A week before *Anya*'s romantic hopes were dashed, *Man of La Mancha* opened downtown at Washington Square, inaugurating a new chapter in the destiny of the romantic show. This adaptation of Cervantes had its detractors—what doesn't?—but the issue here is that the Mitch Leigh–Joe Darion score could enjoy widespread popularity in a day when the country was turning its back on theatre music. Time was when the detritus of theatre scores dominated the airwaves, when Broadway's songwriters led the front guard in pop music, when cast albums were a big industry. But with the advent of rock all this changed. Steadily, theatre songs have been losing their hold on the nation at large. Discounting rock shows, which obviously are aimed at the pop industry as it is presently constituted, few whole scores—that is, a core of four or five hit tunes in the *Brigadoon* or *Kiss Me, Kate* sense—of the recent past have made it big. No, not few. None.

Besides giving the waning celebrity of theatre music a boost with "Dulcinea" and "The Impossible Dream," worn out on the nation's juke boxes to the point of delirium, *Man of La Mancha* proved that the thematic, semifantastic romantic show is still most people's preferred trip, even when the comedy is supplied by a Sancho Panza right out of the twenties-operetta handbook of dialect humor. Brilliantly staged in three-quarters arena style (until it moved uptown) by Albert Marre, the show was a reminder—as if one were needed—that the musical's strong point as theatre is its admixture of the best acting and singing talents. Strong in all things, the cast headed by Richard Kiley and Joan Diener lived up to the demands of myth, a test they wouldn't have had to pass in a chuckling musical comedy, where, for one thing, they would have made no test of an audience's imagination.

"The Impossible Dream" is still with us, of course—nothing can kill that one. But since then, theatre songs with "hit" quality such as *Zorba*'s "Only Love," *Coco*'s "Always Mademoiselle," *Follies*' "Losing My Mind," *The Grass Harp*'s "Chain of Love," and *Mack and Mabel*'s "Time Heals Everything" have remained caviar for the few, hidden from the American mainstream. Broadway's rich heritage—and future—of commercial potential isn't being tapped the way it used to be by the mass media, especially radio. This is only one more example of how the economic factor—in this case, the passing of the show-tune market—has cut into the musical theatre's stability.

26

The Sixties (II)

Decline

By the second half of the sixties, some of Broadway's composers were ready to abandon the overworked Rodgers-Schwartz-Loewe sound hanging on through the fifties and pick up on contemporary developments (distinctly short of hard rock, however). But most patrons preferred the sounds of the past in bright packaging, worked around a star turn. *Sweet Charity* (1966) was a compromise with everybody, but it worked so well it looked like Ultima Thule to those who had sat through (or left during) *Skyscraper* or *The Yearling* a few months before. If *Sweet Charity* was taken to herald a new era in musical comedy, it was because people were starved for a good show and found one in this directed/choreographed supermusical devoted to the direction/choreography of Bob Fosse and the gamine plastique of Gwen Verdon as Charity, the latest meatheaded whore with a heart of gold. Cy Coleman and Dorothy Fields' score sounded fresh and with-it, though Coleman had a difficult time creating a warm tonal ambience for a cold-truckin' book that rivaled *Dolly*'s for heartlessness. Neil Simon's script struck many as palpable evidence that the musical had caught up with Life; certainly its New Yorkers seemed real enough, if a Times Square dance hall is your idea of real. But Fosse had left "real" staging back in *Redhead.* Even in *How to Succeed* his dances overthrew the rigid people-would-move-like-this-if-they-danced steps, giving the "Coffee Break" number a deeper reality by exaggerating it beyond the horizon of belief. Like Harburg, Fosse woos the clarity of real life with fantasy, using his corps the way De Mille did, but with splayed elbows and top hats.

Meanwhile, if *Sweet Charity* could at least act fresh-minted, the shows that immediately succeeded it held true to orthodox patterns. *It's a Bird . . . It's a Plane . . . It's Superman* dressed up a Strouse-Adams score in ignescent Eddie Sauter orchestrations, yet the songs were still vintage Strouse and Adams. Some of *Superman* was played in a cute pow-zowie comic book style, but since a lot of musical comedies unfold like comic books anyway, it didn't make much of a stir. A month later came the most traditional musical of the season, *A Time for Singing,* a beautiful romantic show based on Richard Llewellyn's *How Green Was My Valley* that sighed with too much honest sentiment for its own good. Though it missed the tough undercurrent of Llewellyn's reminiscence of life among the miners of South Wales, it had Welsh atmosphere to spare in its rich choral writing and in Donald McKayle's exuberant choreography. The first five minutes were pure gold, a stirring men's chorus superimposed over a stark mine ballet, but the flashback story was narrated by the adult schoolteacher rather than the boy Huw, as in the book, which rather upended the plot perspective.

Three days after *A Time for Singing* opened, it was followed and totally obliterated by *Mame,* the last of these three unreconstructed musicals and a wonderful treat then and now. Jerry Herman's score did a considerable service to Broadway in repopulating the media with show tunes, while Gene Saks' direction and Onna White's fast drags covered up with a dandy joie de vivre wherever *Mame* lacked the inner life of Jerome Lawrence and Robert E. Lee's 1957 straight play version of Patrick Dennis' book. Playing perhaps the most strenuous role in musical comedy history, the titanic Angela Lansbury sang, danced, acted, spun off ripostes like pebbles on a lake, modeled a breathtaking wardrobe, and sometimes passed out in her dressing room during intermissions. *Mame* pioneered nothing in the musical's history, but what with tunes like "My Best Girl," "Open a New Window," "It's Today," and the title song, with a child actor (Frankie Michaels) in a major role who didn't pout, lisp, freckle, or cavort like Salome at the races, with comediennes Beatrice Arthur and Jane Connell on hand as well as Lansbury, *Mame* was undebatably a luminous occasion.

All together, the semicontemporary *Sweet Charity* and the three holdouts, *Superman, A Time for Singing,* and *Mame,* fairly represented the general run of late sixties musicals, excluding for the moment rock shows. *Charity* was the old brassy musical comedy–*cum*–star vehicle given impetus with a director/choreographer's individual style; *Superman* and *Mame* were charming romps with dutifully integrated scores; *A Time for Singing* was an unabashed romantic show with some legit vocalizing, a fuller use of operatic ensemble, and a setting and time removed from present-day reality. By the sixties, forty years after Romberg and Friml parlayed adventure into the sensation of the era, the format of the romantic shows was merging with musical comedy far more coherently than it had in, say, *Oklahoma!*. Hammerstein and Kern made undiluted romance work thematically (*Show Boat* again), but later commentative shows were finding the satiric, anti-sentimental approach of a *Sweet Charity* useful for establishing a viewpoint. The artistic musical of the modern era needs the best of both heightened musical technique (romance) and dead-on realism (musical comedy) to arrive as music drama.

The merger came to a formidable climax in two Harold Prince shows, *Cabaret* (1966) and *Zorba* (1968). Based on older properties, both were original theatrical conceptions as staged by Prince and choreographed by Ronald Field. The stories unfolded within outside frames that provided a second, subtextual level of meaning. *Cabaret* had its mirror reflecting the audience, its sleazy emcee and cabaret folk controlling the action, watching the drama progress from the sidelines or intruding with vaudeville turns such as "Two Ladies" and "If You Could See Her Through My Eyes" that redoubled the plot implications. *Zorba* had a "let's tell a story" premise and a small chorus to interpret the action or push it along.

Prince was the catalyst in this not very new idea for the sagging tradition of the linear narrative; the three Sondheim-Prince shows of the early seventies developed the conceit as an organic concept rather than a production device—and then, finally, it *was* an innovation. After all, *Allegro* had its Greek chorus too, but *Allegro*'s choristers behaved like choristers while the Prince players are an integral part of the story, *people* rather than a chorus. The unnamed waiters and mädchen of *Cabaret,* the Leader of *Zorba* gave way first to Joanne and Larry, Sarah and Harry, Marta, April, and Robert's other friends in *Company,* then, more enticingly, to *Follies'* quartet's younger selves—people. Everybody on stage is part of the story; everybody interacts musically; the musical is an entity.

Cabaret was more glittering than *Zorba,* yet finally disturbing; *Zorba* was more sullen than *Cabaret,* yet exhilarating—at least, it was supposed to be. Some of the more pungent scenes, such as the murder of the widow and the mine dynamiting, didn't quite work on stage, overshadowed in most memories by their equivalents in the movie *Zorba the Greek.* On the other hand, there are a number of things the theatre can do that no movie ever can. Maria Karnilova's death scene, with the grim reaper personified as "The Crow" and with a touching vision of her vanished childhood in a song, "Happy Birthday," stood out as a luculent piece of music theatre.

Zorba was not as finished a work as *Cabaret,* but this is a faint damn, for *Cabaret* is one of our greatest musicals. If the business of a modern "operetta" is music drama, *Cabaret* and *Zorba* had it galore. Both scores were by Kander and Ebb, rivaled today only by Sondheim for lyrical wit and point and musical dramatization. It was no surprise to anyone that *Zorba* did not open with "It's a Wonderful Day in Piraeus" or whatever, but who could have expected the ruthless matter-of-factness of the first number's statement of purpose:

Life is where you wait
While you're waiting to leave.
Life is where you grin and grieve . . .

or this grim chant of "the crow," watching while the Frenchwoman died:

Soon
We'll see the crow
Perch on the sill, stare at the door;
Then
Make of his wings shadows that spill
Over the floor;
Crow,
Come from the cloud,
Black as the shroud she's never worn.
Crow,
Crackle and cry,
What doesn't die . . .
. . . Never was born!

The updating of theatre music got a little nudge from *The Apple Tree* (1966), Bock and Harnick's most impressive work, so impudent a departure from the *lex scripta* as to border on the radical. Who would have thought the gentle scriveners of *She Loves Me*'s little shop clerks and *Fiddler on the Roof*'s tradition-hugging families would give us such a gambol?—

ah, but remember how sassy their *Tenderloin* rogues were. The pair wrote their own book (with Jerome Coopersmith), knocking convention on its ass with three man-versus-woman one-act musicals tied together, whimsically, by the word "brown." "The Diary of Adam and Eve" was a sentimental comedy. "The Lady or the Tiger" a hot-blooded pagan orgy (with some dynamite mod music and the surprise non-ending of Frank Stockton's famous story), and "Passionella" a mixed-media Hollywood spoof. Bock and Harnick's three separate little scores connected with time present, mirabile dictu, beefing up the pit sound with electric guitars and burlesquing rock singers in "Passionella" while taking a crack at the American success dream as well. Cast to depth with perennial Eve Barbara Harris, Adam Alan Alda, and Tempter Larry Blyden, *The Apple Tree* was a remarkably full-bodied show that fulfilled the promise *Sweet Charity* only flirted with.

Like Bock and Harnick picking up their traces for a more contemporary sound, Harvey Schmidt and Tom Jones recovered from the syrup of *I Do! I Do!* (1966) for the imagination of *Celebration* (1969), a symbolic masque involving a young couple and a rich fat cat pursuing eternal verities on New Year's Eve. No doubt dismayed by *Celebration*'s hazy reception, the team gave up on the commercial theatre to open a workshop on West Forty-seventh Street. There they now present their experiments to a less mass audience. It's Broadway's loss, for if Jones' games on youth, age, innocence, and the like are too abstruse for most theatregoers, Schmidt's music has a transcendent simplicity and freshness that is sorely lacking on the main stem today.

Even more ambitious than *Celebration* in the area of plot material were two unsuccessful adaptations from serious originals, *Here's Where I Belong* (1968) from John Steinbeck's *East of Eden,* and *La Strada* (1969) from Federico Fellini's well-known film. By then, production costs were so huge that flop musicals could disappear after one performance, as these two did—no sheet music, no cast album, movie sale unlikely, just good-bye forever on a Sunday night. On the other hand, the equally ambitious *1776* (1969), a retelling of the first Continental Congress and its epic Declaration, ran 1217 performances because, frankly, it was terribly good. Peter Stone let no showmanship pyrotechnics infiltrate his rock-solid book, and Peter Hunt's excellent staging culminated in a hair-raisingly gentle tableau of the delegates signing the Declaration of Independence, slowly fading behind a projection of the document while the Liberty Bell tolled.

Set aside the artistic dimension of the Kander-Ebb-Prince shows and *1776,* the romantic musical was in bad shape. *Darling of the Day* (1968), based on Arnold Bennett's *Buried Alive,* didn't even name the author of its book in the playbill. The show still got some rave notices, possibly because it was the only genuinely period musical that season, but Jule Styne and E. Y. Harburg's score was below their par and the public's enthusiasm for Patricia Routledge was tempered by their . . . apathy . . . for Vincent Price. *Maggie Flynn* (1968) put Shirley Jones, Jack Cassidy, and a shrill passel of orphans in Civil War–time New York to no great effect, and *I Do! I Do!*'s very long run was mainly the achievement of Mary Martin and Robert Preston (the entire cast) and stage magician Gower Champion rather than the piece itself. In those days of hit or wipeout, few musicals could afford the expense of building an audience (*The Wiz* almost shuttered after a week for that very reason). The winsome *Come Summer* (1969) never had a chance. Another rural American show, *Come Summer* harked back to New England in the 1880s courtesy of director/choreographer Agnes De Mille's superlative folkish dances that somehow always seem to be danced by real folk. Even with authentic New Englander Ray Bolger and the doughty Margaret Hamilton, *Come Summer* gave up after a week.

Another flop romantic musical worthy of better reception was *Dear World* (1969), featuring yet another legendary performance by Angela Lansbury, another diamond-bright Jerry Herman score, and another gifted director/choreographer, Joe

Layton. *Dear World* stuck closely to its source, Giraudoux' *The Madwoman of Chaillot,* causing some people to wonder why so complete and perfect a play was adapted in the first place. Herman once again concocted a title tune for a smashing production number, but this was no formula show; it took its form, most noticeably in Layton's liquid street scenes, from its content, ending up a sort of romantic show with incongruous suggestions of musical comedy. Ultimately, it just didn't happen. Perhaps Giraudoux' complete and perfect original wouldn't succeed nowadays either.

Musical comedy mostly fell short of the gains made by *Cabaret* and *The Apple Tree* or even the half-gainer *Sweet Charity.* Reworkings of past stage, screen, and prose successes were commoner than ever, but *Her First Roman* (1968) from *Caesar and Cleopatra, Henry, Sweet Henry* (1967) from *The World of Henry Orient,* and *Billy* (1969) from *Billy Budd* were more like corruptions than adaptations. *Hot September* (1965) from Inge's *Picnic* and *Breakfast at Tiffany's* (1966) from Capote's story couldn't even survive tryouts. *Walking Happy* (1966) disinterred that old potboiler *Hobson's Choice* to tread a tightrope between period charm and uptempo foofaraw rather nicely, and *Canterbury Tales,* a British import of the 1968–69 season, did to rather than for Chaucer, but at least it did it with a contemporary beat and in a production vastly better than London's limp original.

One unusual musical comedy, *Hallelujah, Baby!* (1967), is probably the only flop to win a Tony Award as best musical of the year. A backstage story with overtones of fantasy and race relations, *Hallelujah, Baby!* brought its principals from 1900 to 1967 without aging them, in a triangular love plot replete with comments on American society then and now. Its chief adornment was neither book (Arthur Laurents), music (Jule Styne), nor lyrics (Comden and Green) but star Leslie Uggams. Another backstage legend, *George M.* (1968), had Cohan's songs and Joe Layton's inventive overview in its favor, but Joel Grey's chilly portrayal of the great song-and-dance man was only a little less hateful than his *Cabaret* emcee.

Broadway's wish for an updating in theatre scores was not quite satisfied by the Nashville sound of *A Joyful Noise* (1966), though the vocal equipment of John Raitt, Karen Morrow, Susan Watson, and Clifford David was a welcome oasis of open-stopped singing. It was inevitable that a pop tunesmith from outside would step in and show 'em how. Luckily, when it happened, *Promises, Promises* (1968) had an anchor of a script by Neil Simon to hold it together. Bert Bacharach, working with his usual lyricist, Hal David, deserted the world of mindless pop with a sure feel for the needs of a book musical so Jonathan Tunick's orchestration could let the "new" sound ride it out in style, even unto a wordless girls' scat back-up in the pit. New York theatre patrons happily accommodated themselves to Bacharach's wily, shifting-meter idiom, perfect for this glass-and-chrome version of Billy Wilder's film *The Apartment. Promises* was all Manhattan in its office-status gaming, company party, singles bar, and West Side studio. *Sweet Charity* was funkier, but *Promises* had cheer.

For those who like to worship their idols from a-near every now and then, Katharine Hepburn obliged with her first musical, playing la Chanel herself in *Coco* (1969). Alan Jay Lerner's book was funny, and the decisions of Cecil Beaton and Michael Bennett on how the fashion sequences should look and move were just right, but André Previn and Lerner let the evening down badly with their ho-hum score. Hepburn, however, was in excellent form, singlehandedly making sense of the star vehicle format.

Tradition continued to be upheld by old classics in two-week stands at the City Center, excellently performed in the choreography, orchestrations, and designs of their premieres. It was a museum of the best of the past. Richard Rodgers' summer season at Lincoln Center entered the act in 1964 with a more limited repertory comparably mounted. When *Annie Get Your Gun* showed up there in 1966, Merman still owned the title role, but with modern stage technology, the ingenue and juvenile were no longer needed to sing "Who Do You Love I Hope" or "I'll Share It All with You" during set changes; the secondary pair was written out of the libretto, giving further evidence that the two-couple layout of old-fashioned musical comedy (which dates back to *The Magic Flute* and beyond) was really dead, allowing the main plot to be treated in greater depth. The ancient form was still shedding snakeskins of convention to renew itself for a new generation.

Meanwhile, the revue and the little musical had all but vanished from Broadway, though downtown theatres were by their very size limited to one or the other. Social satire rather than artistic enterprise was still the raison d'être of the Village circuit, but things were even worse uptown, where the closest approach to revue was an hour and a half of headliners such as Jack Benny or Judy Garland. Carol Channing arrived in 1961 with comedians Jules Munshin and a French singing quartet, but calling it *Show Girl* didn't turn a nightclub act into a revue. Occasionally an evening of song devoted to one composer worked off-Broadway; Bernstein, Blitzstein, Porter, Arlen, and Coward were all granted retrospect in the sixties, not to mention the unkillable *Jacques Brel Is Alive and Well and Living in Paris.*

Led by *The Fantasticks* (1960), *You're a Good Man, Charlie Brown* (1967), and *Dames at Sea* (1968), each at a different level of whimsey, the off-Broadway book show of the sixties was tiny (the combined casts of the three is exactly one-third of a *Carousel*), often informal, and tended to the musically slight, whether in simplicity of composition for new scores or watery three-man combos for revivals of big shows from uptown. There were some bright exceptions, of course. The above three proved their durability, certainly, but there were undertakings of a more adult nature in *Dynamite Tonite* (1967), a devastating antiwar opera set in a bunker; in *Now Is the Time for All Good Men* (1967), questioning the values of middle America with a lively score by Nancy Ford and Gretchen

Cryer; and in *Ballad for a Firing Squad* (1968), a revision of *Mata Hari.* More typical notes of imbecility were sounded by *Promenade* (1969), a free-form flight of imagistic drivel performed by a talented cast, and a disastrously stupid production of the Weill-Brecht *Rise and Fall of the City of Mahagonny* in 1970. No doubt the summit of all this was reached by *Curley McDimple* (1967), with gap-toothed little Bayn Johnson bringing those rotten Shirley Temple movies back to life without a trace of wit. It ran for 931 performances.

27

Rock

In the twenties, when Tin Pan Alley hovered around the theatre district on Twenty-third Street, there were basically two levels of American popular song. Theatre music was of course the higher, musically expressive, lyrically literate, distinctive. Even out of context, these songs had the strength of purpose: they went from point A to point M developing a theme, while the rest of the country's pop tunes merely restated the title premise, going no farther than a sessile idea like "My Blue Heaven" or "Me and My Shadow."

These two worlds overlapped somewhat, especially in the revue and in Hollywood (where every mass market film had at least one song slipped in somehow), but throughout the thirties, forties, and fifties the best songwriters worked for Broadway, forcing the pop world to catch up to them just as Kern and Berlin did in the century's second decade.

As of the fifties these complexly interconnected systems

drew apart. Rock and roll couldn't be used in a play context (as *Grease* inadvertently proved later on), for its unmodifiable sound quality can't express mood or establish tone, nor is it useful in characterization. So-called rhythm and blues is far more adaptable—it adapted nicely in *Pippin,* for example—but rock, the present situation of the nation's pop music, rock in its many forms, is as useless as rock and roll was in the context of a theatre piece for exactly the same reason.

Nonetheless, it was inevitable that somebody try a rock musical. It was also inevitable that the first such show to hit Broadway would succeed if it didn't wait too long, for it was now the late sixties, rock had arrived, and the novelty would amuse New York theatregoers, most of whom are over thirty and don't hear much rock anyway. Now, if some canny producer could find a composer who would cut his rock with a little healthy pastiche, cast his show with young, young!, *young* people to emphasize freshness, and . . . yes! make it a counterculture piece with long hair and love beads and—oh wow!—hippies, and what else do we need? Well, naturally it's going to be antiwar, and how about a little nudity?

Hair (1967), the "American tribal love-rock musical," came at just the right time to make it big. Starting off-Broadway, it got rave notices, dropped in at the Cheetah discotheque, and finally moved into the Biltmore Theatre in 1968, earning mixed reviews. (Channel 2: "the best musical of the year"; John Chapman: "the most dismaying low of 1967–68." Chapman's understatement is correct.) It also earned a mind-blowing fortune on ticket and cast album sales and lasted out 1742 performances.

Hair has two almighty things in common with *The Black Crook* of 1866: musical novelty and skin. But the older show went farther with its materials. *The Black Crook* was proportionately only as big a hit in its day as *Hair* was in ours (which is to say, *very* big), yet *Crook* remained current for fifty years while *Hair* was already dated when it opened. *Hair* does deserve credit for Galt MacDermott's tuneful music, though it was wedded to the inept third-world mouthings of Gerome Ragni and James Rado. There was a lot of score, in fact, but no story: a young man has been drafted and must go off to war, period. This slim scenario was designed to support a series of sketches covering the gap between the hip and square worlds, making a convincing case for neither. Tom O'Horgan, director of the uptown version, is adept at upgrading poor material with staging tricks; he did what he does, and the publicity attendant on that dim moment of youthful nudity at the first act curtain didn't exactly discourage ticket purchase.

The race was on. *Hair*'s fabulous profits were bound to inspire imitations, including a few equally fabulous bombs. MacDermott and Ragni came up with an inflated quest-type of rock show in 1972, *Dude. Dude,* the aphid of musicals, possibly the worst Broadway musical of all time, *Dude,* a mess from its confused non-inception on, *Dude,* a million-dollar holocaust that played on a stage in the middle of its theatre's orchestra, asking what is life and begging the question, *Dude,* the show that teaches a lesson: novelty has no sequel.

MacDermott had better luck in 1971 working with Mel Shapiro and John Guare on an adaptation of Shakespeare's *Two Gentlemen of Verona,* but then this was no rock show. It had a beat, but the musical style was eclectic, and many of the lyrics could be understood in the theatre—a lucky break, for they had a freedom that few song lyrics possess in the tight framework of musical comedy. *Two Gentlemen* was large with freedoms, in fact, for it had a very loose structure, looser and looser yet as it went along. It originated in the New York Shakespeare Festival's free summer season, so it reflected Joseph Papp's bewildering view of Shakespeare as a reporter of ghetto life. The citizens of Verona and Milan were portrayed exclusively by blacks, strange-looking ethnic types, and longhairs, all attuned to the mores of present-day "liberal" America (song title: "Bring All the Boys Back Home"). It might have worked had they engrossed themselves less abstemiously in the pulse and tempo of a plot musical, but work or no work, it *was* a popular hit.

Jesus Christ Superstar (1971), another Tom O'Horgan special, was another rock success, but as with *Hair* and *Two Gentlemen,* the score for this "rock opera" was hardly all rock (it wasn't an opera either; rock operas are usually rock song cycles with a fancy handle). The legit composer Ned Rorem, in assessing *Jesus Christ Superstar,* examined the complicated fund of sources that so-called rock must draw on if it is to tackle a story line on stage: "Within three minutes, and before any solo voice is heard, composer [Andrew Lloyd] Webber has treated his listener to a nearly indigestible stew of Hindu ragas, of Rodgers' 'Slaughter on Tenth Avenue,' Prokofieff's *Age of Steel,* Strouse's *Bye Bye, Birdie,* Honegger's *Pacific 231,* Bernstein's *Fancy Free,* Copland's *Rodeo,* Grieg's Piano Concerto and the heavenly choirs of *Lost Horizon* which blur into Ligeti's stolen for *2001.*" Four years later Webber was still caressing old forms in his music for a British show *d'après* P. G. Wodehouse, *Jeeves.*

Simultaneous with the hot-ticket *Jesus Christ Superstar* was a genuine rock opus, Melvin van Peebles' "tunes from blackness," *Ain't Supposed to Die a Natural Death.* A scene from it turned up on the 1972 Tony Awards show, completely mystifying a television audience ready for their usual quota of production numbers from the season's crack musical comedies. (The problem was, there weren't any crack musicals that year. The hits were *Superstar, Two Gentlemen of Verona,* a *Man of La Mancha* revival, and *Sugar,* the sole new book musical of the four. When the Tonys were aired, everything else had closed or hadn't opened yet, and the pickings were at their slimmest.) *Ain't Supposed to Die a Natural Death,* a moderate success at 325 performances, caught the anguish of Harlem on its own terms in such songs as "Coolest Place in Town," "Catch That on the Corner," and "Lily Done the Zampoughi Every Time I Pulled Her Coattail." It was also the most contemptuous, amateurish piece of garbage ever crowed over by patronizing critics afraid to clip the tender bud of Afro-American art.

Jesus Christ Superstar's spectrum of aural borrowings was presaged by a little rock show, *Your Own Thing* (1968), v-e-r-y gently drawn from *Twelfth Night* and given to crosscutting Shakespearean verse with modern jive quite ingenuously. It also went the *Hair* route in regard to the generation gap, much more cleverly (God to Jesus, projected on slides: "When are you going to get a haircut?"), and it had two things *Hair* didn't have: one, real lyrics, and two, charm. *Purlie* (1970), from Ossie Davis' play *Purlie Victorious,* made a gallant stab at justifying unadulterated rock as a medium for a book show, but Gary Geld and Peter Udell's high-powered score was still bucking rock's intransigent tonal capacities.

Others tried, less successfully. The 1972–73 season was studded with dud rock shows: *Lysistrata, Via Galactica* (through-composed, set in the future, and performed on trampolines), *Tricks* (from Molière), and *Shelter* (man-woman modern) as well as *Dude.* Since then the proportion of rock shows has declined. 1974–75 had only two such items, *The Wiz* and *The Lieutenant;* the latter locked horns with My Lai, rather late for all that.

The Wiz, however, can defend its rock as a black show (a travesty of L. Frank Baum's children's classic, in fact, and a most amusing one), for rock music is to a large extent black music. Charlie Small's score channeled as much variety as rock could ever control, but if his lyrics could not be heard in the theatre, the songs were adorable and/or exciting when called for, though they too subscribed to the pop world's annoying habit of not rhyming when it thinks it is ("side" and "tired"). As far as sheer entertainment goes, however, *The Wiz* went all the way, jiveassing Baum's familiar characters with a wry ear for cultural distance and some genuinely imaginative staging. George Faison's choreography bypassed Broadway's dancing heritage to employ footwork from television and rock concerts (the better ones), giving the production a stand-out, joyous identity. Story sense went out the window when a team of crows straight from Motown pranced nattily behind the Scarecrow, but who cared? (For that matter, who cared when the smash 1903 musical version programmed such irrelevant ditties as "Love Is Love," "The Different Ways of Making Love," and "When You Love, Love, Love"?) *The Wiz* simply wasn't intended to be a story-integral show. It was a musical comedy, a fresh variety of same, true, but like its predecessors peaking in specialty bits, particularly when Clarice Taylor's dizzy good witch and Mabel King's laser beam of a wicked witch were on.

The rock fad has more or less passed now, at least until *The Wiz'* imitators get going. Spawned by *Hair,* it left a treasury of nothing, although *Your Own Thing* may ultimately prove durable through its wise use of pre-rock and the more versatile rhythm and blues, as doubtless will Stephen Schwartz' clown revue of Christian parables, *Godspell* (1971). Unlike rock, rhythm and blues isn't case-hardened by the gestalt of its own sound. It has room to navigate in; it can renew itself song by song; it can interpret; it gives the lyricist a chance to make his points.

The worst thing about the rock musicals was their librettos. This musical medium's limited scope cut its advocates off from the book-musical tradition, resulting in a caravan of all-purpose songs tricked up with sketches thrown in like bench-warmers in the final, frantic moments of play. Sure, it was great to hear something different on Broadway for a change, but while rock scores made amusing listening on the phonograph, on stage they couldn't fulfill minimum dramatic criteria. They were shiftless, without form, and so rapaciously commercial they made the Syndicate look like Winthrop Ames.

As Walter Kerr noted in early 1975 (in general, incidentally, not just about rock), musicals "are turning into concerts with virtually no spoken words at all and little in the way of intelligible lyrics, getting down on their knees and begging choreographers to come in and play tricks with scenery and lighting that may somehow or other save their souls . . . if we're ever going to find a fresh impulse for musical comedy we're going to have to pay some attention to what happens when people open their mouths."

If the rock librettos of the late sixties and seventies can be said to have any orientation at all, it was using the used-up counterculture for its own sake, headbands and beads as totems of nothing, a blowsy worldview that died with Haight-Ashbury and Woodstock. You can't trust anyone over thirty, was the third world's chant. Well, Broadway's rockers will never see thirty again.

28

The Seventies

Fall

Looking back on the first half of the present decade, the dismaying view yields short weight not in quantity but in quality. This should have been the era of totally liberated music drama, neither romantic shows nor aspiring musical comedies, but a composite of both, the "better world" and musical power of the first with the theatrical dynamics of the second. But the *Gypsy*s, *Cabaret*s and *Apple Tree*s of the seventies were damn few.

The 1970–71 season, for example, was, with two exceptions, timid. The two exceptions were *Follies* and *The Rothschilds,* financial failures that each lasted a year. The time was filled out with two Yiddish musicals (who on earth goes to those?); a couple of small shows, *70, Girls, 70* and *Frank Merriwell;* two parlous bombs, *Ari* and *Lovely Ladies, Kind Gentlemen;* a know-nothing rock show, *Earl of Ruston;* a ghetto revue, *The Me Nobody Knows;* the famous revival of *No, No Nanette;* and Richard Rodgers' *Two by Two.* All together, only the last two made it into the black: ten tries, two hits, and two failed first-raters (discounting the Yiddish pair, which are technically not Broadway entries anyway).

Now compare. 1960–61 hosted only eleven book shows, one of them a foreign import, leaving the same total as 1970–71—but *Camelot, Tenderloin, Carnival, Do Re Mi, The Happiest Girl in the World,* and *The Unsinkable Molly Brown* offer a higher general average in entertainment. Even the superflops had more panache in 1960–61: *Donnybrook* and *The Conquering Hero* were certainly more engaging than *Frank Merriwell* or *Ari.*

Go back ten years earlier and the comparison is mind-blowing: *The King and I, A Tree Grows in Brooklyn, Guys and Dolls, Call Me Madam, Out of This World, Seventeen,* and *Flahooley,* charmers all to at least some extent. Discounting the revues, 1950–51 had the same allotment of ten shows, but whether hit or flop these ten had more music, more comedy, more point than their relatives from 1970–71. This isn't nostalgic malarkey either. Almost all fifties and sixties shows mentioned above were recorded; listen to any one of them and give an ear to the cast album of a by no means unpopular seventies entry like *Inner City* or *Over Here!* or *Two Gentlemen of Verona* or *The Magic Show.* Actually, as the better scores have proved, the musicians of the seventies enjoy a more sophisticated compositional technique, but—let's face it—the frequency of melodically appealing and literate scores is down from before.

The economic struggle, escalated in the seventies, added to the general malaise. Broadway's fiscal condition is by now the economics of default. Television is economics. Movies are economics. Rock concerts are economics. Theatre is pin money. While the terrific odds against having a popular success and an artistic entity at the same time threatened to hold the better men in check, unknowns surfaced yearly with famished imitations of the standard sixties uptempo shows or deranged rock items, all taking up unwonted space playing to a music-hungry public who took what they could get, while old grads like Rodgers, Loewe and Lerner, and Styne hadn't grown enough to match the new-style format of the modern musical. There were some promising new names, but with one musical apiece it was hard to tell the comers from the flash in the pans.

Getting the sound of today onto the musical stage in a way that would benefit a specific libretto was still a problem to be faced by the half decent or better seventies shows, for too strong a pop affiliation results in an out-of-kilter collection of undramatic tunes, as if the twenties were here to stay . . . again. Returning to our paradigm 1970–71 season, two of the ten musicals footled fruitlessly with rock while *The Rothschilds, Two by Two, Frank Merriwell,* and *70, Girls, 70* courted the past in their music as well as their plots, or, in *70, Girls, 70*'s case, its cast. Only one show that season came to grips with an advanced musical idiom—*Follies,* which ironically enough also dealt partly with the past.

The previous season had a slightly more upbeat profile. Besides *Purlie*'s galvanizing hullabaloo, there was a new sock in the Strouse-Adams *Applause* (1970) songs. Indeed, it was energy and guts rather than real eminence of material that made the show a sellout, especially in Lauren Bacall's traversal of Bette Davis' *All About Eve* role. Mitch Leigh's *Man of La Mancha* music had already dissolved the operetta shell of the romantic show in 1965, but he outdid himself with an elegant array of modernistic tunes for *Cry for Us All* (1970), an adaptation of William Alfred's verse play *Hogan's Goat* cast for vocal and acting richness that somehow never caught on. Both *Applause* and *Cry for Us All* were updated musical comedy and romance, respectively, rather than genuinely fresh, so the slack had to be taken in at the tail end of the season by *Company* (1970), another landmark show not only for Stephen Sondheim's dazzling score—talk about modern!—but for the insatiable ambition of the show's total concept.

Company: a man in his thirties, surrounded by married friends and available girls, seeks an answer to the married-versus-single, intruded-on–versus–lonely battle, finally deciding he has found one: sharing life is "Being Alive." He doesn't have the girl in mind at curtain fall, but at least he'll be ready for her if they should ever meet. The dilemma in itself was a neat break from Broadway's time-honored love plots, wherein the delights of conjugal amour were never for a moment questioned, but then, if *Company* was no strutting musical comedy, it was all the same the antithesis of the romantic show. Only the expressive power of Sondheim's ballads connected with the musical plays of the forties.

Company was the very ego of today, in score and script, in Boris Aronson's somewhere-everywhere-in-the-East-Seventies set, and in its layout, a series of self-contained sketches enclosing the protagonist's investigation of his world. The players did their own ensemble work, quite sealing up the crypt of the once indispensable merry but dramatically anonymous villagers in Michael Bennett's super choreography. Bennett was on his way to being the best stager of musicals there is, a man who apparently kneels at the altar of concept rather than gloss. Here, and even more in the later *Follies* and *A Chorus Line,* he moved his actors/singers/dancers in the best of all possible ways, renewing musical comedy tradition by developing it. The Bennett patterns suggest the past without living in it, and they flourish, fusing bits of our experience with arrant distinction.

Despite a busy in-group following, *Company* wasn't a lot of people's favorite show. Like *Gypsy* and *Cabaret,* it exposed a few all-too-human faults ruthlessly, but *Company* wasn't about somebody else, such as stage mothers or Nazis; it was about a lot of folks in the audience, and thus cut bone-close on those who like musicals comforting and prancy. *Company*'s Boston tryout was even more uncompromising, for the first version of "Being Alive," "Happily Ever After," presented the hero's savage attempt to unlearn what he can't face having learned—that he is in fact lonely. Ostensibly saying one thing and meaning another, "Happily Ever After" was too complex a situation for the audience to grasp, and the less ambiguous "Being Alive" replaced it.

The romantic show was somewhat on the upsurge in the seventies—there were even a few revivals. The 1972 Lincoln Center *Man of La Mancha* in Albert Marre's original arena staging and with most of the original principals enjoyed a sell-out summer run, but an insufficient *Desert Song* and a retread of Loewe and Lerner's *Gigi* movie from Los Angeles failed to hold a public. Then there was *Ambassador,* based on Henry James' *The Ambassadors,* perhaps one of the greatest novels ever. Ignoring nearly all of the book except its initial premise and staging it ponderously with antediluvian operetta songs in 1972 was akin to falling off the flat edge of the earth. This *Ambassador* did after a week, leaving only the memory of Danielle Darrieux's luminescent Marie de Vionnet.

Richard Rodgers' contribution to the early seventies was *Two by Two,* a Noah and the Ark affair scuttled by Danny Kaye's outrageous scene-stealing and shtick. *Two by Two* ran a year on theatre parties and on the public's apparent ability to settle for the names on the poster, while the far more magical *Cyrano* (1973) couldn't last a month despite Christopher Plummer's adroit junket as Bergerac and Leigh Beery's sumptuous rendition of "You Have Made Me Love." *Two by Two* did have the edge on *Cyrano* as far as levity goes, it's true, but both were examples of the musical that takes itself seriously, a type that seemed ready to reestablish its onetime eminence. Unceasing failures notwithstanding, romance stuck with it undeterred: a second *Cyrano de Bergerac* adaptation, this one by Wright and Forrest, floated around on tour at exactly the time the Plummer show folded.

Neither *Two by Two* nor *Cyrano* was an important show, but they were at least diagnostic of poor old operetta's willingness to grow new gracefully. It was a little late by the seventies, for the romantic shows and musical comedy had already joined as the Musical in the sixties. Check the billings of the best shows of that decade. They no longer call themselves musical comedies or musical plays, just musicals. Still, there they were, *Two by Two* and *Cyrano,* offering palliatives to a cynical modern epoch. They dispensed with the chorus (*Cyrano* had one, just barely), they courted the contemporary idiom in their music (*Cyrano* did. Rodgers simply wrote what he always wrote and got the dynamic Eddie Sauter to orchestrate it; it came out sounding like Eddie Sauter in a training bra), they had staging concepts (earth tones and projections for *Two by Two,* spiffy period "suggestions" in *Cyrano*'s group movements). But it just didn't happen, twice. As with Giraudoux and *Dear World,* Rodgers' Odets source and *Cyrano*'s Rostand weren't adapted, merely revived punctuated by ditties. A good cast and some yearning artistry helps (it helped *Cyrano,* but not enough), but except for youngsters Madeline Kahn, Walter Willison, and Tricia O'Neil, *Two by Two* was senile and lifeless.

A more determined enlivening of the dreamy, antique recesses of the serious show was made by Claibe Richardson and Kenward Elmslie in their score for *The Grass Harp* (1971). "Yellow Drum" and "Reach Out" were pure fifties musical play, "Floozies" and "Walk into Heaven" semipure rock, and "Chain of Love" the timeless, aristocratic art song that musicals produce every now and then, but the spectrum of sound was so character-oriented it held together wonderfully. *The Grass Harp* was another of those shows with a great score and a paltry wen of a book. The second pass at equipping Truman Capote's lovely story for the stage (Capote himself failed the first time, in 1952), it only gave seven performances even with Barbara Cook, Carol Brice, Karen Morrow, and Ruth Ford in its small cast, but retains a following through the cast album. That's one thing that hasn't changed from the fifties: most musicals still get recorded, flops included, even though fewer than half of them repay the record company's investment.

The romantic show made a startling display of numbers in the 1972–73 season with four of the fourteen musicals, though

Cyrano, Ambassador, and the woeful little *Dear Oscar* (with Wilde singing "There Where the Young Men Go" while seatholders stared fervently at the exits) convinced no one that the medium was in fettle. It was up to *A Little Night Music* to hold the fort, singlehandedly to make up for the half empty years after the *Show Boat*s, *Carousel*s, and *My Fair Lady*s (more about *A Little Night Music* later). Two seasons on, musical comedy and romanticized musical comedy were back in the saddle again, nearly total, challenged only by *Shenandoah* (1975), a skeletonized adaptation of James Lee Barrett's original screenplay ignited by Gary Geld and Peter Udell's melodic score.

Shenandoah was a curiosity. It lost control of its story throughout Act Two, its pair of child actors were execrable and sang as sharp as scratched balloons, the songs ranged stylistically from forties musical play soliloquy to doltish country ballads in thirds, and the movie's big scenes seemed facile on stage. Yet many theatregoers adored it, clapping their hands off at each performance. Why? Possibly because they were starved for old-fashioned book shows with heart, with song—the *Paint Your Wagon–A Tree Grows in Brooklyn* kind of evening now in short supply. Despite its Civil War setting, *Shenandoah* wasn't in the tradition of the American shows of the forties, for it slacked in its approach to its subject matter. But it was certainly American in its politics, old, rare, and fine American in John Cullum's towering portrayal of a man who will cede neither property nor children to a cause he doesn't believe in. As Sondheim has pointed out, Hammerstein dealt with a similar theme in *The King and I* in Anna's battle for her rights in a feudal state, but these are uncommon instances of individual integrity in a medium that holds up a *Cradle Will Rock* as a museum piece of hype art while less obvious social-political vessels like *Knickerbocker Holiday* or *Sandhog* fade from view.

This nation's ancient liberty of owing nothing to no one (after taxes, at any rate) is more usually exploited in pop song lyrics of the sixties and seventies, where such sentiments are taken for granted by their audiences. Broadway may be America's theatre capital, but it remains a New York industry, melting potty and pseudoliberal. Popular songs are often written by their performers nowadays, and few of them hail from the Northeastern megalopolis. For every "Let's all hold hands and love one another" ditty by ———— (fill in the name of your favorite capitalist liberal) there is a "leave me alone and I'll leave you alone" item like the Charlie Daniels Band's "Long-Haired Country Boy," to name one of 1975's conspicuous examples.

The one yare romantic show of the early seventies was *The Rothschilds,* way back in 1970 before the rush was on. A period piece, with a Bock-Harnick score redolent of era, this historical pageant chronicled the rise of the famous banking family complete with historical figures, even covering historical developments in its musical numbers. Hal Linden's mammoth Meyer Rothschild deserved a Pultizer Prize (he settled for a Tony), as did Keene Curtis' four "villains" (another Tony), and Michael Kidd's direction/choreography threw out the operetta handbook to stage the work for the seventies instead of the twenties, but the evening's greatest virtue was the material—book (Sherman Yellen), music, and lyrics. This was one Jewish show that denied its patrons the slightest in-group chortle. It was large and lavish, with its own impossible dream, "In My Own Lifetime," but this was no fantasy: the dream was possible, and as with many romantic shows of the past, the family was the unit of bounty. Linden's ecstatic singing of "Sons" was one of the unforgettable moments of the modern musical; we've had poignance and vision, but oh, do we need real. *The Rothschilds* was Bock and Harnick's last partnership. *She Loves Me* may be their sweetest score and *The Apple Tree* their most characterful, but *The Rothschilds* stands with *Fiorello!* as their most carefully theatre-wrought work.

As for plain old musical comedy, it was plainer than ever.

The little show had resurfaced, no doubt because of the financial crunch, but the four-character *Park* (1970), the five-principal *Wild and Wonderful* (1971)—which was neither, but it's so easy to pick on a show with a spoof-me title—*Frank Merriwell* (1971), *Shelter* (1973), and a revival of *The Boy Friend* in 1970 all missed the boat. A more noticeable gaffe was *The Magic Show* (1974), a popular success because of Doug Henning's remarkable bag of tricks but a woeful nothing qua musical.

Off-Broadway's tradition of little musicals grew less fogbound with two delightful adaptations of (full circle!) our two proto-American plays of long ago, *The Contrast* (1787–1972) and *Fashion* (1845–1974), both by Don Pippin, Steven Brown, and Anthony Stimac. Meanwhile, in their workshop on Forty-seventh Street, Harvey Schmidt and Tom Jones presented works in progress in 1974–75, *The Bone Room* and *Philemon,* liberated musical comedies fraught with themes of identity and morality not always skillfully developed, but with the team's familiar touch of simplicity in the songs.

The big musical comedies laid the biggest eggs; think of *Georgy* (1970), *Look to the Lilies* (1970), *The Selling of the President* (1972), all adaptations. *Minnie's Boys* (1970), retailing the early years of the Marx Brothers, gave show-biz legends a bad name, and as far as flops go the seventies brought forth two superlatives for this volume. *Molly* (1973) had to be the most chaotic, pointless musical ever not written, and *Dr. Jazz* (1975) the most loathsome piece of business ever to humiliate a month of previewgoers. Rather less deserving of its sudden death was *Smith* (1973), a travesty of formula featuring a hero literally trapped in a preposterous musical comedy. Oh, well, aren't we all?

Seesaw (1973) was the nattiest of the big flops, emended and ripened so extensively in tryouts that its replacement director/choreographer Michael Bennett was listed as the author of the book. With this transformation of William Gibson's two-character *Two for the Seesaw,* Dorothy Fields closed her forty-five-year career collaborating with Cy Coleman, by now immersed in a contemporary pop idiom. His *Seesaw* music ran the gamut, from the vaudeville hurdy-gurdy of "It's Not Where You Start (It's where you finish)" and the haunting cool of the title song on down to a hateful hard-rock intrusion, "Ride Out the Storm." Michele Lee and Ken Howard (later John Gavin) made a strong impression unraveling the soap opera theatrics at the core of the tale, and their songs struck all the right poses, but the best of *Seesaw* was Bennett's way of filling out the scenario with the occasionally ugly sights and sounds of Manhattan, an island which in 1973 bore little resemblance to the place that so happily informed *On the Town* in 1944.

The unexpected conquest of the *No, No, Nanette* revival in 1971 supposedly signaled a return of (1) hummable tunes, (2) funky antiques with their rabbit warrens of convention and dopiness, and (3) more revivals. This is a misapprehension. Not till two years later was a dopey musical revived (*Irene,* the blockbuster of 1919), and even then it was so diddled and doodled on the road it came out as a new piece. In fact, the revivals didn't fare well at all. Hummable tunes notwithstanding, *On the Town, The Pajama Game,* and *Good News* all crossed the Rubicon of memory and sank without a trace, as did a cringingly bad staging of *Lost in the Stars. Where's Charley?* came back as a little show, also badly directed, at the uptown Circle in the Square, which has enough trouble with Chekhov and O'Neill as it is. More dismay: *Gentlemen Prefer Blondes* chased its own tail as *Lorelei* in 1974, spotlighting Carol Channing's superannuated flapper for matinee mavens. Only *Gypsy* and *A Funny Thing Happened on the Way to the Forum* passed the test of lasting appeal, proving . . . well, God knows what that proves. The second *On the Town* had a wonderful cast and production, if not Robbins' dances, and if it was dated, what was *Irene?*

The hit musical comedies weren't much better than the failures; they just ran longer. *Sugar* (1972) took its best moments from the Billie Wilder movie *Some Like It Hot*. It was certainly a crowd pleaser in Robert Morse's airy clowning, but even Gower Champion couldn't make it memorable. *Grease* (1972) moved north from Second Avenue's cavernous Eden Theatre to merchant, seemingly forever, its fifties parody and its exact re-creations of rock-and-roll song types, while the less resourceful *Over Here!* (1974) couldn't last a season giving the forties the same treatment, even with the Andrews Sisters, forgotten but not gone. Nostalgia was in the air, it was said, but even a novelty show needs material of some worth to please. *Grease*'s leather-jacket-and-saddle-shoes set sprang from life—my God, we were really like that once—whereas *Over Here!* brought back only the fakery of Hollywood's big broadcast movies. One held the mirror up to nature, the other held its mirror up to a stupid mirror.

But the emancipated romantic-realistic musical was still in there pitching, and there were several home runs. Opera creators Stanley Silverman and Richard Foreman deserted elevated haunts for two sensational music-theatre works in commercial precincts off-Broadway, *Dr. Selavy's Magic Theater* (1972) and *Hotel for Criminals* (1974). Both free-form works built on garish situations, they were promiscuous with creativity in Silverman's crystalline cross section of musical styles. *Dr. Selavy* took on mental illness, while *Hotel for Criminals* retrospected Feuillade's ghoulish silent film serials. Both amazed and thrilled while disdaining the genre clues that audiences are supposed to need, and the public took the out-and-out operatic layout of *Hotel for Criminals* in its stride —it's kind of hard not to when the music is that good.

For those who prefer more ostensive story lines, *Pippin* (1972) pretended it had one, and many were ravished. A somewhat pretentious picture of Charlemagne's dim son, *Pippin* had Bob Fosse's imagination and Stephen Schwartz' rhythm and blues score going for it if not Roger O. Hirson's book. Another of those we're-a-bunch-of-clowns-let's-do-a-show jobs, *Pippin* opened with white hands in the darkness, palms front, while Ben Vereen sidled to the footlights to "come hither" his way through "Magic to Do" seconded by the full cast, arms akimbo and made-up like pariahs. It was really something, and by the time Irene Ryan exhorted the ticketholders to join her in a chorus of "No Time at All," *Pippin* was home free. Truth to tell, the show was a joy, but it ultimately proved to be one hundred and thirty-five minutes about a penetratingly ordinary young man.

In the realm of serious music drama, things slowed up a little in the seventies. Besides *Follies,* the closest thing to an earnest story musical was *Raisin,* and then only because it depended so heavily on Lorraine Hansberry's excellent play *A Raisin in the Sun.* Judd Woldin and Robert Brittan's score was strongest in not-very-contextual ballads, and the plot songs simply lacked the appeal of the incidental numbers in, say, *She Loves Me* or *110 in the Shade.* Without the musical depth a strong dramatic show needs, *Raisin* won its plaudits on Hansberry's original script and some electrifying performances by Virginia Capers, Joe Morton, Ernestine Jackson, and Deborah Allen as the black family struggling to move out of the ghetto. Donald McKayle's staging dispensed with props and set changes to focus on the principals and the feel of Chicago's black enclave c. 1955, but his artful pantomiming of doors, kitchen things, and cars was defeated by an unbearably dreary unit set.

The little show tried to turn serious in *Sextet* (1974), a party of six friends and strangers strange-interluding and subtexting all over a multilevel apartment scene. It might have worked if the score had been of any interest, for there is yet more to be said in this format about the course of human relationships than *Company* was able to say in two and a half hours—especially since *Sextet* was the only one of several recent musicals dealing with homosexuality that did more than cruise the public with surface blandishments. As it was, *Sextet* granted one immense boon in its leading lady, Dixie Carter, a stunning raven of boundless talent who seemed born to play those female lead roles that musical comedy seems only recently to have dropped.

Casting is a major factor in production, of course, and sometimes it can be *the* stratagem in the identity of the show itself. This is all very well for a vehicle like Merman's *Happy Hunting* or Verdon's *Redhead,* enjoyed for its strutting ringer and promptly forgotten. But occasionally a show with some artistic aspirations gets embroiled in satisfying both its own concept and the demands of a star turn, thus decosmeticizing the false glamour while yet building it up. This logistical problem dogged *Goodtime Charley* (1975), a well-intentioned Joan-of-Arc-and-the-Dauphin tale with a leaden book, a pleasant score, a great Joan (Ann Reinking), and a Dauphin (Joel Grey) who apparently wanted to satisfy demands of musical theatre and the undemanding New York public at the same time. Grey's role was enmeshed in the drama, certainly, but it still carried the apparatus of the vaudeville parade—the big entrance, whooshed up wide-eyed from the basement on his bed after a nightmare, the undodgeable soft shoe, the fluttering lips and funny walk for age, even an eleven o'clock song, "I Leave the World" (and eleven o'clock wasn't any too soon). Weirdly enough, Reinking, a marvelous dancer, didn't. True, it can't be easy to choreograph a saint who wears armor, but if a dauphin can soft shoe . . .

Then there was *Mack and Mabel* (1974). Like *Goodtime Charley* an amalgam of the sober show and kickier musical comedy, this looked to be the winner of the season, a David Merrick–Gower Champion package with Robert Preston and Bernadette Peters, a Jerry Herman score, a big cast (rarer and rarer in the seventies), and a nostalgia trip to the romance between Mack Sennett and Mabel Normand. This was what everyone was supposed to be waiting for (and didn't get until *Chicago* at the tail end of the season), a splashy musical comedy hit.

Only it wasn't splashy because Champion really tried to tell a story instead of decorating one; it was even unconventional in form and design. It wasn't all that comic and brassy either. And it wasn't a hit. What it was was a terribly good show with some gaping flaws, mainly in book-score coordination and in a pair of deadly Sennett-styled comic sequences that just weren't funny.

But *Mack and Mabel* had a lot more going for it than against. Preston and Peters were the tops as the flick-obsessed Mack and the Mabel who never got to be first fiddle, but the show itself had a flair of its own. No musical's book deserved the Tony that season—especially *Shenandoah,* which won it—but *Mack and Mabel* didn't deserve it least. It began and ended starkly in an outcast movie hangar, and color never quite took over as would befit a show set in the silent era. Robin Wagner's designs pushed stage right to jut into the auditorium of the Majestic Theatre, and called for grips to move props around on stage as if on a movie lot, giving the show a striking presence totally at odds with the decor-elaborate, proscenium-bound stage dressing of a big musical.

There were production numbers, of course, but the fair, faithless brio of musical comedy mostly circled around the principals, pushing their love affair–business partnership into dramatic relief as more congenial lives buzzed on around them. While Lisa Kirk led the dancing girls in "Tap Your Troubles Away," Mabel's disintegration was played out in perfectly inapposite little scenes intercut for irony with the latest of cheer-up-it-could-be-worse songs. Herman's score was as good as anything he had done yet, though still bound to basic AABA song forms. He confirmed his practice of resisting contemporary nuances in his music, yet his melodies were so attractive they sounded refreshing amidst the aggressive smears of the mid-seventies.

Mack and Mabel was Champion's commencement from shiny prefabricated jobs into concept shows; his colleague Michael Bennett had already won his tassel, but his most astonishing work as director/choreographer didn't arrive till late that season. Conceived as well as staged by Bennett, and incubated in a workshop down at Joseph Papp's Public Theatre, *A Chorus Line* (1975) was an integral "whole piece" devoted to the last two hours of an audition for a Broadway musical. Nothing like a narrative, *A Chorus Line* tendered a look at the personal lives behind the spanking-bright nameless robots of Broadway ensembles. If its occasional hints at making a statement about anonymity versus identity didn't pan out, it was still a tremendous evening, mainly for Bennett's staging. He got the bravos he deserved for letting the content find its own form, but thanks go also to Tharon Musser's lighting, an underrated strategy in any show so dependent on the plastique of dance.

Speaking of star director/choreographers, the mummy grinning on a dung hill that Percy Hammond saw in *The Threepenny Opera* came back to death in a Bob Fosse show, *Chicago* (1975). Based on Maurine Watkins' 1926 satire on how publicity tactics subvert justice, *Chicago* was the ultimate Fosse musical, co-authored as well as staged by him. Those strutting, smirking, barbaric clowns lurking at the edges of *Pippin* took over in this one to smashing effect, and at last it was clear what Fosse had been driving at all along.

Chicago's worldview was a tough one, tougher even than Watkins' original. All sympathy for the heroine was dispensed with in Gwen Verdon's nail-hard portrayal of the murderess acquited by the newspaper headline mill—the right dress, a smart performance on the witness stand, a faked pregnancy. Not surprisingly, a Hollywood remake for Ginger Rogers in 1942 changed it around, making a likable innocent out of a killer—but then that's exactly the sort of maneuvering that Watkins' play was about. The musical adhered to the play's thesis, losing the light touch of Watkins' dialogue but on the other hand illuminating the theme with the cosmophysics of musical comedy.

Splendidly produced and hell-bent for slick, *Chicago* looked like the newest show ever imagined, even if playing a courtroom as a circus is at least as old as *Lady in the Dark*. Tony

Walton's fabulous unit set, Kander and Ebb's glittering twenties song tropes, Ralph Burns' brilliantly lewd orchestrations, and a magnetic cast (a pause to huzzah Chita Rivera's sensational second murderess) combined to enpicture a microcosm of such depravity it made *Sweet Charity*'s whores and hustlers look like the cast of *Heidi.* The show worked hard to capture a modern interpretation of Chicago in the twenties, but the final song, "Nowadays," made it clear with a little reverse irony that things are no different today for the American people, "who made it all possible by believing in our innocence"—so the two murderesses explained it while throwing roses at the audience.

It's irresistible to compare *Chicago* to *A Chorus Line,* as they were the two major productions of the last season covered in this book, 1974–75. They do have one gambit in common: conceptual direction/choreography, which was also a major factor in the runner-up *Mack and Mabel* and to some extent in that dark horse *The Wiz.* We are certainly more dependent on production than we used to be, if only because the stage itself can do more (pieces of *Chicago*'s stage even went up and down). As for the material, no two shows could be more divergent than *Chicago* and *A Chorus Line,* the one glancing at the world through darkest glasses, the other almost keening over the frail aspirations of more or less nice people. *A Chorus Line* had a lot of heart, whether or not you're into that—not the heart of *Mack and Mabel*'s central romance or the heart of *Shenandoah*'s family almanac, nor yet the heart of the *Wiz*'s innocence, but the heartfelt reaching out of honesty . . . valor, even. "What I Did for Love" was the lecture of the exhausted chorus-line hopefuls near the end of their trial—possibly because Marvin Hamlisch and Edward Kleban would otherwise have lacked a commercial hit tune. Then, horrifyingly, they materialized one by one in a phosphorescent apotheosis, the dancers who were so painstakingly individualized for us now submerged in a grim, callous, defiant "big number." It was scary, but all the same, one was moved because the characters worked as people. And more: they had hope. Even the losers could go home believing in something.

Not so the inhabitants of *Chicago*. They believed in nothing, registered nothing but meals eaten, money made, rocks gotten off. To the audience at *Chicago,* thrills were to be had not by breathing along with the actors (as in a romantic show of the forties with its larger-than-life score) but by retaining one's alienation. The music had a lot to do with it, of course, added to Fosse's maniacal theatre of manipulation, but then musical comedies always tended to carry a built-in alienation because of their obtrusive jokes and brittle ditties. How could anyone care about a *Girl Crazy,* or a *Mexican Hayride* or a *Hello, Dolly!?* Well, one cared at *A Chorus Line,* at *Mack and Mabel,* even at *Shenandoah,* though its foolish book and now-trendy, now-musico-dramatic score tested one's patience. One didn't care at *Chicago;* one wasn't meant to. This was musical comedy incarnate, diamond-hard, ironic, riveting; it burst with personality; it had point of view.

Fosse had already used parodies of old stage archetypes in *Pippin,* if randomly, and three of the greatest musicals ever—*Show Boat, The Golden Apple,* and *Follies*—turned on entertainment motifs. But *Chicago* used them more heavily, for its theme is media hype, and what else *is* entertainment, after all? Billed as a "musical vaudeville," *Chicago* took its shape from radio microphones and the nightclub spotlight, setting Verdon on a piano for the pointedly vapid "(That) Funny Honey (Of mine)," providing a collegiate quartet complete with megaphones for "When Velma Takes the Stand," even closing *victoriously* with the headline act of the two freed criminals (the italics are Fosse's).

Follies, as will be seen in the next chapter, also recalled the distorted dream-catering of media myths in its score, but *Follies* was about people victimized by bankrupt ideals, *Chicago* about how the falseness thrives. Nothing was ever what it pretended to be, especially not as sold by suave radio crooners or footloose film heroines with their didactic final frames. Even Kern and Marilyn Miller got the rapier thrust in "A Little Bit of Good (In everyone)." Like the pop tunes of bygone days, *Chicago*'s songs proffered the seductive panaceas—but with a twist, for you got to see the corruption below the surface.

This chapter is entitled "Fall" because musical theatre scores sank to a low level in the seventies. The books have always been a problem, but from the twenties through the fifties there was a concentration of talented composers we simply don't have any more. The best score of this 1974–75 season was heard in a revival (*Gypsy*), and though *Shenandoah*'s songs tender melodic appeal, only John Cullum's soliloquies rank as theatre music. The *Wiz* score flutters by when heard without the flavorful stage business, and *Mack and Mabel*'s sudden demise seems to have buried its disarming tunes, and *A Chorus Line*'s expert word-music collaboration seems to have disappointed the public more than pleased.

And *Chicago*? For all their fidelity to outdated pop, these Kander-Ebb songs did their dramatic duty up the yin-yang. And as for those who decry the use of pastiche, let them find theatre songs of the modern era with the sardonic power of *Chicago*'s "All I Care About (Is love)" or "When You're Good to Mama," with the associations they convey from our folk musical panorama (that is, with the exception of Sondheim, rapidly becoming a Christ for today's theatre buffs).

On second thought, perhaps this isn't the fall any more. We may very well be on the cusp of something. For more evidence, we have to backtrack just a bit.

29

Follies, A Little Night Music

"New Art Is True Art"

When the Stephen Sondheim–James Goldman, Harold Prince–Michael Bennett *Follies* (1971) tried out in Boston, the Harvard *Crimson*'s Frank Rich headed his review, "The Last Musical": "The setting is described as 'a party on the stage of this theater tonight.' They are not kidding, and there is no getting around the fact that a large part of the chilling fascination of *Follies* is that its creators are in essence presenting their own funeral."

Economically at least, Rich couldn't be debated. Dig it: the old *Follies of 1907* cost $13,000 to mount, *Oklahoma!* $83,000, *The Pajama Game* $169,000. *Follies* cost $800,000 to produce and had to earn $85,000 a week to break even. True, it was a big show, big even for the seventies. It's not likely that the flagging New York theatre can support many such shows—it couldn't support *Follies,* though the piece lasted a year. Even so, *Follies* didn't prove to be the last gigantic musical.

But that funeral Rich spoke of wasn't economic. *"Follies,"* he said, "is a musical about the death of the musical." Goldman's book dealt with a reunion of aging Ziegfeld-type entertainers just before their old theatre is to be torn down. Prominent among them are two married couples, friends from thirty years ago; one of the wives still loves the other's husband. Throughout the evening black and white ghosts of the cast's young selves float around the action—showgirls, a singing and dancing chorus, and the two couples as they were in the forties . . . young, full of hope, thinking they knew what they wanted of life. As the evening wears on, the mistakes of the past spill out, the dissatisfaction—waste—of the present confronts the principals, and the ensuing pandemonium erupts in a sumptuous Ziegfeldian Follies revue in which the four, their defenses down, face up to the lie and surrender the dream. Dawn breaks, the reality of Manhattan peers in through a collapsed wall, and the couples separate to leave as their ghosts stare after them.

Perhaps the most richly staged musical of the modern era, *Follies* was generically in the new mode of serious music drama neither comic nor romantic (though the specter of Romberg-Friml cut through in "One More Kiss.") It was also one of the few shows to develop its theme in song lyrics as well as script. ("Still playing games, acting crazy," sang two of the leads casually. It's the story of their lives.) The curtain rose on a glorious showgirl ghost posed downstage center. Slowly, ever so slowly, arms extended and body rigid, she was seen to move to a waltz in the style of a Satie *gymnopédie* as Ravel might have harmonized it. The vast Winter Garden stage seemed a wreck of itself in the darkness as other ghosts drifted in, relics tailing the "real-life" characters of the present. This dreamlike waltz set the mood for the whole piece, not only as a stage picture but also as a literalization of the subtext—the values of the past accusing, haunting, bedeviling their present-day selves. As the party guests arrived, threading unwittingly past their own ghosts, the audience clapped for the familiar faces of past decades—Yvonne de Carlo,

Ethel Shutta, Michael Bartlett, Mary McCarty, Justine Johnstone—not realizing the trap it was falling into, reconfirming the old glamorous images only to see them shattered.

Besides the supporting cast, three of the four principals were out of an earlier era of American entertainment, Alexis Smith, Dorothy Collins, and Gene Nelson. The fourth, John McMartin, stood as an unknown quantity at the vortex of the past-present problem. The most ostensibly successful of them all, the one who "got what he wanted," he wants and has nothing. It is he who provides the climax in the elaborate Follies parade of Big Numbers, reminiscent of old forms but composed by Sondheim in progressively contemporary modes. Nelson had a freewheeling baggy-pants vaudeviller, "The God-Why-Don't-You-Love-Me-Blues," Collins a prototypical torch song, "Losing My Mind":

> All afternoon, doing every little chore,
> The thought of you stays bright;
> Sometimes I stand in the middle of the floor
> Not going left, not going right . . .

and Smith got a thumping Star Lady and Chorus turn, "The Story of Lucy and Jessie." All three numbers ceded the unpleasant truths about the characters: their old ideals hadn't held up with time. Maybe they were wrong ideals, or maybe times have changed . . . or maybe our definition of success has. McMartin had the last Folly, a Mister-Broadway-in-top-hat-and-cane specialty, "Live, Laugh, Love"—and McMartin, alone of the four, still tried to put over the lie:

> Success is swell and success is sweet,
> But every height has a drop.
> The less achievement, the less defeat:
> What's the use of shovin' your way to the top?
> Live 'n laugh 'n love 'n you're never a flop . . .

But he can't get through with it. As he stumbles in his words, the conductor throws him a cue and the line of dancers flanking him sing on, eyeing him balefully for ruining the number. McMartin's was the Folly on the brink, dissolving the minirevue and bringing the four back to time present.

When *Follies* opened on April 4, 1971, most critics missed the point. Barnes' suggestion that the cast album come out on 78s may well be the most obtuse piece of theatre criticism since they gave *Tobacco Road* till Saturday night. But the *Times* also gave space to Martin Gottfried: "I am convinced that *Follies* is monumental theater. Not because I say so but because it is there for everybody to see."

Perhaps there was too much for everybody to see at one sitting, for not everybody is certain he saw it. Even the authors themselves are divided over what *Follies* ultimately presented, but one thing is sure: quibbling aside, *Follies* is one of American music drama's few epics. Most musicals don't stretch very far in their two and a half hours of diversion. *Follies* stretched. It was bigger than most shows, structured beyond the ken of formula-hunting mass audiences. Forget exposition and narrative ploys. *Follies* was a mosaic of plot pieces—a mystery, in one sense—played out on multilevels, the *Follies* about follies. In its use of old musical comedy keys, it was a foray into the collective unconscious of our theatre imaginings, a striking use of pet middlebrow totems. Lastly, in its score *Follies* was opera, for its music wasn't there for lift or story enlightenment—it *was* the story. That it ended in Los Angeles opening a brand-new theatre is not ironic, for the *Crimson* was wrong: *Follies* is not the last musical, but the next.

The next but one, a fitting close to this book, was *A Little Night Music* (1973), the ultimate completion of the romantic show. All the formalistic elements were in place—a "legit" score, handsome decor and beautiful people, a semifantastic setting removed from daily life, and the full compensation of beauty. Only the heroes were missing, for like musical comedy and the musical play, romance was now free to deal with realistic human emotions—ah, but with what grace!—and in this show, as in life, there are no heroes. Hugh Wheeler's elegant script borrowed Ingmar Bergman's *Smiles of a Summer Night* characters, but the show went less dark and sardonic than the movie; Sondheim's score soothed and uplifted as so many romantic show scores have determined to, yet this one outranks them all.

The musical has reached a point at which opera-trained voices aren't required to give full expression to lyrical ideas (as they absolutely were in the days of operetta), so Glynis Johns, Len Cariou, and Patricia Elliott could give full measure without having to sound like a failed Red Shadow or Rose-Marie (and how many Red Shadows and Rose-Maries were able to justify the book scenes?). Happily, Victoria Mallory, Laurence Guittard, and Mark Lambert were on hand to supply a more potent vocalism, not to mention a quintet of Liebeslieder singers (Brahms used a quartet, but who's counting?).

Our musical romances no longer envision love as a drug of sanitary affection, lenient beyond belief. Musical comedy got around to sex years ago (and even *The Desert Song*'s tent scene spoke up for the operetta world in a resoundingly phallic sword business), but romances too often lacked that fulfillment of an adult worldview. True, *Man of la Mancha* made up for its lack of a love story with a rape scene, and *Cry for Us All*'s plot turned on the ways of the flesh, but *A Little Night Music* did it with elegance. People are human; they have sex a lot. But they don't necessarily have to snigger about it, musical comedy style.

As it happened, one of Sondheim's more adroit pieces in this vein was abandoned out of town, as so many interesting songs are when a scene isn't working. But this particular song's picture of the battle/affair between a stuffy hussar and a game actress, composed as a polonaise, demands notice, so in lieu of a plot diagnosis or further assessments of format, *voilà* "Bang!":

Carl-Magnus: The war commences,
The enemy awaits,
In quivering expectancy.
The poor defenses,
The penetrable gates,
How terrible to be a woman.
The time is here,
The game is there,
The smell of fear,
Like musk, pervades the air.
The bugle's sounding,
The pistol's steady,
The blood is pounding,
Take aim and ready—
Bang! Twenty minutes small talk,
Thirty at the most.
Bang! Two or three to pour the schnapps.
Bang! Bang! Bang! Half a minute to propose
The necessary toast,
Bang! The tunic opens,
Bang! The trousers fall,
Bang! The foe is helpless,
Back against the wall.
Bang! An hour and a quarter overall,
And bang!
Desirée: Twenty minutes to arrange
Those bloody awful flowers,
C-M: Bang!
D: Can I get away with more?
C-M: Bang! Bang! Bang!
D: Then I have to brush my hair,
And that could take me hours,
C-M: Bang!
D: A fit of vapors . . .
C-M: Bang!
D: No, that's too quaint.
C-M: Bang!
D: A wracking cough and
Then a graceful faint . . .
C-M: Bang!
D: A lengthy lecture
C-M: Bang!

D: On self-restraint . . .
C-M: Bang! Bang!
Quintet: Bang! Bang! Bang! Bang!
C-M: The battle rages!
Q: Bang!
C-M: Whatever ground I gain
I fortify remorselessly.
Q: Bang! Bang!
C-M: The foe engages—
Q: Bang!
C-M: By shifting the terrain,
How pitiful to be a woman.
Q: Bang!
C-M: Attack!
Q: Bang!
C-M: Retreat!
Q: Bang.
C-M: Lay back!
Q: Bang!
C-M: Re-form!
Q: Bang, bang!
C-M: Outflank!
Q: Bang!
C-M: Deplete!
Q: Bang!
C-M: Move up
And then restorm!
Q: Bang, Bang, Bang, Bang.
C-M: The siege succeeding,
Q: Bang.
C-M: The time grows shorter.
Q: Bang.
C-M: She lies there pleading.
Q: Bang.
C-M: I give no quarter . . .
Q and C-M: Bang!
C-M: Foray at the elbow,
Salvo at the knee!
Q and C-M: Bang!
C-M: Fusillades at breast and thigh.
Q and C-M: Bang! Bang! Bang!
C-M: Then when she's exhausted,

Q and C-M: Bang!
C-M: A fresh sortie!
Q: Bang.
C-M: I taste the conquest—
Q: Bang!
C-M: The taste is sweet.
Q: Bang, Bang!
C-M: She lays her arms down,
Welcoming defeat.
Q: Bang, Bang!
C-M: Both sides content,
Q: Bang! Bang!
C-M: Secure positions,
Q: Bang, Bang, Bang, Bang, Bang.
C-M: All passion spent,
Q: Bang. Bang.
C-M: Discuss conditions.
How terrible—
Q: Bang.
C-M: How pitiful—
Q: Bang.
C-M: How glorious to be a woman.
Q: Bang, Bang, Bang, Bang.
D: He is a peacock—
Q: Bang.
D: I keep forgetting.
Q: Bang.
C-M: The quarry senses—
Q: Bang.
C-M: A momentary pang.
Q: Bang, Bang.
D: It's all so foolish.
Q: Bang.
D: Why am I sweating?
Q: Bang.
C-M: The war commences . . .
C-M and Q: Bang!

Great art may spring eternal, like hope, but little of it is totally new. When Moussorgsky wrote *Boris Godunov* he spoke of "the past living in the present": the new renews the old, cossets it, but also moves on to fresh ideas. The romantic show is/was the Hammerstein stronghold, ennobled in the twenties with a story sense and lyrical point, mostly ignored in the thirties but rediscovered and perfected in the forties. Like *The Golden Apple, Cabaret, Follies,* and the later *Chicago, A Little Night Music* reclaimed Hammerstein's linear narratives with their motor themes to voice the thesis at the root of the story in ways Hammerstein tried out only in *Allegro.* All these shows have the maximal bounty of thought. They amuse, but they are to be comprehended.

Where we stand now is the big question. Where do we go from here, if indeed we go at all? The music in musicals is probably our most salient hope as well as, at the moment, our saddest disappointment. The format of musicals is now as flexible as it ever need be; it can incubate a thesis, play with interior meanings, even span time and space as if it didn't exist, which is of course what the theatre is for. The word portions to some of the better shows are like prisms of textual concept, radiating nuances and subtexts with ease, illuminating the dramatic action with a thought process. Okay, fine. What we need now is musical composition on a comparable level—No, we have such composition. We just don't get enough of it.

Follies and *A Little Night Music* had it to spare, which is why these two works close this volume. The outlines of popular song haven't changed all that much from the days when Kern and Berlin transformed it from saltines to cake, but musicals couldn't go on forever using just songs. The sophisticated or poetic or perceptive lyrics of Porter, Hart, Hammerstein, Harburg, and Sondheim have worked their wonders, but this isn't enough. Nor is opera the answer. The answer is music drama, an entity conceived throughout in musicodramatic terms, with the ultimate penetration of art. A play with some cute songs is nothing, and quite aside from the embellishments of dance and incidental music or motivic shufflings, the score of a musical rests on its songs—ballads, comedy numbers, scenes, choruses. Back in the thirties some composers made it clear that these songs could be organically conceived, subtly related to each other as contours of a larger shape. The one- or two-man assembly line gave ground reluctantly, and though tryout tinkerings are still as hectic and haphazard as ever, musicals are often constructed all of a piece, and they at least intend to make sense.

Follies and *A Little Night Music* not only intended to, they did, the one elaborately on several contiguous planes, the other more directly. We will always need solid books, but music above all is the key. Without its rich melodic output, *Night Music* would have been a better than average boudoir-and-country-weekend snafu. The songs defined it, distanced the characters, embodied the drama. God, what a song can do all by itself! No wonder Hammerstein and Harburg had to write the lyrics as well as the books. If a tune like "Who Cares?" could make all the difference in *Of Thee I Sing*'s love plot, lost in the bombardment of political satire, what dimensions are achieved by *Night Music*'s "Every Day a Little Death" or Hermione Gingold's sarabande of a comedy number, "Liaisons." We no longer require a nifty middle strain in our ballads to hold our interest, though we still get them. Sondheim writes organic songs, spun out in one breath with no pop seams showing. Oh, we still like our massed finales, but the stirring oratoriettes-with-dialogue of *Rose-Marie* and *The New Moon* gained sublimation in the close of *Night Music*'s first act, a finaletto for Friml and Romberg to ponder with a wild surmise, called "A Weekend in the Country." Good theatre isn't only pity and terror, and in this extended songthing the plot zips along, the characters reveal a little more about themselves, the sets fly around defying unities of time and place, and voices merge in that consonant but individual mass that so thrilled Victor Hugo when he first heard the musical that Verdi made of *Le Roi S'Amuse*. Or consider "Send in the Clowns," a junction of story and song, ravishingly written, specific and universal, with an accompaniment Franz Schubert would have loved. Sung by the actress (Glynis

Johns, and she was superb), it carries references to the theatre—"making my entrance again with my usual flair"—but its scope is life. Few were the people who heard it in the house to whom the song did not apply an exquisite pain from somewhere in the past.

I don't know about you, but my most enthralling memory in musical comedy is of *Night Music*'s final moments, when "Send in the Clowns" welled up in the orchestra as Len Cariou embraced Johns to confirm their happy ending, something we in the audience could hope for and believe in. We need realism in the theatre but we need our fantasy too, and if life isn't as nice as *A Little Night Music,* well, that's what the *Little Night Music*s are for. And the *Show Boat*s, the *Carousel*s, the *My Fair Lady*s. And they do it through the music. *Follies* may well be *the* superior music drama Broadway has produced, for its statement is a vast one, but moved as we were by those four forlorn ghosts watching their present selves abandon the old haven, it is the romances that capture us most. They gentle us with consoling visions, disdaining urban flux and chatter for the more natural environment of the countryside, sometimes even giving us heroes to emulate. Of all the types of musicals there have been, the romantic shows have the most consistently admirable record, although some of the very greatest works for Broadway stem from less elevated musical comedy.

And that's it, with thanks to Thackeray for an optimum final line: "Come, children, let us shut up the box and the puppets, for our play is played out."

A VERY SELECTIVE BIBLIOGRAPHY

Atkinson, Brooks, *Broadway*. New York, Macmillan, second edition 1974. Do not read Atkinson on musicals; he seems to have forgotten much of what he learned when he was reviewing them regularly. But do try him for a cogent history of The Street from 1900. One is not convinced by Atkinson's grasp of musical values—he calls *On the Town*'s "New York, New York" a "joyless, suspicious theme song"—but his understanding of straight drama is to be trusted.

Engel, Lehman, *The American Musical Theater*. New York, CBS Legacy Collection/Macmillan, 1967. Winningly illustrated and featuring a complete discography of original-cast albums, this is an in-depth introduction from a technical standpoint, with emphasis on how the music makes it work.

Goldman, William, *The Season*. New York, Harcourt, Brace and World, 1969. Easily the most readable and informative book listed here, this one chronicles the hits and flops of an entire season (1967–68) with reasons why. Fascinating, the best book on live theatre that I know of.

Green, Stanley, *Ring Bells! Sing Songs!* New Rochelle, Arlington House, 1971. With pictures and posters galore, this is musical comedy in the thirties, every single show, all viewed with an eye on the way the world was then. The back half of the volume gives ridiculously incomplete data on each play—not very helpful, that.

——— *The World of Musical Comedy.* New York, A. S. Barnes and Company, third edition 1974. This is the preferred all-around reference work for those who require (correct) statistics as well as engrossing reading. Green skips the *objets trouvés* but little of importance is omitted. His discography, limited to twelve-inch LP's, misses a few of the titles Engel caught, but he does mention alternate recordings (revivals, sound tracks, and so on) with brief ratings to assist the tyro.

Kimball, Robert; Brendan Gill; and Bea Feitler, *Cole.* New York, Holt, Rinehart and Winston, 1971.

Kimball, Robert; Alfred Simon; and Bea Feitler, *The Gershwins.* New York, Atheneum, 1973. Here are two dazzling coffee-table trophies, with lyrics, personal and production photos, and reminiscences. They do a remarkable job of bringing a dead era to life for us moderns.

MacKinley, Sterling, *Origin and Development of Light Opera.* London, Hutchinson and Company, 1927. Every bibliography must have its class entry, preferably something arcane and ancient so as to provide (1) tone, and (2) the impression that the author has scouted every imaginable source. As it happens, MacKinley's charming antique (which can be found in libraries) offers the definitive statement on how slightly comedies in music have changed from the days of the old Greek goat songs. This entertaining volume gathers up the loose ends, including such pertinent movements as Swedish Sagospel, Danish Syngespil, and British Carriage-Play. MacKinley's thesis that "the more we seek the dead past the more we find the living present" is proved early on when a theatre slump in pre-Christian Rome is relieved by "vulgar abuse . . . sensual episodes and inconceivable obscenities."

Smith, Cecil, *Musical Comedy in America.* New York, Theatre Arts Books, 1950. Complete through *South Pacific,* this classic history is infinitely worth a search through out-of-print shops. Smith had three virtues: wisdom, wit, and musical training. Any one of these alone is rare in theatre literature; the three together are lightning. This is a must, particularly for its detailed examination of the early years, which I'm afraid I rather raced through.

Wilder, Alec, *American Popular Song*. New York, Oxford University Press, 1972. Taking constant potshots at rock, Wilder investigates the output of theatre composers (and a few pop tunesmiths) through the fifties. He takes an insider's stance, rooting at what made American popular music what it was. Uncountable musical examples, sans lyrics.

Zadan, Craig, *Sondheim and Company*. New York, Macmillan, 1974. Most of Zadan's work consists of direct quotations from Sondheim and his collaborators; as criticism verité you couldn't ask for a more illuminating production. There are also intriguing articles on such items as orchestration, musical direction, and recording the cast album.

ANNUALS

Burns Mantle's *Best Plays* (New York, Dodd, Mead and Company) series featured obtuse digest versions of the season's hits each year from 1919 on (two volumes covered 1899–1919) and others took on the task after him. Mantle rarely picked a musical, but he did list the cast and credits of the whole year's shows, with tiny summaries of the plot for trivia buffs. Far more useful to many for its visual orientation is Daniel Blum's *Theatre World* (New York, Greenberg; Chilton Company; Crown Publishers), now edited by John Willis. This series tackles the subject entirely in pictures and statistics, with bleary one-page introductions. Blum's pictures really did capture the stylistic energies of the times: check out the full-stage shots of *Carousel, Song of Norway,* and *Up in Central Park* in the first of the series (1944–45) for evidential atmosphere. A caveat: the recent volumes have been tending to rather feckless photographs.

BIOGRAPHIES

The situation here is quantity, not quality. Most of the big composers have had their books (not so the lyricists), and the more colorful producers, actors, and whatnot got their titles too, mostly "as told to" some hack. Few of these are recommendable. Richard Rodgers wrote his own *Musical Stages,* but it's something of a drone. Try Edward Jablonski and Lawrence D. Stewart's *The Gershwin Years,* George Eells' *The Life That Late He Led* (Cole Porter), or Deems Taylor's *Some Enchanted Evenings* (Rodgers and Hammerstein, separately and together). Pick of the litter: Jerry Stagg's *The Brothers Shubert*—awfully funny. Howard Dietz' *Dancing in the Dark* offers good reading but doesn't spend much time in the theatre. Who can blame him?

LYRIC COLLECTIONS

Ira Gershwin's *Lyrics on Several Occasions* (New York, Viking Compass paperback, 1974) is the only album of an American lyricist's work still in print and contains amusing notes on the ins and outs of creation. The Overlook Press published a Noel Coward volume in 1973, but its completeness only brings home the appalling lack of resonance of Coward's later verses. Simon and Schuster brought out *Lyrics by Oscar Hammerstein II* back in 1949; this is now long vanished. Sondheim, who knew him well, has been quoted as calling Hammerstein a man of "limited talent and infinite soul." I couldn't disagree more, and if you can locate a copy of this slim book of lyrics set by Rodgers, Kern, Romberg, and including *Carmen Jones* as well, the best of the lot, you may find infinite talent to match the soul. Meanwhile, Crown Publishers has given us *Their Words Are Music*, Lehman Engel's analysis and congeries of theatre lyrics, from *The Mulligan Guard* to Edward Kleban. Another must.

SCRIPTS

By the fifties, most of the more or less successful musicals were published in book form, mainly by Random House; the practice obtains today. Such items go out of print fast though, so be prepared for a safari.

A NOTE ON RECORDINGS

Consider this: since records were invented, virtually all popular artists of some standing have been leaving their specialties on disc, some as many as a hundred different numbers in two or three takes each. Show scores *in toto* weren't recorded at first, but a likely hit or two was sometimes set down by the original singer and a pick-up combo in no particular arrangement. The British started releasing cast albums of whole shows before the twenties, the United States picked up the habit in the forties, and by the fifties most musicals that opened left forty to fifty minutes of their distinctive personalities for the future to hear. Old shows that had predated the cast album era were at last recorded by new people, and 78 RPM sets were reissued on LP in more modern sound. This is not even to mention the pop singles business that still hangs on by a thread, with such as Ella Fitzgerald's 45 of "Roxie" and "My Own Best Friend" (from *Chicago*).

In other words, there's an immense legacy of theatre music on disc, about seventy years' worth all told. I don't see any practical way of listing it all except in a separate book, but a few navigational hints might help those who want to explore on their own.

There is some amusing lore in the history of theatre music recordings—Tamara waxing "Smoke Gets in Your Eyes" for Brunswick with Leo Reisman's orchestra, she hoping to preserve the rubato of her phrasing, the band intent on keeping a steady beat for home dancing; or, *Oklahoma!*'s second "original cast" album, four ten-inch 78s of "Lonely Room," "It's a Scandal, It's an Outrage," and "The Farmer and the Cowman" (in two parts), which disappeared so fast that today Decca isn't even sure it ever existed. In the Secrets of the Industry department there is RCA Victor's speeding up of tape of *The Golden Apple* to fit all that music onto one LP (and thereby pushing it up in pitch), and for History in Your Living Room there is a television documentary of the *Company* recording session, with redoubtable Elaine Stritch apparently spooked by the microphone while doing "The Ladies Who Lunch."

But this note is for those who seek the living testimony of records, not for anecdote hunters (I only know those four stories anyway). Discographies may be found in the Green and Engel books referred to in the bibliography. In the matter of choice, where more than one full-length recording was made, the original cast is always to be preferred, though later productions may offer better sound. Only the premiere casts, which had months to grow into their parts and comic play (and which frequently use snatches of spoken dialogue to provide dramatic context), can be expected to bring a show to life. Original orchestrations and vocal arrangements also merchant the authenticity of period, and students beware: movie casts are to be avoided at all costs.

Only the bigger hits survive on disc after the posters come down; the less prepossessing works go out of print and eventually fetch unbelievably inflated prices at collectors' shops. Check out church bazaars and thrift shops for second-hand items or be prepared to pay anywhere from thirty to two hundred dollars for the weirder titles. These especially are the preserve of a race of the obsessed beings freaked-out on films and theatre; any one of them would trample you to get to a copy of such as *Seventeen, Flahooley,* the 1952 *Of Thee I Sing* revival, *By the Beautiful Sea, Greenwillow,* or *Make a Wish,* all on RCA or Capitol. Columbia's catalogue held on longer thanks to Goddard Lieberson, who recorded almost everything in sight because no one else was willing to and who kept his projects in the stores even after they had proved their financial unviability beyond the shadow of an accountant's doubt. Under Clive Davis Columbia's theatre wing was permitted to lapse, but after Davis' cloudy departure Lieberson came back to rerelease most of the true, the good, and the beautiful.

Just for the record, the all-time collector's item show album, LP class, is probably the Ann Sothern television version of *Lady in the Dark,* which had a limited distribution and thus turns up less frequently than the others. Not as complete as the later Columbia try with Risë Stevens, deprived of Weill's *echt* scoring, and saddled with anachronistic vocal back-ups in the Kay Thompson–Hugh Martin style, it still has the edge in Sothern's high-powered Liza Elliott.

Now for a bit of the long-range. One of the problems besetting the music-historical side of artistic musical theatre is the limitation of one LP record, the only really marketable ambit for commercial recording—and yet the cast album is still the one document that keeps us in touch years later. The best theatre scores today are more than a group of songs that start and end like a pop album. Art takes its own form in no specific length: Strauss' *Elektra* fits neatly on two records, while another not-to-be-disputed colossus, Wagner's *Die Meistersinger von Nürnberg,* has to be squeezed onto five (London's old mono *Meistersinger* originally came out act by act on seven). But with few exceptions, musicals are just going to have to fit on one disc, about sixty minutes maximum—although not all records use all of those minutes. If Tchaikovsky's gigantic *Manfred* orchestration comes out again and again on one stereo LP, why did Capitol shred *Follies* into two twenty-minute sides? (Those in search of the core of *Follies,* one of the six or seven greatest musicals, are advised to buy the piano-vocal score and the Random House text to work it out for themselves.)

I end with *Follies* because it was about ghosts, and so, it seems, is this book—George Fox, Lillian Russell, George M. Cohan, Victor Herbert, Weber and Fields, Florenz Ziegfeld, the Shuberts, Marilyn Miller, Bert Lahr, Fanny Brice, Bobby Clark, Romberg, Kern, Gershwin, Porter, Hammerstein, Joseph Urban, Libby Holman, Clifton Webb, George Jean Nathan, Moss Hart, Gertrude Lawrence, Kurt Weill, Dennis King, David Burns, Helen Tamiris, Billy Rose, Joan McCracken, William Tabbert, Judy Holliday; my God, even Helen Traubel, Bill Johnson, and Judy Tyler in that one show.

INDEX

(*Continued from page iv*)

ILLUSTRATIONS:

The Bettmann Archive Inc.: "Seventeen."

Culver Pictures Inc.: "Showboat," "Porgy and Bess," and "Allegro."

The New York Public Library at Lincoln Center, Astor, Lenox and Tilden Foundations, Theatre Collection: "The King and I," "Redhead," "On the Town," "One Touch of Venus," and "As Thousands Cheer."

Martha Swope: "Chicago."